Major Jesse A. Marcel, an Army-Air Force intelligence officer, had been sent with his team to the crash site. His impression was that the wreckage was of a craft unlike any that he had ever seen. He stated that "it was not a missile, a tracking device, or a weather balloon." The *Roswell Daily Record* carried the story on the crash that quoted Air Force personnel stating that they had recovered the wreckage of a "flying disc of unknown origin."

A press release was issued by the Roswell Army Air Base on July 8. It stated, "Roswell Army Air Field was fortunate enough to gain possession of a disc through the cooperation of one of the local ranchers and the Sheriff's office at Chaves county."

It appears that the military altered its policy immediately afterwards and drew a cloak of secrecy over the entire affair. A report on the case being broadcast from the KSWS radio station in Roswell was apparently interrupted by an incoming teletype message saying, "Cease transmission. National Security item. Do not transmit. Repeat. Do not transmit this message."

ALIEN IMPACT

MICHAEL CRAFT

St. Martin's Paperbacks

ALIEN IMPACT

Copyright © 1996 by Michael Craft

Library of Congress Catalog Card Number: 96-5227

ISBN: 0-312-96287-8

Printed in the United States of America

St. Martin's Press hardcover edition/August 1996
St. Martin's Press Paperbacks edition/September 1997

10 9 8 7 6 5 4 3 2 1

Dedicated to my mother Sandra, for her unconditional love and support. I also wish to express my gratitude to Ralph Blum for his wisdom, friendship, and "coyote."

CONTENTS

Introduction   ix

PART ONE: **MAKING CONTACT**   1
Chapter 1   Strange Days   3
Chapter 2   The Abductions   24
Chapter 3   Hidden Agenda   43
Chapter 4   Unknown Apes   66
Chapter 5   Night Terrors   76
Chapter 6   Thieves of Time   94

PART TWO: **FIGURES OF EARTH**   117
Chapter 7   Vanishing Monsters   119
Chapter 8   The Very Good People   138
Chapter 9   Gaian Message   163
Chapter 10   Alien Genesis   187

PART THREE: **THE ALIEN CULTURE**   211
Chapter 11   Angels From Space   213
Chapter 12   Prophesies and Panics   234
Chapter 13   Cults of Chaos   247
Chapter 14   Planetary Elders   270
Chapter 15   The New Seers   286

Bibliography   301
Index   323
About the Author   333

INTRODUCTION

You can measure a circle
by beginning anywhere.

—CHARLES FORT

The myth of the alien is as old as humanity. Angels, elves, dragons, talking trees, demons, and trolls are the ancestors of our modern Grays, Bigfoots, poltergeists, and channeled spirits. Ten thousand years ago, our ancestors sat by the campfire and told one another tales of nonhuman, even nonphysical, beings possessed of magical abilities. Today those tales continue, though the fire has been replaced by television, and the "magical abilities" with an advanced, alien technology.

Something deep inside us appears to love or require the existence of incomprehensible beings and forces, both hostile and friendly. Whether they are there because we need them, or because they need us, they *are* there for us. Whether or not these things are "real" is another question, perhaps one without a single answer.

This book was not written solely because the author shared humanity's fascination with the mystery. I began exploring the phenomenon because I needed to understand what I was experiencing myself. Like many, many others, I've had my own share of strange, UFO-type encounters. Though such experiences have not made me a believer, hearing the stories of others, from both modern and traditional cultures, has helped expand my understanding.

In my own struggle for some interior balance, all interpretations proved useful, whether they were literal and physical, psychological, religious, or shamanic. We are all complex, multilayered beings with a shared legacy. The truth always has many faces; sometimes we even see our own face, as in a mirror.

After more than twenty years of exploration, I still do not

know what "truth" to believe. Besides the fear of the unknown, my greatest obstacle has always been my own desire to find an answer. "Belief is the enemy."

Rather than try to tell only my own tale, I have outlined the Tale itself as I found it. The UFO community, and its vast literature, is a creaky house built from many different materials. Disappearances and abductions, mysterious strangers, alien animals and apparitions, celestial portents, prophesies, conspiracies, and futuristic technologies join the similar experiences of other times and cultures. Witnesses anywhere and at any time may show vast psychological changes, including false memories, flashbacks, time distortions, paranoia, messianic complexes, even so-called possession states and newly emerged psychic abilities.

The entities encountered include eerie visitors from outer space, underworld cities, and other planes or dimensions. Alien races such as Reptoids, Deros, Pleiadeans, Ashtar Command, and glowing-eyed, hairy monsters rub shoulders with CIA operatives, threatening "Men in Black," the military, scientific institutions, psychedelic researchers, and everyday, normal people going about their lives.

It is these normal people that make the mystery much more than the imagination, visions, or psychosis of a scattered few. The numbers of people who report seeing UFOs or meeting alien beings is constantly rising. According to one recent survey, the number of people who believe in such phenomena is over fifty percent of the population in the United States alone (with similar numbers claimed in Europe and South America).

These growing throngs of believers are paralleled by vast changes in our world and ourselves. Everywhere people are making life changes based in part on a belief system that accepts alien beings. Such transitions leave their mark on us in art, literature, film, politics, and religious beliefs.

I do not deny a real existence to the phenomenon. Many cases show seemingly physical effects on machines, fauna and flora, and people. Instead of chasing these reports, I examined the phenomenon as a whole, and was led to explore the role of consciousness in physical reality.

I acknowledge the impact of the powerful belief systems of those touched by the phenomenon. This includes that most obscure of all cults, the cult of professional skeptics making a lifestyle out of debunking witnesses and "true believers."

Anyone watching television or reading a newspaper can see that our world is undergoing tremendous turmoil, a chaos in which some see the end of civilization. What will be left after these great waves of change have passed; what will we believe in after this violent, creative century has ended?

Can humanity remain open to many meanings in this phenomenon that apparently mirrors our own minds? Looking in the alien mirror, we perceive a shifting reflection, an image of human "reality," and its deconstruction, dissolution, or re-creation.

—Michael Craft

ALIEN IMPACT

PART ONE

MAKING CONTACT

This is how he grows:
by being defeated, decisively,
by constantly greater beings.

—RAINER MARIA RILKE

1

STRANGE DAYS

Who hears may be incredulous,
Who witnesses, believes.

—EMILY DICKINSON

DURING the 1980s, an old friend was visiting near Point Reyes Station, California. Though it was late night and the house was in a rural area, the two women inside suddenly noticed a bright light glaring through the front window. Looking out, they could see a large, eerily glowing sphere hovering just over the treetops bordering the property. It remained motionless for some minutes. They saw no special markings or projecting fins and the object emitted no sound.

My friend was fascinated and wanted to go outside for a closer look, but the other woman panicked and begged her not to investigate. Finally, after calming her friend, she jumped in her car to pursue the object that had begun to float off.

Driving along the deserted highway that led to the sea, she was able to follow the object that seemed at times to be waiting for her to catch up. She noticed that it did not move in a straight line, but instead seemed to smoothly rise and fall with the contours of the land. It also made some remarkable right-angle turns in its trajectory.

She finally parked on a cliff overlooking the sea to watch the object heading west. In a sudden burst of speed it vanished, leaving her alone to contemplate an empty night sky and a mystery.

No matter where on earth you live, someone nearby has encountered a strange flying light or an inexplicable alien creature. The results of one ABC-TV, 1994 poll estimated thirty thousand UFO sightings in the United States alone. Countless people have been awed, confused, kidnapped, harassed, deluded, or awakened. It is easy to find a multitude of support groups willing to provide their own explanation; however, "the truth" may be much more elusive.

People have reported unidentifiable lights in the sky long before the invention of aircraft. Since ancient times, there have been descriptions of encounters with nonhuman entities, frequently dwarfish in size and possessed of seemingly magical abilities. Also in many traditional cultures, witnesses or contactees (those people "contacted") have described their experiences within familiar religious or cultural contexts. Before there were flying saucers, there were "flying ships"; before aliens, there were fairies, angels, and devils.

Some say that these ancient encounters were the foundation of some world religions. It is perhaps understandable if tribal peoples meeting UFOs believed that the "gods" expected them to start a cult. Each successive generation of witnesses created a new layer of superstition to interpret the continuing phenomenon. Only after Rationalism and science disrupted the continuity of belief systems were we forced to grope for new interpretations.

Since the dawn of industrial culture, and especially after World War II and the invention of space flight, most witnesses and contactees describe their experiences in terms of the Extraterrestrial Hypothesis (ETH). This position holds that our planet has been visited by aliens from another planet via flying saucers, or UFOs.

The vast majority of believers in the hypothesis are convinced that we are not only visited, but manipulated by these strange travelers. Ideas of genetic engineering, alien abductions, brainwashing, and monitoring "implants" have become commonplace in Europe, North and South America.

Hand-in-glove with ETH is a belief that our government (at least) conspires to cover up knowledge of the alien visitors. It seems that the growth of the ETH accompanied the rise in public mistrust in propagandizing, bureaucratic nation-states.

The commonplace term "flying saucer" is an unfortunate choice of words. UFOs are sighted in many forms. Over and over, people have seen blobs of light, cigar-shaped objects, spinning tops, triangles, clusters, globes, boxes, and moving streaks in addition to saucer shapes. In many cases, the objects appear to melt from one shape into another, or fade from metallic-looking to transparent.

The phrase "flying saucer" came into use back in 1947 in an Associated Press item that flashed through newsrooms across the nation:

> PENDLETON, Ore., June 25 (AP)—Nine bright sau-cerlike objects flying at "incredible speed" at 10,000 feet altitude were reported here today by Kenneth Arnold, a Boise, Idaho, pilot who said he could not hazard a guess as to what they were.
>
> Arnold, a United States Forest Service employee en-gaged in searching for a missing plane, said he sighted the mysterious objects yesterday at 3 P.M. They were flying between Mount Ranier and Mount Adams, in Washington State, he said, and appeared to wave in and out of formation. Arnold said he clocked and estimated their speed at one thousand two hundred miles an hour.
>
> Inquiries at Yakima last night brought only blank stares, he said, but he added he talked today with an unidentified man from Utah, south of here, who said he had seen similar objects over the mountains near Ukiah yesterday.
>
> "It seems impossible," Arnold said, "but there it is."

At the time, Arnold was flying a Callair plane especially designed for mountain search and rescue. Attempting to lo-cate a crashed transport plane and the bodies of its crew, he was an unlikely choice for a trickster. Bill Bequette, a local reporter, is credited with recording Arnold's statement that the object moved like "a saucer skipping over water." Within a few days, Arnold was surrounded by reporters asking for additional details about the "flying saucer" sighting. He later said that public ridicule caused him to regret ever opening his mouth.

After the initial report, witnesses to similar aerial phe-nomena began to emerge across the country. As the increas-ingly bizarre stories multiplied, many reporters who were originally sympathetic began to ignore them.

The Arnold sightings were not the first publicized UFOs in this country. During the 1890s and 1900s, there was a wave of "phantom airship" sightings in both England and the United States. The then-Prince of Wales was one witness. In many cases, they were thought to be dirigibles, even though the reports described speeds and maneuvers far exceeding technical levels of the 1900s. No known dirigibles were in operation anywhere in the 1890s!

At the beginning of this century, dirigibles were used by a number of governments for military purposes. The United States, Britain, and especially Germany employed these fortresslike, propeller-driven balloons as both spy planes and bombers. In 1909 and again in 1913 there were widespread phantom airship panics in England and Ireland. In newspapers of the day, reported sightings accompanied hysterical rants against German spies and infiltrators. Some of these sightings were undoubtedly of military dirigibles. However, a number of cases on both sides of the Atlantic suggest something inexplicable.

In the 1890s, glowing airships were seen on the East and West Coasts, in the Great Plains, and in Texas. Many of the aerial sightings displayed behavior strikingly similar to that of modern-day UFOs. Ships dropping strange objects, altering course abruptly, changing altitude with tremendous speed, and emitting strange, powerful lights are all documented in reports of the time.

In March 1897, farmer Robert Hibbard from the outskirts of Sioux City, Iowa came much closer than he intended. While observing a phantom airship, his clothing was snagged by an "anchor dangling from the object," which carried him off the ground for several dozen feet before he fell. (There are similar tales of "fairy ships" during the Middle Ages dangling or dropping anchors.)

In *The Houston Post,* April 22, 1897, there was a report from John Barclay, who around 11 P.M. heard his dogs barking furiously accompanied by a strange whining sound. Picking up his gun and heading outside, he saw a huge oblong shape, with side wings and other attachments, hovering outside his home. The object emitted a bright light that "seemed much brighter than electric lights."

After circling a few times, the object settled down into an adjacent pasture. When Barclay moved closer, he was met by a man who told him that no harm was intended and to lay aside his gun. The man said, "Never mind my name; call it Smith." He then asked Barclay to go into town to buy some chisels and bluestone while he waited; for the purchase he provided a ten-dollar bill. When Barclay asked to see the airship, he was told, "No, we cannot permit you to approach any nearer, but do as we request you and your kindness will be appreciated, and we will call you some future day and reciprocate your kindness by taking you on a trip."

After purchasing the items and returning, Barclay asked where the man was from, and where he was going. The man replied, "From anywhere, but we will be in Greece day after tomorrow." He then went on board, after which the object's lights came on and it lifted up. Barclay said that the object was "gone like a shot out of a gun." The same issue of *The Post* reported another sighting of presumably the same object over a Texas village a half-hour later that night.

This encounter contains several examples seen in classic UFO encounters. They include a mystifying flying object that should not exist, an emphasis on unnaturally bright lights, a request for simple, easily obtainable articles, and the promise to return at a later date. The airship sightings suggest a transitionary form of UFO encounter between ancient and modern times.

The contacted phenomena was also going strong in the nineteenth century. The Spiritualist Movement was born in 1848 when the Fox sisters of Hydesville, New York, became famous for seances where rappings from "the spirits" were heard. Messages from the dead, from angels, and from other planets were "discovered" in the rappings. Mediums, mystics, and Spiritualist journals soon became popular around the world.

Trickery was not uncommon, but exposures did little to dampen public enthusiasm. Audiences gathered to observe such phenomena as levitation, automatic writing, telepathy, psychic healing, speaking in tongues, and channeled messages. By 1855, Spiritualism claimed over two million followers.

The first psychological investigation of a medium occurred in the 1890s, when Professor Theodore Flournoy of the University of Geneva began studying the case of Helene Smith. In March 1892, Miss Smith began receiving automatic messages when she held a pen in her hand. She soon began entering trances where she would speak in an Italian accent and identify herself as "Leopold." After Leopold entered her body, poltergeist activity would begin in the room. Leopold was an enemy of the deceased author Victor Hugo, who would also enter Miss Smith's entranced body. The two spirits disagreed violently, and each told Smith to ignore the other.

On September 5, 1896, Helene Smith woke at 3 A.M. with a strange vision of a "beautiful pink-blue lake," where she met a "dark-complexioned man" who flew off in a flying machine emitting flames. The man, whose name was Astane, began to visit her with increasing frequency. He told her that he was from the planet Mars, and on occasion took her there to visit. Everyone on "Mars" seemed to travel around in these flying machines.

Smith learned to speak the Martian language and began to write strange, "oriental-looking" symbols while in trance. These symbols had the same runelike characteristics seen again and again in modern contactee stories. Professor Flournoy was fascinated by these characters and noticed that they seemed to make an actual language rather than gibberish. With Smith's help, he translated the channeled writings into French, eventually emerging in the 447-page book, *From India to the Planet Mars.*

Smith was also visited by other "Martians" possessed of "extremely long fingers and long hair," who took her on journeys to other planets. (Long-haired and long-fingered aliens are a common theme in modern-day contactee reports.) The visions of Mars and the Martians invariably started with a vision of rose-colored or pink light. The pink light also appears in modern-day visions.

Another important feature of Helene Smith's visions were her visits to little men similar to the dwarves of the Middle Ages, who stood roughly three feet tall. The little men presumably enjoy our attention, since they are still being seen a hundred years later.

The phantom airship sightings and the Spiritualist visions represented two distinct streams or traditions still active today. There are people who *see* or *meet* UFOs, and there are those who *channel messages* from the "space people" while in trance. Nowadays these two themes often run together.

One of the first men to speculate that the mysterious lights seen in the sky came from outer space was the iconoclastic philosopher Charles Fort. Born in 1874, Fort was a journalist who spent his youth reading extensively in the literature and history of science. At first as a hobby, he began keeping exhaustive notes on reports of *anomalies,* (recorded phenomena departing from the norm). These notes later became the basis for his still-influential works, *The Book of the Damned, Lo!, New Lands,* and *Wild Talents.*

Fort often employed his celebrated wit to poke fun at the sacred cows of science. He was skeptical about "scientific explanations," and observed that "experts" frequently distorted facts to fit their own theories or to attack competing schools of thought. His books, filled with accounts from the news services of the day, still make fascinating reading. There are exhaustive lists of archeological oddities such as coins and bits of machined metal found in million-year-old coal beds. There are the celebrated and inexplicable rains of frogs, fish, and even raw meat, viewed by spectators around the world. There are accounts of mysterious, disappearing beasts, and of course, the phantom airships.

Charles Fort's legacy continues in the work of numerous investigators of cryptobiology (alien or unrecognized animals) and "Fortean anomalies." Like Fort himself, today's Fortean investigators are not above employing folklore alongside scientific method in their investigations. Also like their spiritual founder, Fortean publications such as the excellent *Strange* magazine or Britain's *Fortean Times,* display an open-minded skepticism and sense of humor.

After years of cataloguing sightings of anomalous objects, Fort wrote:

> "I began with a notion of some other world, from which objects and substances have fallen to this earth; and which had a tutelary interest in this earth and is now attempting to communicate with this earth; modifying into an acceptance that some other world had been for centuries in communication with a secret society or certain esoteric ones of this earth's inhabitants.

"We are too busy to take up alarmism, but extra-mundane vandals may have often swooped down upon this earth, and they may swoop again; and it may be a comfort to us, some day, to mention in our last gasp that we were told about this."

Fort's "extra-mundane vandals" apparently swooped down in Pascagoula, Mississippi, on October 11, 1973, in one of the most renowned UFO cases of this century. Between 7 and 9 P.M., Charles Hickson and Calvin Parker were fishing from an old pier on the banks of the Pascagoula River. Their attention was drawn to a strange, blue light about two miles distant, which raced to a position about forty feet away. In the glow was an oblong object hovering approximately eight to ten feet above the water.

Before the terrified men could withdraw, they heard a "little buzzin' noise," and an aperture appeared in the object. According to Hickson, "Three whatever-they-weres came out, either floating or walking, and carried us into the ship." Eighteen-year-old Calvin Parker passed out from fright or shock; middle-aged Hickson did not.

He described the bizarre creatures as having pale, silvery-gray skin, no hair, large eyes, long pointed ears and hands "like crab claws." Hickson remembered being taken into a circular, brightly lit chamber where he was suspended horizontally in midair. A floating object "like a big eye" scanned up and down his body. After the weird examination ended, the two men were returned to the riverbank, where Parker regained consciousness.

Both men, simple shipyard workers, were stunned by the experience and called the local sheriff. Press reports followed, and journalists flocked from across the nation. Some were True Believers ready to deify the two witnesses, others were skeptics prepared to discredit them. A few investigators, including authors J. Allen Hynek and Ralph Blum, adopted a more even-handed approach.

In this they were aided by Jackson County Sheriff Diamond, who was sternly protective of the two reluctant witnesses' reputation. According to Sheriff Diamond, "First thing they wanted to do was take a lie detector test. Charlie—he was shook bad. You don't see a forty-five-year-old man break down and cry unless it's something fierce that happened. He said to me, 'After what I already went through on this earth, why did I have to go through all this?' "

The sheriff, who observed there was no evidence of alcohol on the men, also said, "I'm not easily convinced, but I heard that boy pray when he was alone and thought that nobody could hear. That was enough for me." Hickson passed his lie detector test.

Though there were no other witnesses, some secondary reports did come in. There were three aerial UFO sightings in Pascagoula on or about the same day, one from a local minister. Two days after the event, a meteorologist from nearby Columbia, Mississippi reported tracking a mysterious object to within three miles of his station. The object suddenly "became stationary and all of a sudden my radar just completely jammed."

Though official interest faded, the case is still cherished as a classic example of an alien encounter. The real meaning of the experience was probably only known by the two men involved. As Hickson told author Ralph Blum:

"You know at night, I lie in bed and think about them.
If I can, I'd like to get in touch with them. I mean it.
Every night when I'm in bed, it's almost a picture that
comes into my mind. Just the same way every time.
All I have to do is close my eyes."

Over the centuries, there have been countless attempts to reproduce images of the strange things people have seen in the sky. Cave paintings, parchments, tapestries, sculptures, painted canvases, and woodblock prints were the available mediums in the past. As interesting as these may be, they can only reflect a witness's or artist's memory. Has this situation changed since the invention of photography? Everyone knows the old saying, "seeing is believing." Aren't photographs real proof of an event? Maybe not.

In 1953, a sixty-two-year-old man named George Adamski published a book claiming that he had met an extraterrestrial in the California desert. The alien, who he described as tall, green-eyed and with flowing blond hair, took him on journeys to the planets Venus, Mars, and Saturn. On each planet, he met beautiful aliens. They had chosen to contact humanity at this time because of the danger to all life from our nuclear program (a common theme for contactees).

Adamski published some of his photographs of UFOs, showing the familiar saucer shapes with a surprising level of detail; one can see ports and propulsion equipment. He also had photographs of much larger "mother ships" that were dark, cigar-shaped objects surrounded by many smaller lights.

Adamski took many of his photographs on the grounds of the Mount Palomar Observatory where he "worked" and kept a small telescope. His claim to be employed there was the cause of his downfall. "Professor" Adamski actually worked at a local cafe near the observatory!

His photographs, while never proven forgeries, were shown to be *possibly* taken of models. This evidence, combined with his assumption of a more elevated job title, sank Adamski's claims for most of his audience. (Of course, one can still find True Believers who say that it was a conspiracy.)

Adamski's photographs closely resembled those of another early contactee, Swiss farmer Eduard Billy Meier. Meier took over one hundred seemingly clear photographs of UFOs that he called "beamships." The beamship pictures were only the beginning of Meier's claims; he told tales of being taken back in time by aliens to meet Jesus Christ and other illustrious figures of history. Like Adamski, Meier formed what could only be called a cult of believers in an alien creed.

His photographs, at first welcomed enthusiastically, were later subjected to much skepticism. Critics noticed that most of them had been taken with the camera facing into the sun, where the glare would obscure details such as supporting wires. The controversy grew when it was found that Meier was in possession of a model closely resembling his beamships. Billy Meier's claim of constructing the model *after* his experiences was met with ridicule.

One contemporary case of UFO photographs occurred in the small town of Gulf Breeze, Florida. On November 11, 1987, home builder Ed Walters noticed a strange glow coming from behind the trees bordering his suburban home. Getting up from his desk to look, he saw a top-shaped flying object with porthole shapes and a luminous ring around the middle. He ran back to his house in order to get his old Polaroid camera.

Walters succeeded in snapping four photographs of the object as it drifted off. As he ran closer, the object emitted a beam of blue light directly at him. He found himself paralyzed and lifted off the ground. A suffocating odor of "ammonia and cinnamon" burned the back of his throat.

While struggling and screaming in terror, Walters heard a mechanical-sounding voice in his head telling him to "Calm down; we will not hurt you." He responded with curses and struggles, whereupon his mind was filled with "flashing dog pictures" moving to the sound of a female voice. Then he was dropped to the ground and the UFO was gone.

Returning to his house in shock, Walters's wife noticed both the ammonia odor and her husband's ashen face. She and their son had seen nothing. Walters had his pictures developed and anonymously printed in the *Gulf Breeze Sentinel*. After the photos ran, several local students came forward to report that they, too, had seen the object.

Walters continued hearing voices in his head, saying in both English and Spanish, "They won't hurt you. Just a few tests. That's all." On December 2, Walters had a nighttime encounter with a four-foot tall humanoid standing by the porch of his house. The being, carrying a silver rod, stared at Walters and then fled. Giving chase, Walters was again grabbed by a blue beam emanating from a UFO resembling the earlier one. The UFO returned on two later occasions, on which Walters succeeded in videotaping it.

He also had an encounter while driving on a deserted country road on January 12, 1988. He was blinded by a white light that caused his hands and arms on the steering wheel to feel "burning pinpricks." As a UFO appeared and hovered over his truck, his head was filled with mental messages telling him to come forward. Walters sensibly ignored the voices and crawled under his truck.

Peering out from under the vehicle, he then saw five separate beams shoot from the craft. Where they landed stood five humanoids carrying silver rods, who then began to step toward him in unison. Screaming obscenities, Walters jumped back into his truck and drove away at breakneck speed.

Walters went public with his stories and photographs, and

submitted to a barrage of reporters, lie detector tests, and UFO investigators, including professional witness debunker Phillip Klass. Though passing lie detector tests, he was unable to convince many investigators that he was not lying.

Walters's UFO photos were subjected to studies by professional optical experts. Physicist Dr. Bruce MacCabee, a government employee working on SDI ("Star Wars") and a pro-UFO, examined the films and pronounced them genuine. NASA's Jet Propulsion Laboratory researcher Dr. Robert Nathan also examined them and pronounced them "suspicious." Apparently, photo experts can prove any photo to be both true and false.

Undaunted, Ed and Frances Walters turned their experiences into a book, *The Gulf Breeze Sightings,* which became an instant best-seller. In a bizarre twist reminiscent of Billy Meier, Walters's credibility suffered a serious blow when a model of the UFO was found in his possession. Like Meiers, Walters's claims of building the model after his experience fell on deaf ears. (Future witnesses might be well advised to avoid building models.)

Besides the human element, one lesson of these cases is that photographs will *never* constitute acceptable proof. Fakery is too easily accomplished, too easily assumed. Short of biological evidence (living or dead aliens), UFOs remain unprovable. Perhaps we must return to the witness experience as containing the primary meaning in a sighting or encounter.

Veteran researcher John A. Keel once noted that a great number of UFO sightings seem to be entirely subjective. That is, "the objects are seen only by specific individuals under very specific conditions, while nonspecific individuals in the same areas see nothing." Others suggested that these "nonsightings" are experienced by people with latent psychic abilities. They theorize that sightings or alien encounters occur at pivotal or significant periods in an individual's life, marking a major transformation in the person's psyche.

Many witnesses and contactees do experience marked personality changes after their experience. In addition to forming cults, writing best-selling books, and hiding from reporters, some witnesses suffer mental blackouts, cryptamnesia (repression or forgetfulness of experiences), paranoia, and hallucinations. Often these symptoms tend to occur *after* their UFO experience, which should be considered the triggering event, rather than another symptom.

More esoteric contactee symptoms include retrocognition (memory of times before one was born), telepathy, and prophetic dreams. Though science is still exploring such phenomena, numerous academic and military studies have concluded that extrasensory perception is real.

Lest these possible side effects lead us to think that all UFO witnesses are crazy, it's worth remembering that most sightings are made by ordinary, God-fearing people who never displayed the slightest interest in strange phenomena. Case studies are filled with eloquent testimonials from family members, ministers, and law enforcement officials vouching to the honesty of witnesses.

While common sense may be on the side of the psychological perspective, it's more difficult to account for physical effects. Witnesses frequently experience chronic headaches, dehydration, anorexia (loss of appetite), ephridosis (excessive perspiration), akinesia (temporary paralysis), inductopyrexia (physical sensations of heat or fever), and conjunctivitis (eye burn). While many of these symptoms might be caused by one's emotional state, conjunctivitis is much harder to self-induce.

One of the most common of witness aftereffects, conjunctivitis is characterized by reddened, swollen and painful eyeballs. The sore and itching eyes can last for weeks, or in severe cases, months. The malady is usually caused by excessive exposure to ultraviolet light; some actors have received mild cases of conjunctivitis from overexposure to glaring stage lights. There have also been studies showing that microwave radiation may cause eye burn.

Some contactees have also found strange marks on their skin after their experiences. Sometimes there are burns or warts in a circle or triangle, other times just a strangely shaped sore place or reddish area. Efforts by physicians to explain these marks have failed, though they are similar to the "devil's mark" for which supposed witches were burned at the stake in less enlightened times.

If the experience is wholly psychological, how do we explain the frequent accounts of suddenly stalled cars? The literature of UFO sightings is full of reports of automobile engines abruptly going dead in the middle of the road just prior to contact. Though it would reportedly take huge levels of power, it is possible for low-frequency electromagnetic radiation (EM) to interfere with electrical systems. The much-feared "electromagnetic pulse" of an air-detonated nuclear attack would do precisely the same thing on a regional or national level. Could EM radiation also cause witness side effects?

Both Russian and American studies, in many cases dating from World War II, explored the physical effects of ultraviolet and electromagnetic radiation on human subjects. All of the physical symptoms felt by the UFO witnesses above showed in these studies.

EM researchers have remarked on the unusual sensitivity of lab animals to EM radiation. If UFOs are somehow connected to EM, then do nearby animals show a similar sensitivity? Reports of both phantom airships and modern-day UFOs do indeed note that witnesses were often alerted to the phenomenon by the howling of dogs, geese, or other domestic animals.

Electromagnetic radiation can also affect telephone systems. (Phones in some parts of Canada and Alaska require special shielding from the EM effects of the Aurora Borealis.) Phones ringing with no caller, bizarre noises, and intermittently dead phones plague UFO contactees and witnesses.

One possibly related experience discussed by both contactees and Spiritualists is the "electronic voice phenomenon," or EVP. This is a modern form of spirit (or alien) communication in which voices are recorded directly onto magnetic audio tape without a visible source of input. In other words, they just turn on the tape recorder and see what happens. Many contactees have also reported EVP coming in, unasked and unwanted, through their telephones.

Though taping EVP can be done with a simple recorder, enthusiasts spend fortunes devising ever-more-complex equipment. (Some early enthusiasts were the inventors Thomas Edison and Nikola Tesla.) There are numerous American and European associations devoted to EVP, with, of course, the obligatory newsletters.

The amazing thing about EVP is that it really works! Blank tapes set recording "space" and played back later may often contain muttered voices, faint whispers, and even clear words and sentences. EVP voices "typically speak in short, cryptic, or grammatically poor phrases." (In other words, they speak like the aliens in typical UFO encounters.)

Critics maintain that the tapes are merely picking up bits of radio and television communications. The faithful, however, hear personal messages from aliens, saints, and departed family members. If one wants to try this at home, remember that it works better listening with headphones.

In most cases, what is immediately noticed about UFOs is their bright light. Many times, all that was ever seen by a witness was a "light in the sky." The flash of light is also extremely common in religious tradition, often seen before the appearance of an "angel" or messenger from God. Sightings of humanoid aliens are also frequently announced by a flash of bright white, pink, or blue light.

The image of an eerie, glowing sphere or disc floating in space seems holy to many people, as if the spiritual realm were manifesting itself to them for divine purposes. There is little wonder that some people interpret such an experience as a personal revelation.

These individuals take the "message" from their encounter and devote their life to communicating it to the world. The literature of UFOs (and religion) is filled with reports of people developing obsessive-compulsive characteristics, even to the point of leaving jobs, home, and family.

A few, rare contactees have become so convinced of the truth and clarity of their visions that they seem more real than their prior life. This True Believer may ignore both skepticism and ridicule, sure that they alone "have seen the light." With such strength of belief, it is no wonder that they have been able to form groups of faithful followers around themselves.

These contactees have become the UFO fundamentalists, literal fanatics who equate their personal visions with the destiny of humanity. Disbelief, an attack on their visions, becomes an attack on the contactee. They spend years writing and lecturing in an attempt to attack their "enemies." In ancient times, they would have used fire and sword.

Most alien encounters seem to have no message at all. On September 19, 1963, four children in Saskatchewan, Canada, were accosted by a "ghost" from a UFO. The children were playing behind their school when they sighted an oval-shaped circle of light in the sky that stopped directly overhead. They saw a box shape drop away from it and hover nearby. When they moved toward the object, a figure suddenly appeared before them. The transfixed children later estimated that it stood ten feet tall, wore a robe, and semed at times to be transparent.

Holding out its hands, the being moaned and floated toward the terrified children, who ran home screaming. One of the girls became so hysterical that she had to be placed in the hospital. Both parents and local authorities were impressed with the real fear of the children. There were other local reports of UFO sightings.

Just another ghost story? Though it is heresy to believers in the Extraterrestrial Hypothesis, I found many correlations between ghost-lore and UFO cases. As in most ghost cases, UFO sightings occur at night. UFOs seem to enjoy buzzing people sitting in cars on lover's lanes; so do ghosts. Investigator Jenny Randles notes that UFOs, like ghosts, may be seen by one or two people in a crowded area while remaining unseen by others in the same vicinity. The marked sensitivity of dogs, cats, and farm animals also appears in cases of ghost sightings.

There are many UFO sightings where the object appeared and disappeared out of nowhere and moved in total silence, seeming wraithlike and insubstantial. There are even UFO cases where the flying shape was seen to glide through a solid object like a wall. This behavior is also typical of ghostly manifestations.

Another area of comparison is found between these two phenomena. The UFO occupants are frequently described as "luminous" or "radiant," the same description used by witnesses of ghosts. The speech of the aliens, like that of the EVP above, is cryptic, grammatically poor, and often whispery or chill-inducing. Those unlucky enough to think they have spoken with ghosts also remark on the unearthly quality of their speech.

The many examples of ghost messages spoken through mediums or channels exhibit this same predilection for murky meanings and cryptic phrases. Though this probably says more about the minds of mediums and contactees than it does about ghosts and aliens, it is another factor worth further exploration.

The strongest case for comparison is not a phenomenon that is seen or heard, but one that is *smelled.* Over and over, UFO witnesses (and contactees) report the burning stench of sulfur or sometimes ammonia. The "fire and brimstone" of ghosts, demons, and apparitions is often equated with the odor of sulfur. Among others, researcher John Keel identified the acid aroma of both UFOs and ghostly encounters as that of hydrogen sulfide. Isn't it odd that supernatural manifestations smell just as bad as the UFO-nauts?

Does the study of ghosts have anything "substantial" to offer UFO research? In *The Ultradimensional Mind,* philosopher Michael Grosso notes that though "it's difficult to explain one unknown by another unknown," there appears to be "a substantive link between ufology and parapsychology." When compared, "UFO data seems less isolated, less anomalous, and more familiar when viewed in relation to parapsychology; they exhibit connections with other areas of knowledge." Looking at the bigger picture helps our feeble attempts to explain the unknown.

This does not mean that UFOs are what people commonly think of as ghosts (that is, the spirits of dead people). Our usual interpretations for both sets of phenomena may be too narrow. What seems to be flying saucers from Mars or the ghost at the local cemetery may be more closely related than anyone previously thought.

It's often been noticed that the phenomenon likes to play with people's heads. A witness or contactee (the "victim") may find him or herself in a descending spiral of meaningless riddles and unearthly portents, attempts to regain unverifiable memories, and eventual delusion or paranoia. What separates this descent from common cases of mental illness is an apparent "outside factor" that delights in throwing out clues leading nowhere. The victim receives a continuing confirmation from "reality."

A typical contactee experience begins with an extraordinary event. It could be an angel, ghost, inexplicable animal, or a UFO with alien occupants. If a UFO experience, the unfortunate individual may then begin hearing monotonous voices repeating strange phrases in unearthly or foreign languages. One version of this is the fairly common "number-calling phenomenon," in which a toneless voice repeats long strings of numbers. Usually first heard over the television or radio, they may move on to mysterious phone calls that repeat the numbers as if they held some meaning for the listener.

The Game intensifies by drawing people into long, convoluted adventures, usually under the guise of aiding the space people. People may be asked to contact other contactees hitherto unknown to them, or to buy commonplace items and leave them in deserted places late at night. John Keel, while researching a UFO "flap" (series of sightings in the same area), actually met people who were instructed to pick up some of these items left by others he'd previously interviewed! These people were both players in the same game without even knowing each other.

Some contactees think that they've been on an adventure without ever leaving their house. There are cases of people who thought they were on actual trips to Heaven, Hell, Mars, Venus, or Fairyland, only to learn later that they were observed home asleep or in a trance.

Keel theorized that some contactee symptoms are based on a form of posthypnotic suggestion. "Certain words or perceptions are introduced into the percipient's mind, and when these words or perceptions reappear again—even years later—the percipient is automatically triggered into a trance or hallucinatory state. The number-calling phenomenon may be one such trigger."

Other post-hypnotic triggers could be the strange letters or scripts seen on some UFOs (or in automatic writing). The April 1972 issue of *Saga* reported the story of an engineer named Wheeler who encountered a UFO parked on a highway. Among other details, he vividly remembered stylized versions of "Greek letters" on the object. Years later, he thought he saw the same letters in another UFO case. Were they the same, or did the sight of the letters create a UFO trance state?

Another possible trigger is the widely discussed "beeping sound" heard by many contactees. A pulsing, beeping tone is heard, then the individual wakes up in another place, in other clothes, or suddenly finds himself meeting aliens. An inability to account for lost time is common for victims of "the beepers."

Mythologists and psychologists have been fascinated by legends found in many cultures of an archetypal Trickster. The Trickster has no permanent form or pattern; he fits his behavior and appearance to the people he tricks. His tricks, often involving supernatural phenomena, are usually rather malicious. Scholar Carl Kerenyi notes that the Trickster is found "playing tricks in the ghostly regions of the psyche, where spirits and poltergeists reign." Maybe he also plays the UFO game.

In 1958, psychologist Carl Jung published *Flying Saucers: A Modern Myth of Things Seen in the Sky.* Jung viewed the rising tide of UFO reports as indications of far-reaching cultural, political, and spiritual changes. He compared sightings of the objects, and their effects upon witnesses, with an alchemical process working to transform the way we view the world and ourselves.

Jung made every effort to leave the ultimate origins of UFOs wide open. He discussed swarming insects, electromagnetic phenomena, ball lightning, parapsychological effects, and alien spacecraft as possible causes. Though he has often been cited by authors who support the Extraterrestrial Hypothesis, his quotations are frequently taken out of context.

Because of these misquotations, he later clarified his position. In *The Symbolic Life,* he wrote, "I expressly state that I cannot commit myself on the question to the physical reality or unreality of the UFOs since I do not possess sufficient evidence either for or against."

Whatever the ultimate nature of UFOs, Jung realized their tremendous psychic impact. He described them as focused projections of powerful archetypal images from the collective unconscious. These projections are comparable to imagery found in folklore and mythology. UFOs, whether real or not, have all the power and characteristics of a myth. Any serious studies of the phenomenon should include its psychic or psychological ability to influence our beliefs and behavior.

Dr. Jung also remained open to physical interpretations.

"So far as I know it remains an established fact, supported by numerous observations, that UFOs have not only been seen visually but have also been picked up on the radar screen and have left traces on the photographic plate. It boils down to nothing less than this: that either psychic projections throw back a radar echo, or else the appearance of real phenomena affords an opportunity for mythological projections."

Jung's point is far from resolved. Examining the wider literature of UFO-like apparitions, mythical monsters, fairy lore, etc., I found many examples of "substantial" physical evidence and apparently real electromagnetic effects. On the other hand, most extraterrestrial believers completely ignore research showing a psychological relationship. The unwillingness of either side to examine the whole suggests a strong, blinding bias toward pet theories.

In modern physics there is thought to be a two-way relationship between experimenter and experiment, or between an individual mind and reality. The human mind influences physical reality; the two cannot be separated.

The UFO experience may never be understood until researchers accept both its physical and imaginal components. As Jung noted, "Should it be that an unknown physical phenomenon is the outward cause of the myth, this would detract nothing from the myth."

Whether people are only seeing things or truly being visited by ETs, (or neither), it's clear that the phenomenon has mythological, psychological, and historical implications. The channeling movement of the 1980s and '90s was preceded by the UFO contactees of the '50s, which merely continued the Spiritualist Movement of the turn of the century. The phantom airship waves preceded the flying saucers "flaps."

Many researchers now consider the Phenomenon to be deliberately deceptive. UFOs may leave behind ordinary debris like articles of clothing, pieces of metal, newspapers, and common place chemicals. Some witnesses describe household litter on the floor inside alien vehicles. Should we conclude that these reports are hoaxes because they don't fit our image of alien spacecraft? Maybe the aliens are merely sloppy housekeepers, or perhaps this confusion and contradiction is *desired*.

Author Jenny Randles coined a term, the "Oz Factor," to

describe the sensation of being "transported temporarily from our world into another where reality is similar but slightly different." For shorter or longer periods of time, many contactees and witnesses live with this sensation. Something happened to shake up their old view of the world. Unfortunately, it sometimes seems that whatever initiated the interior change apparently didn't want them believed by others.

Recurring reports of newspapers and empty Coke bottle strewn about the floor of alien crafts suggest that all is not as it seems. Can exploring the "reports that don't fit" increase our understanding, or will it leave us all stranded in Oz?

2

THE ABDUCTIONS

All knowledge is but remembrance.

—PLATO

SOMEONE scanning the magazine racks in an American supermarket might easily conclude that we are all seized by a hysterical panic. Journals everywhere display the same headlines: "Spacemen Stole My Baby," or "I Was Forced to Have Sex with Aliens," or "Experts Confirm That Aliens Are Abducting Housewives." Just tabloid hype, or is there more to it?

Many people do take the news of alien kidnappings and stolen pregnancies seriously. Therapists, doctors, and a multitude of authors make the talk-show circuits to promote their latest book on the phenomenon. There have been documentary films and made-for-TV-movies supporting the bizarre claims. Recently a distinguished professor of psychiatry at the prestigious Harvard School of Medicine also studied the reports; the book on his findings became a best-seller.

These reports are not lacking in committed witnesses. Whether deluded or not, there are literally hundreds of women in America claiming that aliens have impregnated them and/or stolen their fetus. Many have sought professional counseling to cope with feelings of violation or rape. There are many additional witnesses who insist they were abducted and sexually or genetically examined. Are all these people neurotic or dishonest?

Most of the recent reports describe diminutive alien beings possessed of terrifying psychic and technological abilities. Because of their pale skin color, they are popularly named the "Grays."

This rising tide of forced abductions, rapes, mind control, unwilling genetic experimentation, and stolen pregnancies

are the dark side of UFO literature. Because of their sensational and sexual elements, they are highly attractive to the
media in the '90s, especially television "news magazines."

Tales of sexual encounters with the occupants of UFOs are
nothing new. Many ancient cultures reported experiences that
sound suspiciously like modern alien abductions. It took the
Villas-Boas case of 1957 to carry the notion of alien-human
interbreeding to the twentieth century imagination.

Antonio Villas-Boas was a twenty-three-year-old Brazilian
farmer working at night because of the intense heat of the
day. On October 14, he was tilling his fields alone on his
tractor. Around 1 A.M. he sighted a "luminous, egg-shaped
craft flying toward me at terrific speed." The engine of Villas-
Boas's tractor died as three metal legs descended from the
hovering object.

The frightened farmer attempted to escape, but was captured by four helmeted humanoids who forced him into the
craft. Inside the UFO, Villas-Boas was subjected to an examination by the entities, who took a blood sample from his
chin. He described the aliens as speaking with one another in
a "barking language" similar to the barking of dogs. They
then stripped him and sponged him off with some liquid.

The beings left him on a platform or table, and an "oily
smoke" entered the room from a vent. A nude, red-headed female with "long fingers and slanted eyes" then entered. He
described the woman as "much more beautiful than any other
I have ever known before." She rubbed and embraced the
confused farmer, who became aroused and engaged with her
in sexual intercourse. Villas-Boas repeated the act two more
times, and later said that his partner performed "much the
same way any woman would," except for her unnerving
"barking sounds."

When they were finished, the woman pointed to her belly,
to the farmer, then at the sky. Villas-Boas interpreted this to
refer to the fruit of their intercourse. "What they wanted of
me was a good stallion to improve their own stock." Then
his clothes were returned and he was given a short tour of
the ship. After setting him back on the ground, the UFO
sped away.

After reading a local newspaper calling for UFO reports,
Villas-Boas came forward with his tale. He was examined

by a local physician, Dr. Olivio Fontes, who reported what seemed to be a case of radiation poisoning. Dr. Fontes also noticed a scar under the man's chin where he claimed the blood sample had been taken.

Investigators mentioned that the poorly educated farmer seemed honestly to believe his own story. His tale, widely carried by news services, was seized by the UFO research community as an example of the aliens' need for human genetic materials. Their own race, in serious physical decline, was replenishing itself with human genes.

This motif of required human-alien interbreeding became popular with many UFO authors, though the theme suffered significant alterations in the early 1980s. Some of these reports speculated that the aliens are aware of the imminent end of humanity, and are creating a hybrid race that would survive the coming cataclysm. Others have suggested that they were mating with us to improve our own degenerate stock!

The most famous of all early abduction cases occurred on September 19, 1961. Around 10:30 P.M., Betty and Barney Hill were returning from Canada on Route 3 near the village of Lancaster, New Hampshire. Betty had been following the movement of a bright, flashing object in the sky through her binoculars. The object moved on a strange, spinning flight pattern. Though Barney had dismissed it as an airplane, they both became concerned when it suddenly veered from its path to move closer to them. South of Indian Head, the mysterious object suddenly came to hover eighty to one hundred feet overhead. Barney Hill stopped the car and got out leaving the motor still running.

Walking closer to the blue-lit object, he saw a row of windows or observation ports. When he noticed what seemed to be a dozen "glowing faces with hypnotic eyes" looking down at him, Betty Hill heard him exclaim, "I don't believe it! I don't believe it! This is ridiculous!" Now thoroughly frightened, Barney ran back to the car and drove off at a high speed.

Driving along, they heard a continuous "beeping sound" that appeared to come from the car trunk. They became drowsy and apparently fell asleep. After two more sets of beeping sounds, they awoke to find themselves thirty-five miles away from their last remembered location. Both their watches had stopped. Eventually they reached home.

Betty Hill remained extremely upset by the encounter. Two days after the sighting she began reading at the local library on UFOs, including Major Donald Keyhoe's book *Flying Saucer Conspiracy.* Ten days after the experience, she began having vivid nightmares where she remembered being captured by aliens and taken aboard their craft for a painful medical examination. She became convinced that these were not mere dreams, but actual memories.

In February 1964, the Hills began a series of sessions with psychiatrist Dr. Benjamin Simon of Boston. Simon initially suggested hypnotherapy in order to "relieve the couple's tensions stemming from the encounter." In independent sessions, the two began to remember the "two lost hours" through "inducted time regression." Their sessions were audio taped; listening to them restored conscious memory of the events to the Hills.

They recalled separate experiences. Barney Hill said that he was captured by the aliens and forced into the ship, where he underwent a medical examination. Though he refused to open his eyes, his captors communicated with him through a form of mental telepathy.

Betty also underwent an examination, part of which involved the insertion of a long needle in her navel. The aliens communicated that this was a "pregnancy test." After her exam, Betty was shown a "star map" that supposedly showed the aliens' home world. Her attempts to sketch the aliens' point of origin closely resembled the stars Zeta Reticuli 1 and 2.

The Hills received unexpected confirmation from a military source. The radar at Pease Air Force Base reported tracking an anomalous UFO in the New Hampshire skies the same night of the report!

Dr. Simon tended to be skeptical of the reality of the experience. In his view, the story was "too improbable . . . much of the material was similar to dream material." Simon also speculated that the Hills, who were a racially mixed couple, might be expressing deep-seated conflicts about their relationship. The Hills were not interested in such theories and continued to maintain that the event really occurred. Their experience was recorded in a best-selling book, *The Interrupted Journey,* written by John Fuller.

Skeptics, including astronomer Carl Sagan and professional debunker Phillip Klass, criticized various aspects of the tale. Despite the skepticism, the Hills' story achieved the status of legend in UFO circles.

Another famed case occurred in the Sitgraves National Park in Arizona, north of Payson. The event, on November 5, 1975, was particularly remarkable for the presence of six sworn witnesses to an abduction that apparently lasted five days.

The brothers Travis and Duane Walton were members of a seven-man wood-cutting crew that had received a Forest Service permit to clear trees in a selected area of the National Park. After a long day's work, the team piled into a truck to begin the drive back to their base. On the way, the entire group sighted a hovering saucer shape surrounded by a "golden glow."

When the truck stopped, Travis Walton jumped out and began running toward the object for a closer look. The others in the crew remained by the vehicle and shouted for him to get back. The men saw a blue beam of light shoot from the object and hit Walton, knocking him back into the trees. The horrified woodcutters fled in the truck, driving to the local sheriff and returning with a search party. The searchers found no sign of either Walton or the UFO.

The search was resumed on a larger scale the following day, and lasted for five days. When Walton still failed to turn up, the woodcutters voluntarily took a lie detector test, chiefly in order to clear themselves of possible charges of foul play. The men passed the test, but Walton himself turned up that same night, disheveled and confused.

According to him, he had been abducted by the pale, large-headed and huge-eyed occupants of the craft. He had been subjected to a painful "medical examination" and taken on what he reported as a space flight. He also stated that he had seen a figure of human appearance on the craft who seemed to be allied with the entities.

Walton also took a lie detector test administered by Dr. Gene Rosenbaum of Durango, Colorado, who stated, "This young man is not lying. . . . he really believes these things." Walton later wrote a book describing his abduction, *The Wal-*

ton Experience. His story was made into a sensational 1993 feature film, *Fire From the Sky,* which shows in gruesome detail the examination by the creatures.

In 1993, I camped in the area of the incident and found it to contain very wild sections of forest and mountain; it was easy to picture the presence of the unknown. For many of the local people, the story had attained the stature of a myth. Travis Walton and most of the others still live in the same area, and have kept to their story.

Painful exams by rather fumbling aliens ignorant of human anatomy seem to be a staple of abduction reports. Are they just trying to figure out what makes people tick, or do they have a deeper agenda? The investigations often focus on human reproductive organs (remember Betty Hills's "pregnancy test"?). In 1976 there was another examination case, this time on the opposite side of the continent in New England.

Four men, Charlie Foltz, Chuck Rak, Jack and Jim Weiner, were on a canoe trip along the wild Allagash waterway in northern Maine. The men were experienced outdoorsmen and anticipated some serious fishing. The trout weren't biting, but the men themselves got hooked.

Paddling along in their canoes at night, the men sighted a hovering, glowing ball of light with "oscillating patterns like iron filings around a magnet." Signaling the object with a flashlight to provoke a response turned out to be a mistake. The men were picked right out of their boats by a "beam of light from the sky."

After the beam, Jack Weiner reported struggling to open his eyes for what seemed an eternity. When he finally did, he found himself inside a strange, glowing chamber sitting on a bench next to the other men of his party. All of the men were naked.

Weiner saw that his friends appeared to be dazed and completely unconcerned by their surroundings. Struggling, he found that he was unable to move his body. Then a bizarre, alien form emerged from the light. It was a big-headed, large-eyed, diminutive gray humanoid. The alien was joined by others who busied themselves conducting a physical examination of the men.

Weiner, in a panic, began struggling even more fiercely.

The aliens responded by peering hypnotically at him out of their enormous eyes. He heard a mechanical-sounding voice in his head repeating over and over, "You will not be harmed. . . . You will cooperate. . . . You must do as we direct. . . . You will not be harmed."

Weiner reported that his armpit was scraped by some metal or ceramic instrument. He was also subjected to an examination of his genitals, which included a painful probe being inserted into his penis. A strange device was then fitted over the organ, apparently to take a sperm sample.

After their exams concluded, the men remembered a great light, then found themselves back on shore at their camp with confused memories of the last hours. Badly shaken, the men returned home to tell their story, eventually seeking hypnotic regression in an attempt to regain full recall.

There were a number of factors that were of great interest to investigators. Two of the men, Jack and Jim Weiner, were identical twins. The taking of sperm samples corroborated earlier accounts. Later inquiries also revealed that the men suffered many of the classical aftereffects of abductions, including follow-up paranormal phenomena. Lastly, all of the men were professional artists who were able to make detailed sketches of their experiences. Their story was turned into a book, *The Allagash Abductions,* written by Raymond E. Fowler.

In 1975, Steve Killburn was an earnest young man who had attended informal discussions with investigator Ted Bloecher on regaining lost abduction memories. Killburn was convinced something strange had happened to him a few years back while driving home on an empty stretch of road to Baltimore, Maryland. Bloecher introduced him to a colleague of his, Budd Hopkins.

With Hopkins, Bloecher, and a psychologist, Killburn underwent a series of hypnotherapy sessions. During three sessions over a period of months, he recalled a frightening encounter with two lights in the sky. The memories included a "magnetic force" that pulled his car off the road, followed by hazy pictures of alien beings. He eventually realized that, "I don't want to remember. I'm not supposed to remember." Hopkins included Killburn's story in his work *Missing Time,* published in 1981.

One of the most popular and influential figures in modern UFO circles, Budd Hopkins is an accomplished painter and sculptor whose works have appeared in the Guggenheim Museum, the Whitney Museum of Modern Art, the Smithsonian's Hirschhorn Collection, and others. He is also a best-selling author of a number of abduction studies, including *Missing Time* and the CBS-TV miniseries *Intruders*.

Bitten by the UFO bug after an early sighting at Cape Cod, Hopkins started following up cases whenever he could and developed contacts with many researchers in the field. Because of his personal sympathies, he became a popular interviewer with UFO witnesses weary of accusations of delusion or fraud.

Budd Hopkins is an early exponent of hypnotherapy as a valid means of verifying abductee experiences. From his early days as an amateur investigator, he has since become a father figure for the modern abductee movement. He maintains that the abduction cases contain the answer to the entire UFO mystery.

He early suggested that the key to these cases is in the missing time element of many abductees. If he could unlock the missing time, the real story would come out. This commonsense theory became the sine qua non of many abduction therapists.

Hopkins's final observations stunned his many readers. He felt that the memory blocks experienced by many abductees reflected their role as "human specimens" continuously studied over a period of years. The testimony of these individuals suggests that they "are being picked up as children, implanted with monitoring devices, and abducted a second time after puberty." (The strange scars found on many of his witnesses were evidence of the implants.) The monitoring aliens then returned again and again to check on the progress of their subjects.

In 1983, Hopkins received a letter from Kathie Davis, who reported a number of frightening experiences at her suburban home in Copley Woods near Indianapolis. Intrigued, he responded with an invitation to meet in New York. Her story convinced him that she and her family had undergone a series of genuine, traumatic UFO encounters and deserved further investigation.

Hopkins unearthed a harrowing tale of a family that had been repeatedly abducted for years, beginning in 1965. Their memories, filled with hazy recollections of gray-skinned aliens and suspicious blank periods, began to emerge under hypnosis. The aliens had landed in their yard (where a strange burn mark was to be seen) before removing family members from the home. Inexplicable scars on Kathie were the result of the alien exams and "implants." Worse memories were still to come.

Just prior to her wedding in 1978, Kathie took a pregnancy test and verified that she was pregnant. The wedding was moved up from April to March, but she later began menstruating normally. An additional test confirmed that she was no longer pregnant. According to her normal memories, she had suffered some sort of traumatic abduction experience during the same time period.

Through hypnotherapy, she learned that her fetus had been taken from her in an operation aboard an alien spacecraft. She also learned that she had been originally impregnated by the aliens, not her husband. The baby was an alien-human hybrid! Her mind was filled with the shock and anger of the violation, and grief at her loss.

Convinced of the reality of the experience, additional memories flooded forth. Months after the fetus was stolen, she was taken by the aliens to meet her baby and hold it in her arms. She felt that this was done to check her emotional response to the hybrid baby. "It has something to do with touch, and the human part. . . . They don't understand, but they'll learn." These memories helped her come to terms with the experience.

Kathie Davis's story was reported at length by Hopkins in his book, *Intruders* (followed by the CBS miniseries of the same name). The book and the following miniseries brought the notion of hybrid infants and stolen pregnancies to a wider audience. Letters testifying to similar experiences flooded in from around the nation.

Interviewed in *Fate* magazine, Hopkins said that he was unclear about notions of good or evil in relation to the aliens and pointed to the visit concerning the hybrid baby. "At the end, she had been allowed to see the child, so she had hope for the future." Elsewhere, he discussed his observations of the abductions as a worldwide phenomenon. "We can logically theorize that there may be tens of thousands of Americans whose abductions have never been revealed. . . . We are in the middle of an epidemic."

In 1987, an associate of Budd Hopkins published a book about his own abductions that would reach an even wider audience. That book was *Communion: A True Story,* and the author was Whitley Strieber.

Strieber was the best-selling author of a number of horror novels, including *The Hunger* and *The Wolfen.* Around Christmas 1985, Strieber entered a period of depression so severe that he was unable to write. Living with his wife and young son in an isolated upstate New York cabin, he became convinced that he was being watched constantly. He bought a shotgun, had an elaborate alarm system installed, and began checking in closets and under beds before going to sleep.

The paranoia was accompanied by physical symptoms: fits of chills, extreme fatigue, and rectal pain so intense he was unable to sit for long. His marriage began breaking down after he insisted that his family sell their cabin and Greenwich Village apartment and move to Austin, Texas, then back again to New York. On January 3, 1986, he realized that all his problems were caused by the same event. "The confused swirl resolved into a specific series of recollections, and when I saw what they were, I just about exploded with terror and utter disbelief." He remembered awakening one night and being unable to move. Entities entered his bedroom and removed him to another place, where he underwent a number of operations conducted by small, dark-eyed, gray-skinned aliens.

One of the painful procedures involved a gray, wired device being inserted into his rectum, accounting for the continuing pains. In another operation, they inserted a long needle into his skull. "The next thing I knew, there was a bang and a flash." His captors also made a long incision in his forefinger (the site of a continuing, hard-to-fight infection). The shocking memories ended in a blank space.

He began wondering if he was losing his mind, or if he had a brain tumor. Though he'd never before been interested in UFOs, he picked up a book long enough to note that Bud Hopkins lived in Manhattan. In desperation, he found Hopkins's number in the phonebook and called him. Hopkins was immediately interested, and the two men met.

Strieber saw in Budd Hopkins a man who had wrestled with his own inner demons and won. Hopkins found him "profoundly frightened and clearly disoriented." He assisted Strieber with news of other abductees and their similar struggles; Strieber was no longer alone. Hopkins also introduced him to Dr. Donald Klein, an experienced psychologist working at the New York Psychiatric Institute. Dr. Klein agreed to counsel him using hypnotic regression techniques.

During the course of his therapy, Strieber "recovered" a series of alien abduction scenarios. They started with recent events, but gradually a pattern of lifelong abductions began to emerge. The aliens included both the typical Grays seen by others, and larger, seemingly female humanoids possessed of telepathic abilities. The entities possessed high, flutelike voices and struck him as somehow "insectlike" in appearance and manner (a feeling shared by other abductees).

Strieber still felt that he had many missing or untrustworthy memories, and attempted to verify some of them. His journey only confused him further; on one occasion, he found that memories of an entire year of living in a major city were false! What had happened to him in that time?

His memories had him utterly convinced that the "Visitors" had been monitoring him since childhood. He also realized that the deep and abiding terror felt since childhood had dictated his choice to write horror novels for a profession. He had been unconsciously telling the story of his own life.

During this period, Strieber's wife was also regressed by psychiatrist Dr. Bob Naiman. She found memories that corroborated Strieber's more recent accounts, though most often she was an observer.

> "They came for Whitley and he's supposed to go. But I'm not supposed to go. It has to do with him. I wanted to go too, but I felt I shouldn't."

Strieber's son had also shared experiences of what he called "the skeleton people." Guilt by association?

While still in therapy, Strieber began writing a book on his abductions and subsequent struggle for sanity. Budd Hopkins and others argued that it was too early for him to take this step. He responded by asking Hopkins's publisher, Random House, to delay publishing Hopkins's forthcoming book on the grounds of audience competition. Their friendship eventually failed.

Strieber originally wanted to call his book *Body Terror* because of the high levels of fear felt on a particular incident. However, one night he listened to Anne talking in her sleep. Suddenly she said in a strange, deep voice, "The book must not frighten people. You should call it *Communion,* because that's what it's about."

The voice was wrong, because it did frighten many people. The fear did not harm sales, though. *Communion* held the number-one position on the *New York Times* best-seller list for many months, unprecedented for a book on UFOs. The cover, featuring a portrait of a smiling "Visitor" done by artist Ted Jacobs, was particularly compelling. Buyers were picking it up off the shelves on sight, as if the image somehow resonated in their subconscious.

People around the world flocked to the banner of the "Visitors"; some entered their own abduction therapy or started newsletters and support groups, including a "Communion Foundation." The UFO books of other authors took on a new luster and sales were high while Strieber told his story on national TV talk shows.

He soon came out with a sequel, *Transformation,* an account of his continuing relationship with the entities. In many ways, *Transformation* was easier for readers to assimilate as its "fear level" is much lower; Strieber had come to terms with his experiences.

Transformation was followed by the film version of *Communion.* Starring actor Christopher Walken, it was a financial flop and panned by many critics. Strieber was also coming under increasing attack from fellow UFO researchers and authors. Some of these were probably motivated by jealousy at his success (very common in the UFO community). Others had clearer motivations and pointed arguments.

Hopkins and others were upset when he claimed bizarre knowledge of other contactees and writers, including seeing Kathie Davis (of *Intruders*) on an alien craft, only "it was just her head on a shelf." He made statements to listeners at his lectures that "the visitors will be watching you now."

There were also continuing allegations that Strieber had discussed *Communion* with his publisher long before his initial therapy. Witnesses claimed he'd described it to them as a fiction written under cover of a true story. Despite the attacks, the book remains a classic in its field.

When I first read *Communion* in 1988, I was very disturbed. For many years as a child, I had experienced episodes of waking into a "sleep paralysis" with a sense of beings standing nearby. Now other "memories" began flooding back; disturbing dreams of medical examinations in round rooms, strange machines floating in the sky, even childhood encounters with aliens. Could these things have really happened to me? I was skeptical of my own gullibility, but was also wary of dismissing things out of hand. The feelings were strong.

On an impulse, I purchased fourteen or fifteen copies as gifts for friends in various walks of life, telling them nothing. Some months later, I asked them what they thought of the book. Every single one confessed to strange, disturbing feelings of familiarity regarding Strieber's experiences. Ten of the readers admitted that they were so unnerved by the feelings "it had happened to them" that they never finished reading it.

This admittedly unscientific survey might confirm what Strieber, Hopkins, and others have been saying; that we are in the midst of an epidemic of alien abductions. It could also mean simply that Whitley Strieber is an extremely effective writer, and his subject is a powerful, archetypal theme buried deep in our minds. Maybe the two answers are the same.

The September 1992 issue of *Fate* provided a questionnaire for people wondering if they have been abducted. Some of the questions were:

> "Have you ever awakened paralyzed with a sense of a stranger or presence in the room? Have you ever experienced a period of time, an hour or more, in which you were lost, but could not remember why or where you had been? Have you ever found puzzling, unremembered scars on your body?"

According to the story in *Fate,* a recent Roper Poll of six thousand adults asked these and similar questions showed that two percent responded positively to four or more survey questions, "indicating that they may have had an abduction experience." When extrapolated to the general population, it "indicates that as many as 3.7 million adult Americans may be abductees" (error margin of 1.4 percent). Do such articles and books convince people that it happened to them?

Whatever the initial trigger, more people than ever claim alien encounters. They share common themes: incidents of sleep paralysis, disturbing dreams, missing time covered by "screen memories," childhood alien contact, sexual or genital examinations aboard UFOs, surgical implants, and tales of human-alien hybrids or stolen human embryos. The vast majority of their new memories are recovered through hypnotherapy.

Women claiming that "aliens stole my baby" are particularly popular with journalists and television interviewers. Their claims are shocking and extraordinary; their obvious grief and anger especially heartrending.

Many of them claim to have passed standardized pregnancy tests and even had their abdomen start to enlarge. Then one morning, they woke up to find their belly flat again; their doctor could now find no evidence of pregnancy. A few women have small abdominal scars such as laparoscopic operations might leave behind. Most show no evidence of surgery.

Some people have "recovered" memories of aliens removing ova from human females. The reports also describe tiny monitoring devices that were implanted into the amniotic fluid surrounding a human fetus. In some cases, the device alerted the aliens when it was time to remove the baby; other times, it simply tracked the growth and birth of an outwardly normal baby. These implants are supposed to be too small to register on scans done by our "primitive" science.

Many therapists have emerged to provide services for abductees, (often called "experiencers"). Some of these counselors have solid reputations and skills; others more questionable backgrounds. Some charge hefty fees for helping clients remember the abductions, and then end by writing popular books about their work.

Those who facilitate abduction groups find themselves in a position of responsibility and authority. Trained or not, they automatically become mentors and guides, counselors and comforters.

In *Healing Shattered Reality*, authors Alice Bryant and Linda Seebach discuss not only physical and emotional indicators signaling contactee trauma, but ways for the experiencers to rebuild their lives. Though oriented toward channeled material, this well-researched work also draws upon professional studies of sexual abuse and violence. It's so popular that new age bookstores have difficulty keeping it on their shelves.

Toronto psychotherapist Dr. David Gotlib edits the *Bulletin of Anomalous Experiences* and is no stranger to the history of reported UFO contacts. He focuses on helping his clients deal with fear, depression, and anxiety. Unlike Bryant and Seebach, however, Dr. Gotlib is not committed to one particular interpretation.

In a recent issue of *UFO* magazine, Gotlib said:

"There are lots of interesting theories . . . (but) I feel that it's bad medicine and fundamentally unethical to simply pick one theory and proceed on that basis." He goes on to note, "All experience, positive or negative, is an opportunity for transformation, if you let it be so. Whatever this phenomena is, it's part of the human experience."

Another popular abduction counselor is California hypnotherapist Yvonne Smith, who leads the Close Encounters Research Organization (CERO). She stresses that "CERO meetings are for the abductees. When new members come for the first time, they're always nervous. I always want them to feel at home, comfortable." She encourages people to tell their stories at their own pace and not to avoid reliving the pain. "There is hope. We can get past this fear."

There are many groups of experiencers attempting to process their encounters and get on with their lives. The majority rarely question the environment of belief they find themselves in. For them, these things happened as they (now) remember. They're glad to have found others like themselves and the groups provide a sense of security and family.

When the news spread that psychiatrist John Mack had signed a contract with a major publisher to write about abductees, the entire UFO world was abuzz. Dr. Mack is a professor of psychiatry at the Cambridge Hospital, Harvard Medical School. One of his earlier, non-UFO books, had won the Pulitzer Prize. He'd recently published several provocative and sympathetic papers on his studies of contactees. If anyone had the credentials to make the phenomenon be taken seriously, it was he.

His book, *Abduction: Human Encounters with Aliens,* published in 1994, is a well written analysis of his work with thirteen cases of alien "experiencers." After long investigation, Mack was unable to attribute mental illness to any of his thirteen primary clients and viewed their claims seriously.

Mack says that he originally took the idea of alien abductions lightly. Then in January 1990, he visited Bud Hopkins out of curiosity, and found himself "impressed with his sincerity, depth of knowledge, and deep concern for the abductees, who had often been incorrectly diagnosed and inappropriately served by mental health professionals."

But what affected Mack even more, "was the internal consistency of the detailed accounts by different individuals from various parts of the country, who would have had no way to communicate with one another, and whose stories had emerged only with difficulty, accompanied by distressing emotions."

Mack met some other experiencers and was again impressed with their consistency. He decided to begin taking abductees as clients. Some of them described "multi-generational abductions," saying that they believed their children were also experiencing similar events. Their stories, including more suspected "implants," are told at length in Dr. Mack's book. *Abduction* is a fascinating work, though its chief impact perhaps lies in its respected author, who brings greater credibility to a controversial subject by his mere participation.

In an article in the *Washington Post,* John Mack affirmed his belief in the existence of the Grays and other alien forms:

"We do not know the source from which the alien beings come from. But they manifest in the physical world and bring about definable consequences in that domain. My own impression is that we may be witnessing . . . an awkward joining of two species, engineered by an intelligence we are unable to fathom, for a purpose that serves both our goals with difficulties for each."

It remains to be seen if Mack will suffer as other respected scientists crossing the line in the past have. Like other supporters of hypnotherapy, he has been faulted for his conclusions, but no concerted attacks have yet emerged from academia. Times have indeed changed.

. The idea of recovering "missing memories" of alien abductions did not originate in the UFO research community. America is currently going through a painful self-examination of its high incidence of child abuse and incest. Largely due to better-trained medical and social service staff, reliable reporting of child abuse has greatly improved. Child abuse leaves permanent scars and is a very real social problem of alarming proportions.

A huge industry of therapists has grown to serve individuals and groups of clients seeking to heal the wounds left by child abuse and/or incest. Since victims of such abuse are believed to blank out these painful memories in order to survive, therapies that help recover them have naturally become very important. Of these therapies, one of the most important is "guided imagery" or hypnotherapy.

The reliability of hypnotherapy as primary evidence is now being challenged. There are a few highly publicized cases where individuals confronted their victimizers in court, based on memories recovered by this means. The courts found the parents or adults guilty and put them away in prison or fined them. Then the "victim" suddenly realized, too late, that the alleged abuse was imaginary and had never really occurred. Such poorly treated cases unfortunately erode support for genuine survivors of incest and child abuse.

There are now national support organizations (such as Philadelphia's False Memory Syndrome Foundation), for people accused of child abuse based on recovered memories.

Some of these are currently engaged in lawsuits seeking damages from therapists. The suits claim that the predisposition of the therapist toward finding abuse led them to influence unduly their entranced client.

In the 1993 conference proceedings of TREAT (Treatment and Research of Experienced Anomalous Trauma) is a remarkable paper entitled "Making Monsters," by Richard Ofshe and Ethan Walters. In it they note the preference of mental health practitioners for miracle cures. Recovered memory therapy, they say, is merely the latest "miracle," and is as unreliable as earlier fads such as mesmerism.

> "Practitioners believe repression is a powerful psychological defense that causes one to lose all awareness of physically or sexually terrifying events. Not only is the event repressed but so are memories of the trauma's social context—that is, everything preceding and following it that would suggest to the victim that some trauma had occurred.
>
> "They may remain unaware of the trauma for perhaps thirty years, until they enter treatment where they discover their repressed memories. Once these memories are dredged up and accepted as real, practitioners encourage their clients to publicly accuse, confront, and perhaps sue those they believe to have been the perpetrators. These often turn out to be parents, siblings, and grandparents.
>
> "Therapists feel obligated to do whatever is necessary to uncover their client's hidden traumatic history. The methods employed have generated profound controversy. Critics charge the therapy does not unearth real memories at all. Rather their origin is therapist-induced. Clients are essentially being tricked into remembering events that never happened. . . . If therapists who elicit recovered memories and convince clients of their truth were obligated to demonstrate the validity of these accounts, they would be unable to do so."

All of this happened before in America; we were taught about it in elementary school. A number of fundamentalist preachers and ministers became convinced that "witches" and other agents of the devil were at work in their community. In response, a group of school children "recovered" memories that their neighbors and even parents were witches. The hapless accused were hauled into court, barbarically tortured until they confessed, and hanged or burnt at the stake. Today we call it the Salem Witch Trials of 1692.

If hypnotherapy is increasingly unreliable as evidence, where do we go from here? Many investigators continue to focus on physical evidence such as ground markings, unusual debris, sonic or electro-magnetic phenomena, and multiple-witness sightings. Some are using hi-tech devices like Magnetic Resonance Imaging scanners in an attempt to verify the alleged "implants." Unprovable cases where there are only recovered memories and publicity-seeking therapists are of little interest to these hard-boiled investigators.

Investigators must also be prepared to drop their own preconceived notions. Phenomena that defy set patterns are often overlooked by already-convinced researchers looking to bolster their pet theory. For example, drivers of automobiles being buzzed by UFOs have reported that the passenger in their car "turned into an alien" for a few minutes. Such anomalous elements are quickly erased from reports by believers in the Extraterrestrial Hypothesis.

The entities encountered might indeed be "real," but not necessarily aliens from another world. Veteran researcher Jacques Vallee joined the ranks of Carl Jung and others when he suggested that UFOs and aliens could conceivably be powerful archetypes (complex images embedded in human consciousness). The archetype theory could account for the Phenomenon's ability to change appearance to fit the witness's cultural background. Medieval peasants saw the Devil or fairies, rural workers in the 1950s and '60s saw spacemen from Venus, moderns apparently see whatever their latest therapist believes.

Whatever really happens in these cases, people would do well to keep an open mind regarding abduction reports. The long, transgenerational history of abductions is enough to suggest that something is going on both inside and outside our heads.

3

HIDDEN AGENDA

*We are never deceived;
we deceive ourselves.*

—GOETHE

OVER the past twenty-five years, I have witnessed a fair number of strange objects in the sky. Some of these were doubtless normal objects distorted by atmospheric phenomena, or had some other reasonable explanation. Two unexplained sightings, however, were extraordinarily vivid, and occurred in the presence of scores of other witnesses.

One sighting took place in 1986, in the pristine desert of Joshua Tree National Monument, near Yucca Valley, California. Perhaps fifty of us were there at a group campsite to listen to ethnobotanist-philosopher Terence McKenna give a lecture. Since we were going to stay there overnight, around 5 P.M. I went to my spot to set up my tent. Suddenly, I felt some kind of vibration, like that created by a passing train, and looked up into the cloudless sky.

Approximately two hundred fifty feet directly overhead was a huge black object about the size of a football field. Though it was near sunset, the huge, elliptical object was clearly seen, including the large number of moving lights visible on it. There were no projecting fins, propellers, windows, or painted markings; it was not the Goodyear blimp. I later realized that it was an exact replica of the so-called "mother ships" seen by many others and duplicated in the film *Close Encounters of the 3rd Kind.*

The object hovered overhead for approximately five minutes, then slowly passed over the horizon. I immediately walked down the trail to see if anyone else had seen it; perhaps forty people had. No one had a "normal" explanation.

Some years later, during the summer, I was attending an African dance concert in a hall in upstate New York. The drums were beating and everyone was dancing, when suddenly someone ran in shouting, "There's a UFO outside!" A trickle of people, swelling to a flood, ran out. Eventually at least two hundred fifty people were standing in the field gazing up at the sky.

We saw a large sphere of light passing along some power lines and silently moving toward us in a straight trajectory. The object was self-luminous and seemed to be barely eighty feet off the ground. When it reached the field where the crowd was standing, it suddenly broke apart into four smaller, spherical lights that separated, then flew off in the same direction in a line.

The next day, some of us called the local airports to see if any small planes or helicopters had been reported in the area, with no luck. In both instances, most people appeared happy with the possibility that they had seen an alien craft. However, many other witnesses claimed that if these were alien craft, the government "must already know about it" and perhaps were working with them. Some reported that they were worried that "we were being watched" and mentioned their fear of hostile abduction.

When we examine the literature, it appears that there have always been two camps of UFO believers. One group would be overjoyed if the saucers all landed tomorrow, and the other group suspects that they have already been around a long time, with unpleasant results. In this latter group, a few individuals have dedicated their lives to uncovering hidden government-alien activities. Some of them have found unusual evidence to support their claims.

Conspiracy theories are the lifeblood of the Extraterrestrial Hypothesis and its believers. The latest anonymous rumors of secret military experiments on cattle and humans, government treaties with aliens, CIA-sponsored "Men in Black," even Nazi and U.S. saucer programs are all carelessly tossed around as "proof." One author's secondhand hearsay is rehashed by the next as documented evidence.

Americans who believe what they see on television news magazines must be worried. We can hardly turn on the TV without encountering at least one documentary alleging government conspiracies to cover up the "truth" about alien invaders from another world. Unfortunately, it is rare for these reports to mention any theories outside of the Extraterrestrial Hypothesis. Viewers are led to assume that there are only two possible belief systems: that of the debunkers or that of the Faithful alleging physical space travelers and government conspiracy.

The situation is further muddled by persistent allegations of UFO-related projects at bona fide military bases engaged in futuristic research. The strange sightings and repressive levels of security at these projects only confirms the opinions of the True Believers. Whatever is truly occurring at these bases is probably more bizarre than many UFOlogists can imagine.

Some of the older reports originated in well-documented sightings. Fumbling attempts at obvious whitewashes, such as the Air Force's universally despised Project Blue Book, have bolstered cries of government cover-ups. Against all likelihood, these reports may contain a grain of truth.

UFO-related conspiracy theory originated in the Second World War. When people in the 1940s and '50s began wondering if the shiny lights in the sky were evidence of classified government programs, some recalled the "ghost rocket" and "foo fighter" sightings of World War II.

Cigar-shaped objects called ghost rockets were sighted from 1946 to 1948 in Finland and Sweden close to the Soviet Union. First thought to be Soviet military craft, they were never explained or confirmed and may have been related to the German V-2 rocket program. Throughout World War II, Allied bombers over enemy territory also reported strange balls of light flying near the wingtips of their planes.

The rare photographs of these objects look like glowing balls of plasma, or luminescent gas. Even if one ignores the question of how the hypothetical "balls of plasma" came to be there at all, the reports also stated the objects moved at high speeds with sudden changes in direction. Aerial acrobatics from plasma are even less credible.

They were dubbed "foo fighters" from the French word *feu* for fire, via the comic strip *Smokey Stover* quote, "Where there's foo, there's fire." After the war, it was learned that a number of German and Japanese pilots had encountered similar aerial phenomena. (These foo fighters were later to reappear, in greater numbers, over Korea, Okinawa, and Japan during the Korean War.)

The foo fighters may have had occupants. At least there were associated reports of strange, humanoid figures appearing aboard some of the airborne bombers. Like the leprechauns of myth, these "little green men" behaved in a bizarre, mischievous fashion and wreaked havoc with sensitive instruments. They seemed to appear and disappear out of thin air.

The little men, dubbed "gremlins," were viewed as hallucinations suffered by oxygen-deprived flyers. After the war, the gremlins passed into folklore, living on only in *Bugs Bunny* cartoons and military jargon (where inexplicable equipment breakdowns were called gremlins). Though gremlins were forgotten, the foo fighters were not, and some have tried to connect them to the legendary Nazi flying saucers.

There are countless myths about Nazi survivals, cults, and strange technologies. The French and Americans, in particular, seem fascinated by the Nazis and books on them sell very well in their countries. Though most of the books are either fiction or racist rubbish, some interesting historical rumors have appeared about German UFOs.

At the end of the war, military analysts began investigating reports of flying saucers, ghost rockets, and foo fighters. Could they be products of an earthly military operation? Apparently the U.S. Air Technical Intelligence Command (ATIC) thought so. In 1956, Edward J. Ruppelt wrote:

> "When World War II ended, the Germans had several radical types of aircraft and guided missiles under development. The majority of these aircraft were in the most preliminary stages but they were the only known craft that could even approach the performance of the objects reported by UFO observers. Like the Allies, after World War II the Soviets had obtained complete sets of data on the latest German developments.
>
> "This, coupled with rumors that the Soviets were frantically developing the German ideas, caused no small degree of alarm. Wires were sent to intelligence agents in Germany requesting that they find out exactly how much progress had been made on the various

German projects. The last possibility ... was that the Soviets had discovered some completely new aerodynamic concept that would give saucer performance."

Though ATIC's scientists were later to report that there was "no conceivable way that any aircraft could perform in such a way to match the reported maneuvers of UFOs," rumors that the Nazis had been working on saucers persisted. A number of books and pamphlets supporting the story emerged during the 1950s and early '60s. One of them was *We Want You—Is Hitler Alive?* by "Michael X" Barton.

Among many controversial revelations, "Michael X" reported that German engineer Viktor Schauberger had designed several saucer-shaped aircraft for the Luftwaffe in 1940. The saucers supposedly employed electromagnetic energy and flew by remote control. According to "X," development of the saucers had continued in secret and were responsible for many recent UFO sightings around the world. His story was picked up and repeated by other authors.

Christof Friedrich in *UFOs—Nazi Secret Weapon?*, wrote that the Nazi saucers were called "flugelrads" and reached speeds over two thousand kilometers per hour. The flugelrads were based upon Viktor Schauberger's electromagnetic-propulsion designs and were "used at the end of the war to fly a special cadre (including Hitler) to safety in Antarctica."

Another oft-repeated tale was that the Nazis had been in touch with a secret occult society of advanced adepts, who had given them plans for "vimanas" (a Sanskrit term for mythical flying machines).

According to Wilhelm Landig's *Gotzen gegen Thule,* the foo fighters were actually "Manisolas," or living "bio-machines" that could shift across the spectrum from pure light to solid metal during a seven-stage life cycle.

Landig described their appearance when flying:

"At night the discs shine in glowing or glossy colors, showing on occasion long flames at the edges and red and blue sparks, which can grow so strong as to wreathe them in fire. Most remarkable is their power of reaction against pursuers, like that of a rational creature, far exceeding any possible electronic self-steering or radio control."

These Manisolas were supposedly employed after the war by Nazis escaping to the hidden underworld to plan their eventual return.

Though many of these wild tales emerged long after the end of the war, they are descendants of rumors that investigators have heard since the mid-1940s. Other reports suggested that the U.S. military had taken possession of the Nazi program and were building their own saucers.

The reports of ghost rockets, foo fighters, and mythical Nazi saucers suggested that someone was exploring unconventional means of flight. Sky watchers, military buffs, and some journalists began putting two and two together, and hoped for the "conspiracy" to break. They didn't have very long to wait.

Something "bright and fast" burned through the storm-filled night sky near Corona, New Mexico on July 2, 1947. It smashed into the ground, scattering wreckage and debris over three-quarters of a mile onto William Brazel's ranch. After taking a look at the crash site on their property, William (Mac) Brazel and his children reported the wreckage to Chaves County Sheriff Wilcox. The sheriff called in the Air Force.

Brazel showed the Air Force team the wreckage he'd found strewn about an area over three-quarters of a mile long. Much of the wreckage apparently consisted of a foil-like material similar to the foil of cigarette packages, but non-creasable and untearable. There were also extremely light, I-beam shaped pieces of "unbreakable material." The I-beams were incised with strange, unidentifiable symbols. All the wreckage was carted away by Air Force personnel.

This became one of the most famous mysteries in UFO history, just a month after Kenneth Arnold's highly publicized sighting in Washington state. The Arnold sighting had initiated the first intensive media focus on UFOs; now there was a report of one downed in the Southwest.

Major Jesse A. Marcel, an Army-Air Force intelligence officer, had been sent with his team to the crash site. His impression was that the wreckage was of a craft unlike any that he had ever seen. He stated that it "was not a missile, a tracking device, or a weather balloon." The *Roswell Daily Record,* a publication for the nearby town, carried a story on the crash that quoted Air Force personnel stating that they had recovered the wreckage of a "flying disc of unknown origin."

A press release was issued by the Roswell Army Air Base on July 8. It stated, "Roswell Army Air Field was fortunate enough to gain possession of a disc through the cooperation of one of the local ranchers and the Sheriff's office at Chaves County."

It appears that the military altered its policy immediately afterwards and drew a cloak of secrecy over the entire affair. A report on the case being broadcast from the KSWS radio station in Roswell was apparently interrupted by an incoming teletype message saying, "Cease transmission. National Security item. Do not transmit. Repeat. Do not transmit this message."

Mac Brazel was held by the Air Force for a period of several days and ordered to stay silent on the grounds of national security. Air Force General Ramsey later gave a press conference where he stated that the earlier report had been "a terrible mistake." The material was merely the wreckage of a weather balloon!

Though the story ran down in the media after the Air Force denial, it refused to die in the minds of researchers. Within years, there were reports circulating of four humanoid bodies found in the wreckage. The bodies were said to have been kept under ice and remained the object of intense, classified investigation. Cries of a continuing cover-up were added to the story.

Much of the speculation stems from claims by William Haut, a former Air Force public affairs officer, who said that on July 2, 1947, he was first told to prepare a news release describing the retrieved saucer, and then to change it to the weather balloon story. A local nurse who claimed that she was part of the first autopsy of the aliens subsequently died in a plane crash.

In the years that followed, UFO investigators Bill Moore and Stanton Friedman located over three hundred witnesses to the Roswell Incident, including fifty claiming to know that alien bodies were recovered by the military. Similar testaments were obtained by a second, independent research team. Something strange does appear to have come down from the sky at Roswell.

While the furor over the crashed saucer at Roswell was dying down (or being covered up), there were other significant events. One of these was the strange death of Captain Thomas Mantell.

On January 7, 1948, the air control tower at Goodman Field, Kentucky, reported a sighting of a bright, disc-shaped flying object. The object was still visible nearly an hour and a half later. At that time, four National Guard P-51 Mustang planes were diverted from a training exercise to investigate the object. Captain Mantell was the flight leader.

The aircraft sighted the object and initiated pursuit. At an altitude of fifteen thousand feet, three of the planes turned back due to lack of oxygen supplying equipment. Mantell's craft, supplied with oxygen, continued the pursuit while remaining in radio contact.

Captain Mantell made one transmission stating that the object remained in sight and that he was climbing to investigate. Reports of his transmission quote him as describing the object as "metallic . . . tremendous in size." Then the radio went dead.

The Mustang crashed, with wreckage scattered over a mile. The body of Mantell was found in the wreckage. Examination showed that he had not attempted to eject from the craft. Due to "extraordinary wounds" on the body, he was buried in a closed casket.

Was Mantell's flight shot down by the mysterious object? The final report by authorities was that experienced pilot Mantell had passed out "from lack of oxygen, while mistakenly chasing the planet Venus."

Another wreck was reported to have occurred in the Aztec, New Mexico area on March 25, 1948. At this latter crash it was said that sixteen alien bodies had been found in a damaged but recoverable flying saucer. According to the questionable Air Force sources of newspaper columnist Frank Scully, the craft had been detected by radar units, and there was some speculation that radar signals had disrupted the craft's controls.

The disc was reported to be approximately one hundred

feet wide with a central cabin six feet high. It was said to be made of a light metal so hard that neither heat nor diamond drills were able to mark the surface. There were no signs of rivets or welding. Entrance was obtained through a porthole damaged in the crash.

The report went on to state that the interior of the craft held panels marked with hieroglyphiclike symbols, and a book of these markings seemed to be constructed from some sort of plastic. The object was then transported to Wright-Patterson Air Force Base.

The cadavers were described as three and a half feet tall and slender, with huge heads, large slanting eyes, diminished ears, and gray skin. The report also stated that clinical dissection revealed an atrophied digestive tract, and a strange, ozone-smelling fluid instead of blood.

Whether or not this tale represents a hoax or an actual event, over the following years there have been many reports of saucers retrieved in the Southwest. Both in the Southwest and elsewhere, their living and dead occupants are said to answer to the description of the Grays above.

New Mexico was then and remains one of the most important military research areas on the planet. The world's first nuclear bomb test site is there. White Sands Missile Range is not far from Roswell, as is Holloman Air Force Base. Roswell itself still has the second largest runway in the United States. The "nuclear city" of Los Alamos is a few hours north. There is also a host of smaller or lesser-known military research facilities in the state.

It is a fact that highly classified research in many areas, including the Strategic Defense Initiative (SDI, or "Star Wars"), is under way to this day in New Mexico. Over the years, a number of modern UFO researchers pursuing their own investigations have run afoul of the government's desire to keep these projects free from prying eyes. Is it possible that some of these projects continue to study alien life forms and technology?

By the 1950s, there were numerous publications dedicated to the proposition that aliens were visiting the earth. Some of these were channeled writings from one avatar or another; others were more "nuts and bolts" in their focus. Those of the nuts-and-bolts variety often focused on the "suspicious" silence of the military services on such matters, especially the U.S. Air Force.

In the January 1950 issue of *True* magazine, there appeared a sensational article on UFOs by retired Marine Corps Major Donald E. Keyhoe. Major Keyhoe's controversial article pointed many fingers at the government and was widely read. In it, he speculated that "the planet Earth has been under systematic, close-range examination by living, intelligent observers from another planet." He stated that this was known to top-level officers in the Air Force, who were covering up the evidence. Keyhoe backed up his claims with anonymous reports from members of various military and government agencies.

Major Keyhoe also released a book in 1950, *The Flying Saucers Are Real,* which sold over five hundred thousand copies. This work, and the follow-up *Aliens From Space,* fixed the notion of government-UFO conspiracy in the minds of many of his readers. Keyhoe's books have been justly criticized as sensationalistic and poorly documented. However, they marked the real beginning of hearsay and unsubstantiated rumor as acceptable proof in the minds of UFO conspiracy buffs.

There were many other UFO sightings throughout the 1940s and '50s, including some by military personnel. Despite many investigations, official government policy was that there was nothing "unearthly" or unexplainable in them.

The best-known government investigation was the widely criticized Project Blue Book, conducted by the Air Force from March 1952 to December 1969. This extensive investigation employed highly trained officers to interview hundreds of witnesses and researchers, eventually concluding that there was no evidence to support the existence of flying saucers. The official government investigation is supposed to have ended then.

Many Blue Book documents are still classified and beyond the reach of the public. It is safe to say that Blue Book's public report marked the end of trust in government on the part of the civilian UFO research community.

The '40s and '50s are now being reexamined by modern UFO researchers due to the extraordinary appearance of alleged top secret government documents. One relates the existence of Majestic 12, or MJ-12, a classified government research group founded after the Roswell Incident and answerable only to then-President Truman.

In 1982, UFO researcher Bill Moore and television producer Jamie Shandera received a mysterious wrapped canister containing a roll of unprocessed 35 mm film in the mail. There was no return address. When developed, they had copies of a nine page document stamped PREPARED FOR PRESIDENT-ELECT EISENHOWER: EYES ONLY and OPERATION MAJESTIC. They knew that they held potential dynamite in their hands.

First displayed in 1987 by Moore and Shandera, the MJ-12 document is alleged to have been made for President Dwight D. Eisenhower on November 18, 1952. The document opens with a discussion of the early sightings. It then relates the reclamation of four "extraterrestrial biological entities" (EBEs) from the wreckage of the Roswell crash, and the subsequent examination of the bodies. (The physical descriptions match the Grays earlier at Aztec.) The document also notes a decision to maintain the cover-up in the interests of national security.

A second Southwest crash, in Texas this time, is also described in Majestic. The document states the belief of investigators that the craft "do not originate on Earth." Because of the "ultimate need to prevent a public panic at all costs," it was the unanimous decision of the Majestic group that the future investigations be conducted under the strictest security.

The names of the twelve members of the Majestic group appearing on the document were all prominent senior military and scientific personnel, all now deceased. They include a past chairman of the Joint Chiefs of Staff, past Secretaries of the Army, Air Force and Defense, Admiral R. H. Hillenkoetter (a founder of the Central Intelligence Agency), and other former heads of the CIA. (The CIA itself was created in 1949 under the Central Intelligence Act.)

Award-winning reporter Howard Blum's book, *Out There,* details lengthy interviews and research on MJ-12. Perhaps the finest study to date on the controversy, the book describes the existence of a multi-agency UFO Working Group formed under the auspices of the Defense Intelligence Agency (DIA).

A major focus of the Working Group was the Majestic report and related matters.

This Working Group is reported to have initiated a top-level FBI investigation of the authenticity of the MJ-12 documents. According to Mr. Blum's sources, the FBI investigated the possibility of fraud by Moore and Shandera, disinformation by foreign intelligence agencies, or disinformation or cover-up by the Air Force Office of Special Investigations out of Kirtland Air Force Base.

This reported FBI investigation is supposed to have eventually rejected the first two possibilities and reached a dead end with the Air Force. Every one of the officers interviewed denied prior knowledge or involvement with MJ-12. Additionally, a large number of those interviewed suddenly decided to retire and refused further interviews on constitutional grounds as private citizens. The FBI's final report concluded that the UFO Working Group themselves were now possible candidates for fabrication of Majestic!

Elements of the Majestic document have been endlessly scrutinized by experts in government documents of the era. As usual, some experts consider it genuine while others maintain it is a fraud. Yet others see it as government disinformation using standard format and codes for classified documents of the time.

President Harry Truman's signature on the document has been certified as genuine. Freedom of Information Act requests have established that documents mentioning the name Majestic did indeed exist in the National Archives, though highly classified. Many of those who believe the document consider MJ-12 an ongoing project still active today and kept hidden from the overall intelligence community on a "need to know" basis.

The Majestic story aired on both ABC-TV's *Nightline* and *20/20* news shows. Amazingly, after these remarkable assertions appeared on nationwide television, there was *no* follow-up of any kind by the national media. However, a small number of ex-military personnel and researchers have stepped forward to back up Majestic in books and lectures. One of these was Milton William Cooper.

Bill Cooper is a former Navy petty officer who alleges that he worked on two classified government documents relating to Majestic and similar projects. Two months after the *Nightline* broadcast, he released information about MJ-12 over the CompuServe and Paranet computer networks. He stated that, despite the fear of reprisal, he "couldn't live with the secret any longer" and had to release it. Consumer computer networks were chosen as they possess the capability to broadcast information widely in a short period without immediate controls.

Cooper stated that the two reports he saw were Project Grudge-Report 13 and a Majority-Majestic briefing. The Grudge report that he viewed contained twenty-five black-and-white photographs of "alien life-forms" with physiological reports. The Majority report discussed the government's growing concern regarding alien interference with earth.

The Cooper material describes many classified departments that study UFO phenomena for the government. Project: Pounce was designed to retrieve any crashed UFOs or related technology, and provide subsequent cover-ups. Project Redlight's mission was to test-fly any captured or replicated alien spacecraft. It was postponed after attempts resulted in destruction of the craft and death of the pilots, then resumed in 1972.

Redlight's base of operations is the infamous Area 51 or "Dreamland" at the Groom Lake Base in Nevada. (This area, part of the eight hundred thousand acre Nevada Nuclear Test Site, is the Mecca of alien conspiracy buffs. The fact that Stealth, Aurora, SDI, and other real, highly classified projects are tested there only adds to the speculation regarding aliens.)

Project Guest is concerned with an alien life-form held in an electromagnetically secure facility in Los Alamos, New Mexico. It is supposed to be the last of sixteen captive aliens originally held at this location. The project is responsible for extracting information from the alien.

Other projects, including Aquarius, Luna, and Delta, deal specifically with alien life-forms, including alleged joint alien/U.S. government research! (Senator John Glenn says that he received a letter from the National Security Agency "admitting the existence of an Air Force Project: Aquarius focusing on UFOs.") Projects Gabriel and Excalibur are engaged in researching weapons to be used against hostile aliens, in the air or in bases located underground in the United States.

The Majority document asserts an agreement dating back to the late 1940s in which the aliens are allowed to examine cattle and humans for research purposes. Any humans examined were to be returned unharmed, with documentation of who was taken provided to the U.S. agency responsible for tracking them.

In exchange, gifts of alien technology were granted to the government, who would keep the operation under strict security. The treaty also permitted the construction of underground alien bases at various locations.

The treaty, or communications leading up to it, are alleged to have been started at Holloman Air Force Base, and involved at least one President meeting face-to-face with the aliens. The aliens themselves are supposed to have been the "big-nosed Grays," as opposed to the snub-nosed variety found in the wrecked saucers.

According to Cooper, the document specifically stated that "the aliens had violated their treaty with our government by mutilating animals and abducting humans; that the abduction of humans was supposed to be for medical purposes only." The aliens were also apparently implanting monitoring or controlling devices in people.

The implanted device is said to be a spherical object forty to eighty microns in size, which is placed in the optic nerve near the brain. Based on the original tracking of test subjects, the document estimates more than one in forty Americans have been implanted!

There is (he says), a contingency plan should this information become widespread or the aliens attempt an overt takeover. The government would announce that a terrorist group had entered the United States with a nuclear weapon and martial law would be declared. All persons with implants and all "dissidents" would be rounded up and placed in detention. Anyone resisting arrest would be killed.

Bill Cooper believes that the government is frightened by their lack of control over the aliens, yet have little choice but to continue their same policy formulated by their predecessors in the '40s. If it were made known that aliens were abducting people with government knowledge, he thinks, the massive hysteria could topple the government.

Cooper's DD-214 Honorable Discharge does show that he was working for the NSA (National Security Agency) while stationed at San Francisco, California. The Cooper material is only one of many reporting a treaty between the aliens and the U.S. government, some mentioning the same projects listed above.

Another mysterious figure claiming to have worked on joint alien-human projects is physicist Bob Lazar. In 1989, Lazar created a sensation by stating that he had studied alien propulsion systems at a facility called "S4" near Groom Lake, Nevada. First appearing as a black silhouette on a Las Vegas television program, he later emerged publicly on a nine-part special report, *UFOs: The Best Evidence,* on CBS-affiliate KLAS-TV.

Lazar's claims to have worked earlier at Los Alamos have reportedly been verified. *UFO* magazine has also reported that they have obtained a W-2 form showing that he was employed by the Office of Naval Intelligence (who he says were his employers at Groom Lake).

Lazar claims that though he worked on specific technology, he was aware that "there were alien beings working somewhere in a lab nearby under heavy guard." According to him, some of the guards themselves were aliens. This underscores his conviction that the technology he was studying came by friendly means, and that there is a treaty with the Grays.

The technology Lazar claims to have worked on relates to alien "gravity amplifiers" that are used in two modes; one for short-term, atmospheric flight, the other for long-range space travel. He says that the fuel for the amplifiers is "element 115," which is a very heavy, nonradioactive substance similar to lead.

While at Groom Lake, Lazar also was permitted to view an alien "book" that told the entire history of the human race from the point of view of the aliens. He said that "anytime the word 'human' came up in the book, it was always replaced with the word 'containers.' Containers referred to people; containers of what, I don't know."

Bob Lazar's testimony was hailed as the long-awaited

breakthrough in the alien conspiracy. Others have accused him of being a government intelligence agent spreading disinformation to muddy the waters. Lazar's endorsement of Bill Cooper's material on Majestic added fuel to the controversy.

The belief that the government has retrieved saucers, brokered treaties with aliens, and even joined them in building underground bases is surprisingly widespread. There are literally hundreds of books on the topic that mention government cover-ups. New Age bookstores always carry a few of these popular items.

The cases and reports above produced no tangible evidence that one could see in a museum or lab, yet are articles of faith to thousands of people, rivaling Kennedy assassination buffs in number. Researchers disagreeing with them are often labeled government agents or even agents of the Grays.

Some more skeptical researchers speculate that reports like Majestic are part of massive disinformation campaigns conducted by the U.S. military establishment. Disinformation is a cover story leaked to provide a blind for truly classified projects or events. While reporters and others are off chasing little green men, the real work of the project (such as the Stealth bomber) proceeds unexamined and unhindered.

Conversely, disinformation serves to discredit those who have really seen something. It is easy to see why investigators (and the public) who've heard the same remarkably absurd stories again and again lose interest. Adding pointless or purposely bizarre elements to genuine sightings of classified projects can ensure their protection.

One of the strongest supports of the government conspiracy theory is the persistent appearance of the Men in Black. Though it has never been made clear who these individuals are, they have been seen so often that they've become a separate subfield of study.

These "MIBs" tend to wear black suits and sunglasses and drive around in black, late model Cadillacs. These autos have been described over and over as "smelling brand new" and showing no wear inside or outside. Their drivers are most often deeply tanned, with oriental features and a stilted way of speaking. After they meet the witness, the vehicles and their occupants disappear from sight.

The modus operandi of MIBs is to warn witnesses against speaking about what they have seen, even threatening them with unspecified harm. Many times the MIBs will show a knowledge of the witness's life or the sighting far exceeding anything told to neighbors or reporters. On some occasions, witnesses and contactees have received a visit from the black Cadillacs even before they have discussed their experience with anyone!

One can imagine the impact a meeting with the Men in Black has upon an already shocked or confused witness. It sometimes appears that their sole purpose is to convince people that there is indeed a (rather clumsy) government conspiracy. Others believe that the MIBs are the aliens themselves, or even gypsies.

If this is a neurosis or hallucination, it is an amazingly widespread one. Many independent UFO researchers have heard MIB reports from a variety of credible witnesses with no knowledge of one another or the literature. John Keel reported many personal encounters with the mysterious strangers. He interviewed frightened witnesses just after they'd met an MIB and even attempted following the black Cadillacs on deserted roads only to lose them. He also found motel reservations made in his name by MIBs, including meaningless messages left for him at the desk!

It's easy to locate UFO researchers who point the finger at the government, though researchers who actually interview government personnel are scarce. Was there anyone working directly with the military establishment in New Mexico who would speak with me?

A good friend suggested that I contact Colonel Alexander. John B. Alexander, Ph.D., is manager of antimateriel technology in the Defense Initiative Office at Los Alamos National Laboratory. As a colonel in the U.S Army, he served as the director of Advanced Systems Concept Office, U.S. Army Laboratory Command, and chief of Advanced Human Technology, Army Intelligence, and Security Command, among many other assignments. He is co-author of *The Warrior's Edge* and a contributor to *The American Warrior.* Colonel Alexander is also fascinated by near-death studies, and was a former president of the International Association for Near-Death Studies.

With a lifelong curiosity for both psychic phenomena and UFOs, Alexander has established a reputation as a serious investigator. Because of his military and science establishment ties, he has been accused of spreading disinformation and of being a "CIA agent in league with the aliens." After speaking together on the phone, he invited me over to his desert home during a blinding blizzard.

Since the two-foot deep snow had almost obliterated any traces of the desert road, I nearly despaired of finding his place. Eventually, I made the correct guess and found his property, only to discover that the storm had knocked out the outside lights and his house was nearly invisible. Finally, after much pounding on his door, my quest was rewarded by a warm drink, a hot fire, and Colonel Alexander.

He began by describing the origin of his interest in the subject. "I was ten years old when the first big UFO Flap hit in '47 and I guess that made a big impression on me. I attended a rather unusual grade school with its own radio system. I remember that the school allowed me to give a talk on UFOs over that radio system for the other students.

"After becoming an adult, during a break in my military career, I spent five years as a deputy sheriff in Dade County, Florida. That job exposed me to gunshots, machete fights, even child murders. Still later, during the Vietnam conflict, I commanded a Special Forces A-Team with a force of fifteen hundred ethnic Cambodian mercenaries. There I experienced death by being the one doing the killing as well as commanding others in the same role. At the same time I was studying meditation in Buddhist monasteries.

"Those experiences of death changed me dramatically and began my questioning into the nature of death. I later received a doctorate in Thanatology under Elizabeth Kübler Ross, eventually becoming president of the International Association for Near-Death Studies. The parallels between near-death experiences and UFO abductions further supported my interest in UFO phenomena. In my studies of reported UFO cases I've heard so many wild, improbable rumors that I've become fascinated with the structure of belief systems and 'disinformation.' The last lecture I gave was on belief systems."

Alexander provided examples of wild rumors in the field.

"One tale that I'm tired of is the notion of a government-built tunnel system that is supposed to connect all the different alien bases. Let's forget the tunnels that are said to criss-cross the entire country and just focus on the hi-tech system that is supposed to connect an 'alien base' at Dulce with Los Alamos. We're talking about a tunnel that would be seventy to ninety miles long at least, all of it built in total secrecy. That is one very long tunnel!

"If people would just look at the immense difficulties surrounding the building of CHUNNEL (the trans-English Channel tunnel) they would get an idea of the incredible difficulty of engineering such a monumental project. Yet we are asked to believe that the U.S. government has spent decades building giant tunnels exceeding CHUNNEL many times in length without the public being the wiser.

"What I want to know is, where did all the money for this come from? What would those kind of expenses do to the GNP and taxpayers? Think of all the problems you'd have if you were on the other side of the coin (one of the conspirators). The scale in these stories is so huge, it would be impossible to hide it."

He laughed. "People can make anything fit into their belief systems. Once at a UFO conference this guy came up to me with pictures he said proved that the government had underground bases connected by tunnels to alien bases. I looked at this one, 'Hey, that's the Lockheed Palmdale facility! Hey, this one is the base at Northrop.'

"He basically had gotten a set of photos of different government bases, mainly military, that had underground sections. Now you'll get no disagreement from me that there are indeed underground bases built by the government. There are obvious reasons for that. But just because our government built things underground hardly means that there are giant alien bases or giant intercontinental tunnel systems."

Colonel Alexander did think there was a crash at Dulce and a subsequent cover-up. "I believe that the Dulce crash was actually a prototype Stealth Bomber. The UFO and the "alien body" were part of a cover-up story. I think that the officials involved were *glad* to have people think that there was an alien crash. They would have been happy with anything being said but the truth, that this crash was from a top secret military research program for a new type of bomber!

"It's a perfect example of a successful disinformation that has now become part of a belief system with its own momentum. It's probably very amusing to the people who helped create the Stealth cover-up, who probably never imagined that this particular cover-up would last this long!"

He was less vehement regarding the continuing Groom Lake/Dreamland reports (perhaps understandable in light of the known SDI and Stealth programs based there). "Let me see . . . if you think that 'strange things' happen in the desert, or that the Air Force does fly some weird things out there . . . well, you're right! That doesn't mean that there are any aliens involved, though. That's all."

He made a face when asked about accusations that he works for the CIA to hinder UFO investigations. "That's true; it has happened. Some of my views are not very popular with the True Believers. Many of these people have no scientific background whatsoever, and have arrived at their conclusions by nonscientific, nonprovable approaches. And if you say 'Bullshit!' then you're part of some government conspiracy.

"I always say to people, try to play the part of the government. In general, most governments are large, monolithic, unwieldy bureaucracies that are incapable of pulling off such large scale conspiracies. Look at how small a circle Watergate was. Yet some of these people would rather believe that they are being systematically deceived and betrayed by their entire leadership on a global scale."

Speaking of his own beliefs, he said that "there is some sort of UFO phenomenon that clearly has a mental or psychic component but also leaves behind real physical evidence. You can't make any sense of this phenomenon without studying the role of consciousness. Remember, you can't study anything without the observer being part of the effect. Just the fact that I'm talking about it with you makes you part of it. You can't be a 'neutral observer' anymore."

The paper trail continues growing. The January 14, 1994, issue of the *Washington Post* carried a full-page story on a General Accounting Office probe into reports of retrieved saucers. According to the *Post,* Representative Steven Schiff

(R-New Mexico) had been contacted by constituents after an episode of NBC's show, *Unsolved Mysteries,* which dealt with the Roswell Incident. Rep. Schiff contacted then-Secretary of Defense Les Aspin, who passed along his request for information to the Air Force. Schiff was reached by Air Force representatives who brusquely told him to check the National Archives and then to drop it. Schiff didn't like it.

Rep. Schiff is a member of the powerful House Government Operations Committee, which oversees the GAO. Admittedly on questionable territory, Schiff instituted a General Accounting search for classified government documents. According to Schiff:

> "Generally, I'm a skeptic on UFOs and alien beings, but there are indications from the runaround that I got that whatever it was, it wasn't a balloon. Apparently, it's another government cover-up. If the Defense Department hadn't been so unresponsive, it wouldn't have come to this."

Groom Lake (or Area 51) has also been in the news. The February 20, 1995, issue of *Newsweek* magazine carried a report of a lawsuit against the unknown operators of the base. Attorney Jonathan Turley is representing five former government employees, and the widow of a sixth. They claim that they suffered blackouts, respiratory illnesses, rashes, and open sores after being exposed to toxic wastes at the site.

The case has an unusual twist in that four months after the suit, the government denied the existence of the facility. The case now cannot proceed without the government admitting that the place exists. Since the place has long been an open secret to Russian spy satellites, Turley told *Newsweek* that he intends to call the Russian attaché to the witness stand to testify to its existence. It appears that the facility does exist, despite the disclaimers.

Umberto Eco's novel, *Foucault's Pendulum,* centers on a hoax perpetrated by three bored intellectuals working for an obscure publisher of occult texts. The characters chose all the bizarre or ridiculous theories of underground cults and historical conspiracies they could find, and fed the seemingly unrelated items into a computer named Abulafia (named for the famous cabalist). Abulafia linked the disparate pieces into a consistent story of an incredible secret handed down through the centuries by groups of illuminates. Each group possessed only a portion of the truth; whoever held the key would grasp incredible power.

Unfortunately, the group of hoaxers let some of the random connections from their game slip in the presence of real occultists visiting their publisher. Word of their "discovery" spread through shadowy networks, and before long the protagonists were running for their lives. Groups of True Believers scattered across Europe were convinced that the secret really existed, and were prepared to murder anyone who stood in their way. At the end, they kill the supposed possessor of the secret in order to *keep* it a secret.

As the chief character, Casaubon states:

> "We invented a nonexistent Plan; and They not only believed it was real but convinced themselves that They had been part of it for ages, or rather, They identified the fragments of their muddled mythology as moments of our Plan, moments joined in a logical, irrefutable web of analogy, semblance, suspicion. But if you invent a plan and others carry it out, it's as if the Plan exists. At that point it does exist."

Some conspiracy theories create their own truth, a truth that is essentially unprovable. Do the believers really want the conspiracy to end? Eco's Casaubon thinks not.

> "Through the centuries the search for this secret had been the glue holding Them all together, despite excommunications, internecine fighting, coups de main. Now They were on the verge of knowing it. But They were assailed by two fears: that the secret would be a disappointment, and that once it was known to all, there would be no secret left. Which would be the end of Them."

So far, there appears to be little physical evidence regarding government involvement with alien beings. The many documents and whistle-blowers, while provocative, do not possess the impact of actual alien spacecraft or aliens. They do, however, support many people who wish to believe that aliens are running our country.

If half of these allegations *are* true, then the international cover-up is so massive and pervasive there is little hope of getting to the bottom of it short of a presidential address or overt alien intervention. If the allegations are false, then a lot of people are wasting their time and money. Why then, does the notion of a massive UFO conspiracy remain so popular?

According to author Sam Keen, "Both God and the Devil testify to the abiding human experience of being possessed by alien forces, being out of control, unable to achieve autonomy." The current submersion of the individual in modern bureaucratic society "is equivalent to the surrender of control to a force outside ourselves."

> "But if we cannot stay in control, we can at least define what cannot be controlled as demonic. Propaganda allows us to exteriorize the battle, project the struggle within the psyche into the realm of politics. We excel only by reducing others to the status of inferiors; win only by creating a majority of losers. One man's triumph is another's defeat."

If this is so, then perhaps by "seeing through" a worldwide conspiracy, some people assert their freedom. Learning "secret information," they attain a sense of power and individuality. Whatever the truth is, conspiracies by their very nature project dark, unknown places. If we look into these shadows long enough, we can imagine whatever dark forces we want.

4

UNKNOWN APES

But huge and mighty forms, that do not live
Like living men, moved slowly through the mind
By day, and were a trouble to my dreams.

—WILLIAM WORDSWORTH

BIG, glowing-eyed, hairy monsters are a staple item in UFO lore. Bigfoot, Sasquatch, Yeti, Abominable Snowman; these creatures have so many names precisely because they're seen so often in so many times and places. Most past research in the U.S. focused on the Pacific Northwest, where there are huge wilderness areas that could support a few surviving tribes of large primates. However, in the last thirty years there have been over one thousand documented reports of sightings on the East Coast. How is this possible in such long-settled, highly developed regions?

Despite frequent Bigfoot-UFO sightings over the years, most UFO researchers ignore hairy monsters as too absurd or irrelevant to follow up. The same is true of the (far fewer) Bigfoot hunters, who also ignore possible connections with lights in the sky or paranormal phenomena. If you were trying to get scientific or public acceptance for the possible existence of a large North American primate, then would *you* investigate UFOs?

Unfortunately for wishful researchers in both fields, the association between hairy giants and glowing lights has not gone away. The following case, first reported by Ohio investigator Dennis Pilichis, contains so many striking elements it has become a cult classic.

It was hot on June 1, 1981, and Robert S. and his family were badly frightened. Uncanny things were going on in the virgin woods by their isolated farmhouse near Rome, Ohio. The month before, a group of local Amish hired to haul logs had bolted out of the woods after the sound of gunshots. Their workhorse had huge, ugly slashes along its side. The taciturn Amish farmers wouldn't say what they had shot at; they just left in a hurry and didn't come back.

Then a few weeks later, a bulldozer operator digging for a gas line came to the house saying he'd found a spot that looked cleared for construction. Strangely, there was no road leading to the spot. Robert hiked over and saw a bare, burned area about forty feet square, with four evenly spaced holes like something heavy had rested there.

Then there were the missing family ducks and chickens. Robert's sixteen-year-old son had found them in the woods on the 15th, with their heads neatly bitten off. Their bodies were untouched. It didn't help his son much; he'd been having nightmares about a "creature" staring in his bedroom window at night. The family quietly began carrying their shotguns with them on their chores.

On the night of June 25, all hell broke loose. The dogs and remaining ducks started carrying on in the front yard. Robert and his sons ran out on the porch with guns and flashlights. They saw an unbelievable "thing" that was huge and black with glowing red eyes, which they later estimated to be between seven and eight feet tall. One of the boys directed a flashlight at the shape and Robert shot it with his 4-10 shotgun. The farmer, a good shot, knew that he'd hit it right between the eyes.

The thing screamed loudly, a sound that went from a hair-raising, high pitch to a low decibel groan, and ran off into the field. They could hear the screaming move off into the woods. The family didn't get much sleep that night, waiting up with guns loaded in case "it" came back.

It returned the next night around 2 A.M., making grunting sounds out by the front porch. Robert aimed his light at it, but again all he could make out was a huge, black thing "like a gorilla with glowing red eyes." Yelling to his boys to get back inside and get dressed, he reached inside the door and grabbed his shotgun.

Before he could take aim, the thing emitted its unearthly scream and ran off. He and his boys jumped in their pickup truck and sped down the road in the same direction. Seeing nothing, they stopped at a neighbor's house down the road. The man had seen nothing and they started back home. On the way back, they began hearing the sound of heavy brush breaking and snapping. Right where the sounds seemed loudest, their truck stopped dead, though the lights stayed on.

Clutching their guns and frantically attempting to restart the vehicle, the sounds grew louder and they could hear a low growling. A second car happened along and stopped to see what was the matter. The new arrival also heard the crashing and growling sounds. Another attempt to start the truck worked, and both cars quickly left the scene.

On the night of June 28, family members were supposed to attend a local musical event. Because of the fear they still felt, everyone stayed home. Late that night, one of the family saw some shadowy forms moving near the line of the forest. Driving out on the family tractor, they saw a "black shape waving some sort of blue light." When one of Robert's sons raised his gun to shoot, the light went out. Driving further on the tractor, they saw shadowy figures with glowing red eyes. They opened fire and used two full boxes of twelve-gauge shells. The red-eyed forms seemed unhurt and shifted their position. They kept reappearing, almost as if they were attempting to draw fire.

Finally, the family returned to the house, but were unable to get much sleep. The next morning they found a number of large, three-toed footprints in the area. There seemed to be a six-foot stride between the prints. In many cases, the prints ended abruptly, then began again at some distance.

Against the wishes of most of the family, a relative present at the house throughout the attacks called local law enforcement officials twice. The Ashtabula County sheriff came out to the property twice on June 29. In both his reports on "suspicious activity," he notes that large, three-toed tracks were found. The sheriff, with a sergeant and a deputy, patrolled the area at 5 A.M. and 11 P.M. but found nothing else.

Since June 29, family members had been keeping nightly, armed vigils on the farmhouse roof. On the night of July 1, two of them stationed on the roof noticed four huge lights hovering over the tree line. The lights appeared to change from blue to red to yellow, and were spaced along the treeline. The family also witnessed one of the lights shoot a beam of white light toward the ground. While they watched the light, they heard high-pitched "screams that sounded like a woman" coming from the woods.

Then the lights all disappeared together. Suddenly, the watching family members could see a number of dark forms running toward the house. The terrified family opened fire with rifles and shotguns, drawing hair-raising screams from the things. The things kept running back and forth as if "they were trying to draw our fire." Noticing luminous, red eyes glowing from the woods, some family members began shooting in that direction. Their shots were answered by more of the eerie screams.

The family kept reloading and shooting at the forms and eyes all night. At one point they observed a shadowy figure of a "horse" standing alone in the field where the things were moving about. Certain that this was not their own horse, they opened fire on the form, which responded with another of the screams. Around 3:30 A.M., they noticed a glowing, white light flying over their cornfield. One of the lookouts stationed on the roof said that he "felt the light from the thing hit him in the head," and he nearly toppled over.

Strange lights continued to fly silently overhead all through the night. One "glowing red ball" was observed to change shape into "something that looked like an owl." Another red object, the shape of a cigar box, flew close enough to the house for Robert to shoot at it point blank. They heard a sound like "a bullet hitting glass" and the light went out. The next day, the exhausted family found many three-toed footprints in the area. Their own horse was found safe in the barn where it was kept.

The family decided to ask a local Fortean researcher, author Dennis Pilichis, to investigate the situation. Arriving on July 3, Pilichis and a friend immediately noticed the stressed-out state of the family. He also found a ladder leaning next to the farmhouse roof and coffee cups, coats, and flashlights left on the roof. The yard "was covered with spent shotgun shells."

Searching the area for evidence, they easily found more of the three-toed prints pressed deeply into the extremely hard-packed earth. Pilichis later described the prints as "claw-like in that the toes appeared long and hooked. There was also an apparent twisted heel with scuff marks."

The prints seemed to start from nowhere and to end just as suddenly. Pilichis measured strides between the prints as variously nineteen and forty-three inches. He took plaster casts and photographs of the prints, which were measured at fourteen inches long and six inches wide.

Pilichis returned to monitor the situation on July 6 and again on July 7. The family reported that the phenomenon continued, and that an extremely large, black form had come close to the house the previous night. Pilichis and researcher Williard McIntyre from Maryland scouted the larger area, including the woods, and found more of the strange footprints.

After taking taped interviews of the family, Pilichis and McIntyre decided to spend the night. At one point, the family reported seeing the glowing red eyes and started shooting. The two investigators missed the sighting and walked out to the treeline with two family members.

They all reported sighting a "glowing form" that emerged from the woods and stood there. The excited family members shot at it and it appeared to fall. The group ran over, but found nothing other than a flattened area in the grass, with "a path leading away as if something had dragged itself off."

The two investigators began tossing stones into the wooded area in an attempt to provoke a response. Somebody or something tossed a rock back, nearly hitting them! Later in the night both investigators sighted the red-eyed forms many times, including one close-up encounter where Pilichis swore that he could see body hair on the being. They also observed what they termed "phantom flashlight beams" in the woods, and concluded that they marked the first appearances of the creatures.

As the investigators continued to monitor the farmhouse, the phenomenon continued its pointless tricks for a while longer, then eventually died down with no explanation. There were similar reports from nearby Rock Creek, Ohio during the same summer of 1981. Though no lights in the sky were seen, there were encounters with the Bigfoot-type creatures, and more of the three-toed footprints. It seemed the phenomenon had no purpose other than to terrify some isolated families, and to attract the notice of a few investigators.

* * *

Some of the most interesting Bigfoot reports come from the southern or midwestern United States. On June 30, 1988, seventeen-year-old Chris Davis had just finished changing a tire on a road in Bishopville, South Carolina. Looking up at the direction of a sound, he saw a seven-foot-tall, two-legged beast with glowing red eyes running toward him. He jumped in his Toyota and tried to flee. The creature caught up with him while his vehicle was doing forty miles per hour, and jumped onto his roof. Before it fell off, he noticed that it had three fingers with long black nails.

Many other sightings of the "lizard man" (Davis reported scales on the thing, though others did not) soon followed. Investigators were able to make plaster casts of the three-toed prints, which measured seven-by-fourteen inches. Like most such cases, the reports died out a couple of months later, as if the thing had moved on to darker pastures.

I was raised in the state of Maryland, which despite its high suburban population still contains large wild tracts. Amazingly, hundreds of Bigfoot sightings have been reported from Maryland and neighboring Pennsylvania over the years. I remember from my days in Boy Scouts that we used to tell each other scary stories about such creatures, much as children still do today.

Like many west-of-the-Rockies reports, the Maryland Bigfoot often had glowing red eyes, three toes, and a sulfurous odor. One such beast was active during the staid 1950s. At odd times throughout the decade, the Prince George's County Police office was flooded by reports of a huge and hairy, blazing-eyed beast. As in all such cases, there was a wave of reports bordering on hysteria, then the cases simply faded into obscurity.

In another Maryland case, a man claimed that he hit a seven-foot-tall Bigfoot with his car. On April 28, 1975, Peter Hronek claimed that he swerved his car to avoid a hairy creature on Rocks Road, but struck it with his left fender anyway. State Police helicopters and K-9 patrols searched the area the next day, but found nothing. Police also recovered some hair from his damaged fender and grill, but refused to release the results of their analysis.

East-of-the-Rockies Bigfoot sightings are not limited to

the East Coast. Hairy apes, some as large as twelve feet, have been sighted in Indiana since the 1940s. One Aurora, Indiana couple reported a twelve-foot-tall Bigfoot that attacked and dented their car in 1977. The husband fired fifteen shots at the creature, which they claimed crawled away. An earlier Bigfoot-type creature was seen near French Lick, Indiana, in 1965. A bright green monster with glowing red eyes nicknamed "Fluorescent Freddie," he was reported by dozens of witnesses to be ten feet tall.

Another case from Rising Sun, Indiana occurred on May 18 and 19, 1969. The electrical power was gone for a couple of hours from the farmhouse of Mr. and Mrs. George Kaiser. Though there had been recent sightings of UFOs on a nearby ridge recently, they had not been disturbed. At 7:30 on the following evening, George Kaiser was walking toward his tractor when his dog started barking. He looked up and saw a hairy, man-sized figure about twenty-five feet away.

"I watched it for about two minutes before it saw me," Kaiser later told investigators. "It was all covered with hair except for the backs of the hands and face." At first paralyzed by surprise, Kaiser moved toward his car and the creature ran off. They later found four-toed tracks in the ground. The next night, a neighbor reported seeing a glowing UFO overhead through his binoculars.

Sometimes, the apparitions change shape or disappear in plain view. One witness in 1964 saw a Bigfoot near Point Isabel, Ohio. "It changed into another form right before our very eyes. The thing just crouched down; its hands became paws and it went on all fours, and it all happened like a slow-motion movie. Then it was gone. It vanished into thin air!"

There is a seemingly endless literature of Bigfoot sightings, with more reports added or unearthed daily. A Bigfoot kidnapping has even been used as an alibi in a murder case. Russell Welch was released from Fresno County Jail, California, in October 1987, after he claimed that a Bigfoot had stolen a child, sixteen-year-old Theresa Ann Bier. Authorities claimed that Welch was released to avoid claims of double jeopardy if he was to be charged for murder, instead of the original kidnapping charge.

Bier did not return from a June 1987 camping trip with Welch in the central Sierra Mountains. Investigating police officers stated that Welch seems to believe sincerely that Bier was captured by a tribe of Bigfoot creatures. Russell Welch also claims to remain in communication with them.

There have always been reports of people seeing monsters. Hairy dwarves, smelly "swamp apes," demons, insectoid bipeds, gleaming men of metal, one-eyed giants, animal-headed people, dragons and sea serpents, winged men; the list is found in every time and place, including modern UFO lore. Is there any truth to such creatures? If they are more than mere myth, then where do they come from and where do they go?

Monster hunting gets into some people's blood, and the biographies of monster hunters makes reading almost as fascinating as the accounts of the monsters themselves. Some, like veteran investigators Loren Coleman, Janet and Colin Bord, or the late Ivan T. Sanderson, have made a lifestyle of searching out mysterious creatures across America and abroad. Their well-detailed reports have provided fuel for many late-night speculations.

The monster-hunters owe a great deal to the Fortean "science" of cryptobiology. Unlike most academic naturalists and biologists, cryptobiologists believe that folkloric traditions of monster sightings contain worthwhile clues.

Many cryptobiologists focus on what are believed to be previously unrecognized but natural life-forms (such as the increasingly accepted East Coast mountain lion, for years considered a myth). Real-life, apelike, "missing-links" such as Bigfoot would also fall into this category.

Other researchers delve into murkier corners. Reports of glowing-eyed, disappearing Bigfoots that associate with UFOs and are apparently immune to bullets would seem to suggest a nonphysical phenomenon. Though there are cases of mammals whose eyes reflect a greenish or yellowish sheen from a strong light source, there is no evidence of any natural animals whose eyes glow flaming red in the dark. (There are some reports of dogs suffering an optical condition that causes their eyes to reflect light with a reddish tinge.)

These monsters are not the only ones with red eyes. As in many UFO cases, there have been Bigfoot sightings that left witnesses with cases of conjunctivitis, or eye burn. As mentioned earlier, conjunctivitis can be caused by overexposure to ultraviolet light or electromagnetic fields.

Accounts of tracks starting and ending in the middle of a field or mud also suggest something not quite normal. Unless the creatures can fly, where do they go? Another key indicator of paranormal activity is the frequent reports of suddenly stalled cars, just as in many UFO encounters. It's highly unlikely that primitive, hairy apes would possess an advanced electromagnetic technology. If they did, why would they employ it to halt cars, thereby ensuring a sighting, and then blind the witnesses?

From coast-to-coast, over a hundred years of collected reports agree that Bigfoots stink. Accounts of Bigfoot odors, while agreeing that the creatures do smell *very* bad, seem split into two distinct categories. One version has the creatures bearing an odor "like outhouses and dirty socks" (a combination of feces and sweat that one might expect to find in a huge primate with bad toilet habits). The other reported odor is less easily explained: a stench of sulfur or "fire and brimstone," the same as found in many UFO and ghost sightings. Do they smell the same because they are related to such phenomena?

One of the most commonly found pieces of Bigfoot evidence are huge footprints (there are even museums of collected plaster casts). Like the strange odors, the prints appear to be divided into two sorts: five-toed and three-toed (though a few four- and six-toed prints have been reported). Primates are five-toed, but the three-toed variety seems to be more frequently associated with the hydrogen sulfide odor.

There are also scattered reports of Bigfoot-type creatures that appear to be self-luminous. A few of the "swamp ape" reports from the southern U.S. fall into this category. Many witnesses also insist that their sighting was preceded by a change in the surrounding air temperature. The air suddenly and temporarily becoming noticeably colder or hotter suggests that something else is occurring. Medieval (and Hollywood) accounts of the manifestations of demons is one comparison that comes to mind.

Are there two kinds of Bigfoot-type creatures? There has been a huge amount of evidence accumulated worldwide suggesting that genuine, hairy hominids may linger on in scattered wilderness areas, mostly in inaccessible mountains or swamps. Final proof for these ancient survivals rests upon the dedicated efforts of a few professional investigators and hunters.

If the other sort does exist, these sulfur-smelling, glowing-eyed, vanishing types may not be "real" Bigfoots at all. Their appearances in highly populated areas need not suggest that they are hiding out in a few parks or wooded areas. Instead, they may be just a fragment of that larger, trickster-like phenomenon whose only apparent goal is to terrify or mystify us. Are there really "demons"?

5

NIGHT TERRORS

*There is something over the sky,
like the tongue of an ox.*

—PABLO NERUDA

ARE aliens rustling cattle? For the past two decades, ranchers and farmers throughout the United States and the world have reported thousands of bizarre animal deaths. The manner of the deaths do not fit into natural predator or rustler scenarios. A very high percentage of them remain unsolved after investigation by state and local law enforcement officers.

The deaths are characterized by highly efficient removal of internal organs, eyes, tongues, or genitals. The animal's blood is totally drained or suctioned from the corpse, with none left behind on the ground. Cattle, horses, pigs, goats, sheep, dogs, and even deer have been mutilated, in some cases found mere hours after being seen alive. Many cases apparently took place in broad daylight.

One of the many mysteries surrounding these operations lies in the precise surgical appearance of the incisions. Knives, saws, and scalpels all leave telltale marks, and have been ruled out by forensic experts. Over and over, specialists have stated that they are mystified by the wounds and are unable to imagine what technology was employed to make them.

Some of these mysterious wounds display evidence of high levels of heat. One forensic expert went on record stating that "only advanced laser scalpels could have made these cuts that seem to have been divided and seared along cell walls."

Many of the sites where the carcasses are found show no footprints or tire tracks leading to the remains. Were the cattle dropped? The remains are often centered in circles of flattened or burned vegetation. In some cases, the circle is only one of many such markings appearing in rows or arcs along the landscape. All of this is fact, well documented by a number of state and local law enforcement agencies.

The deaths are frequently accompanied by sightings of "strange lights in the sky" near the site or in the same region. In addition to bizarre cults and clandestine government experiments, UFOs are the most commonly offered speculations offered by ranchers and even police.

Strangely shaped, unmarked, black helicopters have also been seen flying in the vicinity of the carcasses. Because of these sightings, helicopters belonging to Armed Forces have occasionally been forced to change their flight plans to avoid shots by angry ranchers. A number of cattleman's associations have offered cash rewards for information leading to a solution to the mystery. To date, no one has collected any reward.

Though a number of newspaper articles in England, Canada, and the United States have attempted to link the mutilations with Satanic cults, this line of investigation has so far been completely unsuccessful. No arrests have been made, no charges ever filed, no informers or witnesses to such cult activity ever come forward.

The real fear and mystery left in the wake of these mutilations has lent credence to many wild theories. In some cases, the locals are beginning to wonder if there is not a plague of aliens or even vampires on the loose.

Inexplicable animal mutilations have been around for a very long time. Accounts dating from the Middle Ages mention outbreaks of "vampire" attacks on flocks and herds. One medieval German record tells of herds of sheep found slaughtered, their organs, genitals, or eyes removed and missing. The account tells of hysterical mobs hunting for the culprits, at last seizing two peasants as "werewolves" and burning them at the stake.

Unexplained lights in the sky are also mentioned in the old reports, yet were rarely linked to the attacks in the minds of the chroniclers. Was there a connection back then, as is theorized now in modern cases?

Many ancient cultures have myths about werewolves, werebears, weretigers, or vampiric demons who mutilate flocks (or people) and then disappear. There are also repetitive, unsubstantiated reports of large-scale animal mutilations occurring in England, Europe, the Great Plains, and New England in the previous century.

In 1810, there were unexplained slaughters of herds of sheep and cattle along the Scottish-English border. Eight and ten animals a night were being found drained of blood. Mobs of outraged farmers searched the area without success. Just as suddenly as they began, the mysterious attacks ended. Maybe "it" moved to Ireland.

In January 1874, up to thirty sheep a night were slaughtered in Cavan, Ireland. The corpses were drained of blood. Legions of armed and angry farmers searched the surrounding countryside, but were unable to halt the killings. By April of the same year, the killings had moved to Limerick, approximately one hundred miles from Cavan. This time some people were also reported slain before the attacks mysteriously ended.

Similar attacks occurred near Windsor Castle, England in 1906. In nearby Guildford, fifty-one sheep were killed in a single night. The customary mobs of armed, torch-bearing farmers found nothing. The mystery monsters appeared again in Derbyshire, England in the 1920s, leaving behind slaughtered sheep and goats.

For the next seventy years, rumors of animal mutilations and disappearances occurred over and over in areas where there were reports of "strange dirigibles in the sky." There was a wave of mysterious dirigible sightings in both England and the United States throughout the 1890s and 1900s, always denied by both governments.

In some cases, witnesses reported seeing or meeting the occupants. In 1897, a farmer named Alexander Hamilton swore that he and his family had seen a glowing "dirigible" with "six of the strangest beings I ever saw" stealing one of his heifers. The hide of the animal was found in the field the next day.

Many of these sightings, written up in newspapers of the time, occurred in the same areas as modern UFO sightings. It appears that the phenomenon prefers familiar surroundings. John A. Keel has written about "window areas" that may be doorways where other dimensions or times interpenetrate our own. It's as good an explanation as any.

The modern animal mutilation mystery attracted attention in Colorado in September 1967, when an Appaloosa mare named Lady was found stripped of flesh from the neck up. There was an immediate connection made with the current rash of UFO sightings in the surrounding Sangrè de Cristo mountains. Her story made headlines worldwide and is the first example of what became a pattern.

After sundown on Thursday, September 7, 1967, rancher Harry King said good night to one of his family's favorite horses; he didn't know that it was the last time he would see Lady alive. She was a healthy three-year-old Appaloosa who belonged to Harry's sister and her husband. Harry owned excellent pasture land, so Lady grazed on his ranch in the San Luis Valley in southern Colorado.

Each evening Lady went back to the ranch for water where her mother, Snippy, was corralled. But Lady didn't show up on September 8. The next day, Harry King found her near the edge of a small, flat clearing in the brush. He was shocked to see that she had been stripped to the bone from the neck up. The rest of the body was undamaged. The bones of her exposed neck and skull were as white and dry as if they had lain in the sun for weeks. But he knew that he had seen her alive just two nights before.

Police investigated, but came up with no leads or possible motives. Reporters followed shortly to cover a story that later brought many others forward. Lady's death preceded a rash of similar, unsolved mutilations of horse, cattle, sheep, and dogs across the country. By the mid-seventies, there had been so many reports that *Newsweek* magazine published a story on the mutilations in 1974. Some accounts reported that local sheriff's departments were receiving up to three calls a day in problem areas.

Though most modern reports seem to come from ranches in the western United States, one of the most remarkable cases took place in Hempstead County, Arkansas. Early Friday morning, March 10, 1989, Mr. L. C. Wyatt walked outside on his farm. Entering a pasture near an abandoned logging road, he was stunned to see that five of his cows were dead. Their bodies were lying in a straight line across the pasture. Like Harry King, Mr. Wyatt knew that he had seen these cows alive two days before.

Walking up to the bodies, he realized that all five of the heifers had been pregnant. Examining them more closely, he saw that most of the cows had parts of their anatomy removed. Three had rectum tissue removed in a clean, bloodless oval. One had an eighteen-by-twenty-two-inch portion of its belly removed. Another was missing an eye. One cow had its legs drawn up as if it had been running when killed.

He saw no other wounds on the bodies, no sign that the cows had been shot. It was almost as if the cows had allowed themselves to be dissected. As in all the other cases, there was no sign of the missing organs elsewhere on the property. He also saw no blood on the ground next to the bodies.

Wyatt went home and called the Hempstead County Sheriff's Department, who sent out two deputies. They investigated the scene and made out their report. Though they concluded that some kind of instrument was used in the excisions, they were unable to say what was the actual cause of the deaths.

Later that same day, Jim Williamson and Juanita Stripling, two editors from the *Little River News,* arrived at the farm to take pictures. "The first look at the scene gave the impression that the cows had dropped dead in their tracks. One cow was lying on her right side. There was a large, round cut-out area with the calf lying just outside the cut and still in the embryo sac. The cut area was neat and precise. There was no blood on the ground or on the body of the cow or calf. There was also no dampness on the ground from water or other body fluids."

They then walked farther along the line of dead cows, noting the unusual nature of the wounds. As they took photos, Jim Williamson remembered that he had been watching a strange "golden glow" in the sky the evening before. Similar to unidentified lights he'd photographed a year before, this one hovered above the Rural Electric Association substation about fifty miles from the farm.

After sundown, veterinarian James Powell and Hempstead County Sheriff Don Worthy arrived at the mutilation site. Using flashlights, Dr. Powell took stomach and organ samples from some of the cows. The results of his investigation were not made public, and the cause of the killings was never solved.

For the past few years, rural Sweden has been plagued by horse and cow mutilations. Approximately two hundred horse attacks had been reported to police by the time the case received national attention on the TV program *Svar direkt* on February 25, 1992.

In over ninety percent of the cases, the assaults were conducted on horses, all in the same, familiar fashion. Wounds, generally near the sexual organs, were "scalpel-like incisions"; the perpetrators were unknown. An unusual factor in these cases was that most of the animals had been left alive. Over fifty percent of these pitiable creatures had to be put to death when found.

Farmers and horse breeders interviewed on the telecast were unanimous in their fear and confusion. They stressed that several of the attacks had taken place almost in their presence, with no sound or other indications. The perpetrators were "almost like phantoms or supernatural beings." Similar assaults have been reported in Denmark in recent years.

From October 1992 to April 1993, northern Alabama was not a good place to be a cow. Over this period, thirty-two cattle were found mutilated in Marshall and Dekalb counties. The mutilations took the familiar forms of missing lips, genitals, pieces of hide, and an absence of blood. Ranchers and investigating law enforcement officers were extremely skeptical that the deaths were the work of natural predators.

The general region is already known as a window area for UFOs. According to *UFO* magazine, "in 1989 the Sand Mountain village of Fyffe was the scene of several spectacular sightings of UFOs," including "a huge, triangular object doing aerodynamically unreasonable things." Among its witnesses were the local chief of police, his assistant, and an editor of the Rainesville, Alabama *Weekly Post*.

During the time of the mutilations, there were also sightings of the mysterious, unmarked black helicopters in the same area. Witnesses stated that the helicopters appeared to be Bell Jet Rangers. Actually, one witness did claim to see numerals on the side of one of the craft, but when local police checked with the FAA, they were told that the numbers "were not on file."

One carcass was dusted with a "white, flaky powder." Fyffe police officer Ted Oliphant reportedly sent samples to an unnamed eastern university for analysis. At a police press conference on April 7, 1993, he stated that analysis "had determined the substance was composed of aluminum, titanium, oxygen, and silicon in significant amounts." Others later noted that titanium-containing pigments are manufactured at a paper mill in Albertville, approximately fifteen miles away from the mutilation site.

At the press conference, the Fyffe police department announced that they did not believe the mutilations were the work of predators. They also stated that some of the cattle wounds "displayed evidence of great heat, as if they were seared." This report was later countered by the DeKalb and Marshall County Sheriff's Departments, and the U.S. Department of Agriculture, who say the mutilations *were* the results of predators. The investigating officers in Fyffe, they say, simply did not read the indications correctly. They also say they found no evidence of high heat in their samples. This pronouncement by the USDA did not deter the mutilators; more dead cattle were found in the next two months.

If "they" are so interested in obtaining animal parts and blood, why not human blood as well? One apocryphal case reported by John Keel occurred in March 1967. Dark and early in the rainy morning, Red Cross driver Beau Shertzer and a young nurse were driving a Bloodmobile up Highway 2 along the Ohio River (site of numerous UFO reports over the years). The vehicle, loaded down with freshly donated blood, was returning to the Red Cross Headquarters in Huntington, West Virginia.

While driving along a deserted stretch of highway, they became aware of a large glowing object lifting over a nearby hill and diving toward their vehicle. Shertzer rolled down his side window and looked up in time to see a mechanical arm or extension being extended from the object that was cruising just above the Bloodmobile. The nurse simultaneously saw another arm being lowered on her side of the vehicle. It appeared as if the flying object was attempting to grab the speeding Bloodmobile.

While the nurse began screaming hysterically, Shertzer floored the gas pedal and desperately tried to outrun the thing. According to their story, they were saved when the headlights of several oncoming vehicles appeared ahead. The glowing object retracted its "arms" and flew off. To this day, Beau Shertzer refuses to drive along that stretch of highway.

Many pro-UFO-theory writers have come to the conclusion that whatever is behind the animal mutilation-UFO phenomenon is in dire need of internal organs and blood as either (1) a source of food, or (2) a source of genetic materials. Some speculate that an alien race, perhaps suffering from disease or genetic damage, has come to earth seeking an abundant supply of these materials to insure its own survival.

To such intruders, all earth life-forms (including humanity), would merely be "cattle" to be harvested as the need arose. Perhaps Charles Fort was correct when he said that we are all "food for the moon."

> "I think we are property. I should say that we belong to something. That once upon a time, this earth was No-Man's land, that other worlds explored and colonized here, and fought among themselves for possession, but now it's owned by something: That something owns this earth—All others warned off."

Some UFO researchers have been pursuing rumors of an underground alien base in Dulce, New Mexico. Over the past twenty years a small number of people have publicly claimed to have seen the installation containing both alien and U.S. military personnel. Many of their accounts do share similar descriptions of cattle (and human) body parts being processed by aliens for purposes of genetic experimentation and nutrients (especially in the case of cattle).

One famed case is that of Thomas C., who claims to have been a security officer at the underground base. According to Thomas, in his twenties he received classified training in advanced photographic techniques. For the next seven years, he worked in high-security photography for the Air Force. In 1977, he was cleared and transferred to the Dulce facility.

Underground at Dulce, he claims that there is a base of at least seven levels. Only the top levels normally have human personnel. The lower levels are occupied by the alien Grays, with occasional human assistants possessing the necessary clearance. In these lower levels are conducted "monstrous genetic experiments" using material obtained from both cattle and humans. It was the experiments, including many performed on live human captives, that convinced Thomas to flee the project.

After he fled with classified documents from Dulce, he found that his wife and child had disappeared. He was contacted by agents from Dulce, who informed him that his loved ones would now be used in those same experiments unless he returned the stolen documents. According to Thomas's tale, he chose to keep the documents when he realized that the Dulce people wouldn't keep any agreement he made. Grieving for his family, but still free himself, he fled into years of hiding.

Thomas's bizarre tale also describes huge vats where cattle blood and protein is broken down and processed. Some of the resultant glop serves as food for the Grays, who reportedly take nourishment through their skin. Most of it is used for genetic experiments or for "nutrient baths" used in incubating young Grays.

The most gruesome particulars of this story are repeated in a number of "witness accounts" of operations at Dulce (and other sites). Though these unsavory tales hopefully remain unbelievable, it is important to remember that some people *do* firmly believe them. Many of the believers are working-class residents of towns lying close to the reputed alien bases. These are not "fringe" group-type people, and traditionally do not fear and mistrust their own government. Sales of UFO books are up in these mostly Western towns.

It's interesting that recent media reports from scientific researchers state that bovine genetic material is compatible with human material. Because of many similarities, biological material from cattle may be used in studies of human diseases, genetic mapping, and biotechnology. Of course, "Thomas" said some years ago that information from the aliens' experiments at Dulce was being provided to many government projects, including the National Science Foundation and the National Institutes of Health.

One biomedical firm, Biopure, is currently engaged in extracting bovine hemoglobin for human use. The hemoglobin is first processed, then used as a supplement in human transfusions. The greatest problem facing the use of cattle hemoglobin is the danger of transmitting a disease called BSE (Bovine Spongiform Encephalopathy). One of the world's most respected UFO researchers, mathematician Jacques Vallee, dryly notes that someone should warn the aliens about BSE before they catch it.

Vallee also points out that anyone with the money need not resort to lurking around rustling cattle in the dark. (If we assume alien technology, why not alien money?) If "they" required cattle for experimentation, it would not be difficult to rent or buy a large private stockyard safe from prying eyes (at a much lower cost than underground bases). Any Chicago slaughterhouse would be delighted to provide the blood and organs from thousands of cattle to interested buyers.

Vallee is not mocking the real existence of unexplained cattle mutilations, just simplistic explanations. In his book *Revelations,* Vallee notes one of the most puzzling facts of the mutilations. The perpetrators are hardly covert; instead, they appear to seek publicity actively.

> "Avoiding the easy prey of animals grazing in the wild," they deliberately kill "cows and horses owned by civilian farmers near urban areas and on small ranches where they are certain to arouse public confusion and anger. *The mutilations are calculated to create terror.*"

One researcher with a different view is Colonel Thomas E. Bearden (U.S. Army, retired), who holds degrees in nuclear physics and mathematics. While in the Army, he worked extensively on U.S. surface-to-air missile systems to counter the Soviet system.

He is currently "senior scientist and department manager for an aerospace company working with artificial intelligence applications for the Army." Over the past decades, he has also done exhaustive research on the electromagnetic aspects of UFO phenomena. Additionally, he has written persuasively on the interaction between UFOs and human consciousness.

According to Col. Bearden's statistics, over nine thousand cattle mutilations have occurred in the U.S. alone since 1973. Bearden has written extensively on the meaning of cattle, a potent symbol of wealth and security, being mutilated. After all, most of us are nursed or raised on cow milk. In his words, "The cattle mutilations are materialized precognitive nightmares indicating the horror of the Armageddon to come. . . . and the true nature of these times."

It is worth remembering that the missing parts of the slain animals are traditionally proscribed foods. For thousands of years, religious traditions around the world urged their followers to avoid physical and spiritual contamination by avoiding animal blood, internal organs, and genitals. Are those mutilating the cattle aware of the taboo that many people still feel?

Some decades ago, Col. Bearden observed that these phenomena show the workings of a directing intelligence. He then somehow arrived at the conclusion that the phenomenon originated in the Soviet Union and was part of a concerted attack on the American public using "psychotronic warfare" technology.

Psychotronic warfare employs many devices, some physical, some psychological, to influence or adversely affect an enemy's health and/or sanity. It is a matter of public record that both the U.S. and Soviet governments have engaged in extensive research in these areas, research that apparently still continues.

However, there seems to be no hard evidence to support Bearden's claim that UFOs and animal mutilations are part of a long-term Soviet attack on the people of the United States. Bearden's obsession with the Soviets has made him a pariah in the UFO research community (a dubious distinction). One wonders what he has to say now, after vast economic and internal problems caused the dissolution of the former Soviet Union.

It does appear that biological materials are required by the mutilators more during some years than others. Just as there are more frequent periods of UFO sightings (called "Flaps"), there seem to be years in which there are more of these mysterious, unsolved mutilations. There seems to be a general correlation between years in which there are more UFO Flaps and years in which there are more mutilations.

In every year since 1967, there have been unsolved cases of animal mutilation investigated by law enforcement officials. These trained investigators look into every possibility, ranging from deranged cults, psychopaths, and tricksters to government agencies and the military. After following every possible lead, the chief investigator for the Trinidad, Colorado, District Attorney offered his opinion. According to Sheriff Lou Girodo, "It seems very possible that these mutilations are being done by creatures from outer space."

What about the idea that our own government is responsible for such events? After all, there are those persistent reports of unmarked black helicopters sighted near mutilation areas. Carl Whiteside, head of the Colorado Bureau of Investigation, echoes Jacques Vallee on this possibility.

> "If you're talking about the CIA or some government spy agency, it just doesn't make sense that they would be involved in random mutilation of cattle on individual ranches or farms. If they were involved in something like that, they'd have the resources to do it under their own controlled conditions. No one would ever know."

Author and film-maker Linda Moulton-Howe, known among investigators as the "Queen of Cattle Mutilations," has spent decades in researching the mystery. After suitable introductions, Linda graciously agreed to an interview near her home outside of Philadelphia. The site chosen for our meeting was an unusual waterside restaurant shaped somewhat like a flying saucer. Linda was calm, articulate, and chose her words with great care.

"My interest in the animal deaths began in 1979. I was Director of Special Projects at the CBS station in Denver when a rash of mutilations occurred in Colorado. I'd been working on environmental issues and was assigned to investigate the rash of strange mutilations.

"My first thoughts were that there had been some sort of

unpublicized government release of toxic waste. I suspected the strange horse and cattle mutilations were the result of the government's random sampling of animals in the spill area in order to test contamination levels."

However, while interviewing the frightened or angry owners of slain domestic animals, she began hearing one "lights in the sky" story after another. One Wyoming farmer told her that a glowing orange disk "the size of a football field" approached him while he was in his barley field. Shortly thereafter, he found two of his cattle mutilated and bloodless.

Her interviews with owners, law enforcement officers, and veterinary experts eventually led to the Emmy award-winning documentary film, *A Strange Harvest*. The documentary moved away from the environmental contamination to focus on "an accumulation of human testimony that suggested the presence of extraterrestrial mutilators."

After her film was broadcast in 1980, Linda was deluged with phone calls and letters from people with their own tales of lights in the sky and animal mutilations. She also found from newspaper files that the phenomenon appeared to be worldwide. After Lady was found in Colorado, reports began to come in from Canada, Australia, parts of Europe, Africa, South America, Central America, and Puerto Rico. Interestingly, there do not appear to be many reports of such mutilations from Asia.

Since that time, Linda has continued her research and published her book *An Alien Harvest* with a video series exploring the connections between animal mutilations, human abductions, and possible government knowledge of alien life-forms. When asked regarding the possibility of human mutilations, she noted, "This is a very difficult subject, since no one *wants* to believe this could be happening. I have received some reports about human mutilations, but have never received an autopsy report with photographs that could be used as proof.

"However, there are many definite parallels with the human abduction phenomena. Many abductees report surgical incisions have been made, body cavities probed, or body fluids removed.

"And in some cases, people report that a minute device or

object has been inserted into their nose, eye, ear, skull, or genitalia. Some people have speculated that this is some sort of monitoring device. Who knows, really? One man I met personally, who reported a number of abduction episodes, states that minute objects were implanted into his penis by aliens. It's interesting to note that many or most of the animal mutilations tend to focus around incisions in the genital-rectal area.

"I believe that the entire phenomena is wider than most people realize, but has been hindered by the tendency of people to jump to conclusions or onto bandwagons. In general, I'm not very comfortable with hypotheses. There now seems to be undeniable evidence that the worldwide reports of animal mutilations, unidentified lights in the sky, and human abductions are closely linked, whatever their real cause is.

"What we need are trained investigators conducting interviews, raising people's awareness of solid facts, investigators who are aware of the possibility of disinformation when examining evidence."

When investigating mutilations, she always obtains a sheriff's report and photographs, as well as a veterinarian's report. She combines this with as clear a picture as possible from eyewitness reports, and when possible, her own visits to sites. All of this documentation is filed and collated with reports from researchers around the world.

Linda notes that researchers taking the phenomena seriously suffer from the same climate that plagued Galileo when he attempted to communicate his ideas. "Galileo taught that the earth was not the center of the universe and was mocked, harassed, and finally imprisoned for his statements. Now, over three hundred sixty years later and despite evidence from every country on the planet, people are still convinced that they are alone at the center of the universe."

In 1989, and again in 1992, I visited some of the areas in Colorado, Nevada, New Mexico, and Arizona where these mutilations occurred. Many took place in grazing areas, most often National Forest or BLM land, located in some of the most isolated places in North America. Other sites are popular seasonal fishing and camping areas, renowned for their natural beauty.

One of these, the forested preserve of the Santa Clara Pueblo near Espaniola, New Mexico, had suffered a rash of mutilations in the months prior to my arrival. Cattle and sheep had been found sliced up and bloodless in the familiar pattern, with no clue as to the culprits.

The region is archeologically interesting as it contains the Puye Cliffs, site of numerous Anasazi cliff-dweller ruins. The slopes are littered with pottery shards and the rocks hold many petroglyphs (rock carvings). Such artifacts are all that remains of the mysterious cliff dwellers, who vanished for unknown reasons long before the arrival of European colonists.

I found the Pueblos in a suspicious mood. One of the Native American tribes that still believes in evil witches, those that I met were convinced that the mutilations were the result of Satanic rituals. Though there had been many UFO sightings near the ruins over the years, no one that I met connected the two phenomena. They clearly wished to forget the unsettling incidents; anyone interested in such things might even be a witch himself.

Though their tribal police kept an eye on me as I camped in the area near the ruins, I did not mind; their suspicion seemed a small price to pay for the comfort of their presence. No mutilations or UFO sightings occurred during my visit, but I did encounter one of the so-called "zones of fear."

Fairly well known to supernatural investigators, these are generally small geographical areas with easily defined boundaries. You know when you have found one, because ice runs along your spine and the hairs on your neck literally stand up! Turning around to look, you see nothing out of the ordinary, but the oppressive sense of fear remains. Stepping a few paces away, the fear suddenly stops. Stepping back, it returns.

Most often found at so-called "haunted" sites, this strange, admittedly subjective phenomenon has been the subject of many idle speculations. Is it the result of ultrasonic waves, like a dog whistle? Or is it perhaps a psychic residue left by an unpleasant event? If it is a psychological effect, it is a particularly powerful one, able to impact portions of anatomy outside of my conscious control. I have encountered them perhaps six times in ten or twelve years, but can offer no explanation. It would be interesting to return to the spot with equipment that can detect magnetic fields, or measure unusual auditory phenomena.

The "zone" at the Puye Cliffs was on a bare slope below some ancient ruins. Had something strange happened there? Was this a site of "witchcraft" rituals, or had a mutilation been found there? All I know is that I was happy to leave the isolated spot.

On another occasion, I was driving near Joshua Tree National Monument in the California desert with some friends. One of them said, "Hey! We're near the old Giant Rock Airport; I used to go out there in my hippie days. There would be hundreds of us waiting to see the saucers come down. It was a really wild scene."

I'd read many tales about Giant Rock Airport, but had never seen it. It really was an old private airport, owned by one of the earliest UFO contactees, George Van Tassel. In the 1950s, he claimed a number of close encounters with "spacemen," and eventually formed a small cult that did not survive his death. Before he died, he spent huge sums of money building a giant energy condenser of some sort. He called it "the Integretron."

Even though my friend was hazy on directions, we decided to go see if we could find the old airport. We drove another hour or two, and stopped at many bars and gas stations for (often conflicting) directions. Eventually, we saw a silver, silo-looking object on a dirt road, and knew we had found the Integretron.

It was surrounded by barbed wire and was located between two decrepit trailers, each also surrounded by barbed wire. We parked by one of the trailers and sounded the horn until a wizened old woman emerged. She was Mrs. Van Tassel, widow of George Van Tassel, the owner of Giant Rock Airport.

She was suspicious at first, but warmed up when she heard my friends' story of the "good old days." She stood on her side of the fence and explained that the Integretron was not in good working order, but that she intended someday to "rebuild it and open it to cancer patients and people seeking enlightenment." Unfortunately, George Van Tassel's former secretary also claimed ownership of it, and it was her trailer on the other side of the fence!

A graphic symbol of the UFO community if ever there was one, the two women had been locked in a legal battle since George's death. Even though they lived fifty yards apart, and miles from other people, they had not spoken with one another for years! Evidently, the Integretron's healing powers did not include conflict mediation.

Pointing across the desert, Mrs. Van Tassel told us the way to the old Giant Rock Airport, but warned us that there had been a long series of cattle mutilations and human disappearances in the area. A band of local ranchers had finally bulldozed the remnants of the airport building, and though there was nothing left, it was still considered a very unsafe place to visit. Even the rowdy local teenagers did not go there.

With some trepidation, but unwilling to give up after so much effort, we drove out to the site. It was an eerie place, perhaps the most silent desert landscape I have ever experienced. The almost total quiet, the chemical smell of creosote bushes, and the monumental black rocks strewn about joined with Mrs. Van Tassel's story to make our visit an uncomfortable one.

Walking around, we first noticed some swastikas and other occult signs recently carved in a cliffside. When one of us stumbled over the desiccated corpse of a cow, we decided to call it a day. My friend's blissful, light-filled memories of the old days at Giant Rock Airport, when everyone believed the peaceful "Space Brothers" were about to land, had become instead a legacy of fear. On our way out, we did not stop to linger at the fabled Integretron.

Whatever we choose to accept about animal mutilations, that they do occur is indisputable. It is also true that law enforcement officials have for decades professed a total lack of suspects or possible motives. With their domestic stock still disappearing, there is little wonder if locals (and investigators) create mythologies about cults to account for the mystery; most people prefer to ignore this unpleasant phenomenon altogether. Perhaps we are not so far from mobs of torch-bearing, hysterical peasants chasing vampires and werewolves as we like to think.

6

THIEVES OF TIME

The Empire never ended.

—PHILLIP K. DICK

WAS there any way to merge all these outlandish elements together into one clear model? Gray aliens, multigenerational abductions, cattle mutilations, secret government saucer programs, hairy giants, and electromagnetic phenomena may seem to be disconnected topics. Was there someone out there who possessed an informed sense of the "bigger picture"? Through a series of accidents and coincidences, I did encounter two individuals who claimed such an overall vision. However, my experience with them was more a surrealistic comedy than an illumination.

Over the past few years I had heard many wild rumors regarding the mysterious "Montauk Project." The Project is a favorite theme of the "psychotronic warfare" community, a loose network of researchers devoted to strange devices purporting to influence psychic phenomena, human psychology, the weather, and flying saucers.

In 1993, Preston Nichols's book, *The Montauk Project,* became a best-seller at new age bookstores nationwide. This short work is mysterious, provocative, and brings together many previously unconnected elements in the UFO-conspiracy field. It begins with the pioneering work of Wilhelm Reich and Nikola Tesla, takes form in government-sponsored weather control experiments in the early 1940s, and crystallizes in the ill-fated Philadelphia experiment on invisibility during World War II.

According to Nichols, the Philadelphia Experiment was later closed but research continued on clandestine levels. The Montauk Project, operating during the 1970s and '80s at New York's Montauk Air Force Base, was allegedly an attempt to explore, chart, and ultimately manipulate the flow of *time*. The story includes joint human-alien research, abductions and brainwashing, physical age-regression techniques, hairy monsters, psychics linked into Tesla technology, missing Nazi gold bullion, explorers lost forever in alternate worlds, UFOs, pyramids on the planet Mars, and the apparent "end of time" in the year 2012. In other words, just about every possible angle of the UFO theme was in the tale.

Nichols claims to have recovered the blanked memories of his role as chief technician for the Project only after years of struggle. His colleague Alfred Bielek, co-author of *The Philadelphia Experiment and Other UFO Conspiracies*, claimed to be one of two Naval technicians who "fell through time" from the 1940s into 1983, and who later became a consultant at Montauk. Another player, Duncan Cameron, said he was the second sailor who "fell through" and was the foremost psychic employed by the project to navigate time. They claim that their story, the Philadelphia Experiment, was later made into the feature film of that name.

It was not easy meeting Preston Nichols. Those active in the "psychotronic community" are a notoriously close-mouthed lot (some would say paranoid). Research in psychic warfare has been rumored for many years in both parapsychology and intelligence circles. Military attempts at remote viewing, influencing others at a distance, and even making them ill are all a matter of Congressional record. Civilian researchers claim that such reports are only the tip of the iceberg.

Psychotronic technology represents the theory that many of these abilities can be induced or repeated by objects or machines, frequently powered by electromagnetic energy. Supposedly the best efforts in this direction have been made by scientists in the former Soviet Union.

One researcher, retired Army Colonel Thomas E. Bearden, identified twenty-six probable Soviet psychotronic warfare devices. His list included "brain probes, thought implanters and disease radiator rays, antimissile systems, nuclear detonation transmitters, earthquake generators, and weather-control systems." He and others pointed to the severe, freak tornadoes plaguing the central United States as Soviet test runs of these weather-control devices.

Conferences held by members of the psychotronic research community are rather tense affairs. (How would you feel if you thought that your meeting was being electromagnetically "beamed" by others intent on eavesdropping, giving you cancer, and influencing your own thoughts?)

Author Michael Grosso once attended a conference sponsored by the New York Chapter of the United States Psychotronics Association. Though he gave it his best shot, he was unable to endure many hours of "rambling, incomprehensible talks on people burning up, disappearing in time warps, and being gobbled up by psychic monsters." He ended up by "deciding to disappear from the auditorium" himself.

I knew that both Preston Nichols and Alfred Bielek had spoken at this same conference. Did I have to endure one of these paranoid affairs myself to meet them? I finally met Nichols and the others at a public workshop at a workshop center in northern Arizona (since closed).

I knew the organizers of the event, and spoke to them before arriving, even agreeing to pick up the faculty up at the airport myself. They reported that preliminary phone conversations with Nichols had been strange; hints about wiretapping and psychotronic warfare accompanied hair-raising accounts of people abducted and imprisoned in other dimensions.

Just prior to the event, expectations of an unusual audience were heightened by a large number of strange calls to the center's office. Some of the callers demanded to know if they were with the CIA; others blessed them "for having the courage to come out with the truth." There were even a few who said that, yes, they too had been with the Montauk Project.

With a heightened sense of drama (and the absurd), I met the presenters at Sky Harbor airport in Phoenix. Our talk immediately turned toward the weekend's subject matter.

Al Bielek began relating memories that had been surfacing lately during his waking moments. Evidently, he had been on-call as some sort of government "sleeper" to be activated only in case of dire emergency. This plan "was to be accomplished through continued reinforcement of the same government brainwashing program" that initially blocked his role in the Philadelphia Experiment.

Someone had slipped up, and now Al recalled being sent to a secret underground installation on the island of Malta during the late 1980s. Located thousands of feet underground, this was apparently a high-energy research facility built upon an old Atlantean site (yes, Atlantis is also included).

There had been an unexplained accident at this secret facility and Al was the first man sent in. "Once I got in, the first thing that I saw was dead men strewn everywhere along the corridors. None of the staff had survived."

"How did you first get in, Al?"

"I got in from the underground intercontinental subway; they used some of the old Atlantean tunnel systems when they were building, and hooked up into our own government tunnel system. I rode directly over from the States."

"Al, do you mean the underground tunnel system that a number of researchers have reported was built by joint U.S.-Alien workers?"

"Of course; are there any others? I suspect that this facility was another one of the research projects investigating the use of natural energy vortices. You know, of course, that many locations on the planet contain these vortices?"

I nodded.

"For years now, secret research projects have been under way to explore means of exploiting these energy bases. They are not only looking for free energy, but seek to control the actual intelligence of these vortices as well."

I looked at the others, then back to Al. "You mean these energy vortices are actually intelligent?"

"Most definitely! Many of these vortices are geophysical energy patterns many hundreds of thousands of years old; they have certainly evolved their own intelligence. The one at the base in Malta is a relatively young one, only one hundred thousand years or so. It's a real mean one, though."

"What would be the value of contacting such an intelligence?" I wondered. "What could they tell us?"

"It's not for purposes of communication, it's for purposes of control. Through their control of these vortices, they can create hurricanes, earthquakes, all sorts of phenomena. Of course, the vortices themselves don't want to be interfered with; they sometimes get out of hand, like what happened with that mean one in Malta."

When we were leaving the airport, I was immediately commanded to make a U-turn in heavy traffic, as Preston had spotted an unusual "cellular phone" transmitting tower. With my jeep hanging halfway out into heavy lunch-hour traffic, I waited patiently while Preston filmed the tower antenna with his video recorder for later analysis.

He and Al then began discussing the problem of cellular phones, and how they are "beginning to use a wattage many times that allowed by FCC regulations," or even for simple telecommunications. They seemed to understand that some sort of mind control of the population at large is under way, but weren't sure of the goal. More research would have to be done.

At one point, while driving north through the desert on Highway 87, Duncan yelled for me to stop immediately. At first I thought he wanted to relieve himself, but that was not the case. When the car stopped, he jumped out into the highway and began running back down the way we'd come. Preston leaned over and tapped me on the shoulder. "You'd better keep an eye on him; sometimes he'll just run away and get lost." Al nodded irritably.

Was I expected to jump out and start running after him? (After all, the desert was extremely hot and there was fast-moving traffic.) Deciding that losing one of the faculty en route would make an entertaining story back at the ranch, I settled down in my seat. Fortunately Duncan returned to the car without mishap, and we continued toward the mountains. He later said that he'd wished to examine "an unusual energy vortex along the road there."

Duncan is a likable, handsome man with salt-and-pepper hair who makes his post-Montauk living as a carpenter. When pressed, he explained his perceptions. "There's something strange about the energy around here; I have trouble feeling it clearly. It's as if some agency were blocking it." I pointed out that we were passing the infamous Superstition Mountains, reputed site of many hauntings, UFO encounters, and unexplained disappearances.

Duncan nodded; he seemed relieved to have some hypothesis. Preston explained that Duncan was the chief psychic of their group, though Al Bielek was also a sensitive.

Back at the center, the majority of the participants had arrived and were milling around the bookstore before dinner.

The staff were entertaining themselves with speculations of which of the guests was the inevitable "CIA agent." After dinner under the large dining tent, the group gathered in the meeting room. Everyone made it inside just before a tremendous thunderstorm began pouring a torrent of rain.

After introducing himself, Preston asked everyone to say who they were and why they had come. About half was the expected new age audience; surprisingly, the rest seemed to be mostly scientist-types. In addition to engineers, there were a couple of physicists, a chemist, and a university mathematician. There were also two or three German scientists who had somehow heard about the gathering "through the network."

Some of the group were obvious cranks with axes of their own to grind. One launched into a long rant about taxes and the federal government and had to be interrupted twice. The most interesting story was from a sad-faced Idaho woman who said that her father had been involved with the Montauk Project, and later had been murdered under mysterious circumstances. She said that she had come in order to learn more about the reasons for her father's death.

After everyone had spoken, Preston said a few words about the time-travel aspect of the tale. "The top secret Montauk Project created a 'time tunnel' at the base on Long Island. Throughout the 1980s, thousands of brainwashed people physically traveled through the time tunnel to preselected locations. Most people came back, but quite a few never returned. We still have no idea what the ultimate motives were for the Project directors, or who they actually were.

"Duncan Cameron was our psychic who was hooked up to the technology and who navigated time from his seat in the famed Montauk Chair. Al Bielek was involved as a consultant, both because of his engineering background, and his own psychic gifts.

"Of course, both he and Duncan were intimately involved anyway, because they were on the Philadelphia Experiment. The Philadelphia Experiment and the Montauk Project are connected through a timelock, which we'll say more about tomorrow. I myself became involved as a technical person, and was chief technician for the Project. I made the machines work."

Since it was growing late, Preston and Duncan then fielded a few scattered questions about Montauk, and more formal presentations were saved for the following day. For those who were interested, Al Bielek showed a video called *Secrets of the 3rd Reich*. I didn't go, but apparently it was about the infamous Nazi saucer program.

The night ended with hours of loud, spectacular lightning activity directly overhead. I couldn't help wondering if "they" hadn't gotten wind of this event, and had dispatched an angry vortex to thwart our plans. Eventually, the evil vortex went away and I fell asleep.

The morning began with Al Bielek telling the early days of the story and its bizarre cast of characters: Nikola Tesla, Wilhelm Reich, emigrated Nazi scientists, Professor John von Neumann, and the Princeton Institute for Advanced Study.

Nikola Tesla was born in 1856 in Yugoslavia, and later moved to the United States where he worked for Thomas Edison, George Westinghouse, J. P. Morgan, and the U.S. government. A true genius, he is famed as the inventor of alternating current (AC), radar, radio (before Marconi), and the first guided missile systems.

Tesla became involved in the wartime, government-sponsored Institute for Advanced Study at Princeton University, eventually becoming director of the infamous Project Rainbow. Project Rainbow was a study of an "electromagnetic bottle" technique that would render a large object (like a ship) invisible to detection by radar. In many ways, Project Rainbow is the forerunner of today's Stealth technology used by the American military. There was supposed to have been a preliminary test run on a ship in the Brooklyn Naval Yard in 1940. In that test, partial invisibility was achieved, and the go-ahead was given for further research.

Tesla is said to have realized that the technique was extremely dangerous to those involved in the test, and sabotaged the first scheduled experiment with a live crew to gain time for more research. For this, he was dismissed from Project Rainbow in 1942. He is supposed to have died in March 1943, but there are allegations that he was later seen in England. The papers he was working on were removed from his safe by federal agents and remain classified to this day.

Directorship of the Project was given to Tesla's second-in-command, mathematician John von Neumann (who was supposed to have had Nazi ties). Neumann had violently disagreed with Tesla on some of the technology involved, and was willing to continue with the tests.

The keel for the test ship, the *U.S.S. Eldridge*, was laid in Philadelphia in 1942; initial tests were carried out in dry dock. A picked crew, including Duncan Cameron and Alfred Bielek (under an "earlier identity" as Duncan's brother, Edward Cameron) as control-room officers, went into training. Cameron and Bielek had already worked directly with Tesla, von Neumann, and others involved in Princeton.

On July 20, 1943, the test with a live crew on the *Eldridge* was performed. The generators were turned on for fifteen minutes. Not only did the ship disappear from radar, it disappeared from eyesight as well! Bielek and Cameron were in the metal-shielded control room, and suffered no ill effects. The crew on deck experienced nausea, disorientation, and in some cases, lasting mental illness.

At this point, von Neumann wanted an extension, but orders were given from the chief of naval operations for a repeat on August 12, 1943. There was a war on, and human agents were deemed expendable.

According to Bielek, three UFOs appeared over the ship, six days prior to the test. When the test was finally performed, one of the UFOs is supposed to have become caught in the ensuing vortex. The other two saucers departed by "normal means."

To observers on another ship, the *Eldridge* appeared to have completely disappeared from its location. Not only had the ship vanished, but even the outline in the water (visible the first time) was gone. The *Eldridge* had gone "somewhere else."

At this point, Duncan and Al in the control room realized that something was wrong and emerged on deck. The outer world was gone; the crew were either insane, dead, or dying. Some were physically embedded in the steel bulkheads.

Another Cameron brother, stationed on deck, is supposed to have died in this fashion. When Duncan and Al realized that their brother was dead, they both jumped overboard in an attempt to swim away from the ship's electromagnetic field.

"I will leave what happened next for later," said Al. "Suffice it to say that, after four hours, the ship reappeared, and rescue crews came aboard. Most of the crew were later given discharges on the grounds of being 'mentally unfit'; I continued on with top clearance in the Navy, but, like everyone else, was brainwashed to forget any involvement in the Project.

"The *Eldridge* was outfitted for one more test, this unmanned. It disappeared, but upon reappearing, was found to have suffered severe damage to the equipment. The Philadelphia Experiment was voted a failure, and the equipment put into secret storage."

Preston Nichols took the stage next. He began by talking about Wilhelm Reich, the unwitting father of both some of the Montauk technology, and the brainwashing technique employed there.

Wilhelm Reich was a brilliant, highly controversial, Austrian scientist who studied with Sigmund Freud and Carl Jung, and who later emigrated to America. Reich claimed to have discovered what he called "orgone energy," which is the life force intrinsic to all living things and even the atmosphere. His brilliant writings on the function of the orgone in sexuality and orgasm are still studied by many psychiatrists and bodywork therapists. "Neo-Reichian Therapy" is a not-uncommon form of cathartic bodywork still popular today.

Unfortunately, Reich attracted the attention of the Food and Drug Administration when he began claiming that he could heal diseases with orgone energy. He also had published controversial writings on teenage sexuality, which did not help his case at all.

The courts ruled against Reich, and the FDA supervised a massive public burning of his books and destroyed much of his lab equipment. Reich himself was sentenced to prison in a verdict that seemed harsh even in the 1940s. He died in the same prison where he was reportedly permitted to continue his research into energy phenomena. His papers from that time are supposedly classified.

It is a matter of record that Reich worked on a number of federal and state experiments in weather control. His theory was that violent storms accumulate DOR, or "dead orgone." He developed an electromagnetic method to reduce the DOR of violent storms, or simply to break them up. Reich's work with the government resulted in the creation of what is known as the "radiosonde."

The pineapple-sized radiosonde combined Reich's technology with a simple radio broadcasting and receiving device. Used in creating and breaking storms, it was also a potential broadcasting source of "clean" orgone energy. The operation that carried out this "cloudbusting" work was known as Project Phoenix. Eventually the work of Project Phoenix and Project Rainbow were combined in what became the Montauk Project.

Preston cleared his throat, "I have to say here that I only know the material that comes next because I was very lucky. For years, I've been in the radio and radar surplus business. It's been one of the ways that I make my living. Part of how I do this is by going to private individuals who have junk or collections of electronic equipment and buy it off their hands. Sometimes I get lucky.

"I met this guy at a ham radio convention, and he had for sale one of the old Wilhelm Reich radiosonde transmitters, the kind that they used to send up in weather balloons. I bought that one, and asked him if he had any more. He said that he did, in a barn in upstate New York. When I finally got out there, he had a whole pile of junk filling this barn. I bought the whole lot for a few hundred dollars. Well, there was a lot more of those radiosondes there, but there was also an old box full of files and notebooks.

"I was stunned to see that one of these notebooks contained notes of unpublished research by Wilhelm Reich. I had one of Reich's last notebooks!

"Because I feel uncomfortable about speaking about this material in mixed company, I will only touch upon the contents of this research. It involves very sophisticated techniques of programming and deprogramming employing a certain kind of bodywork using sexual energy. These are basically the techniques that they used at the Montauk Project to brainwash the 'Montauk Boys' before they were sent out on missions, and to brainwash us to forget our own participation. If any of the gentlemen present wish to speak with me later, I will be happy to share the information."

This did not go over well with some of those attending. One white-haired, grandmotherly woman raised her hand.

"I'm not very comfortable with this. First you tantalize us with hints, then you piss us off saying you won't share the material!"

Preston shook his head. "I'm not saying that I won't share the material, it's just that I feel uncomfortable saying some of these things in front of ladies. Anyway, basically these techniques are very similar to Eastern tantric techniques. They were used on all the personnel to break them down and program them to behave in certain ways under certain conditions.

"The 'Montauk Boys' were usually blond, blue-eyed Aryan types who fit the Nazi ideal. Remember, we suspect that Montauk had a strong neo-Nazi connection. These kids were kidnapped and brought there, brutally broken down sexually and reprogrammed, then sent out through the time tunnel on missions to different times, places, and alternate realities. Many of these kids never came back."

The room was silent. A few people were quietly weeping for the lost Montauk Boys. I wondered if any of those present had recovered memories of being "one of the boys."

Preston continued on to say that they have since met a fairly sizable number of the Boys, now grown up. Many of them had serious mental or emotional problems, often exacerbated by their "missing time." They had also found that they were gravitating back toward Long Island and Montauk.

The Montauk Boys and other explorers, willing or no, traveled through a "time tunnel" (yes, just like the 1960s TV show) directed by a trained psychic strapped into a chair loaded down with leads to the transmitters. The occupant of the Chair was most often Duncan Cameron.

The Chair surmounted a pyramid of coils broadcasting electromagnetic energy on a frequency that matched the human aura. The signals were run through a digital converter, then fed into a Cray 1 computer interfaced with an IBM 360. The resultant signal was then relayed through the immense radar dish transmitters atop the Montauk Base. Signals were also transmitted through a "Delta-T antenna" that had been found to distort the dimension of time. (It was while working on a homemade Delta-T years later at home that Preston first began to recover his lost memories.)

Essentially, the psychic would think or meditate and the

computers would analyze the signal. This combination allowed the operator to fine-tune the process on a level impossible for a mere machine.

In the early days of the Project, working from the Chair was extremely dangerous. Before the technicians discovered adequate shielding, the operator was inadvertently exposed to lethal amounts of UHF/microwave radiation. In Duncan's case, enough brain matter was destroyed to have his doctors declare him "brain dead"!

According to Preston Nichols, "the only reason Duncan is alive today is due to his strong psychic aptitude. The psychic part of his mind takes over the physical part and runs the body. His brain stem is alive; his body is alive, but his actual higher brain is dead. His psychic energy runs his body through his brain stem."

All heads turned to look at a manifestly-healthy Duncan, apparently unperturbed by the description. The lecture stopped so we could go eat lunch.

In the afternoon, the group backtracked to get the clear story on what happened to Al and Duncan after they jumped from the *Eldridge* in 1943. According to Al, "We fell for a long time through empty space. Then, suddenly we landed on our feet on solid ground. We didn't know it at the time, but we were on the grounds of the Montauk Base on Long Island!

"At this point the movie (*The Philadelphia Experiment*) is wrong. We didn't get attacked by a military helicopter, then escape through a hole in the fence. Instead, we turned to run, and were immediately grabbed by M.P.'s, who took us into the building, then down underground to a huge laboratory. One of the things that we saw there was a flying saucer parked there. It later turned out that this was the same saucer that had been sucked through the vortex created by the *Eldridge!*

"In there we were confronted by an old man who said that he was John von Neumann. Well, we knew that this couldn't be von Neumann, since he was a much younger man whom we had seen yesterday before the experiment. He said that he was indeed von Neumann, and that he had been waiting many years to see us again. He said that it was now August 13, 1983. We knew he was crazy then!"

Al explained that they were taken to a waiting room and

kept under guard there. In that room was a color television, and they began to wonder if the man who claimed to be von Neumann was not right after all. In the 1940s, there was no color TV, and the things that they saw on it eventually convinced them that they were now really in the future. When von Neumann came up to speak to them again, he found a willing audience.

"Von Neumann explained to us that the *Eldridge* had created a dangerous lock in hyperspace, and that they wanted to send us back to shut things down. If we didn't the hyperspace bubble would continue to expand with no end in sight." Al paused dramatically.

"He said that the historical records even showed that we had done it, but *we* knew that we hadn't yet! He said that we had to do anything to shut the machinery down, even if we had to smash it!"

Before returning to the past, Duncan and Al were sent on a number of missions for the Project (why hurry if going *back* in time?). In transit on one of these missions, Duncan went down a side tunnel (theoretically impossible according to Preston), and ended up with a group of aliens. Edward Cameron (Al Bielek, remember?) ended up in the same tunnel soon afterwards.

The aliens revealed that they required a piece of delicate equipment to be retrieved from the saucer kept at Montauk. This was supposed to have been a crystal instrument related to the drive of the ship. The drive was later given to the aliens.

A man in the front row interrupted excitedly, "You mean, they had a working relationship with the Aliens?"

Preston responded, "Much of the technology was derived from that of a number of alien races. The Montauk Chair was based on a prototype given by the Sirians. The Delta-T Antenna, used for bending time, was from the treaty with the Orions."

The man's hand stayed up. "Are you referring to the treaty with Aliens that some people say FDR made?"

"Roosevelt definitely made a treaty with the Orions, exchanging freedom of movement for technological secrets. The Orions are a highly advanced race who control the other alien race that people call 'the Grays.' The Grays are responsible for most abductions of people, and cattle mutilations, too. Many of the underground bases throughout the world have Grays living in them, along with some military personnel."

I raised my arm. "What about these 'Sirians' that you refer to? Are they benevolent or are they malevolent like the Grays and the Orions?"

"The Sirians are relatively neutral, though they also seem to have some sort of treaty and communication with the earth's governments. We think that they disagree with the Orions on a number of issues, but are unwilling to fight them. There is a rumor that they once lost a great battle with the Orions."

I asked Preston another question. "It seems that we humans are in the midst of warring powers with their own agendas, all alien to our plans and purposes. Are there any aliens that you do consider 'friendly,' or useful for humanity to align itself with?"

Preston seemed to think that this was a sensitive topic. He paused for a sip of water, then spoke quietly a little with Duncan. After straightening up, he responded. "The only group that we understand has a right to be here are those from Nibiru. Nibiru, mentioned in Zacariah Sitchin's books, is the planet on an elliptical orbit with our own solar system.

"The Nibiruans are the original inhabitants of this solar system, and the ones who seeded human life on this planet. We are their creations, and they still consider the Earth to be theirs."

Preston smiled dryly, "Whenever they come back, they will probably not be too pleased to see other races experimenting on 'their' humans."

After their alien encounter in a side tunnel, Al and Duncan were returned to the *Eldridge* in midexperiment in 1943. They smashed the equipment, and the ship reappeared, four hours later to observers.

For some still unknown reason, just before the electromagnetic distortion faded, Duncan again jumped overboard, leaving Al behind. Preston and Al believe that he had been brainwashed to return back to the Montauk of the 1980s, to serve the Project.

Al gave his report to his superiors, was of course not believed (especially by von Neumann), and was given a leave of absence. Later he was thoroughly brainwashed to forget that he had ever been involved.

After Edward Cameron (Al Bielek) had aged, the same agency that was tracking the other Philadelphia Experiment survivors employed a sophisticated technique to transfer his consciousness into a baby of the Bielek family. Evidently, someone had decided that Al was to be used again in some capacity, perhaps because of his pivotal role on the *Eldridge*. Now he was truly Al Bielek, yet he had flashes of memory from the earlier life as Edward Cameron. And of course, he was still on call as some sort of "sleeper."

Meanwhile, back in the future, Duncan was also getting a new body. After he had arrived back at Montauk, his body started to age at an accelerated rate. In a short while, he was an old man. In order to preserve him, he was shifted back some decades.

"They" decided to use the same technique on Duncan, a technique vastly improved in the intervening years. A new body, born in 1951, was provided for Duncan, and his consciousness was transferred into it in 1963.

Preston thinks that ITT was the corporation responsible for this operation. "I've often heard accounts of a secret project conducted by ITT at Brentwood, Long Island, in 1963. I believe that transferring Duncan's consciousness to his new body was part of this process."

Preston had met the post-Montauk Duncan some time after his own buried memories began to resurface. After he mysteriously appeared on the scene, Duncan quickly became Preston's assistant in his private lab. Preston grew suspicious, though, and took Duncan to the now-closed Montauk base where they walked around.

Not only did Duncan begin recalling some of the events in the past, but he also remembered that he had been programmed to kill Preston later and destroy his lab! He vowed to resist the programmers, and he and Preston became allies.

Al Bielek's story of remembrance was quite different. He already knew Preston and Duncan well from the annual Psychotronic Conference that they attended. One night at home, he watched on television a movie called *The Philadelphia Experiment*.

As he watched, he noticed that some of the details were

wrong, and then his own memories came flooding back. He traveled to see Preston and Duncan and tell them.

"I went up to them and said, 'I think that I was one of the crewmen on the Philadelphia Experiment, and that both of you were involved in it, too.' They said, 'We know; we've just been waiting for you to remember!'"

That evening Preston showed a videotape he'd made recently on the grounds of the Montauk Base. There was clearly a lot of electrical equipment, some of it quite old, left behind. He pointed out mysterious cables that seemed quite new, leading underground. He explained that there is still a large secret base deep underground at Montauk, with access from some other location. Other than that it was for sinister purposes (what else could it be?), he had no idea what "they" were now doing down there.

The base, as viewed through Preston's tape, seemed vast and dark, permeated with a brooding atmosphere of evil. How much of this was subjective and based on the story we'd just heard? It was difficult to tell. There was one dramatic scene of a grieving Duncan recovering lost memories while in a long bunker full of metal cages. Remembering that it was here that the Montauk boys were tortured and brainwashed, he broke down into loud sobs.

The videotape also showed what Preston termed "an electromagnetic afterimage of the Beast." We could all see a huge, man-shaped, black blur standing in a corner of the picture. But who or what was the "Beast"?

The Beast caused the end of the Project. Worried that the Project was reaching apocalyptic proportions, Preston, Duncan, and others formed a cabal to sabotage the operation. According to Preston, it was a contingency program that only Duncan could activate from the Chair. When the time was right, Preston approached him and whispered the triggering phrase, "the time is now."

Hearing this phrase, Duncan "let loose a monster from his subconscious, and the transmitter actually manifested a hairy monster. It was big, hairy, hungry, and nasty. It showed up somewhere on the base. It would eat anything that it could find, and smashed everything in sight. Several different people saw it, but everyone described a different beast. It was either nine or thirty feet tall, depending on whoever saw it. No one was in any frame of mind to calmly or collectively analyze its exact nature."

While the personnel fled wildly in all directions, Preston's supervisor ordered him to shut down the power. Since turning off the generators had no effect, he was forced to begin ripping out wires and even using an acetylene torch to cut through shielded cables. Finally the Beast faded back into nothing.

The Beast is interesting as a description of the relationship between "big, hairy monsters" and the subconscious. According to Preston Nichols, other similar creatures seen around the world may also be related to this phenomenon. The psychic nature of this being accounts for its ability to continue to manifest on the sensitive film.

Throughout the weekend, there were long digressions into arcane electronics, radio theory, and physics. Certainly no expert on these topics, I was unable to verify if any of the theories were sound. However, the scientist-types present in the audience seemed to eat it up. They stayed up late excitedly discussing the concepts long after everyone else hit the sack.

On Sunday morning, with the heavy rain still present, people eagerly slogged through the mud to the classroom early. Preston started with the Nazi gold that was said to have financed the Project.

"In 1944, an American troop train went through a French tunnel carrying ten billion dollars of Nazi gold bullion. The train was dynamited in the tunnel while carrying fifty-one U.S. soldiers. General Patton was in Europe at the time, and investigated the 'accident,' but could find no explanation or the gold, either. His investigation may relate to persistent rumors that Patton's strange death was an assassination.

"I'm told that the gold ended up at Montauk, where it financed the project for many years. (This was gold worth in today's market approximately two hundred billion dollars.) After that ran out, financing was taken over by the Krupp family, who controlled the ITT corporation."

Later, Al Bielek spoke with me privately about the Nazi Saucer program. He was quite clear that the "flugelrads" designed by Viktor Schoenberger were fully developed by the end of World War II, and supplied me with an impressive array of dates and names to back this up. Unfortunately, he sank his own argument by also insisting that "the Holocaust was just a myth promoted by the international cabal of Jewish bankers." (This bizarre, revisionist theory is commonly found in accounts of Nazi UFOs and underground bases.)

Preston spoke next on a more vital topic, the "End of Time." Because of what went on at Montauk and even during the Philadelphia Experiment back in the 1940s, there is now a "closed loop" in time.

"We are currently in a time loop. This loop extends from where the Montauk researchers penetrated into the past up into where they penetrated into the future. It's all fixed and seems to be unalterable. This all goes as far forward as the year 2012 A.D. Attempts to journey to times after that seem to show a different kind of reality."

Excited questions from the audience drew out more information. Evidently, the Montauk Boys were sent to an empty square in a deserted city. In the middle of the square stood a pedestal upon which rests a metal statue of a horse. At the base of the statue is a plaque that bears the date of 2012 A.D. along with a message. The message was different every time, but the Boys were constantly being sent to record it.

While in the city, the travelers experienced a strange, hazy quality to reality. This haze grew heavier and heavier the farther ahead in time they attempted to move. People don't seem to exist in these future times. According to the presenters, the "end of the loop" in 2012 is best imagined as the extinction of reality as we know it.

A surprising number of authors have spoken of the end of time in similar terms, including the designation of 2012 A.D. as the Big Year, possibly lifted from the ancient Mayan calendar that lists it as its end date. There is some evidence that the ancient calendric systems of North, Central, and South America share a common origin and end point. This may explain why the Hopi, Aztecs, Mayans, and other native peoples believe the world is nearing its end. It does not explain what we are to expect.

The "Martian pyramids" were frequently discussed in the workshop. This story first came to public notice a few years ago when a number of independent researchers were examining NASA photos of the surface of Mars. In an area called on the official maps of the Martian surface "Cydonia," researchers were amazed to see what looked like a huge statue of a humanoid face looking up at the sky!

This face is apparently carved from a mile-high rock plateau. A mile or two away lies a group of large stone mesas that look like a cluster of pyramids. Much has been made of sophisticated computer techniques that showed what appears to be an unnatural symmetry in the structures.

After the publication of Richard Hoagland's book, *The Monuments of Mars: A City on the Edge of Forever,* there has been growing international interest in a closer look. NASA, unwilling to admit officially there is anything to the mystery, seems closer to bending. It's a safe bet that an upcoming Mars Mission a few years away will find some reason to explore Cydonia.

So what does all this have to do with the Montauk Project? According to Preston Nichols, there is already a human colony on Mars. "Mars was interesting to the Montauk researchers, because they knew that there was an old technology there. According to my sources, the entrances to the Face and the pyramids were not accessible from the surface due to their construction.

"The Montauk researchers decided that the best approach would be to project a time portal right into the center of the Martian underground complex. There was little risk, as we had set up remote TV cameras to look through before anyone attempted to enter.

"Duncan was part of the team that eventually went through to Mars in 1982 or '83. I don't know what they did with what they found there. Duncan has tried to access this information, but it is deeply buried and hard to contact. We do know that he encountered Jesus the Christ while there, and Jesus programmed him to fulfill some role in the future."

The last statement (reminiscent of the infamous contactee Billy Meier) caused skepticism even among *this* audience, and a score of hands shot up. Preston repeated that they knew no more than that Jesus was there waiting for Duncan on Mars, and shifted the talk back to the pyramids.

"According to Duncan's recollection, he did go inside the main pyramid and saw still functioning advanced technology there. This equipment was called the 'Solar System Defense.' Duncan had been ordered by the Montauk researchers to turn it off. It had to be shut off before anything else could be done.

"This defense has been shut off retroactive to 1943, which is commonly considered among UFO buffs to be the beginning of the massive UFO phenomenon. There's not much more I can say about Martian pyramids at this time, except that the science-fiction movie, *Total Recall* (from a Phillip K. Dick story and starring Arnold Schwartzenegger) is based on some of the reports from the Montauk Project."

Preston also referred to the infamous "Alternative 3," written about by Leslie Watkins. *Alternative 3* was a BBC broadcast aired on June 20, 1977. It was a satirical story about hundreds of missing people turning up at a secret "slave labor colony" on the moon. The moon base was the "product of an international conspiracy of industrialists who were aware of the coming environmental catastrophe." Presented in a factual exposé-style by "dedicated researchers," the tale was actually concocted by author David Ambrose and filmmaker Christopher Miles. Following the show, Anglia TV was inundated by panicking watchers who believed every word.

Though the directors admitted it was a hoax inspired by Orson Wells's *Invasion From Mars* broadcast, the later book by Watkins claimed to be a true account. Watkins's opinion was evidently shared by Preston Nichols, who also described a similar base on Mars (not in the Cydonia area).

The weekend ended on a upbeat note, with Duncan reminding us that not all was gloom and doom, but also an opportunity to learn and to grow. "Even though much of this material is shocking or horrifying, remember that knowledge is power. Now that you know what has been done and what is being done, you can help educate others and perhaps change things. It's not too late."

The majority of people attending the event appeared to believe wholeheartedly in the material. People displayed tears for those abused, anger at government complicity, and inspiration in their quest for truth.

The obvious grief felt by most of the group was of particular interest. The method of presenting the material was reminiscent of a gathering of incest survivors, or a Twelve-Step meeting. As in groups of abductees, there is no room left to challenge their closely held beliefs. Such skepticism would be heresy, or at the least display an uncouth insensitivity for the "emotional pain" suffered by individuals.

The group shared an esprit de corps of fearless investigators facing off against the neo-Nazi "rulers of time." This struggle against the evil forces behind the government conspiracy is apparently hopeless, yet it seems the only battle worth fighting (according to the players).

Whether we accept the Project's existence or not, it clearly satisfies some deep need in believers. According to author Anthony Stevens, "The shadow projection is pleasurable, to have the Enemy clearly identified and to be locked in conflict with him. There is a real sense in which we do love our enemies, for they complete us."

The presenters themselves were fascinating. Without subscribing to their belief system myself, it was very clear that they believed in it themselves. Though they are accomplished and spellbinding storytellers, there was little sense of the charlatan about them. They did not attempt to fund-raise among the workshop participants.

Preston Nichols, Al Bielek, and others have managed to assemble an impressive array of paper documentation over the years. Among these was an investigation by Congress during the late 1980s to investigate alleged goings-on at the mothballed Air Force base. The results are said to have been inconclusive, with the military denying any knowledge of what had gone on there. Who knows? Entrances into underground portions of the Montauk Base on Long Island have been sealed up with truckloads of concrete (though Preston does not recommend casual visits by the curious).

One thing is certain: the people involved in the Montauk Project, the Philadelphia Experiment, and related events are living in a myth. Not necessarily a fiction; there are many "true myths." But a myth nonetheless.

Their lives have a magical quality impossible to imagine for those of us with more plebeian goals and desires. Like the shamans of old, they remember what other worlds looked like, and what happened in the distant past or the distant future. Additionally, they report strange encounters with alien intelligences.

At first glance, these are not insane people; they hold jobs, make money, lead lives of their own. Yet like Odysseus or Sinbad or Rip Van Winkle, they are questers on a timeless journey with no end. In a sense, they have given up some of their humanity to become myths themselves.

PART TWO

FIGURES OF EARTH

*The world grows thin in these
vibrating geometries until it
becomes the edge of a reflection.*

—Octavio Paz

VANISHING MONSTERS

These our actors, as I foretold you, were all spirits, and are melted into air, into thin air.

—WILLIAM SHAKESPEARE

RESEARCHING absurd phenomena sometimes leads downwards to equally absurd results. If events are impossible or unbelievable, but they happen anyway, what conclusions should we draw? Even when there are no real answers forthcoming, only more questions, we become forced to drop our preconceived notions. Some investigators actually take the leap, risking their remaining credibility or sanity, and venture into case material rejected by most as just "too plain weird."

After my first bewildering foray into monster territory, there was no surprise when I encountered Bigfoot's "cousins," the hairy dwarves. Though they share a hirsute appearance, reports of the two types' behavior are very different. The hairy giants shamble through our lives like a storm, wreaking havoc on fences, leaving tracks, and frightening people and livestock in a very physical way.

On the other hand, the hairy dwarves sow confusion, not violence, in their wake. They seem to delight in tricks of the most malicious sort, much like the gremlins of World War II and their fairy ancestors of the Middle Ages. Also like fairies, the literature of hairy dwarves mentions their attempts at kidnapping children.

Most U.S. reports of hairy dwarves date from the 1950s or earlier. They seem to have been supplanted by the hairless Grays around the beginning of the 1960s. Does this represent a change in the cultural attitudes or collective unconscious of North Americans, or did one alien race literally replace another? Where did the American dwarves go? To find modern-day reports of these beings, one must turn to the Southern Hemisphere where they are still "active."

One encounter was reported in Roque Saenz Pena, Argentina, on May 31, 1985. Three boys, ages five, seven, and eleven, were playing near an abandoned house when they saw a being no taller than two-and-a-half feet. The hair-covered being attempted to abduct the five-year old but the children escaped. He was seen again in the same neighborhood on June 2 and 4. The sighting on the 4th was made by Hector Maidana, age twenty-two, who ignored the creature as it strolled past him. He told investigators that he acted as he did because his parents had told him to remain motionless if the being ever appeared! The same creature (or others like him) was seen on two more occasions that June.

There are other strange beings mingled with the hairy dwarves. South America is a source of many fascinating monster-UFO reports. While the reports share similarities with those of Europe and the United States, there are also many inconsistencies. It appears that either another race of aliens are visiting the Southern Hemisphere, or else people from different cultures perceive the same phenomenon differently.

John Keel reported one bizarre account that took place in Belo Horizonte, Brazil, on August 28, 1963. Three boys playing in a residential garden were amazed when a "one-eyed giant" approached. The being was described as "vivid red in color, with no ears or nose and a strangely shaped mouth." One of the boys tried to throw a brick at the intruder, but was paralyzed by an "orange beam that shot from a square lamp on its chest." The boys were later examined by investigators, including a Professor Hulvio Brant Aleixo who pronounced that the boys were "apparently telling the truth."

The one-eyed creatures were back two years later in the village of Torrent in northeast Argentina. In a report reminiscent of the Rome, Ohio, attack the village was attacked by tall, one-eyed aliens in February 1965. According to one report, the beings invaded a farmhouse and tried to capture a peasant. The man and his friends fought the surprisingly weak creatures off, but they returned in force the next day. The frightened villagers responded with gunfire, which apparently had no effect. Though unharmed, the one-eyed hunters withdrew.

South American researcher Jader Pereira catalogued more than twelve different types of UFO creatures. They range from the one-eyed beings to little green or hairy men to lizard-type creatures. Many of the beings are sporting clawed, "pincer-type" hands instead of four or five digits. Web-footed or web-handed, water-loving types are also reported.

One Argentinean case occurred on April 22, 1980, near Santa Rosa. Farmin Sayago was driving his car when he noticed a "room-sized," black object falling near some high-tension cables. His car stopped suddenly and Sayago got out to check the motor. While doing so, he noticed a sudden, cool breeze and looked up.

He was shocked to see first one, then another seven-foot-tall entity approaching him. The beings had webbed hands, little hair, and protruding mouths. Sayago observed no nose, and said that they "had skull-like faces."

The strange beings were apparently speechless, and moved their lips while gesticulating wildly. One placed his hands on Sayago's head, who then began to feel faint and lost consciousness. Bewildered, he awoke a few minutes later and drove to a friend's house.

Another Santa Rosa, Argentina, case mentions similar creatures. On May 29, 1986, Oscar Alberto Flores was home in bed when he heard a buzzing sound outside, accompanied by a bright light. Looking out his window, he saw an object floating over the trees. He started to back away when he realized that someone else was in his bedroom.

Turning around, he saw two eight-foot-tall beings facing him. Flores could see no mouth, nose, or ears on the beings. He described their hands as long and thin with three fingers each. They were dressed in silver coveralls, and wore medallions on their chests.

Once again, the beings gestured quickly, then vanished. Flores drove to the Third District Police Office in Santa Rosa where he made his report. His account also notes that he sighted a flying, ball-shaped object in the sky on his way to the police station.

Though the Grays so often reported in U.S. sightings are conspicuously absent in South America, some beings roam freely in both continents. The tall, blond spacemen on peaceful missions seemingly appear as often in South as in North America. The contactees associated with them report the same "channeling type" messages as elsewhere.

A number of South American reports also mention tall beings with extraordinarily long chins. Another incident, again in Argentina, happened to Gilberto Gregorio Coccioli on October 4, 1972. At 3:30 A.M., he heard a strange sound outside his house near Buenos Aires. Going outside to check, he reported being hit by a beam of light that caused him to black out.

When he awoke, he found himself in a metallic room with two very tall, thin men with "long chins that reached down to their chests." The aliens apparently spoke to Coccioli by telepathy, and took blood samples. He was then "forced" to engage in sexual intercourse with two women. The encounter ended with him receiving a gift of a small stone to wear on his neck. Coccioli said that "they kept in contact with me by a tingling in the nape of my neck."

Though there are more reports of the big-chinned men, they are outnumbered by encounters with "little green men" related in size and behavior to the hairy dwarves. One group of four young Argentinean men met six green ones on October 28, 1988. The men were walking along a road when they ran into the gremlin-type beings. The little men were indeed green, had only one eye, three-fingered hands, and were "growling." Walking together in lockstep (a frequently-reported feature), they left behind small, frog-like tracks.

Nineteen eighty three was a year for green men hysteria in La Plata, a city on the Atlantic coast of Argentina. Reports of the strange beings accosting children were so commonplace that the local police were deluged by frantic parents and forced to go on alert status. Some of the children reported that the green entities had only one eye in the middle of their forehead. Interestingly, a number of the accounts mention the beings emerging from a well or tunnels, just as in Medieval accounts of fairies (who also reportedly accosted children).

The green men may have briefly visited the United States in the 1950s. Late in the morning on December 15, 1956, a man was gathering Christmas greens in Derry, New Hampshire. Turning around, he saw a two-foot-high green dwarf standing right next to him. Paralyzed, he could only stand there and watch the creature that had "floppy ears and reptilian eyes." After watching the man, the creature screeched and lurched forward, prompting the man to flee. Very few reports such as this one have emerged from North America.

Though alien descriptions from South America differ greatly from the others, some elements are recognizable. Witnesses again report the smell of sulfur, a sense of missing time, and bright lights or a buzzing/beeping sound at the beginning and end of an encounter. Familiar physical symptoms such as conjunctivitis, dehydration, and even apparent radiation poisoning accompany the more mundane psychological aftereffects. The phenomenon appears to be the same.

My own favorite report of little, goblinlike entities occurred near Kelly-Hopkinsville, Kentucky on August 21 and 22, 1955. This old, multiple-witness sighting remains interesting for its similarity to more current South American sightings.

Elmer "Lucky" Sutton and eleven other family members and friends were all present at the isolated Sutton farmhouse. One friend, Billy Ray Taylor, went outside to the well for a drink around 7 P.M. Standing outside, he was amazed to see a flying object overhead that was "real bright, with an exhaust all the colors of the rainbow." He returned to the house with news of his sighting, but the general consensus was that he had seen a shooting star. No one bothered to go out and investigate.

Approximately an hour later, the family dog began barking wildly. Lucky Sutton and Billy Ray went outside to check the animal. They came face-to-face with a nightmarish creature straight out of a Disney film. The being was a luminous, hairless dwarf with huge, shining yellow eyes and enormous, elephantlike ears. The glowing being was approaching the farmhouse with its arms outstretched over its head.

True to peasant tradition when faced with inexplicable aliens, the two farmers grabbed guns and began blasting away at the strange intruder. Their bullets appeared to have no effect other than forcing the being to scuttle off.

Back inside the house, the family heard sounds like someone was climbing on the roof. The men ran out into the back yard, where they sighted another of the glowing creatures. This time the entity fell when shot, but it seemed to float down rather than fall! When it reached the ground, it ran off on all four limbs.

Frightened by the uselessness of their guns as much as the creatures' appearance, the group barricaded themselves inside the farmhouse. For three hours, they watched as a number of the weird little beings sauntered around the house and on the roof. They finally decided to attempt escape, and dashed to their two cars, which they reached without incident. They raced to the police station in Hopkinsville, where they babbled their incredible story.

Impressed by their fear, Sheriff Russell Greenwell, five other officers, and a local journalist accompanied the group back to the farmhouse. On the road, the posse sighted two strange "streaks of light" overhead, accompanied by a loud "banging" sound. When they arrived at the Sutton farmhouse, there was no sign of the strange invaders. After taking a look around the property, the officials left.

When the exhausted family was finally preparing for bed, one of the friends noticed that there were huge, glowing eyes at the window! She motioned to Lucky, who ran outside and unleashed another barrage with his shotgun. The eerie goblin scampered off, and this time did not return.

Though later faced with considerable local harassment and journalistic skepticism, the group refused to alter their story in the least detail. To the relief of the family, the strange creatures were never seen again.

Many reports of alien-type monsters describe creatures that are either winged or birdlike. Though such reports appear in every decade and in many countries, few have attracted as much attention as the West Virginia "Mothmen" seen in the mid-1960s.

These beings were strongly associated with multiple UFO sightings, animal mutilations and disappearances, electromagnetic phenomena including stalled cars and misbehaving telephones, Men in Black sightings, and a wave of contactee-type, channeled messages. The huge, flying Mothmen were reported as featureless and headless except for their glowing red eyes, and easily appeared and disappeared into thin air.

The best investigative work on this phenomenon was again conducted by John Keel; his fascinating book, *The Mothman Prophesies,* remains the classic text in this specialized field. During his investigation, Keel interviewed over sixty-three direct witnesses of the Mothman in West Virginia, Ohio, and Kentucky. This region is part of the so-called "Bible Belt"; the inhabitants are levelheaded, fundamentalist, and non-drinking.

Many of the sights occurred in the "TNT area," a sprawling region of hundreds of acres of abandoned tunnels and concrete bunkers that once housed a munitions installation near Point Pleasant, West Virginia. The TNT area adjoined a two thousand five hundred-acre nature preserve, and was a favorite haunt of the local teenagers.

One classic sighting occurred on November 15, 1966. Two young couples, the Scarberrys and the Malettes, were driving through the TNT area around midnight. As they drove past the deserted remains of a power plant, they sighted a huge, eerie figure by the road. They later described it as "shaped like a man, but bigger, and it had big wings folded against its back. But it was those eyes that got us. It had two big red eyes, like automobile reflectors."

Stunned by the apparition, the two couples just sat in their car and watched as the being shuffled toward an open door of the old building. That was when they decided they'd had enough. Roger Scarberry floored the gas pedal and the car raced down the road.

As they drove, one of the women looked behind and shouted that "it" was following them. Though their speed was nearly a hundred miles per hour, all four later swore that the creature kept up effortlessly, soaring about ten feet over the car. They saw no sign that its "wings" were flapping. They also heard a high-pitched sound, "like a big mouse squeaking."

The thing ended its pursuit at the outskirts of Point Pleasant. The four drove directly to the Mason County Sheriff's office and told their story. According to Deputy Millard Halstead, "I've known them all their lives, and they've never been in any trouble. I took them seriously."

Deputy Halstead returned with them to the old power plant, but found nothing other than a noise like "a speeded-up phonograph record" emitted from his police radio. The four told their story the next day to reporters, and the following report was carried by Associated Press. Reporters and investigators (Keel among them), descended on Point Pleasant.

The Mothman was seen again and again by people in Point Pleasant and in neighboring counties. The reports were unanimous that the creature had glowing red eyes, stood taller than a man, and could fly at unbelievable speeds. There were additional reports of flying saucers (including many daytime sightings) and large, hairy, Bigfoot-type creatures.

Keel began meeting witnesses who reported additional paranormal activity after their encounters. "About half of the witnesses appeared to be people with latent or active psychic abilities, prone to having accurate premonitions, prophetic dreams, ESP, etc." Some of these informants began channeling information from the "space people" to him.

One piece of information was a warning, repeated to him by other contactees, that "something awful is going to happen." He was told this over and over by bewildered people who often had no idea what was happening to them. Among other things, he was warned that Robert Kennedy would soon be killed in a hotel kitchen. Kennedy was indeed killed in such a place shortly afterwards!

The final version of the imminent disaster was that there would be a huge, damaging power failure on December 15, and that he should prepare the people in Point Pleasant. The disaster did strike, but on *November* 15, not December!

On that day, an old bridge into Point Pleasant was overburdened with traffic, and collapsed into the Ohio River. Fifty automobiles fell in, with the bridge's steel superstructure on top of them. Divers and rescue teams recovered thirty-eight bodies, but more were assumed missing. Among the dead were several UFO or Mothman witnesses. The day before the wreck, there had been scattered reports of both Men in Black and UFO activity near or on the bridge.

This tragedy, and the pointless messages leading up to it, led Keel eventually to conclude that the Phenomenon is deliberately deceptive. He also observed that the many sightings appeared to be senseless manifestations designed only to terrorize and confuse people. No one has ever come forward to prove him wrong.

During the same time span, there were a few reports from Kent, England, of a similar, headless "Batman" with glowing red eyes and shrouded wings. Taking a cue from its West Virginia cousins, the Batman chose young couples in lovers' lanes for its witnesses.

Though rare, there are occasional sightings of "winged humans," ranging from an 1877 sighting of a bat-winged man flying over Brooklyn, New York, to the front lines of the Vietnam War. In either July or August of 1969, members of the U.S. 1st Division Marine Corps were serving near Da Nang, Vietnam. Private Earl Morrison was on guard duty with two other Marines sitting on the top of a bunker. According to Morrison:

"We saw what looked like a bat, only it was gigantic compared to what a regular bat would be. After it got close enough so we could see what it was, it looked like a woman. A naked woman. She was black. Her skin was black, her body was black, the wings were black. But it *glowed in the night*—kind of a greenish cast to it.

"She started going over us, and we still didn't hear anything. She was right above us, and when she got over the top of our heads she was maybe six or seven feet up, and she still didn't make any noise flapping her wings. . . . looked like pitch black then, but we could still define her because she just glowed. Real bright like . . . And she just started flying off and we watched her for quite a while."

There are also many reports of alien beings with reptilian characteristics. An early "Reptoid" case occurred on November 8, 1958, in Riverside, California. A man named Charlie Wetzel apparently encountered a "fluorescent-eyed, man-sized thing with a protuberant mouth and scale-covered body." The creature emerged from the shrubs near the Santa Ana River, and jumped on Wetzel's car. The aggressive being then fell underneath the car and was dragged. Wetzel did not linger to see if the being survived.

In British Columbia in 1972, a strange, scaly "gill-man" rose from Lake Thetis and accosted four witnesses over a four-day period. The being reportedly had large, pointed ears, huge eyes, and webbed feet.

There have been a number of reports from the Southwest linking reptilian beings with the smooth-skinned Grays. They are reported to have vertical, cat-like pupils in glowing red eyes. Their scaly skin is said to be grayish-green.

The widespread reports of the underground base at Dulce, New Mexico (mentioned earlier), describe six-foot-tall, scaled Reptoids working there for the Grays. These bizarre tales mention that the Reptoids seem to possess some kind of teleportation technology, appearing on one occasion in a researcher's living room!

Linda Moulton-Howe told me that her "government informants" described the aliens from crashed saucers as possessing a "greenish-gray, reptilian hide." According to this rumor, the cadavers also "had hollow bones, like a bird."

Is there any scientific basis for humanoid reptilians? I found an old article in the February, 1982 issue of *Discover* magazine. According to Dale Russell and Ron Seguin of Canada's National Museum of Natural Sciences at Ottawa, a "dinosauroid" descendant of the ancient dinosaurs might have had large, yellow eyes, scaled skin, and a large brain. The creature was a result of a computer-modeled "speculatory exercise" based upon the carnivorous *Stenonychosaurus inequalis,* which lived near the end of the Age of Reptiles. Scientist Dale Russell stated, "There is a trend in evolution toward increasing brain size."

Regarding a theoretical language spoken by the creatures, Russell speculated that they would sound "avian rather than mammalian . . . their voices would be more birdlike than grunting." Many people reporting encounters with Grays and other aliens report their communications as sounding "fluting, birdlike, and songlike."

Perhaps the Woodbine creature seen in the mid-1980s was descended from flying dinosaurs like pterodactyls. In a letter to the editor of *Strange* magazine, Mrs. Ruth Lundy of Woodbine, Maryland, described an encounter with a reptilian being.

Driving home in Carroll County around 3 A.M., she passed a large graveyard near her turnoff. Making the turn from

Highway 140 to 91, she noticed a man-like figure standing on the edge of the cemetery.

As she drove closer, she was shocked to see that the being resembled a pterodactyl! The creature stood on two feet like a man, and was approximately six feet high. The being began flapping its huge, leathery wings, and took to the air. When it flew over the car, she heard "a sound like a helicopter."

Though the event had occurred ten years ago, Mrs. Lundy wrote that she still feels nervous when she travels through that area. "I feel scared knowing the old story that strange things always go around twice."

Though the name "sea serpent" has become synonymous with hoaxes and bad films, reports of them continue to come from the same locations again and again. Many of the freshwater variety, called "lake monsters," seem to represent paranormal rather than biological activity. Some have the glowing eyes and sulfurous odor that monster hunters have grown to love. They are even associated with UFOs, as if the aliens also find them interesting. Or do they both come from the same source?

Assuming that they do exist, it is remarkable that reportedly huge creatures such as Nessie (at Loch Ness) and Champie (at Lake Champlain) disappear so quickly after a sighting. A startled fisherman or tourist comes face-to-face with the monster, then in the blink of an eye it's gone. Such behavior does not suggest a conventional beast.

People are often at a loss as to whether they've seen an animal or an object. One sighting that may or may not have been a lake monster took place in Nova Scotia on October 4, 1967. Witnesses around Shag Harbor sighted a series of lights that appeared to fall into the water. Members of the Royal Canadian Mounted Police arrived and also saw something strange.

According to the report of Constable Ron O'Brien, "After it hit the water, we were called to the scene. I saw a light floating on the water about half a mile offshore." Rescue boats were sent out, but all they found was an eighty-foot-wide patch of bubbling foam. Captain Bradford Shand reported that it was yellow-colored and that he'd never seen anything like it.

Other witnesses reported seeing a dark, sixty-foot-long object with glowing lights moving along the surface of the water, then dive underneath. Divers searching the area on following days found nothing. The area also has a rich tradition of monster sightings dating back to Native American tribes.

Like UFOs and Bigfoot, lake monsters are remarkably difficult to photograph. According to monster hunters Janet and Colin Bord, "on the few occasions they have been photographed, the image the camera has caught is of a blurred, indistinct nature that presents very little evidence and serves simply to compound the enigma and increase the argument."

Though sightings have continued uninterrupted for centuries, the Loch Ness monster is a classic case of the failure of technology in the face of the unknown. To date, millions of dollars have been spent on sophisticated sonar arrays, tracking devices, and underwater cameras. Despite all this high-technology, the few photos of Nessie remain subject to controversy.

Photographic controversies have not hindered sightings of the creature. "She" seems to choose especially the times when the weather is bad, researchers are absent or exhausted, or have shut down their equipment. In their book, *Alien Animals,* the Bords mentioned a strange inertia that plagues witnesses.

> "One sighting was made by Mr. and Mrs. R. Jenkyns whose house stands on the shores of Loch Ness. On 30 September 1974 they viewed the monster half an hour through binoculars. It appeared fifty or sixty feet long with a trailing tail or neck.
>
> "Although a loaded camera was nearby, neither of them thought to use it, nor did they think to telephone any neighbors. Even stranger is the fact that during the sighting Mr. Jenkyns sat on a sofa and went to sleep for a few minutes."

The Bords also mention an earlier Swedish report of a journalist who sighted three humanoid aliens on a strange craft in

Foyers Bay. Although the man had a camera, he was hit by some kind of "paralysis" and could only lift the camera as the craft departed.

Most sightings of Nessie, Champie, Chessie (a Chesapeake Bay monster), Manipogo (from Lake Manitoba), and the Okopogo (from Lake Okanagan) report a long-necked creature similar to the extinct plesiosaur. In addition to the dinosaur-survival buffs, the plesiosaur description is familiar to millions of people exposed to news reports of the Loch Ness monster.

Supporting this theory are the popular, much-disputed photographs of a long-necked, small-headed, humped beast familiar to many people. The few, also disputed, sonar images suggest a creature with a similar appearance. Many authors have speculated that the deep waters of Loch Ness (and other lakes) provided a safe refuge for this aquatic dinosaur when the great saurian extinctions occurred hundreds of millions of years ago.

There are reports of similar beasts seen on land, though theories about where they go leave much to be desired. John Keel once investigated a dinosaur sighting in Texas during the 1960s. Though there were multiple-witness sightings and footprints were found, hordes of police and journalists failed to locate it. Keel noted that the footprints ended mysteriously, as if "it" just disappeared. Was the Texas Dinosaur just an extremely expensive, well-planned hoax perpetrated on a few rural people, or something more mysterious?

Not all lake monsters are serpentine or even huge beasts. "Mermaid" sightings, far from being the hallucination of ancient seamen, still continue to be seen in the twentieth century. One report was made by a Norwegian fur hunter near Punta Arenas at Cape Horn in 1936. The creature was as beautiful as legend would have it, with human face and breasts, green eyes and hair, and a fishy tail.

Another mermaid was frequently encountered at Kilconly Point, County Kerry, Ireland, between 1960 and 1962. She reportedly resembled a normal woman but emerged from and disappeared into the sea in front of startled witnesses. There are many cases of this kind, and may actually represent marine alien encounters (whatever they are) rather than ocean-loving nymphs.

The literature of lake monsters, sea serpents, and surviving dinosaurs is fascinating and extensive, and some cases do suggest a biological entity. However, many other sightings seem related to *apparitions* rather than to living monsters.

If some of these sightings are only temporarily physical, then where do they come from? Legendary explorer and Buddhist scholar Alexandra David-Neel wrote about "thought forms" in her book, *Magic and Mystery in Tibet*. David-Neel had heard much about the "tulpas," or illusionary beings created by Tibetan Lamas, and tried to create one of her own during her meditation studies. Without the approval of her teacher, she decided to focus on the image of a monk.

After months of concentration in solitude, she was able to see the being, who appeared to take on a life of his own.

> "The phantom performed various actions of the kind that are natural to travelers and that I had not commanded. For instance, he walked, stopped, looked around him. . . . He became more troublesome and bold. In brief, he escaped my control. Once, a herdsman who brought me a present of butter saw the tulpa in my tent and took it for a live lama."

She was eventually able to dissolve the being, but not without a six-month struggle. The "monk" didn't want to go! After the being had left, she wrote, "There is nothing strange in the fact that I may have created my own hallucination. The interesting point is that in these cases of materialization, others see the thought-forms that have been created.

> "Tibetans disagree in their explanations of such phenomena; some think a material form is really brought into being, others consider the apparition as a mere case of suggestion, the creator's thought impressing others and causing them to see what he himself sees."

The same words might be applied to many modern cases of disappearing monsters. Psychotronic researcher Colonel Thomas Bearden also believes that most lake monsters,

UFOs, and Bigfoots are electromagnetic creations similar to tulpas.

> "These entities are materializations from the collective human unconscious shaped and formed by the layers (race, culture, nation, territory, state, region, family, etc.) between the collective and individual unconscious minds of the observers. The exact format depends on the higher 'tuning' that is being forced into materialization."

He also describes these "tulpoidal phenomena" as easier to evoke the more interest in one intensifies. Taking a cue from modern physics theory, (i.e., researchers *looking* for a particle create one where none existed before), he believes that we'll be seeing more monsters in the near future.

> "With this intensity of belief, it is getting easier to evoke a tulpoid, and as it continues, the creature will probably be tuned in and stabilized. . . . There is probably going to be a family of plesiosaurs living in Loch Ness eventually, and space-time will be changed to accommodate this small shift in the collective human unconscious."

Bearden is convinced that our growing belief will not only manifest monsters as temporary apparitions, but eventually as real, living creatures!

Partaking of both Bigfoot and ghostly characteristics are the so-called "ghost dogs." These spectral beings appear and disappear in the same haunted spots over and over, often accompanied by the distinctive odor of sulfur. Though most sightings are of black dogs, some white or gray ones have been seen. The majority of ghost dogs have glowing red eyes.

Ghost dogs are often associated with the disappearance or mutilation of livestock animals. Some of the older accounts maintain the bizarre, bloodless deaths ended with the killing of a mysterious "black dog."

The creatures have a preference for shrinking or growing huge in front of startled witnesses. They have also been reported to walk through walls, fences, or into stones (though many of them are solid enough to leave behind footprints). Some reports also record that the creatures seem immune to gunfire.

There is a rich heritage of folklore associated with ghost dogs, especially in Britain and Europe, though they also appear in American legend. Traditionally they are harbingers of bad weather or the death of the witness. In many historical accounts, they appear only during thunderstorms, usually at churches and graveyards, ancient temples, bridges, crossroads, and hedgerows.

There are also reports linking ghost dogs with UFOs. One case occurred in Burnley, Lancashire, England, on August 23, 1977. A couple awoke at 2:25 A.M. when they heard a knock on their door. The wife got up and opened the door, only to see a huge dog staring at her. She closed the door, but heard the knocking again. She again opened the door, but there was no one there. Closing the door, the knocking was repeated with the same result.

The next day, the couple heard news that a UFO had been sighted in their neighborhood. They also recalled that August 23, 1977, was one year to the day after they had seen a UFO themselves. Their 1976 sighting had also occurred at 2:25 A.M.!

I can never forget my own ghost dog experience. In 1976, my graduating high school class was sorrowing over the inexplicable suicide of a classmate. After attending his funeral, I drove with a group of friends to an abandoned house nearby in Towson, Maryland, where we had often spent time with our friend.

The isolated house, located on a hilly, overgrown estate, had a local reputation as "haunted" and was reputedly the site of a suicide two decades earlier. Its haunted reputation, including UFO sightings, had made it an interesting place for our group to hold large parties in the past, though no "ghosts" were ever seen.

The group of fourteen teenagers started a fire in the ground floor fireplace and began reminiscing about our lost friend. When someone began crying hysterically, we became uncomfortable and the gathering slowly broke up. The last five of us to leave noticed a strange, greenish glow coming from a dark, unvisited room.

Fearing that a fire had been started, we investigated only to see a luminous, green fog pouring in from an empty fireplace. Though there was no wind, the "glowing fog" was extremely cold and there was a pungent, chemical odor. The uncanny sight was my first experience of my hair literally "standing on end."

Terrified, we fled toward our car parked at the bottom of the hill. As we descended the front steps of the house, we glanced behind us and saw the shape of a huge, black dog with burning red eyes standing in the doorway we had just left! Though there was little light except for the stars and we had no flashlight, the dog's brightly glowing eyes were clearly seen.

We continued to see the huge dog's eyes and shape as it followed us down the successive flights of overgrown stairs. At the bottom of the nine or ten long flights, the "dog" stopped, as if it had reached some sort of boundary. Feeling safer by our vehicle, we stood and observed the chilling creature for two or three minutes before it suddenly vanished.

We drove home without further incident, and never returned to the house. Though I attempted to talk about the experience later, the others said that "it" might come back, and refused to discuss it.

What did we see? Admittedly grief over the suicide, coupled with the brooding atmosphere of the "haunted house," may have played tricks on the five teenagers' minds. However, the association with death, lonely places, and invisible boundaries also fits the profile of the legendary ghost dogs.

By a roundabout way my research returned to the images of aerial lights and alien ships. Turning previous comparisons around, it seems that UFOs and aliens exhibit many similarities with spectral monsters. Like ghosts, hairy dwarves, and ghost dogs, UFOs are often accompanied by a sulfurous odor, electromagnetic effects, sudden disappearances, movement through walls, and often appear in the same areas again and again. Like witnesses to ghosts and monsters, those who sight UFOs may develop the psychological contactee syndrome or physical symptoms such as conjunctivitis.

Some people think that UFOs are ghosts. There was a report from England in the 1960s of photographs taken of UFOs flying over a cemetery. When the photos were developed, they were the expected pictures of luminous objects in the sky. When these were enlarged, however, they showed what appeared to be glowing human heads and faces!

Some witnesses told me that the UFOs they encountered felt somehow "alive." According to these witnesses, the alien beings they met seemed to be extensions of the larger, overall entity. Such thoughts are heretical to the die-hard True Believers in abductions by the Grays (and to therapists making a living from their beliefs).

In the classical Greek text *Theogeny*, the poet Hesiod described wars between the gods and primitive, inimical forces. In his poem, the Earth Mother birthed many monstrous forms, including immense giants with only one eye (the Cyclops). Violent, unruly, and connected to storms, the powerful creatures could not be destroyed by the later gods, only imprisoned so our world might survive. Hesiod believed that the forces of Chaos hold a necessary place in the universe, but when unleashed will always disrupt or destroy human society.

These monsters, apparitions, and weird beings certainly seem to be forces of Chaos. Like Col. Bearden's "tulpoidal" phenomena, they manifest in fearsome shapes, perhaps drawn from the human unconscious. After committing destructive or meaningless acts, the beings vanish into mystery, leaving behind a confused or terrified population.

It's interesting that many monsters appear during violent thunderstorms. Janet and Colin Bord suggest that the creatures manifest at these times because of the huge increase in electrical energy available. They refer to the Black River lake monster seen near Lyons Falls, New York. "The monster has been reported seen in this isolated section of northern New York three times in the past ten years, but always when there was an electrical storm in progress."

The Bords also theorize that running water may be a contributing factor, perhaps as an electrical conductor. Ghost dogs, phantoms, and Bigfoots also frequently appear during violent storms.

Many of these creatures may not seem to be related to UFO activity. They could be unidentified life-forms, or perhaps a collective psychosis. However, even absurd reports like the glowing goblins of Hopkinsville may be worthy of investigation precisely because they challenge our accepted belief systems. In an ever-more credulous environment where "one in four people may have been abducted by the Grays," studying alien monsters may paradoxically provide greater objectivity.

THE VERY GOOD PEOPLE

Constantly playing music and singing songs,
they teach what no man knows or can ever know.

—DON JOSE MATSUWA
(HUIHOL INDIAN SHAMAN)

MODERN reports of meetings with alien beings often bear a striking similarity to traditional accounts of fairies, goblins, and elves. The beings' appearance, speech, mode of travel, taste for trickery and kidnapping, and witnesses' aftereffects seem much the same. Were they already here on earth many centuries ago?

Though skeptics may scoff at using folklore as evidence, it often represents the only documentation of our ancestors' beliefs. When old traditions replicate the findings of modern researchers, one begins to wonder what those investigators are so afraid of.

The "fairy tradition," legends of diminutive, magical beings, exists in pretechnological cultures on every continent. Though these beings are said to dwell underground, it is unclear whether "under the earth" meant the same thing to different generations. Many accounts describe what can only be called different worlds or realities accessed through the underworld portals.

Though most popular accounts of fairies were written down during the eighteenth and nineteenth centuries, they often represent oral traditions far older. It's been estimated that many of the tales from the brothers Grimm, for example, contain echoes of pre-Christian initiatic and religious experiences thousands of years old. Viewed in this way, the fairy tradition is a last remnant of the old pagan worldview.

Though a worldwide tradition exists, the largest body of fairy literature available to most Westerners is the European tradition. Most of us in the English-speaking world were raised on fairy tales. Is it possible that our early education prepared us to encounter aliens?

Most folklorists agree that the fairies of European tales are shadowy memories of the ancient pagan gods and goddesses. Once immense, powerful beings of light, they slowly shrunk under Christianity into the flower-dwelling sprites and pixies found in greeting cards and children's cartoons.

The oldest Irish legends tell of a glorious race of gods, the Tuatha Danaan, who colonized primeval Ireland and defeated the giant, demonic Fomorians. These "Children of the Goddess Dan" later made room for succeeding races of mankind by retreating to the "fairy raths" under the hollow hills. Though they faded from the surface, the Tuatha, later called the Sidhe ("shee") maintained a continued influence over humanity. Their involvement included granting favors in wars, stealing cattle or crops, and sexual relationships with selected individuals. People who were able to see them told wild tales of visiting the elfin kingdoms under the hills.

The Welsh national epic, *The Mabinogion,* also mentions individual Sidhe by the same names as the Irish sagas. Though some of these beings had become superhuman mortals rather than gods, there is little doubt that the chroniclers were speaking about the same entities. *The Mabinogion* also associates them with the underworld or otherworld. The epic refers to an underworld adventure of King Arthur, whose sword Excalibur was fashioned and protected by the fairy "Lady of the Lake."

Faith in the ancient gods was violently suppressed by the Catholic Church. To the early Christians, all supernatural beings outside their own pantheon were servants of the Devil (evidently, passage of time has not changed things). Though public worship was forbidden, peasants continued to leave offerings of food or milk for the beings. As the centuries passed and the beings shrank in stature and memory, the offerings were left for fairies and "the good people" rather than ancient deities. Even as recently as the first half of this century, Catholic priests admonished Irish parishioners to discontinue the practice of offering to the fairies.

The "shrinking" of the fairies may not have been due only to religious intolerance and man's forgetfulness. Traditions around the world testify to the beings' ability to change size at will. Perhaps nineteenth-century novelist G. K. Chesterton was correct when he said, "The fairies do not grow, but shrink, when they would mix with men." When speculating on the fairies' "real" appearance, we would do well to imagine them as tall beings.

Hiding from blundering humans may not have been the only motivation for fairies to shrink. Numerous myths describe the natural state of the ancient deities as too bright and awesome for earthly eyes. One Greek tale describes the god Zeus' appearance as burning a woman to ashes. The unfortunate woman had insisted on seeing Zeus as he really was.

As the ancient philosopher Iamblichus wrote in *The Mysteries:*

> ". . . in the case of gods and goddesses they sometimes cover the whole sky and the sun and the moon, whilst the earth can no longer remain steady when they descend. . . . their magnitude visibly fluctuate." He goes on to say that "in the case of gods who make themselves manifest, what is seen is clearer than truth itself; every detail shines out exactly and its articulations are shown in brilliant light."

The gods and fairies of ancient Britain were also said to possess this aura of blinding light. When they took to the skies, they were seen as moving, glowing lights. The fairies were also said to be gaseous, or not made of the same kind of matter as earthly creatures.

According to eighteenth-century investigator Robert Kirk, they had "light, changeable bodies, somewhat of the nature of a condensed cloud, and best seen in twilight. These bodies are so pliable through the subtlety of the spirits that agitate them, that they can make them appear or disappear at pleasure."

This viewpoint was supported by seer Geoffrey Hodson in his 1925 work, *The Fairies at Work and Play.* Hodson wrote that "elves differ from other nature spirits in that they do not appear to be clothed in any reproduction of human attire, and that their bodily constitution appears to consist of one solid mass of gelatinous substance, entirely without internal organization."

Medieval authors linked the fairies and old gods with angels. They were members of the "divine order that disobeyed the Creators' commands, but went not to Hell to serve Satan." According to this tradition, the fairies partake of the same light-filled essence as God's angels, but are bound to earth by their disobedience. There are a number of fairy tales that describe a fairy's quest for either a human soul or God's forgiveness.

The current wave of popular interest in angels has spawned a number of speculations about fairies. According to the iconoclastic, New Age "angel movement," fairies are just one culture's term for the beings of light seen all over the planet throughout history.

One well-known writer on angels and fairies, Dorothy MacLean, considers both to be forces of nature under Divine guidance. The fairies are humanoid, tutelary spirits of plants and wild places, while angels are larger entities protecting huge natural areas, lakes, mountains, and even planets. Both may change size or temporarily manifest in physical reality. MacLean's vision is a modern echo of Iamblichus' view of the ancient gods as intangible, size-altering, beings of light.

Old accounts report the experiences of people who have been taken away by fairies or elves. Some who never came back are supposed to still be alive "under the hills." Just as in UFO abductions, those taken include both voluntary and unwilling travelers.

Perhaps the most famous medieval abductee was a man called Thomas the Rhymer. Thomas of Ercledoune, also known as Lord Learmont, lived during the thirteenth century and was renowned as a prophet and seer. A nationalist agent during King Edward's war with Scotland, he was also a talented writer who reputedly authored the earliest version of the Arthurian love story, *Tristram and Iseult*. His prophesies are known to have influenced the writings of William Shakespeare.

Thomas apparently made many accurate predictions, and his prophesies were published after his death. One of his less-accurate predictions forecasted a tremendous natural disaster in the nineteenth century, which reportedly caused mass panic and hundreds of English peasants to head for the hills.

Thomas claimed that his prophetic abilities resulted from contacts with denizens of "Elfland," where he had been taken by the fairies. While in Elfland, he received initiation and teachings from the "Queen of the Elves." His story alleges that he was gone from earth for seven years.

W. Y. Evans-Wentz reported many cases of British fairy abductions in his classic work, *The Fairy Faith in Celtic Countries,* published in 1911. His sources among the country folk of his day were quite clear that the fairies still existed in their own places, though fewer people saw them than in the past.

They told tales of people who were kidnapped by the fairies and carried to their otherworldly kingdom. Most of these were abducted against their will, often due to some trifling offense accidentally given the "good people." Others were chosen because they were especially attractive, or were wet nurses stolen to nurse fairy children. In some cases, worried relatives were told of the abduction by an apparition resembling the missing person. After so informing their family, the "doppelgänger" faded away.

Independent sightings of the fairy realm were made by seers, who either inherited or learned their ability to perceive the entities when no one else could. These seers may correspond to the stories of modern-day contactees claiming to be chosen by aliens. Many of the seers' reports provided the only explanation for the missing abductees.

Both seers and abductees reported a realm filled with light and unearthly music. The music of the fairies was reportedly so compelling that listeners were forced to dance against their will; some hearers became poets. There were "fairy feasts" complete with nectar and ambrosia, as well as stolen mortal food. Duplicating the Greek myth of Persephone in the underworld, the legends warn that anyone tasting fairy food would be unable to return to earth. This could account for the persistent tales of people thought to be dead appearing at fairy gatherings. They may not have "died," only eaten from the wrong dish!

Robert Kirk (1744–97) was a minister who inherited the ability to see into both the fairy realm and the future. As an influential leader in his community of Aberfoyle, Kirk was in a position to elicit many private accounts of the entities. His book, *The Secret Commonwealth of Elves, Fauns and Fairies* is perhaps the most complete study of fairy lore ever made.

After comparing the writings with other mystical, initiatic traditions, Scottish author R. J. Stewart concluded that Kirk was sincerely attempting to formulate and express his personal experience of another world of life parallel to our own. Stewart believes that Kirk also drew upon the remnants of an age-old tradition that had indeed survived from pre-Christian times.

Because he was indiscreet regarding their activities, Kirk was severely punished by the fairies. Though a dead body resembling his was found beside the infamous Fairy Knowe (hill) of Aberfoyle, the local people whispered that it was a "double," or simulacrum. The story tells that the real Reverend Kirk was taken under the hill, and remains trapped there to this day.

The literature of a magical underworld is vast, ancient, and convoluted. Authors such as Walter Kafton-Minkel and Joscelyn Godwin provide exhaustive, entertaining studies far beyond the scope of this book. Among their bizarre tales of Nazi scientists, Atlantean adepts, and Mongolian God-Kings are reports of miners' encounters with dwarfish, elusive creatures variously called spriggans, kobalds, knockers, goblins, or "dark elves." The dark elves guard the treasures and entrances of the underworld.

These rather frightening creatures reportedly played havoc with human trespassers in their dark domain. German, English, and French miners all swore encounters with these beings, and feared to enter tunnels where they had been seen. Offerings were frequently made to ensure the goodwill of the beings.

In many ways closer to modern images of Grays than the taller, godlike beings of light, dark elves supposedly possessed a magical technology. The entities were renowned as smiths and artificers, and tales describe their curses on swords or jewelry they were forced to make for foolhardy humans.

Not all underworld encounters were so dangerous. One Welsh tale describes a young shepherd who became lost and wandered for hours. At last he came to a hollow place with a number of round rings in the grass, which he recognized as a place other shepherds had told him was dangerous. He attempted to leave, but was accosted by an "old, merry, blue-eyed man." The man told him, "Do not speak a word until I tell you."

The old man led him to a menhir (standing stone) and tapped it three times before lifting it. Underneath was a stone stairway leading down into a bluish-white light. "Follow me," said the man, "and no harm will come to you." The youth did so and eventually came to a palace in a beautiful, wooded land. The land was filled with exquisite music.

He was greeted by an old woman leading three young women. Though they were beautiful and he wished to speak with them, he was mute until one kissed him. Then his speech returned and he eventually became the maiden's lover. The story goes on to say that "he lived with her for a year and a day, not thinking it was more than a day, for there was no reckoning of time in that country."

Eventually he returned home only to find that everyone had thought him dead, and would not believe that it was he. He eventually returned to the underworld and his fairy bride.

The sixteenth-century philosopher Paracelsus called the beings of inner earth "gnomes" and said that they were paraphysical beings close to the element of earth. He wrote that the gnomes could pass through solid rock as air, or could turn invisible if the situation demanded it.

> "Yet the Elementals are not spirits because they have flesh, blood, bones; they live and propagate offspring; they eat and talk, act and sleep. They are beings occupying a place between men and spirits, resembling men and women in their organization and form, and resembling spirits in the rapidity of their locomotion."

Paracelsus went on to describe other tribes of spirits dwelling in the elements of water, air, and fire, who possessed even less physical limitations than gnomes.

Like the fairies above ground, gnomes and dark elves made exquisite, enchanting music. Folklorist Robert Hunt recounts one Cornish tradition of Christmas carols being sung by the beings!

> "On Christmas Eve, in former days, the small people, or Spriggans, would meet at the bottom of the deepest mines, and have a Midnight Mass. Those who were in the mine would hear voices, melodious beyond all earthly voices, singing 'Now well (Noel)! Now well!' and the strains of some deep-toned organ would shake the rocks."

R. J. Stewart alludes to the occult tradition of the "justified men" or initiates into the mysteries of earth and spirit. Possibly contactees, many were known historical figures, including authors of fairy tales or prophetic works (such as Thomas the Rhymer). In their works they dropped hints on the paraphysical activities of the entities surrounding humanity, many times dwelling "under the hill."

One "justified man" was nineteenth-century Universalist minister George MacDonald, author of *The Princess and the Goblin, Phantastes, Lilith* and other works of fantasy still loved today. Though many of his tales deal with underworld fairy races, MacDonald also anticipated Carl Jung by making clear the imaginal or psychic nature of the otherworld.

When his characters enter the fairy realm, physically or in dreams (he saw no great difference between the two), their moral or psychic actions have the same consequences as physical ones. The world of fairies is a distorted mirror where human beings see themselves in reverse; fairy magic could only be fought by self-knowledge. One might say the same of modern abductees.

It's interesting that a colleague of MacDonald's was Lewis Carroll, author of the famed *Alice in Wonderland,* beloved by children and physicists alike for its reverse logic of dreams and alternate worlds. Carroll's original title for his book was *Alice's Adventures Under Ground.*

When studying material as ephemeral as fairy lore, works of "fiction" may offer many clues. A fairy in John Crowley's *Little, Big* has the final word in describing both the otherworld and the human mind, "The further in you go, the bigger it gets."

There are countless native legends of the "little people" across the Americas. The Venezuelan reports of child-stealing, hairy dwarves, and "Little Green Men" mentioned in the last chapter fall under this heading. University of Chicago Professor Lawrence E. Sullivan recorded a Yupa Indian tradition of magical dwarfs, the *Pipintu,* who dwell in the underworld.

> "In one tradition, a Yupa man is trapped in a cave, from where he travels to the underworld, where the Pipintu dwell. Eventually he marries a woman of that place." Besides echoing tales of fairy marriages, the end of the story has a curious parallel with modern reports of Grays.
> "The Pipintu die when they try to imitate the Yupa, who puts food in his mouth. Because the Pipintu are without true anuses or intestines, the food they put in their mouth crushes their bodies from the inside, and they die. The Pipintu can eat only by allowing food to roll down their backs."

This is strikingly similar to modern abductees' reports that the Grays have an "atrophied digestive system," and "obtain nourishment through their region." Probably sheer coincidence, but ancient tales of diminutive, magical beings living in the underworld are widespread across the South American continent.

Farther north, in Belize and Guatemala, local inhabitants have tales of the *Duende,* a hairy, goblinlike being fond of stealing human children and cattle. In the Yucatan Peninsula, the Maya tell of the *Alux,* a term used interchangeably for little people and glowing-eyed, hairy giants. Apparently, both kinds of Alux share the same magical abilities, and haunt the Mayan ruins dotting the region.

The smaller Alux treat intruders with hostility, frequently hitting them with magical, hardened clay pellets that penetrate the skin. An article by Bill Mack, titled *Mexico's Little People,* appeared in the August 1984 issue of *Fate* magazine. In Mack's search for the Alux, he interviewed locals who swore that the entities were still to be seen protecting the ancient ruins. One gatekeeper at an archeological site, named

Xuc, even showed him a pile of the clay pellets that the Alux had shot at him!

When I visited Yucatan and Chiapas in 1988, I met an eighty-year-old local shaman named "Don Juan" who described an initiatic tradition involving the Alux. Similar to the seers of ancient Britain, prospective healers cultivate a relationship with the beings to obtain "special powers and visions."

These modern seers especially cherished small quartz crystals given by the little people as magical tools. The accepted method was to send a "virgin child" into the deep woods; if they returned at all, they would come back bearing the stones. Don Juan would not say what benefit the Alux obtained from the relationship. Interestingly, the Yucatan Peninsula is chiefly composed of limestone and quartz crystals are quite scarce.

Heading North into the United States, I found many accounts of similar beings. Most of these were traditions held by Native Americans, or inherited from them by settlers. The Cherokees long held that strange, elflike creatures lived in Chimney Rock, North Carolina. They were also seen by later whites.

In an 1806 issue of the *Raleigh Register,* Reverend George Newton reported a multiple-witness sighting of "thousands of beings in the air" at Chimney Rock. The story describes the beings as having a "glittering appearance" and being "white, phantomlike beings." According to a Mrs. Reaves, "Their clothing (and filmy as it looked, I can only call it clothing) was so brilliant a white that it almost hurt my eyes to look at them. Although I felt weak, somehow it left a solemn and pleasing impression on my mind."

Another haunted place supposedly inhabited by fairies is California's Mount Shasta, famous in channeling lore as a Lemurian UFO base. According to the Modoc, Shastika, and Wintun Indians, Shasta has been variously the abode of giants, gods, and little people, all possessed of magical abilities. There are many tales, ancient and modern, of people hearing elfin laughter and "bells" coming from underground. The area is also a "window area" where UFO sightings are commonplace.

A big window area for fairies, UFOs, and bigfoots is West

Virginia. Supposedly, invading colonists were warned by Native Americans that the area was off limits to human beings, and was "the home of spirits." While there are no records of modern tribes living in the area before the whites came, there are strange archeological ruins in wild, inaccessible sections of the state. Some of these areas continue to report high numbers of UFO sightings, or glowing mountain tops associated with the tiny spirits.

During my childhood, I visited a relative living in an isolated section of the Appalachian mountains. I remember being told by my great-aunt Ruth and her husband of a night when the sky was "glowing real bright in the East." The man went outside to observe the strange phenomenon, then retired to bed. The next day he found that he was badly sunburned! Many of their backwoods neighbors also reported the light. My great-aunt told me that the light came from "the mountain where the little people lived."

In 1990, I began working with anthropologist Luis Eduardo Luna to develop a conference on botanical shamanism. Luis had been working closely with the Peruvian shaman, Pablo Amaringo. Amaringo was an *ayahuascero,* or healer skilled in preparing the hallucinogenic brew, ayahuasca. Containing the high-powered hallucinogen DMT, ayahuasca is a necessary component of the fairy-rich Peruvian shamanic tradition. A primary stimulant of the optic nerves, DMT-induced visions are often said to "seem more precise and bright than real life."

As a child, Amaringo heard tales of his grandfather, who was said to have joined the world of spirits through high doses of the visionary substance. Later studying the family tradition himself, Amaringo had countless visions of fairies, UFOs, and plant spirits in his role as community healer.

A highly talented artist, Amaringo began to paint vivid pictures of his experiences and visions of the spirit world. His detailed, luminescent paintings are perhaps the most perfect examples one can find of the unearthly appearance of the fairy realm. The paintings, now published in Luna's book, *Ayahuasca Visions,* show paraphysical giants, dwarves, wise spirits of the dead, and UFOs in connection with fairies. An interesting feature of these works are exotic images of fairy cities hidden in the sky or under the earth or water. Amaringo himself makes little distinction between fairies and UFOs from other worlds.

Since esoteric culture in modern Peru is a strange blend of native and European elements, it is difficult to ascertain how much of Amaringo's visions come from traditional sources. However, reports from other scholars do confirm that the main elements of his visions are held by shamans throughout the Amazon and the Andes.

Like other seers such as Thomas the Rhymer or Robert Kirk, Amaringo has devoted his life to communicating his visions. He currently operates a free art school for the local peasant children, where he teaches them to paint botanical jungle scenes with the same vivid precision he learned in his fairy visions (without drugs). Even after one or two years of training, the work of his young students are remarkably beautiful. North American buyers are often shocked when told the ages of the artists!

I was once invited to smoke synthetic DMT in a unique setting. Five of us walked out into a spectacular desert setting and laid out a small Persian carpet brought for the purpose. Our "guide" carefully explained what we must do. "First take a hit and hold it in as long as you can; then exhale and take another. If you've reached your capacity, then lie back down on the carpet, close your eyes, and hold your breath until you must exhale. Otherwise, take another hit and then lie back.

"At that point, you will see a mandala of light that I call the 'chrysanthemum.' When something pulls you into the chrysanthemum, let go and you will find yourself in another world. When this vision eventually starts to fade, open your eyes and sit up, or you will forget some of it."

We were all nervous (terrified, actually) and held back. Finally, I went first, and took three hits of the chemical-tasting substance. I laid back, observed the wheel of light, and went in as instructed. To my astonishment, I found myself in a sunlit land of glowing, bejeweled "gardens" filled with dancing fairies and elves, right out of the film *Fantasia*. The air was filled with the warbling, munchkinlike songs of the joyful beings. It did not seem imaginary or hallucinatory at all; I felt like I was physically there. The joy was infectious; I could feel a big grin spreading itself across my face.

The vision seemed to last an hour. When I looked closely at the dancing or bobbing creatures, they began breaking down into pixels of light, like a television image close up. I realized what I had been perceiving as "elves" were not even humanoid creatures, but rather mobile holograms of light. Because they were emitting sounds and seemed to display intelligence (and humor), my mind was assembling them into a digestible image. I had turned something very alien indeed into munchkins!

Per the instructions, when my vision started to fade, I sat up and opened my eyes. Since DMT is extremely close to natural brain chemistry, it wears off quickly; I felt totally alert, with no hangover or sense of intoxication whatsoever. Only ten minutes had passed!

Did I see "elves," or was it just a "hallucination"? I have never taken this substance again, but I still wonder—did it make me see something that wasn't there, or did the drug allow me to see temporarily what is *always* there? Did I see into the apparitional reality?

India and Asia have their own share of fairy-type traditions. Tibet, Nepal, and India have countless tales of *Devas* (beings of light), *Dakinis* (flying female spirits), *Nagas* (underworld serpent beings), and *Lokapalas* (little people protecting sacred places). The literature of Hinduism, Buddhism, and Chinese Taoism contain many references to these magical beings, who frequently carried mortals off to their hidden realm.

Buddhist texts also note that the founder of Tibetan Buddhism, the magical Buddha Padmasambhava, came from the realm of the Dakinis. Later in life he returned to their otherworld to teach them his wisdom (and may still be there). Tibetan tales of the historical Buddha, the Indian prince Shakyamuni, also refer to his teaching the invisible beings.

Chinese and Japanese traditions describe elflike beings who often formed relationships with meditating hermits. Some of these were as students and teachers; others were frankly hostile. The hostile variety were often called "Fox

Spirits," though they took human form to steal the souls of their victims, mostly through sexual intercourse.

Taoist legends also record that the ancient dead were seen in the fairy otherworld. Uncannily similar to European tradition, these beings had obtained immortality through eating the "fairy food." The Taoists also viewed cave entrances into the underworld as doorways into different dimensions inhabited by fairies. One tenth-century text lists ten "Cave Heavens" and thirty-six "Small Cave Heavens" located under one mountain range in China.

A typical Taoist tale tells of a man who became lost in a tunnel and walked until he found himself in a lovely country "with a clear blue sky, shining pinkish clouds, fragrant flowers, towers the color of cinnabar, and far-flung palaces." He soon encountered a group of beautiful women, who brought him into their house and played exquisite music while they plied him with a "ruby-red drink and a jade-colored juice."

Suddenly remembering his home and family, he returned to the tunnel and followed a "dancing light" back to the surface. After arriving at his village, he was stunned to find that he recognized no one. At his house, he met his descendants who told him of a family tradition of an ancestor disappearing into a tunnel three hundred years before.

Meetings with the fairy folk are still reported in parts of Asia and India. In June 1992, a five-year-old boy named Bhagavat was lost while swimming with others in the river near Navadvipa, West Bengal, India. His parents and the other boys were searching the water when they spied just Bhagavat's finger protruding above a swift-moving current. After he was brought from the water, they found he had suffered no effects of drowning, though he had been submerged for nearly ten minutes.

When his mother asked him what had happened, the boy replied that when the current swept him underneath he saw a "beautiful lady." The woman was "dressed like a princess, with a crown and earrings." She held the boy up until rescuers came. The area has an ancient tradition of the *Jeladevata,* an elfin being of the rivers and lakes who protects people lost in the water.

The fairies were often characterized as mischievous tricksters. A classic trick was to offer a starving or thirsty person food or drink, only to have it turn into urine or dirt. More malevolent was the fairy trick of luring mortals into dangerous traps, such as chasms or quicksand. The legends of many nations describe water fairies who delighted in luring swimmers to their death by drowning.

Even when bearing gifts, the trickster element may be present. Glittering fairy gold was said to turn into cowpies in the sunlight. Perhaps even more distressing, fairy lovers would turn into aged crones or even animals (such as frogs). On the other hand, the reverse logic of *Alice in Wonderland* may come into play, and an animal or diseased beggar might suddenly transform into a handsome prince or princess. Such illusions were often a test of the mortal's wisdom or compassion.

No description of fairy tricks would be complete without mention of the "missing time" elements in their abductions. Like the aforementioned young shepherd or the man lost in the Cave Heaven, people would spend a short time in the fairy realm only to find that many years had passed when they returned home. In the case of fairy lovers longing to see their native land "for just a little while," they were sent back with a prohibition against dismounting their horse or touching the Earth.

The mythical Irish hero Fergus was supposed to have returned to Ireland in this fashion hundreds of years after the arrival of Christianity. When one of his men dismounted against orders, he turned into a pile of dust. After taking a good look around, the others returned to Tir Na Nog, the undersea realm of the Sidhe. (In another version of the tale, the unfortunate rider is the hero Ossian, who lives long enough to tell his tale to a monk.)

A nineteenth-century Welsh story tells of two farm workers, Rhys and Llewellyn, walking home at night. Rhys heard the sound of beautiful music, but Llewellyn heard nothing. He went on, leaving Rhys dancing to the sound. When Rhys never returned, the peasant was jailed on suspicion of murder. A local seer guessed what had occurred, and persuaded a group of men to go with Llewellyn back to the spot days later.

Following the seer's advice, when Llewllyn's foot touched

a "fairy ring" at the site, he, too, heard the sound of harps. The other men heard the sound when they placed their foot over Llewellyn's. Soon, the group could see Rhys dancing in a group of the fairies. They were able to pull him out, but Rhys insisted that he had been dancing for only five minutes. He refused to believe the men, fell ill, and soon died.

Perhaps the most familiar of such tales was set in seventeenth-century North America. Based on Hudson Valley legends of "little men," Washington Irving wrote the story of *Rip van Winkle*. Winkle was a lazy farmer who preferred wandering the woods to working his land. One day he encountered a group of mischievous dwarves playing ninepins on their own outdoor bowling green. He joined the group in their game but made the mistake of indulging in their potent liquor and fell asleep. When he awoke, his beard was long and gray, his clothes tattered, and he was an old man. Returning to his village, he found that a generation had passed and he had been long forgotten.

What was this "fairy food" that evidently induced hallucinatory and missing-time effects? Early investigators such as Sir Walter Scott, Evans-Wentz, or Robert Kirk report that fairies stole the "essence" of food or milk, leaving behind only a useless dross. The belief lingered on into medieval Christian mythology of witches "souring the milk of cattle and blighting the crops." Accusations of doing such things led many peasant women to a fiery death at the stake by the hands of the Church.

Anticipating the UFO-cattle mutilation mystery, malevolent evil fairies were said to drain blood from both men and cattle. These spirits were said to flock around battlefields to partake of the lost essence from hordes of dying men.

The "theft of essence" was not limited to food. Many accounts describe the souls or shades or recently dead people seen at the fairy feasts. In some tales the shades spoke to witnesses saying that only a certain ritual behavior by mortals would release their spirits. Robert Kirk is supposed to have appeared to witnesses asking for such a release.

Other times seers would observe the fairies attending human wakes or funerals. Such attendance was supposed to portend the theft of the soul of the deceased. In many cases, this association of the dead with fairies led to the two being seen as the same. The description of fairies as the "silent people" probably stems from this belief.

Fairy foods were said to include fungus, and many tales describe gold, gems, bread, wine, etc., returning to the fungus from which they were made. The connection between medieval accounts of witches, fairy visions, and fungi has led some authors to speculate on peasant use of hallucinogenic mushrooms. Though there are few known examples of psychedelic mushroom usage in Northern Europe, there may be a connection.

A rather common experience of modern eaters of "magic" mushrooms is an encounter with elves or fairies. These beings act exactly the same as the medieval precursors, and many "witnesses" claim that the beings appear to be made of light.

On the nonhallucinogenic side, the fairies of Europe were also said to raise their own crops of grain and beans in wilderness areas. Travelers reported seeing mazelike or circular designs high on remote hillsides, though these may have been nonagricultural fairy "raths" or circles.

Whatever their source of grain, the fairies were great bakers of bread, and on some occasions shared it with human visitors. Both Vallee and Keel have reported the Wisconsin story of fairylike occupants of a flying saucer that offered Joe Simonton a tour of their craft in 1961. Inside the object, the beings fried up some pancakes on their stove and gave three to the witness.

Simonton ate one and later reported that it "tasted like cardboard." A later analysis reportedly stated that the cakes were made of a mix of earthly grains, mostly buckwheat hulls. Jacques Vallee later found a book from 1910 that included a poem by William Allingham referring to elfin pancakes.

> Up the airy mountain,
> Down the rushing glen,
> We daren't go a-hunting
> For fear of little men.
>
> Down along the rocky shore
> Some make their home;

They live on crispy pancakes
of yellow tide-foam.

Eighteenth- and nineteenth-century peasants told investigators that they referred to the fairies as "good folk" or the "very good people" for fear of their wrath. The fairies' displeasure was often felt directly and immediately, through an attack of "fairy shot" or a "fairy stroke" (the modern medical condition "stroke" is named after fairy-strokes).

Fairy shot or elfstones were small pellets that the entities were supposed to shoot invisibly into their victims. The recipient would feel a pang and fall down dead, or slowly wither away.

Though these were most probably superstitious accounts of actual diseases, there are historical reports of seers identifying the cause as elfstones. A good seer was supposed to be able to remove magically the offending object and restore the individual to health.

It seems clear that such traditions are memories of shamanic practices still practiced in many parts of the planet. Shamans are people that by accident, ordeal, or training, are able to perceive the underworld and other spirit realms. They generally penetrate these realms in order to obtain practical information, such as methods for healing, or finding a lost flock.

Shamans believe that many diseases come from attacks by unfriendly spirits, who will often leave solid objects behind in the bodies of their victims. Like the fairy seers, shamans remove stones or other objects from the sick in order to heal them.

Elfstones were not only for killing. The Scandinavians had myths of magical objects that spirits would insert into seers seeking special abilities. Implanted during an initiatory ordeal, the stones were often crystals charged with some kind of energy. These beliefs are continued today by shamanic practitioners around the world.

Mircea Eliade describes one Australian aboriginal ceremony where an initiate is killed inside a cave by two spirits, who then open his body and remove the organs. Then the spirits will replace the organs and sew him back up with magical substances, including rock crystals. The parallels with modern-day abductees claiming "implants" left by the Grays are obvious. We might have a lot to learn from these old tales.

European fairy stories frequently mention circular markings in the grass, often called "fairy rings" or "raths." I remember being taught about these rings in high school biology class. The rings were supposedly formed by clumps of mushrooms dying off, then resprouting in progressively larger arcs and rings. The center of the ring, nourished by the decayed growth, has richer grass than outside the circle. Though such rings can be found, some quite large, they do not seem to account for all the circles appearing in crops or in dryer areas. The connection with fungi is also intriguing.

Pre-industrial scholars naively speculated that the circles were caused by storms. A 1789 couplet by Erasmus Darwin says:

> *"So from the dark clouds the playful lightning springs,*
> *rives the firm oak or prints the fairy rings."*

It is almost too easy to connect fairy rings with the circular "landing marks" of modern-day UFOs.

The literature clearly connects the raths with fairy gatherings and doorways into the underworld. As with most fairy sites, the sound of unearthly music and sightings of fairies dancing are common at the rings.

One encounter is said to have occurred in Stirlingshire in March 1936, very close to that same Aberfoyle hill where Robert Kirk's body (or simulacrum) was found. The witness was tending his sheep when he beheld ten fairies dancing in a ring to a "wonderful tune." The sheep showed an attraction to the music, but shied away if the fairies came too close.

The same person also heard the fairies later in Aran, but left because their "silvery voices" seemed angry about some matter. Still later, he witnessed another fairy dance, this time near Loch Rannoch. Multiple sightings from the same person over a period covering years would seem to suggest a seer or shaman. The man told folklorists that he "could never forget the incredible grace of their dancing."

The preference of the entities for dancing has been commented on in every continent. Lawrence Sullivan mentions a multitude of South American tribes who imitated the dances of these spirits in their own spiritual practices. For such tribes, ceaseless dancing in a ring was at once a recapitulation of cosmology and a method of inducing ecstasy.

The fairy rings were traditionally the site of glowing, bobbing lights that nowadays we would call UFOs. Many times peasants interpreted these sightings as aerial battles between different tribes of fairies. One case occurred during the Irish potato famine of 1846. The witness told Evans-Wentz, "I saw the Good People fighting in the sky over Knock Ma and on towards Galway." Evans-Wentz included many stories of this sort, some of which described the entities as flying in a heavenly chariot with glowing, spinning wheels.

UFO-researcher Jacques Vallee mentions an 1850's account of another "chariot" that was seen near the Egray River in France. A group of women saw an object that "leaped over a vineyard and was lost in the night." They described it as a "chariot with whining wheels," drawn or occupied by hairy dwarves, which local lore called *Farfadets.*

Vallee also mentions that similar objects were sometimes seen as sky-roving ships rather than chariots. One "cloud-ship" was mentioned in Gervase of Tilbury's *Otis Imperialia.* Apparently, a dangling "anchor" from the ship caught in a church steeple at Gravesend, Kent, England. The witnesses first heard voices from above, then a man slid down the rope to cut the anchor free. He then climbed back aboard the ship, which sailed on its merry way.

An object that may or may not have been a fairy ship was observed in 1920 near Nontron, France. A group of young people returning home from a dance (!) saw "luminous balls of light" floating in the air over a wooded area. There appeared to be small figures inside the lights, and the teenagers heard "musical sounds."

The ability of some people to see fairies or other supernatural creatures could have been induced by an ointment, possibly hallucinogenic. Many old tales, particularly in Wales and Ireland, tell of a "fairy ointment" that bestowed second sight. An individual would rub the cream in the eyes and immediately see apparitions, fairies, and even the future.

Because people with the "Sight" were supposedly unable

to refuse to answer questions, the ability was called "the tongue that cannot lie." Many fairies were also subject to this constraint, though they could answer in complex verse if they wished. One story tells of a seer who vainly attempted to avoid speaking his vision, only to become a part of it.

A man entered a tavern and seated himself next to a known seer who immediately attempted to leave. The newcomer, perhaps already deep in drink, insisted on asking why the man was suddenly in such a hurry. At first reluctant to respond, the seer admitted he had seen the man's death only two days away. The enraged man pulled out his dirk and stabbed the seer to death. Two days later, the man was hanged for the murder.

Some tales, occurring inside the fairy realm, reverse the use of the ointment. The fairies used it to dispel the Sight or dissolve illusions. There are several accounts of young male or female abductees imprisoned or enslaved in the glamorous fairy kingdom (the word "glamour" refers to a fairy enchantment). Noticing that their captors were daubing something in their eyes, the mortals surreptitiously did the same. Immediately, they could see that what was once a magnificent palace of blinding light was now a primitive hut. The beautiful fairies were shown to be beggars clad in rags.

In 1830, Sir Walter Scott wrote:

> "The young knights and beautiful ladies showed themselves as wrinkled carles and odious hags; the stately halls were turned into miserable damp caverns—all the delights of the Elfin Elysium vanished at once. In a word, their pleasures were showy but totally insubstantial—their activity unceasing, but fruitless and unavailing."

In some version of the tale, an observant fairy noticed the unsanctioned use of ointment and put out the eyes of the new seer. While modern cases of alien abductions do not mention a fairy ointment, the connection between blinding and the conjunctivitis of modern witnesses is easily made.

Many of the hereditary accounts of the Sight seem derived from an ancestor who used the ointment. Descendants who continued their elders' relationship with fairies would probably be called examples of "multigenerational contact" nowadays.

Like many modern UFO witnesses, those who saw the fairies were often reluctant to report what they saw. In addition to the threat of ridicule or the harsh arm of the Church, the entities themselves warned silence. As noted above, a loose tongue could result in a permanent abduction if lucky, or death by "fairy stroke" if not.

The poet William Butler Yeats wrote in 1888:

> ". . . you will not readily get ghost and fairy legends. You must go adroitly to work, and make friends with the children and old men. . . . The old women are the most learned, but will not so readily be got to talk, for the fairies are very secretive, and much resent being talked of; and are there not many stories of old women who were nearly pinched into their graves or numbed with fairy blasts?"

Were these beings motivated by more than a desire for privacy? According to Paracelsus, Evans-Wentz, Robert Kirk, and others, the fairies fear human attempts to control them. Evidently, there were rules or principles that *could* be used to control them. In a more modern parallel, our own Men in Black also warn and threaten witnesses not to reveal their experiences.

Besides their magic, appearance, and secretiveness, one of the strongest similarities between fairies and "modern aliens" is in the theft of human beings. Both kinds of cases often involve stolen children or young men and women. It appears that, like modern cases of abduction, the chief reason was for sexual or breeding purposes.

Folklorist Edwin Hartland mentions this explanation given by country folk in Europe for the abductions:

> "The motive usually assigned to fairies in northern stories is that of preserving and improving their race, on the one hand by carrying off human children to be brought up among the elves and to become united with them, and on the other hand by

obtaining the milk and fostering care of human
mothers for their own offspring."

In the fairy tradition, a human child raised by fairies, or a
fairy child nurtured by humans, was called a "changeling."
Though changelings may appear to belong to the host race,
folklore says that their genetic characteristics will someday
emerge. This may be one reason for the elves to steal women
as nurses for the hybrid offspring. UFO investigator David
Jacobs describes cases of modern abductees who meet alien
or hybrid children:

> "Abductees are also required to touch, hold, or hug
> these offspring . . . apparently it is absolutely essential
> for the child to have human contact. Although the
> aliens prefer that the humans give nurturing, loving
> contact, any physical contact seems to suffice."

Among many other pre-industrial writers, Robert Kirk reported seductive female fairies that molested young men:

> ". . . for in our Highlands, as there be many fair ladies
> of this aerial order (of spirits of fairies) which do often
> tryst with lascivious young men in the quality of suc-
> cubi or lightsome paramours and strumpets. These are
> called *Leannain Sith* (fairy lemans or lovers) or famil-
> iar Spirits."

Evans-Wentz reported the case of a man named Laughin,
who was in love with a fairy woman. The woman visited him
nightly, until he became so worn out that he grew afraid for
his life. He finally emigrated to America, but she is supposed
to have followed him there!

The feeling of a sexual relationship with alien entities was
described by contactee Whitley Strieber to journalist Ed
Conroy:

> "She is a human being, like all of her kind. But she is
> of the next level of man. I would like to take her away,
> for my own self. . . . And when her passion comes on

her, she appears out of the night. I'm afraid that my
succubus is quite real."

Author Richard Thompson also mentioned a case of a
modern "succubus" in India. A young Brahmin man from
Tamil Nadu told him that he had been dabbling in occultism,
until he had a frightening encounter with a naked, not-quite-
human female being who appeared before him suddenly one
night.

"A Tantric expert later explained what he had seen:
'You saw Mohini, a demon from the underworld. Had
you known how, you could have entered into a pact
with her. . . . You promise to satisfy her lust once a
month, and she will do your bidding in return, protect
your property, destroy your enemies, whatever.
'But a pact with Mohini is very dangerous. When
she comes for sexual satisfaction, she may assume
eighteen forms in the course of the night, expecting
you to fulfill the demands of each one. If you cannot,
it will cost you your life. And if during the twelve years
of your relationship with her you have an attraction to
another woman, that will also cost you your life.' "

Why are we so fascinated by fairy tales? Many psychologists and mythologists have described the transformative
power of enchantment. The late J.R.R. Tolkien, author of *The
Lord of the Rings* and *The Hobbit,* spoke persuasively about
the healing quality of stories about "talking trees, wise animals, shining magicians and enchantresses, and magical
realms." Deep down inside, there is a part of us that wants to
believe that nature contains other forms of intelligent life,
that we are not alone.

Both fairy tales and UFO reports challenge us to move beyond confusion and find models of healing and personal
integration. These images are easily seen in the thousand-
year-old fairy tradition, but are less clear in the "modern"
tale of UFO abductions. Perhaps abductees struggling to
make sense of their experiences should read fairy tales.

Both fairies and aliens communicate a paradoxical, nonsensical mode of action and speech. Assuming their reality,

many of their acts were senseless then and now. Comparing these less-pleasant similarities may help investigators decipher the perverse logic of alien encounters.

If we believe, as many people do, that aliens from space began visiting our planet during the 1940s, then the old literature will be of little use. However, if these reports of little green men and magical, long-fingered beings of light come from the same alien source, then the fairy tradition becomes relevant indeed.

GAIAN MESSAGE

Even now this landscape is assembling . . .
And the soul creeps out of the tree.

—LOUISE GLUCK

OVER the past decade, there have been many reports of mysteriously swirled markings in fields of grain or grass. The circular formations, often of complicated design, caused no damage to the grain. Their stalks are flattened down in widening rows, not broken. These "crop circles" have been associated with both ancient archeological sites and UFO sightings. Though the most complicated circles were found in England, they also occurred in many other countries.

Theories attempting to explain the phenomenon range from the prosaic to wild and woolly. The explanations include freak winds, hoaxes, magnetic anomalies, dancing fairies, alien communications, and the Gaian consciousness (the mind of the living Earth). The international teams of researchers include UFOlogists, physicists, biologists, psychologists and parapsychologists, archeologists and folklorists, Native American shamans, and stage magicians. Though many have pronounced their "solution" to the mystery, the circles continue to appear without witnesses.

One of the most challenging aspects of the mystery are corroborating reports of crop circles from earlier times. Though less elaborate than modern circles, similar designs were documented in medieval Europe. Closer to modern times, some UFO sightings of the 1950s and '60s left behind circular markings in the grass. These early reports present the strongest hurdle to believers in the Hoax Theory.

During the summer of 1978, British farmer Ian Stevens was driving his harvester through his wheat fields when he noticed something strange ahead. It appeared to be a very large, flattened area in his wheat. Concerned about damage to his crop, he stopped his vehicle and waded through the grain into the area. The wheat stalks were pressed to the ground but not broken, and were swirled in a clockwise pattern radiating outward from the center. What could be responsible for such a thing? Could it have been the wind?

He realized that he stood in a very large, perfect circle, and that it was surrounded by four smaller circles in the grain. Stevens had heard about other mysterious circles found in their crops by his neighbors, but this was the first time he'd seen one this large or perfect. Like the other farmers, he could not imagine how someone could have come onto his land unseen and created the strange marking. He found himself remembering a tale told by a neighbor, Mrs. Bowles, about a UFO seen in the vicinity some weeks before.

Ian Stevens drove his harvester around the area, and later invited family and friends to come out and take a look. Though they scratched their heads and discussed the matter over pints of beer, none of them could imagine a plausible explanation. Similar circles have appeared in the Hampshire area every summer since that date.

In the summer of 1981, the circles began spreading out. Two were found at an ancient burial site in Litchfield, England called Seven Barrows. Though near a busy highway, there were no witnesses to the phenomenon that apparently formed overnight.

Close to two of the ancient hills, the circles were the exact diameter as the barrows. The angle formed by a line running through the centers of the two circles was exactly the same as an angle formed by lines through the two barrows. Though inexplicable, the connection to the two mounds seems obvious.

The site lies near electrical cables carrying four hundred thousand volts over the national power grid, and a parallel railway line. The original construction of the power line and train tracks demolished some of the ancient graves. Were the disturbed spirits of the dead responsible for the mysterious crop formations? Similar circles appeared in the same spot in 1982.

Another set of circles was found in Cheesefoot Head, England in July 1981. Again appearing overnight, the precise series of three circles appeared in a field of grain unmarked by any human or mechanical tracks. As in Litchfield, the circles were swirled clockwise out from the exact center of each design.

The Cheesefoot Head circle marked the beginning of intense public interest in the phenomenon, and was investigated by national news services. Some experts, who had not examined the circles firsthand, pronounced them the work of "whirlwinds." Others felt that these were simple hoaxes done by rustics at the expense of gullible city folk. However, no one offered convincing evidence to support either theory.

Public interest grew even stronger in 1982 and 1983 when the circles again appeared at Litchfield, Cheesefoot Head, Headbourne Worthy, and other locations. Many investigators, including pilot-photographer "Busty" Collins, began to take a greater involvement. (Mr. Collins is responsible for many of the breathtaking aerial photographs of the phenomenon.)

Whoever was responsible for the circles continued to show a liking for ancient sites such as earthworks, mounds, and barrows. It was frequently noted that these archeological sites are also the setting for many repeated UFO sightings. What was (and is) the connection between ancient mounds, UFOs, and crop circles?

The circles continued to appear year after year in an ever-growing area across rural England. Most of the circles were groups of smaller circles surrounding a larger one, or just one large circle alone. Some of the most beautiful free-standing circles were surrounded by concentric rings. All of the circles were again formed by swirled, not crushed, crops of grain or grasses. Most were swirled in a clockwise direction, but a few were found that ran counterclockwise.

The phenomenon took on new dimensions in the summer of 1991 with a wave of circles of extraordinary complexity. Farmers, researchers, and journalists were stunned to find squiggles, heart shapes, triangles, and mathematical shapes intertwined with the familiar "single-ringers." Once again, strange lights in the sky appeared prior to many of the circles. The UFOs were so common that teams of sky watchers were formed to observe the skies near crop circle areas.

On July 16 around midnight, a group of researchers were

driving on the A4 road, west of the ancient site of Avebury when one of them noticed a huge object overhead. Shouting for the driver to stop the car, Gary Hardwick and the others emerged to watch the pulsing green object slowly move west across the sky. As it disappeared, the watchers saw another light following the first. This was followed by a black triangle shape that passed eastward "at an incredible speed" without a sound.

The observers were growing cold and were considering leaving when they saw a succession of pulsing lights in colors ranging from pink and white to green and blue. One of the lights appeared to emit a "thin white beam" that reached to the ground. The tired watchers eventually left and drove home without incident. Later they realized that the spot where they had made the sighting was Needle Point, site of the 1990 crop circles.

Their sighting took on additional significance the next day, when the most spectacular crop circle of all was found a few miles away, near the Iron Age hill fort of Barbury Castle. The first observers "could hardly believe their eyes" as they flew overhead in a small plane. The field of wheat, which had been blank the day before, now contained the largest and most complex pictogram of all.

The design was centered around a huge equilateral triangle surmounted by three concentric circles. Each corner of the triangle ended in a different symbol, all approximately twenty-seven yards across. One design was a spiral "ratchet" line spinning out from the center. Another was a plain circle pierced to the center by a straight line from the apex of the triangle. The last corner was a "sun wheel" symbol, a circle with six equally spaced, curving spokes leading from the center to the outer ring. The huge, perfect triangle itself had lines leading from each angle to meet at the center, giving the impression of a three-dimensional pyramid. The first researchers luckily took hundreds of photographs, as the design only lasted one day, blurred by a heavy rainfall the following night.

That same summer another design appeared. On August 12, 1991, an Ickleton, Cambridgeshire farmer named Hugh Raybone found an "agriglyph" (as they were now being called) in his cornfield. The formation was aligned with the nearby site of a circular design found the previous June and was close to the prehistoric roadway of Icknield Way.

Seen from the air, the markings showed a precise, heart-shaped design with two circles hanging from the "point" of the heart. At measured intervals along the upper edges of the heart were six smaller circles. One of the first locals to walk the circle was neighbor Dick Wombell. According to Wombell:

> "The corn was laid down in a clockwise manner, each stem was bent over at the same height above the ground, about half an inch, the stems were not crushed, and the ears of corn were intact. No one could have made this in the dark, and if there were any lights to aid them we would have noticed them from the farm-house."

Pictures of the formation were published in the local newspaper, and copies made it to nearby Cambridge University. The Cambridge scientists quickly recognized it as a "Mandelbrot set" from fractal geometry. Considered the most complicated design in mathematics, the sets were discovered by Dr. Benoit Mandelbrot in the 1960s. Dr. Mandelbrot had been working with computer-generated fractal designs when he found the set of infinite dimensions that bears his name.

Despite ensuing speculations that "only a Cambridge mathematics or engineering student could have done it," no one stepped forward to claim credit. Today the Ickleton Mandelbrot set is hailed by believers as the finest example of intelligent, nonhuman design, and branded as a hoax by skeptics.

Many other extraordinary designs appeared through the summer of 1991, including "insectograms," serpent, dolphin, flower, snail, and key shapes. Some agriglyphs seemed to be more of the mathematical symbols. Other designs, termed "whale shapes" by investigators, closely resemble the phantom airships seen over the past century in Britain and the U.S.

The phenomenon showed no sign of abating in the following summer. The most outstanding formation appeared on August 17, 1992, just north of the ancient Silbury Hill earthwork in Wiltshire.

In the traditions of mandalas (sacred designs containing spiritual truths), the Silbury formation was in the form of a great wheel with eight individual points spaced along the edge. Each point held a different shape of (presumably) astrological or mythological significance.

The points included a half-moon, a full circle, antler shapes, a trident, and a vulval shape. Aligned along a North-South axis, the circle drew immediate attention as a spiritual message from the "crop circle makers." Some saw it as the Buddhist Wheel of Life, others as the pre-Christian Aryan mystical symbol, the "Great Turning."

Many observers were quick to point out the symmetrical proportions and ancient motifs in the crop circles. Some researchers have compared them to ancient writings and the principles of sacred geometry, the "language of the gods."

Sacred geometry is a heritage left by many ancient peoples around the world. The Sumerians, Egyptians, Hebrews, Greeks, Romans, British, Indians, Chinese, Incans, and Mayans all possessed advanced mathematical and astronomical knowledge that they employed in artistic and architectural motifs. For these cultures convinced of the divine harmony of numbers, the images of sacred geometry provided a visible reminder that their world was based on universal principles of order and wholeness.

Though these geometric images are found in jewelry, weavings, and pottery, their chief purpose was in temple design and the construction of monuments and gravesites. These spiritual centers of a community or nation required construction according to balanced principles, or disharmony would befall crops, animals, and the people.

Whether their technological level dictated building with piled earth, timber, rough boulders, or smooth masonry, these ancient people left behind countless artifacts holding clues to their knowledge. In many cases, following cultures ignorant or uncaring of their purpose built right over the ancient works.

Other examples were either too large to destroy (as in the case of Silbury Hill or the Pyramids of Egypt), or were even kept in use by the people. The marvelous Gothic Cathedrals of Europe are textbook cases of the laws of divine proportion.

A few authors have speculated that some ancient alphabets are related to or derived from the same astronomical principles as the sacred geometry of temple layouts. Since both written symbol and architectural design bear similar meanings, one could theoretically "read" a message from the ancients in their earthworks, monoliths, and temples. The same sort of message theoretically exists in some agriglyphs.

Another ancient people who preserved their ancient geometric traditions are the Native American Hopi tribe. Alone among the original inhabitants of North America, the pacifist Hopi have preserved nearly the entirety of their ancestral religious tradition.

The most famous of their traditions are the "Hopi prophesies," which tell of the coming end of the modern world. They believe that the Creator has created and later destroyed three earlier "worlds"; we are now living in the fourth. The prophesies, recorded in geometrical images carved in the cliffs of their homeland, warn of a time of worldwide corruption and war presaging the end of the age. According to Hopi elder Thomas Banyaca, the British crop circles display designs similar to these Hopi petroglyphs foretelling the imminent end.

Though it tells us nothing of their origin, researchers are correct in stating that many British crop formations display the principles of sacred geometry. Perhaps the hoaxers, aliens, or nature spirits are telling us that we could profit by studying the healing images of ancient times, or to prepare for the end of the world.

By the summer of 1992, over three thousand crop circles had been documented around the world. The vast majority of formations outside Britain were the classic "single-ringer" circles. These circles possessed the familiar swirled-from-the-center design in flattened grass, either in clockwise or counterclockwise directions. There is a well-documented association of these international circles with UFOs.

Though there were scattered earlier reports, the first Japanese circles to attract widespread media attention occurred in Fukuoka Prefecture, Kyushu Island on September 17, 1989.

Rice farmer Shunzo Abe woke to find two wide circles in his fields. His first thought was "that a wild boar had run amok. But there were no signs of footprints to show that anything or anyone had entered the field." Newspaper reports noted that Mr. Abe was angry because he did not know where to file a complaint.

The circles appeared two weeks later on Kyushu Island, this time near the Yoshinogari archeological site. Several additional Japanese circles appeared in 1990 and '91.

A Canadian farmer named Edwin Fuhr may have witnessed a circle forming in his wheat field back in September 1974. He was driving a swathing machine when he noticed a round, shiny object "like a tin duck-hide" ahead. As he walked toward the thing, he saw movement.

> "All of a sudden, I noticed that the grass was moving, turning near this thing. Then I saw the whole thing was turning. I backed up slow; I wasn't going to turn my back on the thing.
> "When I got back up on the swather I noticed there was another four to the left of me, all revolving. I just froze on the seat and didn't move."

Fuhr sat there for another fifteen minutes watching the "stainless steel" globes floating a foot off the ground. He later said that he had wanted to run, but could not move his arms and legs.

> "I was terrified. I froze. . . . couldn't do a thing. Then they took off straight up. There was a grayish vapor coming from underneath them and a strong downwind which knocked the rape down. I had to hang onto my hat."

After he was sure that the things had really gone, Fuhr approached the spot. The spot where he'd first seen the "duck-hide" was now a circle eleven feet in diameter. The grass was flattened down and twisted in a clockwise direction. He checked the other spots and found four more circles. After word got out about Fuhr's UFO sighting, over two thousand journalists, photographers, and New Age believers tramped over his farm to see the spot. Since then, scores of circles have appeared in various wheat fields in Canada, with over a dozen in the summer of 1990.

The same summer, the phenomenon also visited the American Midwest. Circles, some ringed, appeared in Kansas, Missouri, and Illinois. Again the vast majority formed in crops of grain.

The circular mysteries have also been active in other parts of Europe. Germany, Holland, Italy, and Greece have all experienced the phenomenon, with most reports coming from Germany. Strangely, France seems to be completely ignored by whoever or whatever makes the circles.

The circles have not ignored Eastern Europe. Simple circles and ringed ones have been reported from Bulgaria, Romania, Czechoslovakia, and Hungary. Russian circles from a number of regions have been documented. One June 1990 formation in the town of Yeisk in Krasnodar was preceded the night before by UFO sightings. The aerial objects were reportedly "blue and white, like a welding arc."

Outside of the United Kingdom, the country that has the earliest modern reports of crop circles is Australia. In January 1966, a number of news services carried the sensational discovery of "flying saucer nests" in Queensland. Though the term "nest" implies a creature laying eggs in a protected spot, what were really being reported were circular markings found in fields after UFO sightings.

Among the investigators was naturalist Ivan T. Sanderson. In his speculative work, *Things*, Sanderson recounts a number of the sightings that were associated with the circles. One of the sightings, made by a hard-boiled police officer and his wife, was curiously absurd.

The event occurred during a UFO flap of sightings across Queensland. Sergeant R. Hagerty of the Cookstown, Australia police force was driving home from Hopevale Mission with his wife. They were startled to see a number of large, floating "bubbles" moving along the road at a "fast walking pace." The objects headed straight for the Hagerty's moving vehicle, and vanished right under the radiator! The bewildered couple reported their story to police, who took it right in stride with the scores of other reports.

Other sightings followed the more familiar patterns of

glowing saucer shapes leaving the ground or flying in the sky. Local farmers began finding eight-to-thirty-foot-diameter circles in their fields or marshes, with stalks swirled in both clockwise and counterclockwise directions. One element stood out from among modern reports; some of the circles were reportedly full of reeds torn out by the roots! Once again, there was no sign of human or animal paths made to the circles before they were found.

The circle-makers must have perfected their technique since the '60s, as the formations now appear in South Australia and Victoria with the grasses unharmed. These recent "down under" crop circles appear during the Australian summer, near the close of the British circle season.

Something like crop circles was seen and documented long ago. In a 1789 work titled *The Botanic Garden,* Charles Darwin's grandfather Erasmus described the rings:

> "There is a phenomenon, supposed to be electric, which is yet unaccounted for; I mean the Fairy-rings, as they are called, so often seen on the grass. . . . Now as a stream of electricity (during thunderstorms) displaces the air as it passes through, it is plain no part of the grass can be burnt by it, but just the external rings of this cylinder.
>
> "I know some circles of many yards diameter of this kind near Foremark, in Derbyshire, which annually produce large white funguses and stronger grass, and have done so, I am informed, above thirty years. These situations, whether from eminence or moisture, which were proper once to attract and discharge a thundercloud, are more liable again to experience the same. Hence many fairy-rings are often seen near each other, as I saw this summer in a garden in Nottinghamshire, or intersecting each other."

The "fairy rings" were seen and documented numerous times in England and Germany. One of the most famed scholars in seventeenth-century England, Henry More, debated whether the circles were made by fairies or by witches (in whom he believed). He was followed by Dr. Robert Plot, the apocryphal author of *The Natural History of Staffordshire,* who felt that there must be some natural explanation. Like Erasmus Darwin, Plot speculated that "hollow tubes" of lightning were a likely cause. He also noted that cattle would not go anywhere near the circles he investigated.

There was a pamphlet found independently by investigators Bob Skinner and Jenny Randles, published in 1678, entitled *The Mowing Devil*. It concerned the presence of mysterious rings in the fields that local farmers attributed to the Evil One. Though the account is disputed, folk accounts of the work of witches and devils frequently mention high winds that curse or taint the crops. "Injuring the crops" was a charge that sent thousands of supposed witches to their deaths. Were they being blamed for crop circles?

In December 1648, folklorist John Aubrey was passing through the village of Wiltshire with some friends when he suddenly realized that the village stood within the remains of a tremendous prehistoric temple. Though people had been living for centuries within its precincts, the locals ignored the stones or broke them up to make room for cottages or farmlands. No one even noticed the monolithic patterns anymore.

Incredible as it may seem, the ruin was the now-famous, enormous site of Avebury. Aubrey, by training or inclination, was able to see a pattern where no one else did. Yet, after he pointed it out, everyone saw it.

Aubrey was followed at Avebury by an antiquarian mystic, Dr. Stukeley. Stukeley perceived huge, interconnected roads, astronomical complexes, and megalithic temples scattered across the region. His writings of his vision have since been confirmed by generations of archeologists. The British landscape was indeed covered by the artifacts of a forgotten, earth-moving culture.

The emerging vision was carried further by yet another antiquarian gentleman. In the early 1920s, Alfred Watkins was riding his horse over some hills near Hereford when he was struck by a peculiar image. In a flash, the ancient landscape unfolded before him and he realized that ancient groves of trees, hills and mounds, megalithic sites, holy wells, and old churches were all laid out on some sort of interconnected grid.

He found that he could follow this "ancient track" from

one sacred site to another without a map. Speaking to many of the rural inhabitants, he was surprised to find that many of the same family names kept cropping up again and again in association with the places. Among frequent surnames such as Red, Black, White, Merry, and Cold was the name "Ley." He chose to name these ancient roads or paths "ley lines," and the term has stuck.

Though a few conservatives in the archeological community remain unconvinced, it has become generally accepted that leys do interconnect many of the old pagan sites, or churches built upon them. A few researchers have noted that these sites, by accident or design, also delineate the paths taken by migrating birds and animals.

Some dowsers and engineers claim that flows of underground water follow the patterns of the leys, and were a possible energy source for ancients "tapping the grid" through prayer, ritual, or some scientific means unknown to moderns. Besides underground streams and holy wells, the known piezo-electric effect from heavy masses of crystalline stone (the monoliths) are thought to have been another potential source of this earth energy.

In recent years, more has become known in the West about the venerable Chinese tradition of *feng shui*, ("wind-water"). This intricate system of aligning earthly and cosmic energies with human buildings and roads is still in use in parts of China, most notably Hong Kong. Many investigators are convinced that the ancient Britons also had their own form of feng shui.

Less-widely acknowledged is the fact that many sightings of specters, ghost dogs, and UFOs traditionally occur along the ley lines. Is this based upon some mystical form of "earth energy" or is there another factor at work? Whatever the cause, it is true that a high number of crop circle formations also appear on or close to the supposed leys. Many of them, such as the remarkable Kennets pictogram, point at the ancient monuments.

"Captain" Bruce Cathie, a New Zealand researcher, has written extensively on the possibilities of a "worldwide grid" that reflects the ley knowledge of an ancient, worldwide civilization. Though his books are filled with rather unreadable mathematics, he has amassed an impressive amount of UFO reports along this very same grid, which has many correlations with the earth's magnetic field.

The association or paranormal or alien phenomena along the leys added fuel to a host of theories and investigations in Britain and around the world. American psychologist Greg Little, in his book *The People of the Web,* notes that similar phenomena have appeared for centuries in association with the ancient Mound Builder sites in the Mississippi Valley. Crop circles, ghost and fairy-type sightings, electromagnetic phenomena, UFOs, and ancient temples all seem aligned according to some forgotten map.

Are these ancient sites somehow necessary for ghosts, crop circles, and UFOs to manifest? In the Native American traditions of religious ceremonies conducted at the Mounds and Medicine Wheels, Little found evidence that they were.

> "The sites were sacred circles used to commune with and call forth spirits. Only the shamen and chiefs were permitted to reside within the sacred circle during the entire ceremonial period. Through rituals that stressed participants both physically and mentally . . . they literally changed their neurochemistry and massive levels of endorphins undoubtedly permeated their brains altering their perception. Because the sites were built over areas with high 'magnetic aberrations' their brain chemistry was further altered. As they tuned themselves into the spirit world, the realm of spirit emerged at the site in a rush of experiences both mental and physical."

Little also noted that his informants' traditions spoke of the spirits appearing as alien monsters, giant birds, and "little people." The beings "appeared to each participant differently, adjusting their form to the needs and expectations of each individual. We are told that the *maiyun* would appear in the form of little people so that they could directly communicate."

> "Many reports indicate that the *maiyun* sometimes took individuals away for periods of time during the process of communication. Thus, the *maiyun* are similar to the

humanoid entities encountered in the typical UFO abduction."

Little and other writers also note that shamans around the
world spoke of a dangerous imbalance in the land and the
spirit world. "The whites' lack of concern for life, both animal and plant, was a symptom of the lack of harmony in the
world." According to this belief, the rise of UFO and crop circle phenomena are the spirits' attempt to get us all to wake up.
Unfortunately, we've all forgotten how to speak the language.

In his book, *Earth Lights*, researcher Paul Devereux described the phenomenon of ghostly lights that appear and
reappear along the same routes for years, often along what are
called leys. Devereux coined the term "earth lights" to reflect his conviction that such UFOs are indeed an earthly, not
an extraterrestrial phenomenon.

"These earth lights haunt specific terrains: faulted geol-
ogy, mountain peaks and ridges, bodies of water, and areas of
mineral deposits." This kind of terrain, often a source of magnetic eccentricities, are precisely the kinds of areas ancient
people chose as temple sites; in other words, ley areas.

There are at least one hundred areas in the United States
alone where these eerie lights are seen regularly. Some sites
are rich in ghost or UFO sightings; others lie near train tracks
and are associated with the mysterious "phantom trains" (a
moving light sometimes thought to be the lamp of an invisible train). One of the most famous regions of earth light activity is Marfa, Texas, near the Chinati Mountains.

The "Marfa lights" have been seen for centuries, and have
been documented since 1883. Racing along with sudden,
right-angle turns, hovering over the ground, skipping over
the prairie, merging with or splitting off from other lights
and disappearing quickly, they act in ways indistinguishable
from what most people call UFOs.

The Marfa lights have been seen up close by geologists and
photographed on a number of occasions. It has been established that they have a close relationship to fault lines, and appear in greater numbers just before or immediately following
earthquakes. (The first man to point out a connection between strange, flying lights and earthquakes was none other
than investigator Charles Fort.)

A possibly related phenomenon is the glowing or streaking lights emanating from mountain tops. Called MPDs ("mountain peak discharges"), they are clear evidence that nature can produce many-colored, moving lights. According to researcher Michael Persinger, low-level tectonic stress may be responsible for both MPD and the earth lights phenomenon. The stress and pressure at the faults produce powerful electromagnetic fields, causing the lights. Some phosphorescent gases may also be released at these times.

Persinger has also speculated that these electromagnetic fields, coupled with the flickering lights, may induce changes in brain functioning and perception. These changes may be both physical and mental, and could conceivably include hallucinations. If such a phenomenon is possible, it's also possible that these effects were studied and used by ancient people.

In 1979, a group of researchers, including Paul Devereux and archeologist John Steele, undertook a detailed investigation of electromagnetic and ultrasonic phenomena of British leys and standing stones. Their team, dubbed "the Dragon Project," did find a number of interesting readings that may bear some relation to the mysteries.

The Dragon project found a strange electrical resistance between the stones of the famous Castlerigg megalithic site. They also recorded ultrasonic signals from the eastern side of the circle at dawn. Magnetic anomalies, unusual levels of radiation, and unexplained radio signals joined the strange perceptual effects and "time slips" noted by the researchers. Their experience lends credence to the notion that something odd is happening at these ancient monuments.

The preceding data suggest that crop circles are part of a larger tapestry of geological, electromagnetic, historical, and religious events. Just as there are linkages and common motifs among these areas, so are there consistent patterns in the formations themselves.

Even the simple circular shapes show a variety of patterns in their swath. The grain or grass may be swirled fully or partially clockwise or counterclockwise, at right angles, in "S" shapes, or even divided into two folds. The interior coils of a circle may be tight wheels of many windings, or a few loose revolutions. Inexplicably, groups of circles together may have the same swath or completely individual designs.

On top of all this, many circles have been found with successive layers of grain. These multilayered circles may have designs swirled in one direction atop another level swirled in an opposite one. Can it be possible that this astounding variety results from the landing of a physical, flying craft?

Though more complex markings were discussed earlier, one intricate shape deserves a further look. There have been a number of formations that show what appears to be a classical labyrinth design. According to *Webster's Dictionary,* a labyrinth is "an intricate, winding structure of interconnected passages; a maze." Many ancient cultures drew or built labyrinths as part of their temple complexes, and these mazes are associated with both leys and megalithic construction. The spiraling labyrinths found in the crop circles seem to be mazes of this familiar, ancient sort, rather than "modern innovations."

There are also patterns in the experiences of witnesses. A fairly common experience is a sense of a faint humming heard from the areas of the circles. Often noticed the night before a formation, these sounds may be related to the electromagnetic effects found near megalithic sites. If so, the sounds may be internal (inside one's head), rather than external.

Other electromagnetic disturbances associated with crop circles and megalithic sites are the ubiquitous stalled automobiles. The sketchy reports are not clear whether these come from overflying UFOs or some other source.

EM effects may also be responsible for the "ghost images" experienced by photographers taking shots of the formations. There seem to be strange after-images of ghostly "people" and black, flying objects in some of the photographs of the circles. Some film crews have also experienced unexplainable equipment failures within the circles.

Many people feel that the circles contain messages to humanity. While the symbols of sacred geometry admittedly exemplify esoteric principles, they are not *words*. If "they" want to talk to us through our wheat fields, why don't they write messages instead of circles? Perhaps they already have.

One of the strangest agriglyphs of all appeared at Milk Hill, Stanton St. Bernard, Wiltshire, in 1991. It consisted of sixteen or eighteen "letters" in a straight line, all twelve to fifteen feet high. Was it a message from the circle makers?

Though the script (if that is what it was), was unknown, someone claimed to recognize it. Archeologist Michael Green, in an article entitled *The Language of the Circle Makers,* described the runic characters as belonging to an ancient language called "Senzar." According to Theosophical teachings, Senzar is supposed to be "the ancient sacerdotal language of Atlantis."

Though he obtained his Atlantean connection through a channeler, Green conducted an impressive amount of research comparing many ancient alphabets in an attempt to find a common, prehistoric source. Surprisingly, there are a number of runic shapes in these old alphabets that look just like those of the Milk Hill agriglyph.

What does the formation mean in Senzar? Green says that it reads as the name of a deity, very close to the ancient Egyptian earth god, Ptah. If it really was Ptah, why did he bother to sign his name in the English crops? Strangest of all, a week before the markings appeared an American researcher had written in the same spot the words, "Speak to us."

The British researcher Brinsley Le Poer Trench describes a number of forms an extraterrestrial or paranormal communication might take. They include "symbolic communication" and "conceptual communication."

In symbolic communications, "the recipient is shown a symbol or group of symbols that will affect his mental machinery like a punched card fed into a computer, and he more or less automatically delivers the message.

> "Conceptual communications are achieved by implanting a whole concept in the mind of the recipient, at a level just above that at which he normally functions. He may or may not be aware, immediately, of his having received an impression. . . . He may be completely unaware that anything has happened to him. Then later, when his mind is not busy with something

else, the concept will register at his ordinary level of conscious awareness."

Trench notes that recipients of such communications will translate the message into their own frames of reference. ". . . The recipient will express the concept in his own ordinary language, or he will adopt some more or less unusual form of speech depending upon where he believes the concept came from and his own personal emotions, attitudes, and acceptances." This is precisely the explanation many crop circle researchers have adopted regarding possible information and messages in the formations.

Rather than Egyptian deities or UFOs, many investigators speculate that the mind behind the circles is that of the Earth itself. Named "Gaia" for the ancient Greek Earthmother, the notion that Earth could be a thinking entity has become widely accepted.

The Gaia Hypothesis is the brainchild of scientist James Lovelock. Trained in biology, chemistry, climatology, geophysics, and cybernetics, Lovelock is a visionary maverick responsible for many far-ranging ideas now common in the scientific community, such as the possible "greening of the planet Mars." One of his inventions, the electron capture detector, was instrumental in providing important data for studies of pesticide contamination and in monitoring the depletion of the Earth's ozone layer.

After his studies of other planets in the solar system, Lovelock noticed that Earth is particularly remarkable for the constant disequilibrium of its atmosphere. "In a violation of the rules of chemistry of the highest order of magnitude," highly reactive gases such as methane and oxygen co-exist on Earth without reaction.

On other planets, these gases would violently react together and then cease to exist when the atmosphere found its equilibrium. No life-forms could survive such a reaction, yet on Earth, where life depends on this balance, the gases avoid this reaction. "Something" must be regulating the atmosphere.

Lovelock also found evidence of other regulating mechanisms on earth. Oxygen, methane, ammonia, nitrogen, and temperature have all been somehow maintained in ranges optimal for life for millions of years. This homeostasis implied some kind of constant controls.

These controls include large-scale "thermostats" such as volcanic activity, icecaps, and temperature-regulating ocean currents, atmospheric regulators such as cloud density, rain forests and algae, and sophisticated chemical and organic processes on the microscopic level. Somehow, all these phenomena have found a way to work together to keep earth livable for hundreds of millions of years. Based on these factors, Lovelock posited that the entire Earth is one self-regulating organism, which he called Gaia.

An elegant piece of scientific detective work, the Gaia Hypothesis is having a continuing impact on hundreds of disciplines. Though still subject to criticism in academic circles, it seems clear that children in high school biology classes will be learning about the concept. Provided people are still able to live here in the future.

It is common knowledge that humanity is swiftly decimating the few remaining rain forests, polluting the oceans, and contaminating the atmosphere, all of which are the "regulators" Gaia uses to keep our planet livable. What will happen if humanity does not cease its assault? No one is sure what to expect, beyond tremendous environmental devastation.

If Gaia is the most complex living organism in the solar system, then why not assume some intelligence capable of communication? These predictions of massive destruction are precisely what the Hopi elders claimed to read in the crop circles. Perhaps, as some researchers believe, Gaia herself is attempting to warn us of our folly.

Even if the Gaia Hypothesis is someday proven, many will remain unconvinced of her sending us cosmic mail through crop circles. Humanity is not getting that particular message, if a message it is. Other, simpler explanations for the enigma must be examined.

Though the circles' connections with leys and megaliths have been well established, one wonders how geologically induced lights could write complex patterns and even messages in the fields. Are there other factors? Maybe they are the work of inventive hoaxers after all.

In an attempt to prove the plausibility of man-made formations, several magazines, including the crop circle publication *The Cereologist,* promoted a crop circle competition. Held over the weekend of July 11–12, 1992, the event took place on a private field in West Wycombe, Buckinghamshire, England.

British, German, and American teams tried out a number of techniques, including hand-held ladders with attachments, special rakes, and pole-and-chain devices that were used to swirl grain out from a central point. Many of the circles were not up to the high standards of the "real" circles, but others were.

The prize of three thousand pounds was taken by a three-man team from Yeovil, England, who entered under the name "Masters of the Cereal Universe." The team was able to replicate a very authentic-looking, complex insectogram. Of course, say believers, the fact that one can make a crop circle does not mean that hoaxers account for them all. How can people tell the difference between obvious hoaxes and others?

One of the most difficult hurdles hoaxers must overcome is to enter and leave the area without leaving trails or footprints, all in total darkness. Though conducted in the daytime, the competition above proved that some people can indeed remove evidence of footprints. Presumably, they could also wear night-vision goggles, or have some other means of illumination.

Many crop circles have been found out as frauds immediately. In some cases, a concealed hole was found in the middle of a formation, probably the site of a pole used as fulcrum for a "sweeping device" (like the one used in the competition).

Another formation was immediately suspected by investigators. Found in Wiltshire in 1990, it showed the familiar "smile button" face known around the world. The reports do not say if it was considered a hoax only because of the subject matter, or if there was other evidence. (Why shouldn't Gaia like the smile button?)

The classic case of a hoax occurred on July 25, 1990 in an area close to the ancient mound of Silbury Hill. The entire region had been in the midst of a crop circle wave for weeks, accompanied by frequent UFO sightings. The British Army had shown great interest in the circles, and Army helicopters had been sweeping the hills over the month.

On the day of the formation's appearance, a team of investigators grandly announced through BBC-Television that they had video-recorded a "major event" the night before, with orange UFOs appearing above a brand new formation of circles. Their major event turned into major embarrassment when it was discovered that the crudely made circles were a hoax.

In a strange twist, the circle makers left behind a ouija board and a wooden cross at the center of each formation. It was later suggested that the Army had made the circles in an attempt to defuse the public hysteria. The ouija board and crosses were an attempt to link the idea of forged circles to the New Age-type investigators.

Whatever the case, the damage was done. Local and national newspapers loudly trumpeted that the mystery was at last solved and that *all* the circles were fakes. One tabloid carried the story of a man named Fred Day who claimed that he had been faking the circles as a hobby for the past forty-seven years. For his revelation, Fred Day demanded the reward of ten thousand pounds offered by another paper. Meanwhile, other circles kept appearing all over the countryside, most of which investigators were unable to prove as fakes.

The final nail in the coffin comes from two men, "Doug and Dave," who have claimed that *they* are really the ones who made the circles. Many researchers have since thrown up their hands in disgust.

It does seem likely that hoaxers account for a significant portion of British crop circles. The complex agriglyphs only appeared after speculations of alien intelligences became widespread in 1989. It's quite possible that somebody saw this as a great opportunity to play a joke.

Crop formations of insectograms, labyrinths, scripts in "Senzar," and geometrical shapes are the best bets for hoaxes. However, there is little joy in hoaxing small circles that everybody ignores in favor of fanciful designs. Are the "single-ringer" circles also hoaxes?

If they are, we must imagine a worldwide conspiracy of hoaxers forming circles in out-of-the-way parts of Japan,

Australia, Canada, the United States, Eastern Europe, and elsewhere. This theory falls apart when one remembers that these circles have also been seen for hundreds of years.

One is reminded of Charles Fort's old tale of the "mad fishmonger." On May 28, 1881, the residents of Worcester, England awakened to find heaps of crabs and periwinkles piled in gardens, yards, fields, and roads. The learned consensus in the local paper was that a fishmonger, with dozens of assistants and carts, had gone mad and dumped the fish around the town.

The fact that no one had seen the fish appear, or any persons connected with them, made no difference. Any other explanation was unthinkable.

John A. Keel attended the Crop Circle Conference in England in the fall of 1992. He heard many theories and viewed many photographs, but left no wiser.

"I still have no explanation for this Phenomenon. I remember seeing the same thing in Ohio and West Virginia back in the 1960s and was baffled by it then. Maybe it's happening to call attention to itself."

The twentieth-century Jesuit philosopher, Teilhard de Chardin, wrote that humanity, and all earthly life, are integral parts of one interconnected mind. Through this interconnectedness, interior events are mirrored in the outer world and vice-versa, in some vast circular process.

In *The Phenomenon of Man,* published in English in 1959, he anticipated the crop circle prophets by predicting the rise of spiritual forces and a transforming, culminating event:

"Is it not possible that by the direct converging of its members, humanity will be able to release psychic powers whose existence is still unsuspected? The entire complex of inter-human and inter-cosmic relations will be charged with an immediacy, an intimacy and a realism such as has been long dreamed of.

"With this we are introduced to a fantastic and inevitable event which now begins to take shape in our perspective, the event which comes nearer with every day that passes; the end of all life on our globe, the death of the planet, the ultimate phase of the phenomenon of man. . . . What we should expect is not a halt in any shape or form, but an ultimate progress coming at its biologically-appointed hour; a maturation and a paroxysm leading ever higher into the Improbable from which we have sprung."

Whether or not one accepts crop circles as genuine evidence of "a fantastic and inevitable event," they are making their mark on our world. Since Gerald Gardner wrote about the "old religion" in the 1950s, there has been a rebirth of paganism, or white witchcraft. Devoted to healing and spiritual growth, these modern "witches" worship the forces of nature, primarily through the form of the Great Goddess.

This rise of paganism, on both sides of the Atlantic, was strengthened by the feminist movement, growing ecological awareness, and scientific ideas such as the Gaia Hypothesis. Many modern witches tend to worship outdoors, preferably at ancient sacred sites. The crop circle phenomenon provided a great boost to these and all believers in intelligent forces existing in nature, and the magic of the megalithic sites.

Though there are a few claimants to "family traditions," it seems clear that modern witchcraft is mainly a reconstruction of the ancient European religions exterminated by the Church. Those who made the stone circles, and who might have known about such strange phenomena, left no heirs in Europe.

On the other side of the world, one "pagan" tradition has continued without a break. The Aborigines of Australia, the oldest culture in the world, have their own beliefs about ley lines, sacred places, and even crop circles.

Traditional Aborigines call the natural currents of lifeforce through the earth "songlines." Various sacred points on the lines are remembered for special events or significant teachings, and a journey along the songlines is a recapitulation of Aboriginal culture and history.

Like modern witches and Native Americans, these "original people" believe that the world is full of conscious, nonhuman beings. These beings, and all traditional humans living close to nature, revere the circle as a symbol of the divine.

The crop circles are messages from the Creator, messages warning of dangerous, changing times ahead for the planet. Perhaps some of us have heard the message of the crop circles after all.

10

ALIEN GENESIS

Language is a virus from outer space.

—William S. Burroughs

COUNTLESS people around the world have speculated that ancient civilizations show the influence of an extraterrestrial intelligence. As proof they point to ruinous structures built with stone blocks of incredible size. As is often said, many of these stones defy the abilities of our own technology to move them. How were they quarried, shipped long distances, and then fitted into place? Do conservative theories of lines of miserable slaves rolling them over big logs really stand up to scrutiny?

Less obvious but equally impressive is the high level of astronomical knowledge possessed by many ancient cultures. Their extraordinary awareness of planetary orbits and faint stars is only now becoming truly appreciated in astro-archeology.

Other lines of inquiry bearing fruit are extensive linguistic studies that trace ancient languages back to a common source. Researchers have also found a surprising number of ancient symbols, in widely separated regions, sharing the same meaning. Does all this signify a once universal civilization?

During the 1960s and early '70s, there was a surge of popular belief in "ancient astronauts." Like all fads, after the initial wave of successful books and author appearances, the popularity faded away. The questionable scholarship of some researchers served to further discredit the notion.

The idea of an early alien influence lived on mainly through the sources that have always sponsored it: the trance channelers, tribal shamans, and UFO contactees. Though the merits of each of these deserve individual consideration, they are hardly the best endorsement with which to attract scientists and mainstream readers.

The topic would still be lying in limbo if not for two recent factors. The first is the enormous growth of interest in alien abductions, alien-government conspiracies, and information on historical UFO sightings. The other factor lies in the groundbreaking work of one man with superior scholarly training and methods, Zacariah Sitchin. His work, first published by mainstream publishers in the late 1970s, has gained tremendous international popularity, even claiming some respect within the scientific community.

These factors have combined to bring the discredited Ancient Astronaut Theory back to public attention. If only a tiny percentage of its premises are proven true, we may soon be rewriting our history books.

Physical anthropology has made impressive advances in recent decades. It seems that every year new discoveries of skeletal remains push back the dates of humanity's origin. However, such revelations only add to the confusion.

Though it is undisputed that *Homo erectus* first appeared in Africa approximately 1.5 million years in the past, the first *Homo sapiens* (modern man) is now said to have turned up suddenly some three hundred to five hundred thousand years ago. And there lies another mystery.

The theory of evolution posits one species being superseded by another more advanced type, in a continuing succession leading up to the present. The *Australopithecus* of 3.5 million years ago was gradually followed by *Homo habilis* (two million years ago), who preceded *Homo erectus*. The trail of genus *Homo* disappeared after that, until the advanced, present humanity suddenly arrived.

Though many of us had been taught that so-called Neanderthal man (*Homo sapiens neanderthalis*) was the missing stepping stone, this is no longer believed. Based on new excavations, it is now estimated that both Neanderthals and Cro-Magnons (*homo sapiens sapiens*) lived alongside one another in the Middle East as far back as one hundred thousand years ago. Some findings in Israeli caves actually suggest that Cro-Magnons *preceded* the Neanderthals.

Unlike the old elementary school images of Neanderthals as brutish "cave men," it is believed that they had languages, religious ceremonies, villages, and herbal medicines. According to Harvard neuroanatomist Terence Deacon, "Neanderthal's brain was bigger than ours. ... he was not dull-witted or inarticulate." The general conclusion is that Neanderthal was just another form of *Homo sapiens,* one who did not survive into modern times.

In May 1994, Reuters news services carried reports of a new archeological find raising even more questions. Shin bones from a six-foot-tall, male *Homo sapiens* were found in a quarry in Sussex, England, of all places. Boxgrove Man, named after the site, apparently ate elephants, rhinoceros, deer, and other animals. "Scattered animal bones showed that he had cut up carcasses with stone tools made from flints taken from a nearby cliff," said Geoffrey Wainwright, chief archeologist with the ten-year-old English Heritage excavation. The remains of Boxgrove Man have been dated as approximately five hundred thousand years old!

The sudden appearance of modern humanity so close to *Homo erectus* flies in the face of past evolutionary theory. It was supposed to take millions of years for a new genus to develop and then supplant earlier ones. We should not have developed so suddenly, and without a recognizable precursor (the much sought-after "missing link").

This question supports many "ancient astronaut" believers, who have long pondered the universal myths of "gods from the skies" that created the human race "in their image." Some ancient peoples went so far as to describe the gods as intentionally "mixing their blood" with hairy, primitive men.

Scholars have shrugged off records of ancient people's encounters with the gods as myths. It is interesting that most modern translators will give total credence to archaic reports of grain yields, but completely dismiss multiple-witness encounters with gods told in the same series of clay tablets.

Is there any solid archeological evidence to suggest that human beings resulted from some forgotten genetic engineering? According to modern abductees, the aliens claim to have created us in this way long ago, but those reports could just be cases of psychological projection or hallucinations. What did those ancient civilizations really believe about their origins? Were they as advanced as some people claim?

The late naturalist Ivan T. Sanderson coined the term

"OOPARTs" for "out-of-place-artifacts." These enigmas include anything that does not fit into conventional academic models of history and technology. Famous examples of OOPARTs include: optical lenses thousands of years old; electric batteries fashioned millennia before Christ; ancient maps accurately showing the coastline of Antarctica without the icecaps; cement cylinders over seven thousand years old found on Pacific islands; even pieces of machined iron found buried under tons of virgin coal. The great majority of such artifacts languish in the storage sections of museums, never to be placed on display and embarrass archeologists. Such bizarre artifacts led anomalist Charles Fort to conclude that aliens had indeed visited the earth in the past.

A "fossilized" piece of technology was reported in the Pays d'Auge region of Calvados, France in 1968. Speleologists excavating in a chalk quarry found five, reddish-brown nodules of smooth metal embedded in the rock. The objects are of different sizes, but have identical semi-oval, hollow shapes.

At first the investigators thought they were fossils, but later tests showed them to be made entirely of metal. Experiments at a forge showed the objects to have a higher carbon-content than most castings today. They were found in chalk over a hundred million years old! The "artifacts" were turned over to the Geomorphology Laboratory at the University of Caen.

Some of the megalithic buildings or monuments referred to above may also be considered OOPARTs, though their size keeps them where they stand for all to see and wonder. Besides the technology used to erect them, many of the buildings are "out of place" in that they apparently belong to ancient cultures from another continent.

The once-popular theory of "cultural diffusion" has come into extreme disfavor during these nationalistic, politically correct times. Researchers suggesting a Polynesian or Chinese influence in South America, for example, run the risk of being called racists for their trouble. The work of Thor Hyerdahl and others aside, people would much rather claim their ancestors started from scratch than admit any outside influence. Even so, the imponderables continue to pile up.

Since space-based photography became commonplace, high-resolution imaging of large regions of the planet has become another tool of archeology. Satellite technology has un-covered dozens of huge, artificial earthworks previously un-noticed. Immense canal systems in Mesopotamia, advanced networks of canals in Florida, and sophisticated irrigation systems in Central and South America have appeared to puz-zle archeologists.

Though these findings confound some academics, they do answer persistent questions of how the vast populations esti-mated for many ancient cities were fed. The ancients simply built dams, irrigated dry fields, drained swamps, and carried on a high level of waterborne trade; in fact, the same kind of systems associated with our own science of civil engineering.

Another source of large-scale artifacts are the mining and metallurgical projects of ancient man. Ancient iron smelting in North America where no one supposedly used iron, pro-cessing of tin ore and bronze manufacture in stone-age South America, huge, aboriginal copper mines with no sign of where all the metal went; there is a long list of questions.

Archeological fads may come and go, but these OOPARTs, from tiny nails inside rocks to impossible pyramids, remain real. Until we learn to account for their presence, they will continue to shake the foundations of our science and belief.

Like most people, I first heard of ancient astronauts from the sensationalistic writings of Erich von Daniken. His 1966 book, *Chariots of the Gods,* was an international best-seller. By 1974, it was already in its forty-fourth printing. It was followed by additional works, including *The Gold of the Gods,* and a number of popular documentary films.

Amazed by the size and complexity of ancient temples, von Daniken had begun investigating possible explanations for the artifacts. Borrowing from earlier writers, he amassed an immense accumulation of ancient art, statues, and struc-tures that to him, suggested alien technology. He supported his case with esoteric writings, ancient myths, and OOPARTs.

Von Daniken believed that enormous symbols visible only from the air, such as the famed Nazca Lines of Peru, once functioned as landing markers for spacecraft. He echoed So-viet author Professor Agrest's notorious theory that the impossible-for-us-to-build stone platform at Baalbek, Lebanon, was a landing pad for spaceships.

He also drew upon the Old Testament and its tales of the

"Elohim" (literally the plural term, "gods") breeding with the "daughters of man." He took this as evidence that ancient beings from another planet landed on earth in ancient times and engineered the ancestors of mankind. The cave paintings, stone and metal images, and carvings of large-headed "gods" were human attempts to portray our ancient masters.

Erich von Daniken's conclusions were viciously attacked by academics around the world. Since von Daniken's work was poorly researched and documented, his enemies had a field day. Museum of Northern Arizona archeologist Peter Pilles spoke for his colleagues when he said:

> "He makes statements that are totally opinion and states them as fact. He also completely fails to mention that there are hundreds of other possibilities for his findings. Not only is such bunk making a profit, but more important is the fact that his ideas are having a greater impact on the public than those of archeologists."

Archeologist Paul Fish continued the attack by saying, "If it can't be explained, then it's the result of extraterrestrial activity. He has the attitude that without modern technology man is incapable of doing anything on his own without extraterrestrial help or stimulation." Astronomer Carl Sagan was also incensed by "the notion that our ancestors were apparently too stupid to have built the monuments of the past."

The heated criticism was published in nearly every serious news and science publication. When it was reported that von Daniken had falsely claimed in later books to have visited certain ruins, his case was considered closed by the press (though he still fills auditoriums for his European lectures).

I found it interesting to read these twenty-year-old attacks. While some criticisms briefly alluded to the real errors in von Daniken's research, most of the attacks were based on the premise that they are "obviously ridiculous." In other words, few of his critics bothered to scientifically refute his conclusions, which says more about them than it refutes von Daniken's theories.

I was reminded of those old fantasy films where the intrepid explorer brings a living dinosaur back to London, only to have the Royal Society pooh-pooh the evidence of their eyes, because "everyone knows it is impossible." Dinosaurs probably are extinct, but public opinion is not scientific evidence. Of course, some people still believe that the world is flat, or only five thousand years old!

Erich von Daniken's work was picked up by a few maverick investigators. One of these was Austrian engineer Josef F. Blumrich, who joined the NASA space program in 1959. Blumrich helped develop the Skylab space station and the Saturn 5 rocket, and was chief of the systems layout branch of the Marshall Space Flight Center.

When he read a German edition of von Daniken's book in 1970, he was "convinced it was the same old nonsense." After coming to the section on the Prophet Ezekiel's encounter with a UFO (according to von Daniken), he found a Bible and told his wife, "I will show you where he was wrong."

Much to his surprise, Blumrich found that Ezekiel's story did make sense to him. "In chapter one, Ezekiel speaks at length about the structure of the 'fiery chariot.' It just so happens that I have myself designed such things here at NASA."

The biblical passage in question has been translated into modern English.

"One day late in June when I was thirty . . . the heavens were suddenly opened to me . . . I saw in this vision, a great storm coming toward me from the North, driving before it a huge cloud glowing with fire, with a mass of fire inside that flashed continually; and in that fire there was something that shone like polished brass. Then, from the center of the cloud, four strange forms appeared that looked like men except that each had four faces and two pairs of wings . . . and beneath their wings I could see human hands."

Blumrich followed up on the measurements given in the passage and applied his own aerodynamic knowledge on the assumption that it was a technological craft. He determined that the craft was shaped like a child's spinning top and was concave on the bottom and had a crew compartment on its top. He estimated that the object was fifty-five feet in diameter, and had rotorblades thirty-five to thirty-six feet long.

"The thrust of the engine would be about two hundred eighty thousand pounds, not much by our standards when you consider the Saturn goes into the millions." Based on his estimate of engine thrust, Blumrich believed that the "fiery chariot" was used as a shuttle vehicle between the earth and an orbiting mothership, just as employed by American astronauts on the Apollo moon landings. Blumrich's book, *The Spaceships of Ezekiel*, sold well in a number of languages and encouraged the millions of von Daniken followers.

Many believers in the ancient astronaut theory consider the Egyptian, Mayan, and Incan ruins to be alien artifacts. For decades, the untranslatable written texts on Mayan ruins, stelae, and some manuscripts have been the object of intense speculation, much of it centered around an alien theme. Some authors predicted that the eventual translation of their esoteric contents, including advanced "crystal technologies," would transform civilization as we know it.

When they were finally translated during the late 1980s, they did astonish the world, but those hoping for esoteric secrets were disappointed. The texts mainly describe the rise and fall of successive city-states, and the deeds and dynasties of their rulers. Archeologists were mainly astonished by the Mayan predilection for ceremonial warfare and human sacrifice; they had long believed the ancient Mayans were peaceful. The texts also stated that many of their wars followed the commands of their gods, communicated through their priestly class. Historians have dubbed them "Star Wars," since they followed the movements of certain constellations.

When I visited the Mayan cities in Central America, I was awed, but agreed with the archeologists that they were clearly human constructions. On the other hand, science still cannot duplicate or even explain the enormous walls of the Egyptian Great Pyramid, the platform at Baalbek, and many ruins found in the Andes. The stones used are just too big, the level of construction too skillful, for modern technology to compete with. These constructions remain the province of the ancient astronaut theorists.

Author Zacariah Sitchin is currently the strongest voice in ancient astronaut studies. Unlike von Daniken, Sitchin's works are extensively documented, and he does not fail to examine conventional explanations for his subjects. Rather than focusing on "impossible" ancient technologies, he prefers to demonstrate how modern science corroborates the ancient traditions. As he says, "I deal with facts and not with fiction."

He attended the London School of Economics, graduated from the University of London with a degree in economic history, and eventually became one of Israel's leading economists. A lifelong biblical scholar fluent in a number of modern and ancient Semitic and European languages, he is a contributing member of the Israeli Exploration Society and the Middle Eastern Studies Association of North America.

Though born in Russia, Sitchin was raised in Palestine, where he was taught to read the Old Testament in the original Hebrew. At age eight, his Hebrew class was discussing the famous quotation from the Book of Genesis, "Those were the days when there were Giants in the earth and they married the daughters of the Earth."

Young Sitchin raised his hand and asked the teacher, "Why do we say 'Giants' when the original translation of the word 'Nefilim' means 'Those who come down from Heaven?'" His teacher told him, "Sitchin, sit down! You don't question the Bible!" He remembers that he went home fuming over this incident, which initiated a lifelong interest in the original meanings of biblical texts as opposed to translators' interpretations.

After European scholars learned to translate the cuneiform tablets of Babylon, Assyria, and Sumer, Sitchin also began reading them, especially Sumerian. Like other translators, he was startled to find that the biblical Book of Genesis was an abbreviated copy made from six thousand-year-old Sumerian texts. The stories of Adam, Nimrod, the Deluge and the Ark, the Tower of Babel, Abraham, the finding of Moses in the river, and the destruction of Sodom and Gommorah were all in these pre-Hebrew records. Sitchin eventually incorporated his findings into the four volumes of *The Earth Chronicles,* now international best-sellers translated into nine languages.

What was Sumer, often called the world's first civilization? As scholars began excavating Assyrian and Babylonian sites, and then to translate the clay tablets found there, they came upon frequent references to an earlier language both peoples called "Akkadian." They eventually found the remnants of the kingdom of Akkad, and the court of its greatest King, Sargon. The age of Akkad stunned archeologists; it was a Mesopotamiam kingdom from the third millennium B.C. The later realms of Babylon and Assyria were "only branches off the Akkadian trunk."

Sargon's full title was King of Akkad, King of Kish. The records stated that before he was King of Akkad, he had been a counselor to the rulers of Kish. The investigators wondered if this Kish was an even earlier civilization. They found evidence suggesting that Sargon had been the Nimrod of the Bible, of whom it was said, "And Kush begat Nimrod; he was the first to be a hero in the land . . . and the beginning of his kingdom: Babel and Erech and Akkad." Perhaps this "Kush" was Sargon's "Kish."

If there was independent corroboration from the authors of the Bible, then perhaps the rest of the Akkadian inscriptions referred to actual places. They read the following passages, "He defeated Uruk and tore down its wall. . . . he was victorious in the battle with the inhabitants of Ur . . . he defeated the entire territory from Lagash as far as the sea." Was this Uruk the biblical city of "Erech"?

It gradually dawned on scholars that the Akkadian inscriptions were not only a different form of writing (cuneiform), but an entirely different language, neither Semitic nor Indo-European. As they learned more of the language, they began discovering words borrowed from it in later languages spread throughout the ancient Middle East.

The largest find of Akkadian texts was in the library of King Ashurbanipal in Nineveh. Many of Ashurbanipal's tablets noted that they were copies of "olden texts." One statement by Ashurbanipal himself provided the strongest clue.

"The god of scribes has bestowed on me the gift of the knowledge of his art. I have been initiated into the secrets of writing. I can even read the intricate tablets in

Shumerian. I understand the enigmatic words in the stone carvings from the days before the Flood."

It was finally suggested that recognition be provided to the existence of a pre-Akkadian language and people. Since many early Mesopotamian kings legitimized their rule with the title "King of Sumer and Akkad," the name of this earliest of civilizations became Sumer, and its people Sumerians. It has since been realized that the biblical name of "Shin'ar" means "Shumer" (the most correct spelling).

Nowadays the existence of Sumer is taken for granted and proclaimed in basic history courses as humanity's earliest civilization. The ancient cities of Sumer have all been found, including Ur, Uruk, Akkad, Sippar, Nippur, Adab, Larsa, Umma, Kish, Shurrupak, Lagash, and the earliest incarnation of Babylon. Their oldest city, Eridu, was first built in 3800 B.C. That date is when human civilization, as we know it, first appeared.

The many "firsts" of Sumer included humanity's first agriculture, yokes and plows, irrigation canals, boats and navigation, brick-making, kiln-fired ceramics, multistoried buildings, arches, walled cities, metallurgy, petroleum products, surgical implements, metal jewelry and mirrors, plastered walls and mosaics, textile industries, weights and measures, fashion wardrobes and cosmetics, beer and wine, wheeled carts, zoos, and judicial systems. They invented the wedge-shaped cuneiform writing that they used to record religious texts, histories, legal codes, shipping and trading records, ship passenger lists, genealogies, love songs, epic poetry, astronomical records, and advanced mathematics. They even wrote down musical scores and recipes for gourmet meals. Even many of their poems, lullabies, and humanitarian beliefs echo our own sentiments. Zacariah Sitchin sums up their incredible accomplishment when he says:

"As we contemplate the great Sumerian civilization, we find that not only are *our* morals and *our* sense of justice, *our* laws and architecture and arts and technologies rooted in Sumer, but the Sumerian institutions are so familiar, so close. At heart, it would seem, we are all Sumerians."

Anyone who studies the sudden appearance of Sumerian culture may justly feel amazed. After a hundred thousand or more years of *Homo sapiens* using just a few crude, chipped stone tools, there appeared a full-blown civilization out of nowhere. This civilization did not slowly develop; it was "instantly" there, writing, buildings, art, everything. This mystery is the real foundation of the Ancient Astronaut Theory.

Respected scholars endlessly repeat their astonishment. In *The Masks of God,* Joseph Campbell wrote, "With stunning abruptness . . . there appears in this little Sumerian mud garden the whole cultural syndrome that has since constituted the germinal unit of all the high civilizations of the world." How did this happen and where did they come from? What did the Sumerians have to say for themselves?

Since we are to believe their accounts of wars, shipping, and genealogies, could we suspend our disbelief when we read their own report of their origins? They wrote, "Whatever seems beautiful, we made by the grace of the gods." Many texts make clear that this was not just poetic invention, but what the Sumerians really believed.

The Sumerians venerated a pantheon of Great Gods, who ruled over an assembly of lesser gods. The gods were divided into three groups: those who lived before Earth was created and who never or rarely came down from the heavens; those who lived on Earth; and those who seemed to live in the skies and "watched" the earth. The symbol of all the gods was a cross inside a disc, often winged, found in Sumerian and the later Babylonian, Assyrian, Hittite, Egyptian, Canaanite, Hebrew, Persian, and even South American art. No matter where it is found, this symbol always stands for the gods from space.

Like the gods of Greek mythology, the Great Gods and their chief offspring on Earth were members of one large, interrelated family or clan. Human in appearance and emotion, they spent much of their time in clan struggles for dominance, negotiations, love affairs, and infidelities. Despite these attributes, they were immensely old, intelligent, and powerful.

Sumerian texts said clearly that many of these beings lived

among them in the sacred temple precincts in the center of their cities, and often issued commands or messages from them. Though each city was controlled by a particular god, they would sometimes make "state visits" to each other's territory. Some Sumerian texts detail elaborate ceremonials that the people of the city used to pay homage to the visiting gods.

They were ruled by Anu, who remained in the heavens except for rare visits. Anu's firstborn son was named Enki, but the earthly rule was held by Enlil, who may have been the son of Anu by a sister or daughter. The divine succession was passed along to the firstborn son, unless there was a son by the father and his sister or daughter. This law of dynastic incest was emulated first by the Sumerian kings, and later by the Egyptians, Babylonians, and others (including the Hebrew chiefs Abraham and Isaac).

Enki, Enlil, their children, and followers were believed to have come down to Earth in "divine birds" and "whirlwinds," which they kept stored on the flat tops of their walled temples. Sumerian depictions of these objects show either round objects with legs, or tall, conical shapes that emitted flames. The gods themselves were shown as tall humanoid beings wearing helmets that bore curling lines like horns or coils. To show that they were capable of flight, they had stylized wings behind them.

Descriptions of their flying ships used the word *"mu,"* which means variously "fiery stone," "heavenly chamber," and "that which rises straight"; in Hebrew the word is *"shem."* The biblical story of the Tower of Babel (Babylon), mentions an attempt to "raise a shem" in "the land of Shin'ar" (Shumer or Sumer).

> "The people of Babylon said, 'Let us build a city, and a tower whose top shall reach the heavens; and let us make a *shem,* lest we be scattered upon the face of the Earth.' And the Lord came down, to see the city and the tower which the Children of Adam had erected.
>
> "And he said: 'Behold, all this are as one people with one language, and this is just the beginning of their undertakings; now, anything which they shall scheme to do shall no longer be impossible for them.'
>
> "And the Lord said (to those who were with him),

'Come, let us go down, and there confound their language; so that they may not understand each other's speech.' And the Lord scattered them from there upon the face of the whole Earth, and they ceased to build the city. Therefore was its name called Babel, for there did the Lord mingle the Earth's tongue."

The Sumerian word "Babili" means "gateway of the gods." Sumerian seals and sculptures depict angry gods confronting men led by another god who are building some kind of smooth, conical object atop a ziggurat. Was this conical object the shem? If, as Zacariah Sitchin infers, the shem was a rocket, the meaning seems clear. "The flying machines were meant for the gods and not for mankind."

The Sumerian *Epic of Gilgamesh* speaks of "the land of Tilmun ("Land of the Living") where the shems were raised up"; it was also called "the landing place." Based on hundreds of references from Sumer and later cultures, Sitchin concluded that Tilmun was in the Sinai Peninsula (a long journey on foot from Sumer).

Gilgamesh, the King of Uruk, was mortal, but only half-human; his mother was one of the gods. Lamenting his mortality, Gilgamesh decided to go confront the gods in Tilmun to petition them for his own shem. After many adventures, Gilgamesh at last makes his way to Tilmun and its holy mountain. "At the Mountain of Mashu he arrived; Where daily the *shems* he watched as they depart and come in." Sitchin calls it a landing field.

After safely passing through a protective beam "that sweeps the mountains," he petitioned the gods for his own shem. He was told that this was impossible, but was permitted to meet his ancestor Utnapishtim, who had achieved immortality and dwelt with the gods. Utnapishtim told him a long version of the great Deluge, and how the god Enki had warned him to build a huge ark. Utnapishtim did so, bringing his family, animals, and "the seed of all living things" aboard his ark, which survived the Flood and eventually landed on Mount Ararat.

The earthly gods, the "Annunaki," who refused Gilgamesh's request possessed advanced magical artifacts in addition to their shems. These included fearsome weapons of light, "healing radiations," and special "tablets" that kept an open connection between Earth and the heavens. If these remarkable beings were not from Earth, where did they come from, and why were they here?

One of the oldest Sumerian texts, the "Enuma Elish," describes a time before Earth existed, when huge "gods" formed out of the primordial gases. These great gods condensed into the sun and the planets.

The "Enuma Elish" records a tremendous battle between Nibiru (the "Planet of the Crossing") and Tiamat, a huge "monster" planet. The Sumerians left many diagrams of the various planets, including Niburu (called by the Babylonians "Marduk") and Tiamat, which orbited between Mars and Jupiter. Except for Marduk and Tiamat, all the other planets are recognizable by their relative sizes and position, including the outer planets as far as Pluto.

According to Sitchin's version, the planet Marduk was a wanderer from "outside" and was "many times larger than the Earth." Caught by the sun's gravitational field, it now moves in a wide, elliptical orbit that periodically swings it into outer space and then back into the solar system. According to the Sumerians, Marduk's orbit brings it near Earth every three thousand six hundred years.

On its first entry into the solar system, Marduk's huge mass caused perturbations in the orbits of the outer planets, shifting Pluto away from its position as a moon of Saturn and into its own orbit. Marduk moved farther into the solar system, eventually sending its own moons crashing into Tiamat (except for the largest, which fell into orbit around Tiamat). Then Marduk swept on in its huge ellipse. The next time around, Marduk struck Tiamat directly, smashing the huge planet in two. One half became the asteroid belt; the other, a molten ball of rock on a new orbit closer to the Sun. The new planet was the Earth; the new moon from Marduk was our Moon.

The catastrophes had also seeded Earth with genetic and bacterial material from Marduk. As the planet cooled, this seed of life began to sprout, eventually resulting in the plants, insects, fish, and animals.

The orbit of Marduk accounts for the strange numerical system the Sumerians applied to the solar system. Like other ancient cultures, they counted the Sun and the Moon as planets. Unlike these later people, they counted the planets inwards toward the center, starting with the outer planets. Counting the nine planets, the Sun and Moon, there were eleven planets. Marduk was the twelfth planet.

Sitchin has pointed out that counting "from the outside in" only makes sense if the ones doing the counting are entering the solar system. Then, Pluto is number one, Uranus number two, and so on until the Sun.

The Sumerian symbol of the gods is also found in their representations of the solar system. This winged disc with a cross inside it stands for the planet Marduk. It is the symbol of the earthly gods because Marduk was their home planet.

The Sumerian tablets say that the gods came to Earth looking for gold four hundred fifty thousand years ago. Sitchin believes that the planet Marduk, heated by some internal source, eventually developed atmospheric problems, which threatened its life. The Annunaki found that they could strengthen their atmosphere by suspending gold particles in it. Since their earlier surveys had shown high amounts of gold on Earth, when their own supply was exhausted they mounted an expedition to our planet.

Sitchin's translation of the Sumerian creation epic covers billions of years, from the first entry of Marduk into the solar system and the creation of Earth, to the eventual rise of life on Marduk and its transfer to our planet. Strangely enough, many of his conclusions are supported by modern science.

Astronomers have long wondered about the erratic orbit of Pluto, and why an object of its size wandered so far out to the edge of the solar system. By all rights, it should be a moon of one of the outer planets.

They also suspect that the asteroid belt is the remains of a broken-up planet. However, there is not enough mass in all the asteroids to have been a planet, though their position occupies a place where a planet should have evolved. The Sumerian answer to the puzzle is that the missing mass is Earth, pushed into a different orbit!

Scientists have also found evidence of tremendous heat and destruction occurring on the moon well after its creation. As NASA officials reported in *The New York Times,*

"The most cataclysmic period came four billion years ago, when celestial bodies the size of large cities and small countries came crashing into the Moon and formed its huge basins and towering mountains. The huge amounts of radioactive materials left by the collisions began heating the rocks beneath the surface, melting massive amounts of it and forcing seas of lava through cracks on the surface."

Scientists are also concerned about the origin of life on Earth. They believe that the basic elements of life were already present on Earth only a few hundred million years after its formation. Their findings pose a challenge to researchers, since this is much too soon for life to evolve from inorganic gases and minerals (according to accepted theories).

Some researchers have suggested a "cosmic seeding theory," where the first living matter was introduced from outer space. Nobel Prize-winning scientists Francis Crick and Leslie Orgel have advanced a theory that "life on Earth may have sprung from tiny organisms from a distant planet." This accords with the Sumerian tradition that some of the "seed of life" was transmitted from Marduk to Tiamat (proto-Earth).

The Sumerian tradition of the composition of the outer planets has also startled those astronomers aware of it. For example, the Sumerians believed that Neptune "was blue-green, watery, and had patches the color of swamplike vegetation." This picture was confirmed by the space probe Voyager 2, which astonished scientists who had long thought Neptune was a gaseous planet with no water. Voyager confirmed that Neptune was blue-green, and had a "slurry mixture of water ice" on its surface. The "swamplike patches" were giant blue and yellowish-green patches.

The Sumerian picture of even more distant Uranus was of a planet battered by a monumental collision with Marduk on its way into the solar system. They had also described it as a "double" of Neptune in terms of green color and water. When Voyager passed Uranus in 1986, it not only confirmed the watery color and presence of ice, but showed that Uranus had been "knocked on its side" by some incredible catastrophe billions of years ago!

Astronomers were also excited by a wide, hundred-mile-long mark that looks like something impossibly huge had scraped by Uranus' moon, Miranda. Because of its squarish, right-angle appearance, it has been nicknamed "the Chevron" by scientists. Astronomers have called the Chevron "one of the most enigmatic objects in the solar system."

The Sumerians may have been accurate when they talked of a primordial collision in the solar system, but what of the mysterious "twelfth planet," Marduk? Is there any modern astronomical evidence for it?

The search for a "Planet X" has been making headlines for decades. Astronomers around the world have been searching the skies for a tenth planet (our numbering system) on a huge, elliptical orbit. Quite a few have announced evidence of it. In a 1983 edition of the *Washington Post,* one story announced a possible suspect.

> "A heavenly body possibly as large as the planet Jupiter and possibly so close to the Earth that it would be part of this solar system has been found in the direction of the constellation Orion by an orbiting telescope called the Infa-red Astronomical Observatory (IRAS). . . . When IRAS scientists first saw the mystery body and calculated that it could be as close as fifty billion miles, there was some speculation that it might be moving toward Earth. . . . Conceivably, it could be the tenth planet that astronomers have searched for in vain."

In 1985, the "Nemesis Theory" was proposed by physicist Luiz Alvarez and his son, geologist Walter Alvarez. Noticing that Earth has regularly suffered massive extinctions of life at periodic intervals, they speculated that a "death star" or planet passed by at regular intervals. The theory received a boost when other researchers found rare, nonterrestrial elements evenly distributed around the Earth at a depth associated with the great extinctions. For many astronomers, the eventual discovery of our tenth planet is just a matter of time.

Zacariah Sitchin found numerous Sumerian chronicles discussing the early days of the Anunnaki on Earth. They left their "Igigi" (watchers) in orbit overhead, while the main party descended to the surface. They splashed down in the Indian Ocean and made their way to Mesopotamia. After building their landing base in the Sinai, they began to mine gold in a region of Africa (where incredibly ancient mines have been found by archeologists).

The toil was initially carried out by the rank and file Anunnaki three hundred thousand years ago. There were many hardships, and eventually the miners rebelled, even to the point of holding the commander Enlil hostage. Things looked dark until Enlil's brother Enki had a brainstorm.

> "I shall create a lowly primitive; 'Man' shall be his name. I will create a primitive worker; he will be charged with the service of the gods, that they might have their ease." When asked by skeptical gods where Enki proposed to find this being, Enki replied "This creature whose name you have uttered—it exists!" All we have to do, is to "bind upon it the image of the gods."

Sitchin believes that this being was the apelike *Homo erectus,* already genetically related to the Anunnaki by reason of the seed of life from Marduk's early passing. The gods "mixed their blood" (genetic engineering?) with the apelike species, creating a being they named "the Adammu" (the Earthling). The beings were also called the "Lulu Amellu" (the mixtured worker). The experiment was a success, and the "black-headed ones" were put to work in the gold mines, ". . . to the Black-headed people, they gave the pickax to hold."

Most hybrids, such as mules, are sterile. Sitchin believes that early man, a hybrid of alien and ape, was incapable of procreation without the "hand of the gods." In an unauthorized attempt to remedy this, Enki meddled with the primitive workers and gave them the ability to reproduce. This angered the other gods, who forced the mortals to leave Eden.

The biblical story of the Garden of Eden tells of the "serpent" who tempted man to "know himself" by "eating of the fruit of the tree of knowledge." The term "knowing" is often used in the Old Testament as a euphemism for sexual relations. The symbol of Enki is the intertwined, double-serpent, still used today as the symbol of medicine. Was Enki the biblical serpent, and the forbidden "fruit" our ability to "be fruitful and multiply"?

Whatever the case, people spread over the Earth in growing numbers. Because there was still a need for "primitive workers," the gods decreed homelands and kingdoms for them. The first home of man was the region later known as Sumer. It was followed by Egypt (close to the mines), and lastly the Indus Valley, where other extremely early cities have been excavated.

Though his interpretations are his own, Sitchin did not concoct these events from imaginary sources. The tales themselves come directly from Sumerian mythology and history. The ancient sites in Sumer and in later Egypt and the Indus Valley are confirmed as the world's oldest civilizations. Linguistic and mythological research has suggested a Sumerian influence on Egypt and the Indus Valley.

These ancient cities were in close contact with gods, including those who ruled from the central temples of each city. It was from this association that disaster later struck both men and gods.

The first catastrophe rose from the situation referred to in the biblical quotation about the Nefilim mating with the "Daughters of Man." Human women (and men, probably) attracted some of the younger gods, and children from such unions began to appear. The chief of the gods, Enlil, decided that this was an unhealthy situation and cast about for a way to destroy the experiment. He was relieved of this task when informed that the coming pass of the home planet, Nibiru, would cause tremendous gravitational stress on Earth.

The gods had discovered that the ice cap of Antarctica was dangerously unstable, with large sections of ice slowly moving over a layer of slush. Nibiru's coming gravitational pull would cause a huge portion of the icecap to slide into the sea. The crash of millions of tons of ice into the ocean would not only create vast tidal waves, it would permanently raise the planetary sea level. Anyone on the surface would be drowned by the Deluge.

Forewarned by their science, the gods could depart Earth in their flying craft, but humanity would be overwhelmed. Enlil swore all the gods to silence on this issue, especially Enki, who favored his creations.

Enki swore the oath, but circumvented it by telling the secret to a wall, behind which was Utnapishtim (the biblical Noah). Speaking rhetorically, Enki suggested that "if I were a human, I would build a great ark to survive the coming flood." His monologue contained detailed measurements on the construction of this hypothetical ark. Utnapishtim got the message and built the ark in time.

When the Deluge struck in 11000 B.C., the gods flew to their orbiting base to observe the destruction of all they had built. After the waters receded, they returned only to find Utnapishtim and others, with grain and domestic animals, camped out on top of Mount Ararat. Enlil was enraged until it was pointed out that the humans would be needed to rebuild the gods' lands.

They chose to rebuild over their most ancient homes, now covered by tons of mud. They began, of course, with their spaceport in the Sinai. After thousands of years, they gave permission for the humans to build their own cities in Sumer in 3800 B.C.

The second great disaster had its origins in the jealous rivalry between the houses of Enlil and Enki. Thousands of years after the deluge, this rivalry had extended to the two gods' many sons. Key to ascendancy among the gods on Earth was the rulership of the various human cities and the nonhuman spaceport in the Sinai desert.

The gods had hit on the unpleasant strategy of using human conflicts as a way to settle their own differences. Armies of humans devoted to one god or another functioned as pieces on a chessboard; the control of the sacred cities were their prize. Many of these cities contained rare technology originally brought from the planet Marduk, motivating the competition.

The struggles between the gods led to civil wars and unrest in Sumer, Egypt, and Canaan. In the greatest of these conflicts, Abraham of Ur was sent with a cavalry force to Canaan in 2048 B.C. In this war, the nuclear forces of rival gods attacked and destroyed Sodom and Gommorah in 2024 B.C., along with the gods' great spaceport in the Sinai.

Recently, satellite photography has discovered a "great scar" in the Sinai desert. Scientists have no explanation for this burned, blackened plain that stands out from the surrounding white rocks. Could it have been the Sumerian spaceport? "That which was raised toward Anu to launch they caused to wither, its face they made fade away, its place they made desolate."

Sitchin and others locate the lost cities of Sodom and Gomorrah in a former valley, now an inlet of the Dead Sea. Archeologists have discovered that the entire region "was abruptly abandoned around 2500 B.C." and that the water of springs around the Dead Sea are contaminated with "enough radioactivity to induce sterility and related afflictions in animals and humans." It is interesting that local natives call the inlet "Lot's Sea," after the biblical survivor of Sodom.

In an interesting parallel of modern fears, it seems that the gods' reckless use of nuclear weapons backfired. A great radioactive cloud arose from the blast area and drifted east toward Sumer. So-called "lamentation texts" have been found in most of the major cities of Sumer, bemoaning an "evil wind" that killed off most of the population.

> "On that day, when heaven was crushed and the Earth was smitten, its face obliterated by the maelstrom— when the skies were darkened and covered as with a shadow. . . An evil blast heralded the baleful storm, an evil blast the forerunner of the baleful storm was; mighty offspring, valiant sons (the warring gods) were the heralds of the pestilence. Awesome weapons were used; they spread awesome rays toward the four points of the Earth, scorching everything like fire; dense clouds that bring gloom rose up to the skies, that bear the gloom from city to city.

> "On the Land befell a calamity, one unknown to man; one that had never been seen before; one which could not be withstood. The people, terrified, could hardly breathe; the Evil Wind clutched them, does not grant them another day. . . . Mouths were drenched in blood, heads wallowed in blood; the face was made pale by the Evil Wind."

As the Evil Winds "spread to the mountains as a net," the gods realized their miscalculations. "The great gods paled at its immensity. . . . the gigantic rays reach up to heaven and cause the Earth to tremble at its core." Most of the gods fled to other parts. "Then all the gods evacuated Uruk; they kept away from it, they hid in the mountains, they escaped to the distant plains." The mortal population that stayed behind were devastated. "The people were piled up in heaps; a hush settled over Uruk like a cloak."

Hundreds of ancient texts describe this immense catastrophe, which ended the Golden Age when humans and gods dwelled together on Earth. In his *Alien Identities,* mathematician and Vedic scholar Richard L. Thompson describes the parallel wars of the Hindu gods of the Indus Valley (the cradle of Hindu civilization). These wars were memorialized in the *Vedas,* the most ancient of Indian scriptures.

The *Vedas* describe the gods as traveling in *vimanas,* or flying objects. These vimanas are described variously as rocket-shaped and saucer-shaped. The gods themselves are strikingly similar to the Sumerian gods, from their travel to other planets to their clan intrigues.

Their great wars are also similar to the Sumerian gods. Weapons of destruction, such as huge "spears" that rained death upon cities or scorched the countryside, deadly mists that carried plagues, and "Evil Winds" and clouds that wiped out entire populations. Thompson's research echoes the work of many other authors who suspect the ancient Indian gods were advanced beings possessing frightening technologies.

The works of von Daniken, Sitchin, Thompson, and many others have influenced a substantial part of the populations of North America and Europe, at the least. Believers in Erich von Daniken's theories alone number in the millions. It remains to be seen what impact this huge shift in belief regarding our origins will have on education and religion.

Though other interpretations are always possible where religious beliefs are concerned, scholars may shortly be rewriting large sections of the Old Testament. The well-documented finding that Abraham was a Sumerian immigrant from the priestly class of Ur created waves in the biblical research community. Visits from space aside, the Sumerian origin of the stories of Adam and Eve, the Deluge, and the Tower of Babel cannot be discounted.

Perhaps it will be easier to assimilate Sumerian, Egyptian, and Babylonian confirmation of events recorded in the Bible, such as the destruction of Sodom and Gommorah, or the captivity of the Hebrews in Egypt. Yet the notorious "Dead Sea Scrolls scandal" over material withheld from the public for thirty-five years does not inspire confidence in scholars. The researchers and universities involved in the scandal bowed to heavy theological pressure from Israel to withhold controversial documents dating from the origin of Christianity. They were reportedly enraged when exasperated scholars outside their small group recently obtained and publicized the texts.

Sumerian knowledge of astronomy is definitely making its mark on astro-archeology. If modern astronomers searching for a tenth planet (or twelfth to the Sumerians) do find it, it will be the strongest endorsement yet of Sumerian science. If the Sumerians were correct as to the planet's inhabitants, then by the time Marduk is found again, it will be too late for reflection. The Anunnaki could already be back.

Those who refuse even to examine the ancient evidence are still confronted by the world's largest and most influential OOPART; the civilization of Sumer, from which our own culture is descended. Is it more believable that an entire race of geniuses appeared in the Stone Age and invented architecture, agriculture, cities, the wheel, metallurgy, surgery, writing, and literature from nothing, in only two or three lifetimes?

Whether we believe in the reality of ancient astronauts or not, it is indisputable that the Sumerians believed in them. We are forced to acknowledge that the veneration of alien gods from space is humanity's first organized religion, thousands of years older than Hinduism, Judaism, Christianity, Islam, and Buddhism. Perhaps modern believers are merely returning to our religious roots.

PART THREE

THE ALIEN CULTURE

*All visible objects, man, are but as
pasteboard masks.
But in each event—in the living
act, the undoubted deed—there,
some unknown but reasoning
thing puts forth the mouldings of
its features from behind the
unreasoning mask.
If man will strike, strike through
the mask!
How can the prisoner reach outside except by thrusting through
the wall?*

—HERMAN MELVILLE

11

ANGELS FROM SPACE

They are in awe of the star.

—THE BAYEUX TAPESTRY, CIRCA. 1066 A.D.

HOW many people do you know who speak with angels? Over the past fifteen years, I have met so many of them that it now seems almost commonplace. These meetings were not always sought out. The fry cook at a truck stop, a therapist on vacation, a nurse in an emergency room, some rock climbers met in a national park; people from all walks of life have similar stories of helpful or holy beings of light.

The word "angel" comes from the Greek *angelos,* meaning messenger. Most people are not aware of this Greek derivation, yet anyone will tell you that angels are God's messengers. In the Christian, Muslim, Jewish, and Sufi traditions, angels were often said to bring messages to a prophet or saint. Nowadays you do not have to be a saint to receive your own message, just someone with open ears and mind.

Numerous polls announce that people from all walks of life are returning to a belief in guardian angels, astral guides, or totem spirits. In some cases, they consider flashes of intuition to be the promptings of an angel; others claim to have witnessed holy apparitions. Many others believe in the existence of guiding spirits that communicate through certain people, or "channels" (as they are now called).

One of the world's oldest religious phenomena, "channeling" is the practice of communicating with spirits while in trance. The person who moderates between our world and that of the spirits has been called at different times a shaman, an oracle, or a medium. From Amazonian shamans, to the Oracle at Delphi, to the nineteenth-century Spiritualist Movement, people have always been fascinated by mediumship.

Quietly active throughout the early twentieth century,

channeling made a huge comeback within the modern "New Age" movement. This international, social, and spiritual movement is really a number of unrelated traditions (no matter what the Fundamentalist preachers say). One of these is the "Human Potential" movement, founded by Gestalt therapist Fritz Perls and many other authors and helping professionals, which is devoted to psychological integration and expressive communication. The ACOA Movement ("Adult Children of Alcoholics") comes under this heading.

Another is an extremely loose yoga-massage-vegetarian-health network, mainly linked through magazines, health food stores, and professional groups. Still other groups are concerned with the revival of traditional Asian and Native American religions. There are New Age Christians, New Age scientists, and New Age educators. Mixed somewhere into this diverse blend are millions of people who believe in spiritual (or alien) contact through channeling.

In the past ten years alone, channeling has spawned thousands of books, films, TV talk shows and documentaries, and magazines. It is nearly impossible to find a mainstream American who has not watched, listened to, or read about at least one channeler (in the tabloids, if not elsewhere). Channeling has even become a profitable industry in upscale places such as Maui, Los Angeles, San Francisco, Phoenix, Sedona, Santa Fe, New York, and Atlanta. Residents in these places will joke that "you can find a channeler on every street corner."

Channeling owes much of its recent popularity to mainstream film stars and other notables, such as Shirley MacLaine, who wrote favorably about channeling in her popular autobiographies. Some of the channeling "personalities," such as Ramtha or Lazaris, have made fortunes for themselves through dramatic, sensationalistic public appearances (often accompanied by huge scandals). Other channelers, including Kevin Ryerson, Dorothy MacLean, Bartholomew, and Emanuel Swedenborg, may be genuine spiritual leaders.

The influence of channeling cannot be understated; followers of channelers have left their jobs, families, and homes on the strength of personal communications from their "source." Others have found in their experiences the strength or wisdom to face their troubles. For them, a channeler was the spiritual friend they needed for inspiration or healing.

Anyone who believes that channeling cannot change people's lives should take a look at the venerable Aetherius Society. This organization was founded by the British contactee, "Sir" George King. In 1954, King was a London taxi driver when he heard a strange voice "from nowhere" speak to him in his apartment. The voice said, "Prepare yourself. You are about to become the voice of an interplanetary parliament."

Since George had already "met" an Indian sage who telephoned to London just to meet him, he took the voice's pronouncement in stride. He began allowing spirits, aliens, and even Jesus Christ to speak through him to audiences. The first contact was with a Venusian alien named "Aetherius," so George named his society in his honor.

The Aetherius Society grew to the point of having branches in Britain, the United States, Canada, Australia, New Zealand, Ghana, and Nigeria. George and his students have appeared on TV shows to millions of people, and the organization still exists today.

Their modus operandi includes influencing world events through the power of prayer. The organization took credit for saving countless lives during a disastrous Mexican earthquake. Though hundreds of people were killed, the Aetherians "saved many people who should have died." They also possess a "prayer battery" in which they store the power of seven hundred hours of prayer, to be drawn upon during emergencies.

In his 1961 book, *You Are Responsible!,* King describes his first out-of-body adventures on the planet Mars. After being attacked by an evil dwarf armed with a beam pistol, he assisted the Martians in destroying an intelligent meteor that was headed for Earth. Though the Martians were unable to stop the creature, King defeated it "with a weapon of love."

Not surprisingly, George King's followers believe in UFOs. According to one of King's present-day disciples:

"We believe that life exists on many levels and frequencies of energy manifestation. That is why some UFOs are reported as disappearing and reappearing again. They have control of matter to the point where they can travel through the frequencies, including our own. They construct physical objects on whatever plane they choose through advanced scientific methods, including thought control."

During the 1980s, the Aetherius Society gathered from across the globe on an isolated mountain top. They had come in response to King's message that the destruction of Earth was imminent, and only the faithful on the mountain would be "lifted off" by the friendly saucers. As might be guessed, the world did not end and the saucers never came. Evidently, the dates were mixed up, or perhaps it was a test of faith by the space people.

One of the earliest and most influential channelers was Emanuel Swedenborg, who died in 1772. A scholar and mining assessor to the court of the Swedish King, his mystical experiences began late in life. In 1759, when he was fifty-six years old, he had a series of prophetic dreams, ecstatic trances, and visions where he saw heaven and hell, met with God, Jesus and angels, and communicated with the dead. Some of his catatonic trances are said to have lasted for days. His modern followers call him a prophet rather than a channeler.

Believing that he had been chosen for a divine mission, Swedenborg began to preach and publish his automatic writings (texts written without conscious control of his hands). His writings deal with the hidden order of the universe, and the experience of souls after death. One of his most famous quotations was, "The departed Spirits are often terrible liars and on no account are you to believe their words."

After Swedenborg's own death a "Swedenborgian movement" grew and is still practiced by a small group of believers. His chief legacy was in reviving the validity of meeting angels outside the auspices of the authoritarian Church. His writings, combined with the principles of Mesmerism, gradually became the foundations of Spiritualism.

Mesmerism was the inheritance of Franz Mesmer, who believed that people were surrounded by a "magnetic fluid" that could be activated for healing trances. Practitioners placed patients in a trance by making mysterious passes over the bodies of patients, or slowly moving a light before their eyes.

Many people reportedly experienced definite healing from their Mesmerism sessions, and doctors of the time felt threatened enough to bring court actions against some practitioners. Besides its influence on Spiritualism, Mesmerism was the precursor of modern hypnotherapy, indispensable to alien abduction therapists.

Mentioned earlier, Spiritualism grew out of the table-rapping seances of the Fox Sisters in 1848. Though not originally intended to be a distinct religion, it quickly became one that still claims many followers in the United States and Britain. Its one notable difference from channeling appears to be its focus on materializations. Many mediums claimed to be able to temporarily manifest a spirit or other discarnate entity physically, in the presence of witnesses. A surprising number of these materializations, showing spirits and a glowing stuff called ectoplasm, were captured on film. Some of these were proven hoaxes, yet many others perplexed investigators.

The nineteenth-century mediums offered their listeners much practical advice, such as where to move, when to leave a job, leave a husband or wife, etc. Like today, most mediums were emphatic that they were unable to remember what was said during a trance. A famed Dr. Dexter, who claimed to channel Emanuel Swedenborg, said of himself:

> "I know nothing of what is written until after it is read to me, and frequently, when asked to read what is communicated to me, I have found it utterly impossible to decipher it. Not only is the thought concealed, but after it has been read to me I lose all recollection of the subject, until again my memory is refreshed by the reading."

Nineteenth-century investigators also noticed that many mediums displayed unusual characteristics, such as affected gestures and accents, when in trance. These were supposed to be proof of the personality of the inhabiting spirit. Mediums danced, played instruments they had never touched before, and even painted portraits of the beings themselves. Such actions are continued by many modern channelers.

Some mediums manifested poltergeist activity, or levitated in the view of witnesses. These effects were often enacted to convince people of the reality of the spiritual realm. In other words, they were miracles to gain converts!

Just as there are New Age meccas for modern channelers, so there were congenial watering-holes for Spiritualists. One of these was Auburn, New York, the home of a large community of believers in the teachings of Reverends T. L. Harris and James Scott. In 1850, Harris and Scott published a paper entitled "Disclosure from the Interior and Superior Care for Mortals."

Their document was filled with rambling "spirit messages" from St. John the Divine, the prophet Daniel, and the poets Shelley, Coleridge, and others. After gathering their disciples, Harris and Scott announced that "the faithful should yield themselves and their possessions to the perfect medium, James Scott." Their isolated community of about one hundred faithful was plagued with problems and infighting almost from the start.

For the first two years, Scott was able to defeat internal opposition with "messages from the spirits" that admonished the rebellious to place their trust in the "perfect medium." The community finally fell apart when allegations that they were practicing "free love" became widely known. This charge was common in many of the early Spiritualist communities; evidently the spirits did not look favorably upon monogamy.

The first modern contactee was neither caught in a beam of light from a UFO, nor was a Hollywood actress embarked on a journey of self-discovery. She was instead the daughter of an officer in the Russian Czar's army; her mother was a popular Russian novelist. Born in 1831, Helena Petrovna Blavatsky was a remarkable individual who hated the orthodoxy of her times. She once said, "When I was young, if a young man had dared to speak to me of love, I would have shot him like a dog who bit me."

Besides her disgust with marriage, she was from early childhood a seer. She used to frighten her brother and sister by telling them of the ghosts and fairies she saw in the nearby forests. She eventually overcame her loathing of marriage and wedded a Russian general, with whom she traveled the world.

Though she kept her married name of Blavatsky, she had many notorious affairs and indulged her interest in the occult.

After working as a medium in Cairo, Egypt, she was reportedly caught manipulating a cloth "spirit arm" during a seance
and forced to leave the country. She made her way to America and set up shop as a Spiritualist.

There she met the journalist Colonel Henry Olcott, who
supported Blavatsky in starting the Theosophical Society,
named after the Greek word for "God-knowledge." Supporters arrived slowly until Blavatsky produced a massive vol-
ume entitled *Isis Unveiled.* This book, filled with the ancient
secrets of the "Hidden Masters," drew thousands of followers and Theosophy became an international spiritual movement. It exists today with branches all over the world and
headquarters in India.

The literature of Theosophy is filled with tales of reincarnation, underground kingdoms, deathless masters, and angels and spirits from other worlds. Though its popularity has
waned, Theosophy had a tremendous impact on both channeling and the literature of UFOs.

Isis Unveiled and Blavatsky's follow-up work, *The Secret
Doctrine,* brought many esoteric oriental terms to the West
for the first time. Most modern contactees who speak of
auras, thought-forms, and chakras, for example, have little
idea that their vocabulary is Blavatsky's legacy. Though she
was to be accused of fraud many times in her life, she always maintained that she truly was in communication with a
secret order of immortal masters and beings of light.

While studying the channeled literature of the 1950s and
'60s, I encountered the words, "I Am," endlessly repeated.
Among the many groups and solitary mediums who used this
term for God (taken from the prophet Moses' encounter with
an entity stating "I Am That I Am"), perhaps the most successful was Guy W. Ballard.

Guy Ballard was a mining engineer who claimed an enlightenment experience with a Hidden Master atop California's Mount Shasta in 1930. The Master, who claimed to be
the legendary occultist Saint Germain, took Ballard on a journey to a mysterious sanctuary hidden under the Grand Teton
mountains of Wyoming. In the sanctuary, Ballard was shown
"golden spindles" that held the wisdom of the universe from
the days of Atlantis. He published his experiences in *The
Magic Presence,* written in 1934 under a pseudonym.

Later Ballard published *Unveiled Mysteries,* which followed the author on a trip through magnificent, secret cities in Colorado, Egypt, and India. Anticipating UFO-contactee lore, he was shown a "low-frequency radio" that enabled him to speak with beings hidden under the Earth and on other planets. Ballard wrote that the Masters were "wholly Pure, Perfect, All-powerful beings who never make a mistake."

His books were filled with anecdotes showing the Masters' penchant for helping people in need. In one case, a Master cured a disabled girl in less than a minute; another time, he drew miraculous food out of the air to feed his disciples. The Masters were aligned against "sinister forces" dedicated to preventing the evolution of humanity.

Touring the country in his cream-colored Cadillac, Ballard and his harpist wife, Edna, were successful in attracting disciples (and money). They told audiences that the coming age was going to bring the Masters out of secrecy to usher in a time of love and light. Some of their followers also claimed to see the Masters' "flying boats" entering or leaving Mount Shasta.

Though they sang spiritual hymns and preached love, the Ballards were violently intolerant of labor unions, communists, and other servants of the forces of darkness. Facing his large audiences, Ballard would wave his arms and shout, "Everyone who opposes the Light, silence them forever!" His devotees would respond by shouting, "Annihilate!"

Though Guy died in 1939, Edna Ballard hung on by claiming that Guy had not died, but instead "ascended." She was indicted in 1940 for obtaining money under false pretenses, and the case went all the way to the Supreme Court, who acquitted her. Though her movement dwindled, it still exists as the I Am Foundation near Shasta City, California.

By emphasizing underground bases, UFOs piloted by Hidden Masters, and magical "rays" from space, the I Am Movement strongly influenced channeling and interest in UFOs in the United States. Perhaps the most lasting legacy was their belief that evil, paranormal forces were the controlling influence behind communism. This statement was endlessly repeated by some later channels.

Some of the Ballards' ideas reappeared during the 1960s in a book titled *The Secret of the Andes,* penned by a mysterious

"Brother Phillip." One of a handful of books that started the esoteric counterculture of the '60s, Brother Phillip's work described Hidden Masters who dwelt in a secret valley in the Andes Mountains. Their secret abode was said to be powered by an advanced Atlantean and Lemurian "crystal technology." The Masters' lands held incredible orchards where "grapes and cherries grew to the size of oranges."

The Hidden Masters were not only vegetarians, but fruitarians, "the highest, purest diet prior to breatharianism." These highest Masters of all did not eat food made of base matter, but existed on the power of divine light and the pure mountain air.

UFOs were the vehicles of the Masters and their servants, and were used in their age-old battle against the "Brothers of the Left-Hand Path." These UFOs were powered by the fabled, giant Atlantean crystals.

This influential book was filled with odd bits of occult lore from Theosophy, Spiritualism, and UFO literature. Written in a dreamy, semibiblical style, and illustrated with fantastic mythological images, it rang a bell in the minds of those dissatisfied with mainstream society.

Literally hundreds of Americans and Europeans sold their homes and made their way to South America seeking the Hidden Masters. Many of these settled down in regions mentioned in the book. They are still there; in 1994, a *New York Times* article reported the Peruvian locals' unhappiness with "Gringo hippies" who have "taken over" their rural areas. According to the article, many of these modern hippies emigrated because of *The Secret of the Andes* (which is still in print).

There were also many stories told during the early 1970s concerning the Findhorn community in Scotland. Founded by three people with a strong faith in channeling and beings of light, their community became famous for the lush gardens flourishing on the cold, barren Scottish coast. The three gardeners claimed that elves, fairies, nature spirits, and angels were responsible for the incredible plant growth. One of their friends, a retired mathematician named Roc, experienced encounters with the pagan god Pan, who introduced him to the nature spirits.

Paul Hawken's best-selling book, *The Magic of Findhorn,*

carried the Findhorn teachings to an international audience. Well written and entertaining, it explained that the nature spirits were returning to humanity's awareness as a last-ditch effort to awaken them to the environmental crisis. They offered humans a partnership with them that could help restore the world by creating "centers of light." Findhorn was to be the first such center.

For myself and many of my friends, Hawken's book was (and is) a source of great personal inspiration. His story permitted me to hope that all those magical tales I loved as a child held a grain of truth. There *was* a consciousness in nature, and it desired us to live in harmony with the Earth.

One of Findhorn's founders, Dorothy MacLean, spoke with devas and angels on a regular basis, most often in a state of repose. For her, close contact with angels is humanity's lost birthright, one that elevates us closer to nature and God.

> "If the angels bring anything new, it is the quality of joy—appropriate now, because humanity is at the stage where we can express joy in ourselves as we make that giant step from intellect to intuition and leave behind the days of martyrdom and suffering."

Currently, Findhorn is a mature, international community with thousands of residents. The early emphasis on nature spirits has faded to make room for a new focus on humanitarian, spiritual, and family values. A vigorous, positive community, it does seem to have become a real "center of light."

One of the leaders of the Findhorn movement was channel David Spangler. Taking the work of its founders one step further, Spangler began channeling not only angels but "Space Brothers" dwelling in UFOs. According to Spangler's contacts, UFOs were scouts from a fleet of paraphysical extraterrestrials who would help raise Earth to a "new vibration" for the coming age.

> "The journey of the space brothers to your planet was partially for the purpose given of rescue and assistance, as well as for educational reasons. Your planet—our planet—ensouls a mystery deeper than the surface struggle between light and dark, a mystery dealing with

the very creation and nature of the forces of involution, evolution, and chaotic darkness.

"Because of your contacts with these in terms of dealing with the obstructiveness of your daily lives, you gain in strength and in wisdom, preparing yourselves for a destiny in the universe of considerable power and stability and earning the right to minister to other systems of evolution that are only now emerging from the cauldron of primeval creativity."

The Findhorn Press, which published Spangler's books, also reprinted another remarkable work, *A World Within a World.* Circulated within a select circle of mystics since the late 1950s, the document was said to be telepathically transmitted from a being known only as "X-7 reporting." According to X-7, he was a member of a group of intellectuals purged during Stalin's reign of terror in the Soviet Union. (Millions of "politically incorrect" Soviet citizens lost their lives at the hands of their comrades during that time.)

X-7 was herded into a group of intelligentsia bound for salt mines where they were to be worked and starved to death. Deep underground, he found himself slaving in dark tunnels with a small group of similar individuals. Eventually nearing death, a few of the group who were praying for solace observed a small, bluish light in a corner. At first visible only to those praying, it gradually became visible to all. The light provided them with a sense of peace and greater physical energy. Though they had been starving, they did not die.

Returning to the light after their shifts, the group began noticing physical changes, such as the ability to see in the dark and that their bodies were lighter and finer. These transformations, and their ability to survive starvation diets, frightened their brutal guards who nailed shut the gates leading into their tunnels. The prisoners immersed themselves in the light.

Eventually, the light took physical form as a being identifying itself as Jesus Christ, who then instructed them in a series of meditations on the various colors. Practicing meditations on the colors, they found that they could see through and even physically pass through solid rock. Their physical changes were accompanied by an expanded awareness that allowed them to peer into the past and the future.

X-7 said he communicated this story with the British mediums in order to provide guidance in the coming times of trouble. He predicted that after great turmoil, the coming age would be a time of light and love, and that hidden beings of light were preparing the way under the Earth and in space. In preparation for this, the great vessels of light in space were sending down beams of higher vibrations.

Nearly every channel since the 1950s mentions these "rays" coming from outer space. Is there anything to the idea? Even if scientists bothered to investigate, how could they prove such a thing? Perhaps the only value of such ideas is in our own subjective experiences and changing beliefs.

I once visited the ancient Mayan city of Yaxchillan, near the Usamacinta River on the Mexico-Guatemala border. Our party reached the ruins by dugout canoe from upriver. The famous site, located in the rain forest, is especially remarkable for the presence of many carved stone lintels. These wide, ancient doorways were not directly exposed to the weathering action of rain, so the beautiful, intricate carvings survived relatively intact.

On top of one of the temples, dubbed "Temple 33" by some poetic archeologist, there is a crude monolith in a small plaza. The stone looks out of place; it seems rougher than the surrounding masonry.

I was walking late at night and climbed up to the top of Temple 33 to look at the stars. The night air was warm and I decided to practice my Tai Ji (a relaxing martial art form). While I was moving through the slow, graceful postures, some sort of "outside force" seemed to grab hold of me and began dictating my every move. Though it was startling and uncharacteristic, I remained a calm observer. If it was possession (or psychosis), it seemed benign.

There seemed to be some kind of tingling energy shooting from my hands toward the monolith in question. Then when I took notice of the stone, my attention suddenly shot upwards toward the sky. The constellation of the Pleiades, among many sacred to the ancient Maya, was directly overhead.

As I gazed upwards, still moving slowly, I felt as if some

other awareness, outside of my own, awoke within me. Whatever it was, it merely looked around, as if more interested in the state of the old temple than in its temporary host.

Eventually, my strange fit wore off, and I returned to "normal." At the time, I couldn't help but wonder if I had not somehow linked up with a forgotten piece of psychic machinery used by the ancient builders of Temple 33. With the passage of time, my sense of wonder faded, and the experience was not repeated.

Perhaps no channels have produced as many books as Tuella, who communicates with the "Ashtar Command." According to Tuella, this military-sounding organization leads a fleet of Space Brothers waiting in UFOs on the outskirts of our solar system for the end of the age. When the time is right, these ships will evacuate the faithful from Earth before the "great disaster" that will destroy civilization as we know it. The Space Brothers will then return the "positive humans" to the Earth, or transfer them to a new world.

This disaster is usually described as a divine act of nature, such as a pole shift, or the collision of an asteroid with Earth. These disasters are said to be drawn to humanity because of our own negativity. Like other channels, Tuella teaches that if we can transform ourselves, Earth will not need to be destroyed.

Many people sometimes feel that the Earth needs to be cleansed; its problems (humanity) appear to be insurmountable. Some channels say that if you have even that much consciousness of the planet you live on, then you are unique and may even be a partial descendant of alien beings.

There are many ways of saying that we all come from the stars. Some spiritual traditions believe that souls can reincarnate from planet to planet, or even from the future to the past. Others are inspired by the fact that all physical matter on Earth, no matter how transformed or in what state, originally came from the heart of a star. And some believe that a few "Star People" are descended from alien-human interbreeding.

Veteran UFO investigator Brad Steiger describes the mass phenomenon of people who feel that they do not really belong on Earth, but are extraterrestrial in origin. He believes that there are numerous ways of identifying these individuals.

In addition to a lifelong feeling of alien origin, they often have unusually sharp senses; loud noises are most painful to them. For this reason, they dislike crowds. Their sleep habits are unusual in that "they appear to need little sleep, many averaging no more than three to four hours a night."

He notes that though they come from all ethnic types, they have in common compelling, heavy-lidded eyes, and other physical distinctions:

> "Nearly all of them have RH negative blood type, and they all seem to have some kind of problems with their spines. Some have extra vertebrae. Others have undetermined pain in their lower backs. They all have low, normal body temperatures. For them 98.6 degrees is a fever."

Most of them have experienced forms of supernatural phenomena throughout their lives. Upon entering adulthood, they generally experience a gradual awakening to their extraterrestrial origin. "All of them share a feeling, a knowing, an awareness that their ancestors came from another world, another dimension, another level of intelligence." Steiger speculates that they are indeed possessors of a genetic inheritance from alien ancestors.

> "Why would such long-dormant memories, if memories they be, be surfacing suddenly today? Why should this genetically transmitted awareness be breaking forth as if implanted by some chromosome time-release mechanism?"

Many of these people gravitate toward channeling groups, or start their own. Though they differ on many details, they tend to agree on their reason for coming to Earth. They came to improve the genetic stock, and to offer us the gifts of their spiritual awareness. Steiger later took to calling them "Star Maidens" instead of Star People. In his book, *The Other,* he wrote:

> "The 'people,' as they call themselves, are predominantly women. One explained to me that she knew of

only a small number of men who are fully qualified,
and only three of them had enough awareness to be
fully aware of who they were."

An interesting subgroup in the contactee-channeling community are those who believe dolphins and whales to be angelic alien beings. Not to be confused with those believing
cetaceans are an intelligent but natural earthly species, these
mediums channel dolphins as readily as they do Space Brothers or Hidden Masters.

I once attended a "Dolphin Council" held near Los Angeles in 1984. Among the many presenters was Australian Peter
Shenstone, who told the "Legend of the Golden Dolphin"
(his ongoing exploration of the myth of dolphin hyperintelli-
gence; new encounters are added as they appear).

Shenstone's introduction to the dolphin-angels occurred
during his private meditations at home. He began to hear a
high-pitched squeaking sound, which he later realized was a
dolphin speaking to him. The communications led him to
cultivate a more spiritual lifestyle, one centered around reverence for the Earth.

Unlike some who report similar experiences, Shenstone
did not devote himself to woolly minded pronouncements
designed to garner followers. A pleasant, vigorous man, he
stood out for his willingness to "walk his talk."

I later had my own encounter with a pod of wild dolphins.
While swimming in Baja's Sea of Cortez, I found myself surrounded by the playful, leaping creatures; it was an unfor-
gettable, joyous experience. If they were the aliens, then I
belong with those who wish them to land. These beautiful
creatures were supremely "normal" (as in healthy) rather than
"alien." The world would be a much poorer place without
dolphins and whales.

Revised Christian mythology is incorporated in the works
of many channels, including the "dolphin channels." In *Dolphins, Extraterrestrials and Angels* by Timothy Wyllie, the
fallen archangel Lucifer makes the statement, "The rebellion
is over and I am prepared to negotiate in the profoundest
way." According to the channeler, the forces of darkness have
recognized the futility of their struggle, and we are to expect
a new age of light and love.

The immense popularity of channeling is underscored by the multitude of "guides" available to channelers. Beings like Hilarion, El-Morya, Djal Kul, Astara, Bashar, and Sananda join biblical-sounding names such as Moses, Elijah, Samuel, John, Michael, Mary, and Jesus. One advantage to this ecumenical movement is that people feeling attracted to a particular spirit being may choose to channel it, thereby tapping into the pool of wisdom represented by its name. For example, there are hundreds of "Michael therapists" in the United States, all apparently channeling the same being.

Like the early spiritualists, it has become customary for channelers to begin with one "name" source of information, then move on to contacting additional famous beings. Some channels purport to speak for *all* the great spiritual beings of history, whatever the religion.

Perhaps the most notorious of these individuals is Elizabeth Clare Prophet, spiritual leader of Summit University and the teachings of the Ascended Masters. She survived the death of her husband, organizational founder Mark Prophet, by taking a cue from Edna Ballard and proclaiming that he had really "ascended." Prophet now heads an international organization of thousands of devoted followers, with headquarters in the American West.

Enthroned on a stage like a divine being herself, Prophet channels the Blessed Mary, Jesus, Mohammed, Buddha, Krishna, Merlin, St. Germain, and the Violet Fire, moving indiscriminately from one to the next. She has been criticized for the harshly jingoistic tenor of her speeches; for example, the now-defunct Soviet Union was an "evil empire controlled by soulless, non-human robots." On the other hand, "the forces of light have chosen North America to represent the spirit of love in the coming age."

Representatives of her "church" have reportedly been jailed for tax evasion, mail fraud, stockpiling illegal arms, holding members against their will, and hurling boiling water in the faces of receptionists at abortion clinics. Despite many of these allegations, her loyal devotees consider her a divine avatar incapable of error. Prophet's critics are shrugged off as "the unfaithful who will not survive the End Times."

Another famous channeler who fell into scandal is Ramtha,

otherwise known as J. Z. Knight. Knight was a housewife who began to trance-channel the "250,000-year-old" spirit of a wise warrior from Atlantis, named Ramtha. Well known for her dramatic television appearances, Ramtha adopted dynamic, "warrior like" poses and spoke in a lofty, "noble" tone. People would save their money to meet the hefty seminar fees, and then cry tears of joy in Ramtha's presence.

After Knight made a huge fortune from her Ramtha appearances, she began warning her followers of an impending catastrophe due in the late 1980s. The one safe place was in the Pacific Northwest, where she conveniently had large investments in real estate. Hundreds of people reportedly spent their life savings to buy land in this "safe area."

Ramtha's popularity suffered when the predicted disaster did not occur, even though she issued statements that it had been staved off by the power of prayer. A final blow came when her business manager quit, claiming that it had always been a hoax. Interestingly, he stated that J. Z. Knight had come to believe in the hoax herself.

The spirits of the recently departed are also fair game for channelers. There are books written by the spirits of John Lennon, Martin Luther King, Jr., John F. Kennedy, Albert Einstein, and even Jim Morrison and Jimi Hendrix. There is an implication that death has supplied some public figures with a wisdom that they lacked in life.

Are channels and mediums "possessed"? Throngs of scholars have noted measurable, physical changes that occur when someone is "taken over" by spirits. There is extensive documentation of practitioners in groups ranging from Voodoo to Christian Holy Rollers displaying temperature changes, epileptic fits, even huge increases in the production of saliva. The majority of these physiological changes are indistinguishable from those suffered by many UFO contactees. Whatever is going on, it affects these people physically as well as spiritually.

Anthropologist Felicitas Goodman has made a lifelong study of the phenomenon of spirit possession. In her book, *How About Demons?*, she notes that participants in belief systems accepting possession have a very different worldview than most moderns (though this situation appears to be swiftly changing).

> "What can we say about the reality of spirit beings? We can at least point out that the evidence of their presence during possession is accompanied by observable physical changes. Whether these changes are internally generated or created by external agencies is not discoverable.
>
> "As contact with such experiences in an evershrinking world becomes more frequent, it behooves us to treat what others experience with respect, and should we encounter the believers as suffering human beings, to confront them on their terms and not on our own."

Many channelers speak to the Mother of God. The Blessed Virgin Mary not only whispers to channelers, she has appeared to huge crowds of believers at Medjugorje, Lourdes, Fatima, and many other locations. Since her awe-inspiring manifestations, tens of millions of believers have made pilgrimages to the sites. Some of these pilgrims have experienced miraculous healings or had their own close encounters.

Investigator Sandra Zimdars-Schwartz notes that Marian manifestations are significant religious experiences for many of the pilgrims.

> "It is as if these persons have been able to transcend time and to enter into the experiences and meanings that first drew attention to these sites, encountering Mary for themselves in ways that reflect and build on these earlier experiences and meanings. . . . Even very simple images of these experiences are very highly treasured by their subjects."

Marian manifestations are frequently indistinguishable from UFO contacts. They display glowing lights in the skies, bizarre atmospheric phenomena, and typical witness aftereffects. Though some claim to have seen images of a white-robed female form, this in itself does not separate the xperience from other UFO encounters. Meetings with a white-robed, beautiful woman surrounded by an aura of light is a not uncommon experience in UFO literature.

What separates these experiences from most are two elements: the first being the immediate Roman Catholic interpretation placed upon the visions. If such an event had occurred in Tibet, Mecca, Haiti, or Hollywood, the interpretation would probably have been very different.

Actually, with the possible exception of Hollywood, these places *have* experienced similar spiritual manifestations. In each case, the prevailing belief systems incorporated the event into their own framework. For example, Tibet has had many sightings of Arya Tara, the Compassionate Mother who appears to those in need. Outlined in light, she looks just like the Virgin Mary.

The other distinguishing element in Marian manifestations is the fact that hundreds and thousands of people all see "something" at the same time. Theories of mob psychology aside, it is clear that at least a belief in "beings of light" remains important to humanity.

As the channeling phenomenon builds a new atmosphere of belief in Europe and the Americas, one might expect to see increasing numbers of Marian-type visions. Such manifestations are indeed reported on the rise, from the Virgin Mary appearing to Christians to "angels from space" appearing to UFO believers.

During the mid-1980s, thousands of people filed into a house near Mount Shasta to experience a "space angel" manifestation. The being kept up its appearance for days; everyone who wanted to see it had an opportunity. Some people even brought their personal quartz crystals to touch to the being, perhaps absorbing some of its sacred quality. Was the being floating in the air, or standing near a wall? No; in a uniquely American spiritual manifestation, it appeared on television, on a station tuned to an empty channel.

Many channelers focus on a coming end of the Age or the world. Real or metaphorical, it will be a catastrophic event representing a final test for a humanity already reeling from tremendous cultural changes. Perhaps channeling fulfills an important societal function by reminding us to examine what is happening around the planet.

Author Hastings addressed this aspect in his important study of channeling, *With the Tongues of Men and Angels:*

> "The entities who are making these prophesies are in the minority, perhaps a few dozen among the thousands of channelings now occurring. Still, they receive much publicity, and followers often have strong emotional reactions to the prophetic messages. Undoubtedly this is because the channeled messages are correctly perceiving the dangers and dissatisfactions of the times, as well as reflecting generalized fears and anxiety. They fit into a social archetype of prophesy—warning of catastrophes and destruction and advising that personal transformation will enable us to survive or avoid the cataclysm.
>
> "They are a reflection from unconscious levels of our individual and collective minds telling us that the situation is serious. They are not to be dismissed, inasmuch as they correspond with data from other sources of knowledge and evoke our own concern about the problems that we have created and must confront."

Some channeled books are beautiful works of modern mythology. The three volumes of *The Mind Chronicles* by astrologer Barbara Hand Clow describe a fascinating journey through a New Age, archetypal landscape. Through the persona of various players in ancient ceremonies around the world, she encounters animal spirits (including dolphins), extradimensional angels, prophets, priestesses, and alien beings. With each encounter, she must overcome some challenge or reverse evolutionary impulse to rise to the next level of existence.

Though she takes her own journey seriously, she does not lecture her readers on actions that they must take. She sees the necessary emergence of some kind of planetary consciousness, but trusts that it will unfold according to the dictates of each soul. Her approach is open enough that people may integrate her channeled material on whatever level they may, whether it be as divine revelation or simply as inspirational poetry.

The widespread belief in angels and in channeling is quietly making an impact in many areas. This impact is subtle and unseen, because it lies within our own minds and hearts. Many people describe profound life changes after such experiences, such as a greater reverence for life, or a new sense of meaning. Some report prophetic dreams, or an increased trust in their intuitive hunches. Something inside them has opened.

The growing multitude of believers and experiences has found a new way of perceiving the world, one where humanity is not alone but part of a vast cosmic tapestry of benevolent and helping beings. "Only when we dwell in the company of angels do we approach nearness to God."

Whatever one may feel about meeting spirits in person or through a channel, it is impossible to deny that it offers many people the possibility of spiritual contact outside of traditional religious dogma. There are many examples of angels or channeling helping people through difficulties, or inspiring their inner development for the first time. At its most fundamental level, banal messages and greedy charlatans aside, it is simply personal, spiritual revelation.

PROPHESIES AND PANICS

> *It's a poor memory
> that works only backwards.*
>
> —LEWIS CARROLL

EVEN if we do not believe in the real existence of alien beings, we still enjoy films about them. Who among us has not seen at least one science fiction film depicting aliens? Since the advent of video, most young people in the U.S. and Europe have seen very many of them. They have become such a commonplace aspect of our culture that few people even realize how recent and far-reaching a change this is.

As we have seen, those involved with the UFO "community," such as the Montauk Project people, often refer to their experiences in light of popular films and television shows (i.e., *The Time Tunnel*, *Total Recall*, *The Philadelphia Experiment*, and *Alternative 3*). Perhaps such films gave all of us our strange ideas.

Even when attempting to describe supernatural experiences, it seems that we are forced to use the common language of popular culture. More and more, this culture (books, TV, film) is reflecting an alien theme. Is reality being reflected in our literature and entertainment, or is our collective reality actually being created by media?

One of the strangest aspects of the UFO mystery is that many people's experiences mirror exactly the descriptions put forward in popular entertainment. Practically every alien encounter ever reported can be easily matched with a corresponding film or television show. From *Star Trek* to *Blade Runner* to *Earth Versus the Flying Saucers*, people have reported encountering beings similar to those portrayed in film. Are people then hallucinating encounters based on films that they've seen or books they've read? In many cases they have ever heard of the film or book.

Hollywood has caused great shifts in opinion. Films such as *JFK, Gandhi, "X,"* or *The Deer Hunter* galvanized an entire generation. Films have such power that they are often pointed to as a chief factor in the swift absorption of native or traditional Third World cultures into our own.

In a paper titled "Possible Extraterrestrial Strategy for Earth," Oregon State University atmospheric scientist James W. Deardorff speculated on the obvious chaos that would accompany any widespread, public alien contact. Governments would founder, mobs would panic, religious and military fanatics would react with extreme fear and violence.

Deardorff points out that any advanced, intelligent alien race would know to expect all of this from such barbarians as we. He speculates that the aliens would have a number of long-term strategies for peacefully introducing their presence and establishing communication.

One scenario would be opening communication with just a few recipients scattered about the world. The contactee would be urged to communicate their alien message, but no particular care would be taken to help the missionary. These isolated messengers would publish their books in lonely isolation, branded as kooks.

Though the unfortunate messengers are laughed off, some people will read the books. (Remember, this hypothetical alien plan covers centuries, not a few decades.) As more and more messages are disseminated over the years, the "climate of disbelief" is softened, preparing the population for full-scale contact. Deardorff notes that the mass media, such as TV and film, would be ideal vehicles for this alien contact. The decades of movies showing "friendly aliens," such as *E.T.* or *The Abyss,* would be examples of our nearing full and open contact with aliens. Are we being set up?

Early films focused on showing hostile alien contacts more than they did potential friendships. The aliens were depicted as forbidding monsters harboring evil designs on Earth and her inhabitants. I loved that old *Outer Limits* TV episode, *"How to Serve Man."* A race of advanced (large-headed) aliens establish contact with Earth's governments and media, offering vast benefits—cures for cancer, longevity, etc. Later in the episode, they begin inviting huge crowds back to their home world for a "friendship visit."

Meanwhile, teams of scientists had obtained an alien text and were feverishly racing to translate it. The book's title, *How to Serve Man*, soothed the military, who granted permission for the travel to the aliens' world. Only as the first ships were leaving did the scientists realize that the alien text was a cookbook!

Nearly a decade later, millions of Asians and Westerners watched giant alien monsters such as Mothra, Gidra, Ultraman, etc. These low-budget films and shows blended the myths of dragons and other monsters with those of UFOs. Monsters such as Gorgo or Gidra are radioactive; they jam radar and radio and witnesses come down with radiation poisoning. Many of the flying dinosaurs, such as the three-headed dragon Gidra, came from outer space.

Most of these monsters were personified forces of chaos, like an earthquake. They would stomp and crash their way through our insignificant armies on their way to the cities, usually Tokyo. Japan did not fare very well during these visits.

Other alien monsters were intelligent and benevolent. The helpful monster Gammera (a giant turtle), could retract its legs and head to turn into a scaly flying saucer emitting jets of flame. The immense caterpillar Mothra was not only a sapient monster, it was a deity with an ancient revelatory cult. Communications from Mothra were channeled through two diminutive flower fairies. Mothra often faced off against the other creatures to protect humanity.

These films took care to show that these beings came from places outside of the normal world. Whether from a watery abyss, an ancient cave, an island of monsters, or another planet, there was always an otherworldly element present. In an echo of many contactee messages, the monsters were originally disturbed by humanity's unwise experimentation with nuclear weapons. Perhaps most telling of all is that many of these beings possessed an electromagnetic aura that could stop cars, watches, etc. They seemed to be forerunners or harbingers of our future encounters with vast alien forces.

There was a rash of films in the 1950s and '60s about alien invasions or messengers. The prophetic classic, *The Day the Earth Stood Still,* starred Michael Rennie and Patricia Neal. ennie played Klaatu, a dignified alien being who landed in ashington bearing a message of peace for humanity. Once again, the cause of the alien arrival was humanity's burgeoning nuclear capacity. We were deemed ready to join the Galactic Federation of Planets.

As Klaatu emerges from his saucer bearing a scroll containing the message, a frightened soldier guns him down. He survives for a time only to be imprisoned and later killed. Klaatu's monstrous robot, Gort, picks him up and returns to the saucer. Once in the ship, Klaatu's technology temporarily brings him back from death. The Christlike Klaatu departs, after warning humanity that its freedom to war and destroy itself is nearing an end. "We are watching you now; someday, we will return."

In *Five Million Years to Earth*, construction workers in London uncover a huge missile shape, which they believe to be a German V-2 rocket left over from World War II. It is really an ancient spaceship from the planet Mars, from a time when Mars was moist and fertile (five million years ago). The ship contains the mummified corpses of insectoid aliens.

Interestingly, the ship is found on an old street called Hob's Lane, dating back to Roman times. Hob is an old name for the devil, and the street has a reputation for ghosts and a history of violent crimes. This old "power place" has an unsavory influence, caused by the buried artifact.

As our hero (a maverick scientist) begins to delve deeper into the mystery, he realizes that the Earth was once a Martian colony. The insectoid Martians, realizing their planet was doomed, sent an expeditionary force to Earth. For "primitive workers," the aliens bred humanoid apes into humanity (did Zacariah Sitchin see this film?). We are all descendants of the Martians, who did not survive on Earth. The only aliens left are us.

The ship somehow gets activated, and the majority of London's populace falls into a collective trance, or "hive mentality." Anyone who does not have the Martian genes is ruthlessly slaughtered. London is destroyed, though our hero is able to disable the ship before the disaster spreads to the surrounding countryside.

.The message of these early films was simple; the aliens were the Bad Guys, and humanity was good. Generally, the aliens came because of our nuclear weapons, and were often repulsed through the same technology. The films of the Cold

War years, in particular, displayed a paranoid fear of the stranger and a love affair of nuclear weapons. It seemed as if our God was the Bomb, and the devil was the alien. Now the Cold War has ended, the Bomb partially dismantled, and we are left with only an alien pantheon.

An entire generation, we so-called "Baby-Boomers," were raised on television shows portraying alien invasions: *The Twilight Zone, The Outer Limits, The Time Tunnel* (pre-Montauk Project), *U.F.O., Voyage to the Bottom of the Sea;* the list seems endless.

My personal favorite was *The Invaders,* starring Roy Thinnes. I especially remember the opening credits, depicting a long line of flying saucers headed toward Earth. The grave voice of an announcer said, "They came from a dying world . . ."

The invading aliens, bent upon world conquest, infiltrated into all levels of society. Only the character played by Roy Thinnes could recognize the beings (often by a strange deformation of their hands). Each episode showed him locked in one investigation or another, pursued across the country. The intense, noble Thinnes was an inspirational role model for the modern UFO investigator struggling to uncover government cover-ups.

The series' description of the aliens as conservative businessmen dressed in black and driving expensive sedans showed a marked similarity to the Men in Black phenomenon, a prominent feature of UFO lore dating back to the 1950s. In addition to the Men in Black, the show described the aliens as cold and emotionless (a characteristic our hero often used to identify his hidden opponents).

Did such TV shows influence the subconscious minds of viewers, making them susceptible to such ideas? Certainly, everyone has been exposed; the UFO-related TV shows of one generation were continued to the next one. The concepts of *The Time Tunnel* were recycled into the long-running BBC show, *Doctor Who.* The theme of *The Invaders* continued in the short-lived series, *"V,"* also about an alien invasion.

Some of the strongest influences in UFO culture come from books. *Childhood's End* by Arthur C. Clarke (who prophesied communication satellites), predicted a future of alien contact and the end of civilization as we know it. The beings contacted Earth directly, knowing full well that human civilization would collapse under the impact of an alien culture. Calling themselves the "Overlords," the aliens adopted the role of benevolent dictators, rarely interfering directly in human affairs.

The people who met the Overlords turned out to be the last human generation. Children born after that time felt, thought, and acted differently; an alien race was being born to humanity. The Overlords had merely come to midwife the birth of the new race. Normal humanity meant nothing to them at all. It remains to be seen if this is fiction, or another of Clarke's prophesies.

The South African feminist author Doris Lessing entered the field with her remarkable *Shikasta,* a book she hinted to have channeled. Written as a record of the original colonists of Earth, the work covers a period of millions of years, dating from the first seeding of life on Earth. According to *Shikasta,* the aliens consider us a lost colony of theirs, one that has forgotten its true origins. Immortal and able to exist in spirit form, the benevolent aliens frequently incarnate as human beings to help us rise back up. The greatest danger facing such alien envoys is to forget their own origins and become lost as another member of suffering humanity.

> "We sent down a technician, or two, or several. It might happen that all but one or two would be working quietly, unknown to the populace. This one would have to be born, through Zone Six, and bred in the ordinary way by suitable parents, in order that what was said by him could take effect.
>
> "As our envoy or representative grew to maturity in the chosen culture, he or she would become notable for a certain level of perception and understanding demonstrated in conduct which was nearly always at odds with the local ideas and practices. . . . The major religions were all founded by Grade 1 emissaries.
>
> "It has not been unknown for some of our own envoys, not more than a few, however, to fall victim to the pressures, either temporarily or permanently. In the latter case, they were subjected to a long period of reha-

bilitation on their return to Canopus, or sent to a suitable planet to recover."

Shikasta ties together a number of loosely connected threads, such as the beings of light seen in near-death experiences, after-death "Bardo realms," crop circles, and geomancy, ancient astronauts, experimenting aliens abducting humans, and an apocalyptic view of our approaching turn of the century. While the aliens do what they can to help, they are unable to prevent great loss of life as we destroy our planetary environment. They look forward to a time when war, disease, and natural disasters reduce humanity's swollen population to saner levels. There is perhaps a grim truth in Lessing's vision.

No discussion of "alien fictions" would be complete without mentioning the hallucinatory *Etidorhpa or The End of Earth*, written in 1894 by John Uri Lloyd. A man who enters and then betrays a secret society of initiates is punished by being sent to an alien underworld deep within the Earth. Condemned to relative immortality, he accepts his fate as a disciple of an eyeless, gray-skinned humanoid who leads him into the mysteries of underworld physics.

The recurring underworld theme among many alien contactees, including secret civilizations underground, might have been lifted verbatim from *Etidorhpa*. The work also implies a connection between psychedelic mushrooms and alien or elfin beings. Ethnobotanist Terence McKenna has uncovered evidence that the author of *Etidorhpa*, an organic chemist, knew about the hallucinogenic fungus *stropharia cubensis*. There is so much interesting material in *Etidorhpa*, ranging from the scientific to the poetic and spiritual, that one wonders what source of information John Uri Lloyd actually used.

It is clear that alien, esoteric literature influences many people. People leave their jobs, homes, and families on the strength of a channeled communication informing them that they are descended from aliens. Others descend into serious paranoia, sometimes requiring hospitalization. What causes such drastic changes? Anthropologist Desmond Morris made waves in the 1960s with his works *The Naked Ape* and *The Human Zoo*. Both works observe that much of what passes for normal human behavior is really standard primate behavior (including male dominance rituals, territorial games, and wearing makeup).

We are not so far from the apes after all. The irrepressible Robert Anton Wilson coined the term "domesticated primates" to describe normal humanity. When we are panicking in a hysterical mob chasing witches or fleeing from aliens, we are very much the domesticated primate. Encountering the alien, or our simple fear of the unknown, is one of the fastest and surest ways of uncovering our hidden primate face.

The classic modern case of apelike mob behavior occurred during H. G. Wells's radio broadcast of the novel *The War of the Worlds*. Though the work by H. G. Wells had been in print for years, listeners around the region panicked upon hearing the reports of a Martian invasion. Families barricaded their houses or fled to the hills; others armed themselves to the teeth and went looking for the Martians.

A similar hysteria occurred in the late 1940s when a man named Richard Shaver published a story entitled "I Remember Lemuria," in the pulp magazine *Amazing Stories*. His tale, which he apparently believed, described a vast underworld inhabited by degenerate, evil beings called "Deros" (for "detrimental robots"). These loathsome Deros, inheritors of a forgotten Atlantean science that included space travel and telepathy, were responsible for most of the ills plaguing humanity. In Shaver's words:

> "The Deros of the caverns could depopulate the Earth within months if they were free to do so, with the antique mech-rays. Yet you are told that there are no hidden caverns, there could not be any 'antique miracle machinery.' And I myself am to believe that I am the victim of delusions. Even though I have felt the searing rays, been tormented by invisible devices, seen impossible projections of things that do not exist on Earth today and talked to the people who manipulate and use these devices every day—and have been down in there and seen and touched it all with my own hands."

The editor of *Amazing Stories,* puckish Ray Palmer, was reportedly amazed when he received a flood of letters claiming similar experiences with the Deros. Knowing a good thing when he saw one, Palmer published more of Shaver's work and encouraged correspondence with the author. The "Shaver Mystery" rocketed the magazine to a huge subscriber list, with thousands of die-hard believers hanging on every word.

Such a seeming desire to believe in devilish aliens, or alien underworlds, is with us now. The hysteria over the fictional BBC production of *Alternative 3* continues to generate controversy. There are people who insist that this and other works of fiction are actually true stories. To them, if you think that they are just good stories, then you are "in denial."

Other than as examples of the depths to which we can sink, some fiction with an alien theme is worthwhile research material. The incredible *Miracle Visitors* by award-winning British author Ian Watson is an excellent example.

In it, a character sighting a UFO later experiences contactee symptoms, including a painful radiation burn. When seeking treatment from a sympathetic psychiatrist, he regains memories of typical alien contact. After a hypnotic session appears to create another sighting, the psychiatrist theorizes that there is a "UFO state of consciousness."

While the psychiatrist is exploring his theory, the witness loses his fundamentalist fiancée and experiences other contactee-type life changes. After meeting other contactees, the characters realize that they have been chosen to carry a message to humanity. This simplistic solution falls apart when they realize that they have constructed their own explanation. The Phenomenon is taking the answers to their questions from their own heads!

Ian Watson incorporated many of the cutting edges of UFOlogy in his work, including "phantom dinosaurs," correspondences between medieval demons, ritual magic and the aliens, and the deliberately deceptive nature of the Phenomenon. Penetrating to the heart of the "conspiracy within the conspiracy," the chief protagonist eventually realizes a pattern underlying reality, entering into a new worldview. He has become a seer on a journey through time and space. The other witnesses remain behind, locked in their own belief systems.

Watson's work is especially relevant because there does

appear to be some sort of "UFO state of consciousness." There are countless examples of witnesses and contactees reporting "strange thoughts and feelings" (some even fall asleep) just before their sighting or encounter. Did they create their experience? Perhaps, but it is also possible that their unusual frame of mind enabled them to perceive what was previously invisible. Whatever they saw, there is little doubt that it was filtered through their own belief systems, colored by their own fears, desires, and limitations.

One of the greatest names in science fiction was the late Phillip K. Dick (creator of the stories behind the films *Blade Runner* and *Total Recall*). Dick's stories are a strange, cynical blend of far-reaching vision, illusion, scholarship, and humor. What few people knew before his death was that he considered himself a seer who experienced much of what he wrote about.

His last work, found on his desk after his death, was called *VALIS,* an acronym for "Vast Active Living Intelligence System." The book is at once a scathing indictment of life in 1970s Southern California and a religious text exploring alien visitors, Gnostic Christianity, psychedelic drugs, psychotronic warfare, and illumination. It is also an autobiography.

The main character, (Phil Dick himself), is a neurotic who was attempting suicide when he was hit in the eyes by a "beam of pink light." The beam fired information into his brain, including obscure medical knowledge that allowed him to save his son's life (a real event). Though he was able to accomplish some good with his new awareness, it eventually left him more confused than ever. Glimpses of alternative worlds, communications with dead Apostles and extraterrestrials, and paranoid encounters with government mind control experiments shattered his already fragile psyche. The beam came from VALIS, described as an ancient machine orbiting the Earth.

> "VALIS is a construct," Mini said. "An artifact. It's anchored here on Earth, literally anchored. But since space and time don't exist for it, VALIS can be anywhere and at any time it wishes to. It's something they built to program us at birth; normally it fires extremely

short bursts of information at babies, engramming instructions to them which will bleed across their right hemispheres at clock-time intervals during their full lifetimes, at the appropriate situational contexts."

It takes an encounter with a self-proclaimed avatar of VALIS to help Dick put his life back together again. The avatar, a precocious child, dies suddenly, precipitating a crisis of faith for the believers. Only a few of the believers are able to rise above their old belief systems.

Though Dick highlights the connections between aliens and early religions, enlightenment and fanaticism, he was too honest a thinker to commit himself to any belief system. His works should be required reading for any student of UFOs or occult systems.

If *VALIS* is required reading, then the David Lynch/Mark Frost-produced television series *Twin Peaks* is required watching. This weekly series set new standards in cinematography and themes for mainstream television. Though the series received critical acclaim, it was too esoteric to sustain a large audience and was canceled after three seasons. The series has generated follow-up films, books, and fan magazines.

The star of the series was actor Kyle MacLachlan, who played FBI agent Dale Cooper. Cooper is called to the rural town of Twin Peaks in the Pacific Northwest to investigate the murder of a beloved high school senior, Laura Palmer. Immediately the series suggested that aliens or demons or drugs (all mixed together) were somehow responsible for Palmer's death. Agent Cooper, an unconventional sort, employs dream therapy and synchronicities (meaningful coincidences) to locate clues in his dead-end case.

The murderer is revealed as the evil spirit, "Bob," who lives in a strange otherworld populated by giants, dwarves, and doppelgängers of real people. Bob possesses various individuals in order to commit his evil deeds. This strange otherworld (where everyone talks backwards) is also home to some sort of benevolent alien race that is being investigated by the local Air Force base. The bizarre cast of characters also includes the "Log Lady," a spinster representing the forces of Light who channels significant messages from the wooden tree limb she carries around with her.

A skillfully-directed blend of humor, terror, spirituality, and soap-opera, *Twin Peaks* explored connections that researchers in many fields are only now beginning to discuss. Connections between fairies and extraterrestrials, the concept of doppelgängers as parallel selves or souls, and the distorted passage of time in the alien otherworld were all themes on the show. The series portrayed a group of invisible spirits manipulating humanity for their own ends, and the many contactee symptoms affecting those who encountered them.

Twin Peaks also examined links between alien writing and psychological symbolism, between ancient ruins and "ghosts," and between secret military projects and UFOs. Perhaps most crucial to the plot was the situation exploring repressed memories, incest, and multiple-personality disorders (MPDs). A few researchers have noted the correspondences between MPDs and so-called "possession states" in traditional societies. Linking possessing demons, mischievous fairies, and paraphysical aliens with repressed psychological traumas may be a fertile avenue for exploring the age-old alien phenomenon.

Twin Peaks was far ahead of its time. Is it possible that someday researchers will be reviewing this series for clues to the mystery of UFOs and apparitions? This appears unlikely; there was one *Twin Peaks,* but there are now at least five new, low-budget "news magazines" talking about Grays and the Government abducting housewives. If someone wants a message broadcasted, it is a simple one.

University of Denver Professor Carl Raschke writes of UFOs as "agents of cultural deconstruction." Cultural deconstruction refers to "a process whereby long-standing structures of thought and action are dismantled so that new models may take hold" (in other words, an evolutionary process).

"The work of deconstruction is not sudden, but slow and inflexible. . . . So far as UFOs are concerned, the deconstructive movement works upon human culture as a whole, although it may also have devastating effects at times on individual lives."

Deconstruction is not always pleasant to undergo, especially if it is your culture that is being dissolved. In the popular film, *The Gods Must Be Crazy,* a !Kung tribesman finds a Coke bottle dropped from a plane and brings it home to his village. The alien artifact soon causes such trouble that he embarks on a quest to the realm of the gods to return the object.

It is apparent to nearly everyone involved that Western civilization is undergoing a deconstructive process, and our films and literature mirror it. The impact of the alien is perhaps best understood as one facet of this process. Is there a new world waiting to appear after the process has ended? Raschke points out that "the deconstructive process is essential to the fashioning of new information structures that can be used to scan portions of the universe hitherto inaccessible to human intelligence." In other words, we will glimpse new worlds when the old structures have dissolved, just as the aliens have been telling us all along.

The alien voice is now heard most often through fictional films and books. Just as the shamans of the past couched their experiences in terms that hunter-gatherers could appreciate, so will our modern shaman speak in a vocabulary that moderns understand. Perhaps the best shamans will be the ones who have seen the most films.

13

CULTS OF CHAOS

*They worship the heaving earth and the ripping
sky and the rampant flame and the flooding
waters.*

—*THE NECRONOMICON*

ONE of the world's most famous scholars of ceremonial
magic reported an alien contact gone bad. The initial meditations and days of fasting were over, and his attempt at conducting a particularly difficult ritual was well under way.
After surrounding himself with the sacred circle and inscrib-
ing sacred names around the border, he began the First Call,
following it with the preliminary invocation from Abramelin.
Suddenly, a dim, glowing shape appeared in a corner of the
candlelit room. The air became colder and he swallowed with
a suddenly dry throat. His invocation had been answered too
soon!

He repeated the name of the being he had summoned, or-
dering it to manifest in the painted triangle on the floor. "Hear
me O spirit, and appear before this circle in a fair human
form. Come peaceably and visibly, in the Triangle of Art!"
When he could make out a ball of light inside the triangle, he
issued his command.

"Spirit, I summoned you that you might help me receive
communion with my Holy Guardian Angel. Identify yourself
and offer me your wisdom in controlling the fallen spirits of
your order. I command this as a duly sanctified representative
of the Most High. Do you hear and understand me?"

When he neither heard nor felt a response, he repeated the
command, adding the potent Names of God. There was no
answer; something had definitely gone wrong. He quickly
banished the spirit he'd summoned (not really sure that this
was the one he'd called), then purified the room and himself.
Maybe tomorrow he could piece together what went amiss.
He was mistaken.

All night, he heard indistinct voices murmuring in his ears. The next day, exhausted, he began to pore over his books of magic. Suddenly, he heard a crashing noise and turned around. The south wall of his garret was bursting inwards! A huge, rectangular shape of light floated into his room, upsetting his writing table and hovering before him. He fled in a panic out into the streets of Paris.

During the following days, he was haunted by poltergeist phenomena, unpleasant visions, nightmares, and feelings of extreme paranoia. He finally found relief at the hands of a more experienced occultist, who assisted him in purification rituals. In later years, he wrote down this experience in his famous magical journals as a warning to others.

The man was the legendary French occultist Eliaphas Levi, and his experience was part of a long series of mishaps that occurred when he began evoking the spirits listed in *The Sacred Magic of Abramelin the Mage*. This book is one of hundreds of *grimoires*, magical texts containing ancient formulas for calling upon angels, demons, and the spirits of the dead.

Many of the beings said to respond to these rituals were long-haired, long-fingered "beings of light," similar to the entities seen by some UFO contactees. Other spirits, sometimes employed as guardians, were huge and hairy, and had blazing red eyes. These darker, "demonic" manifestations usually emitted a stench of sulfur, or "fire and brimstone."

There were many purposes for employing ceremonies involving these beings. On the lesser side, magicians believed that they could obtain treasure, sexual favors, hidden knowledge, or cause harm to their enemies. The real purpose of magic, however, was to obtain true knowledge of God and the Holy Guardian Angel, or higher self.

The lesser pursuits were called "Low Magic" or "Black Magic," and the pursuit of spiritual knowledge was called "High Magic." A master of High Magic, as an earthly representative of the Divine, was also supposed to have dominion over the spirits of Low Magic. There were many gray areas, and the boundaries between the two systems were often blurred. On this topic, master magician Aleister Crowley wrote:

"The single supreme ritual is the attainment of the Holy Guardian Angel. It is the raising of the complete man in a straight vertical line. Any deviation from this line tends to become Black Magic. If the magician needs to perform any other operation than this, it is only lawful in that it is a necessary preliminary to that One Work."

Nowadays, the magical cults are the dark side of UFO studies. There has been a tremendous surge in the popularity of the darkest or strangest of these cults in recent years. Many of these groups focus specifically on alien beings and alien communications. Traditional UFO researchers usually ignore the beliefs and impact of such cults, even if they claim a high number of alien encounters. However, if one is really looking for "the truth," then no stone should be left unturned, even those lying in the shadows.

There have been many scholarly studies of the extraordinary rebirth of occultism in the twentieth century. The most important influence started in England, where a mystical group calling itself the Hermetic Order of the Golden Dawn was formed in 1887. The Order numbered among its members the scholar Samuel Liddell Mathers, occultist Dion Fortune, author A. E. Waite, poet William Butler Yeats, and the Astronomer Royal of Scotland.

The Golden Dawn was interested in High Magic, and its studies incorporated Hebrew Qabalah and gematria, Egyptian mythology, Greek Hermetics, medieval alchemy, Abramelin magic, and the Enochian magical system discovered by Elizabethan scholar John Dee in 1582. In their magical training they practiced visualization, chanting, prayer, fasting, astral projection, and convoluted mental exercises based on chess.

They were committed to keeping detailed magical diaries of all their experiences. Some of the members later wrote about their magical perceptions of alternate realities, gods and goddesses, spirit communications, and each other. Most of these books are now back in print.

One of the Golden Dawn's members was Aleister Crowley. Educated at Cambridge, he was a mountaineer, chess champion, poet, and a world traveler fluent in many tongues. He was extraordinarily skilled in magical studies, but grew impatient with the magical hierarchy of the Golden Dawn. Notorious for his sarcastic wit, Crowley's maneuvers eventually contributed to the dissolution of the British branch of the Order.

Crowley continued with his magical research and branched off into exploring drugs and sex as magical adjuncts. For this reason he became a notorious subject of many Sunday newspapers, who titled him "The Most Evil Man in the World." His notoriety was fed by his own ego, and he especially enjoyed donning robes, turban, and an "evil persona" for his tongue-in-cheek interviews.

Most of his in-jokes went over the heads of his newspaper readers, and contributed to his infamous reputation. For example, he told one interviewer that he sacrificed "a male child of perfect innocence" one hundred fifty times every year during his rituals. Though the papers printed this as somber truth, it later became clear that he was jokingly referring to a questionable practice of sex magic; the "one hundred fifty children" were his ejaculations (potential children).

Unsavory and arrogant as he undoubtedly was, Aleister Crowley's knowledge of magical studies was profound and sophisticated. (He himself used the spelling "Magick" to distinguish it from the stage variety.) All of his books, including the famous *Thoth Tarot* deck, are still in print. His *Magick in Theory and Practice* became the standard text in the field, eagerly read by High and Low magicians today.

The pioneering work of the Golden Dawn and Crowley's own organization, Ordo Templi Orientis (OTO), carried the mystical knowledge of the ancient world into the twentieth century. Coupled with the channeling-type practice of Spiritualism and the pseudo-Asian mysticism of Theosophy, the magical tradition formed a pool of knowledge that birthed the esoteric New Age movement of today. It also provided a system of reference that many now use to activate and interpret "alien phenomena."

Crowley defined magic as "the science and art of causing change to occur in conformity with Will." By "Will" he meant personal acts or decisions made with power or deep understanding. "Every intentional act is a Magickal act," he wrote.

Training the Will is only the first step of the aspiring magician; he or she must also endeavor to discover their True Will, or destiny. Since most magical systems teach the existence of the soul and reincarnation, each individual has different lessons or purposes for each life. Their appointed destiny is their True Will.

When people are is in touch with this Will, their intentions are aligned with the spiritual and physical laws of the universe. What they Will then comes to pass, whether it is material wealth, harm to others, healing, or self-knowledge.

As in modern physics and environmental science, magic teaches that all things are connected at a fundamental level. This web of interconnection implies that things may be manipulated by acting on corresponding factors. The principle, called "Sympathetic Magic," is behind the notion that "voodoo dolls" affect the person they represent. Besides a connecting link such as hair, blood, jewelry, or a photograph, the magical operator must *believe* that the connection is real. Belief is essential, not for the victim, but for the magician.

Magicians believe that the universe contains other forms of intelligent life: spirits, gods, demons, shades of the dead. There are two main methods of communicating with them, invocation and evocation. Invocation is done by inviting a being to share the mind and body of the practitioner, thereby elevating the magician's consciousness to the being's level. Temporarily, the magician thinks and acts as the deity does. Voodoo possession and channeling are forms of invocation (though most magicians consider unfocused channeling to be a loathsome practice).

During evocation the magician remains in control. Entities are evoked to appear outside the practitioner, often in a focus area, such as a triangle. Generally, magicians surround themselves with a circle to symbolize their identification with the Divine. When they stand within the circle, they *are* God or the gods; their commands for a spirit to appear carry divine authority.

Many of these beings are said to come from other planes or dimensions. Since magical training often includes astral journeys, magicians may decide to evoke the being on another plane, using their astral perceptions to see it. It is said to be much easier to evoke an entity this way, rather than "commanding visible appearance."

Besides the circle and triangle, there are many magical tools used in classical magic. Fairly common ones are a wand (symbolizing the Will), a dagger (the mind), a cup (emotions), a lamp (divine light), incense, and a pentacle or tablet engraved with sacred symbols. These artifacts are really just props to create the proper associations and atmosphere of belief for a magician. A very experienced magician may not need any such tools, instead using intense mental imagery.

Some magicians have wondered whether the beings they call up are real, or are just powerful, unconscious aspects of their own selves. Crowley wrote, "The spirits of *The Goetia* are the portions of the human brain." As magicians of a more practical bent have pointed out, it does not really matter so long as the magic works. The enormous popularity of magic in modern times, as great as at any other time in recorded history, suggests that many people believe it does work.

A key element in the majority of magical operations is the name of the beings called. The countless chants, prayers, and calls are loaded with names from ancient cultures. Many of the names of demons in the medieval grimoires can be directly traced to a corresponding pagan deity. The lustful demon Ashtaroth in *The Goetia,* for example, has been identified with the fertility goddess Astarte. The names changed over many generations of handwritten manuscripts passed down in secret. Mere possession of such manuscripts could be cause for prolonged torture, followed by a fiery death at the stake.

In addition to the known names of the various entities evoked or invoked, there are many words and phrases that no one understands anymore. These "Barbarous Names" are considered effective methods for entering trance states or accessing the deeper mind.

Many of these Names are repetitive, monosyllabic words that have a strange effect upon both speakers and listeners. One can easily believe them to be the last remnants of forgotten languages, or even memories of "speaking in tongues." Magicians practice reciting them in sonorous voices, "vibrating" them, or even shouting them for maximum emotional effect. The word "Goetia" itself means the "howling."

Magical literature contains many different scripts used for ritual or security purposes. Some of these alphabets are from languages long considered inherently sacred, such as Hebrew, Egyptian, and Sanskrit. Others, however, are unique; no one knows their origin. These scripts are considered to induce the same kinds of effects as the Barbarous Names, opening the mind of the reader up to alternate realities. In a sense, people seeing the characters by accident are already involuntary participants in magic, though conscious use of Will is always more powerful.

Many investigators have noticed that the strange names of magical beings closely resemble those of aliens in UFO literature. The mysterious writings attributed to alien crashes could also have been lifted directly from ancient grimoires. It does seem wise for UFO investigators to keep a good dictionary of demons and angels handy, if only to know what some of their witnesses are talking about.

One of the fountainheads of ceremonial magic is the Egyptian magical tradition. Viewing the divinities of Egyptian tradition quite differently from Zacariah Sitchin and his scholarly peers, magicians stand closer to the position of mythology. They believe that the Egyptian gods and goddesses are mythological figures with a life of their own. Some say that the Egyptian gods were paraphysical beings who once lived on Earth. Others see them as remnants of lost Atlantis, who by their sheer antiquity are worthy of evocation. For most purposes of invocation or evocation, they do not have to be "real" in the accepted sense (nor do our alien visitors).

Reading the ancient texts much as conservative scholars do, magicians see descriptions of countless "god realms" where these beings dwell. The various texts of *The Egyptian Book of the Dead* are seen as containing useful information of this sort. Some magicians claim to astral travel to these places.

A complex, sophisticated system, Egyptian magic is seen as potentially holding all the information one would need to understand the universe, or to meet the "Holy Guardian Angel." The vivid, multidimensional deities and their elaborate realms and attributes are reminiscent of Tibetan Buddhism's multitiered heavenly hierarchies. Crowley described the Egyptian Gods as ". . . so complete in their nature, so perfectly spiritual and yet so completely material."

Egypt is universally considered the birthplace of magic;

even the word "alchemy" comes from "khem," an ancient name for Egypt. Though only magicians practice the ancient Egyptian religion anymore, its influence was felt in Sufism, Gnosticism, Hermeticism, and the complex mythology of the Dogon of Africa. The gods of Egypt live on today not only through the magical renaissance, but in channeling, where people claim frequent contact with nearly all of them.

Another heavenly hierarchy comes from more obscure origins. Though there are claims that it originated in antiquity, Enochian magic was first recorded in 1582 by the British occultists John Dee and Edward Kelly.

Dee was one of the outstanding scholars of his time, a mathematician, astronomer, geographer, and antiquarian. He was also an alchemist, a magician, and the Royal Astrologer to the Queen (a respected title in those days). In a time when few people could even read their own name, Dee's keen intelligence and world travels made him a good choice as a spy; his cryptographic skills were apparently used to encode secret communications from the many royal courts he visited.

Nearly every biographer considers Edward Kelly the complete opposite of Dee. After being forced to flee his studies at Oxford for some unknown infraction, he was apparently pilloried in Lancaster for forgery. He is always depicted as wearing a low skull cap to cover his ears, which were supposedly lopped off for theft. Despite these failings, he was fascinated by the occult and is said to have been a student of Thomas Allen, a magus like Dr. Dee.

When Kelly visited Dee's home in Mortlake, the two men became friends and began one of the most fruitful collaborations in the history of magic. Dee would direct ceremonies where Kelly gazed into a black "shew-stone" (a black crystal now in the British Museum), and communicated with strange entities. He would repeat what he saw to Dee, who faithfully transcribed each detail. The operation lasted from 1582 to 1589.

The communications were in a strange, "angelic" language called Enochian, after the biblical "Enoch, who walked with God." Kelly would see an "angel" pointing to letters on tablets with hundreds of horizontal and vertical rows. Letter by letter, the angel would spell out lengthy communications to the two men. Since the Enochian language is supposed to be so powerful that speaking it aloud summons the forces involved, Kelly would just refer to the column and row numbers, never speaking the words aloud. Dee would refer to his own copies of the tablets and write down the correct letters and words.

It is somewhat unlikely that Kelly invented his visionary communications, since as an added precaution the angel dictated its messages in reverse order. At the end of the session, Dee would rewrite everything backwards, causing familiar words and names to appear. A number of scholars have declared that Enochian really is a fragment of an actual language, possessing an elementary grammar and syntax.

The names and attributes of the gods, spirits, and angels called through Enochian Magic are found by reading the various tablets and "crosses." Like sophisticated crossword puzzles, practitioners may read the rows and columns in different directions to obtain different information. The multileveled and complex but internally consistent system of Enochian magic has made it popular with many computer-friendly, modern magicians.

Practitioners of Enochian Magic claim that it really is effective. As a system of High Magic, its goal is the Great Work of illumination, rather than Low Magic. Though the Enochian hierarchy includes chaotic beings called for convenience's sake "demons," they are considered unsuitable for practical contact. Both the angelic and demonic forces are said to turn on anyone who misuses them for personal gain.

The entities of each magical system tend to have a certain reputation. The demons of the Abramelin system must be watched carefully; though they will bring you treasure or willing sexual partners, they *bite*. Less troublesome are the fallen angels of *The Goetia*, though they are unwilling partners who must sometimes be coerced. The Egyptian deities are almost too large and complex to fit into worldly concerns; practitioners contact them when concerned about life after death, astral travel, or influencing world events. The beings of Enochian magic are said to have an independent nature; when you are ready, *they* will come for *you*.

Though the beings described in magic are referred to as demons, angels, and spirits, there is little doubt that they are similar to both channeling's Hidden Masters and the abducting "visitors" from UFOs. Besides entity names and appearances, contactee aftereffects are common in magical literature. Magicians have their own history of hearing voices and experiencing paranoia, messianic delusions, or prophetic dreams. Tales of occultists whose "spirits turned on them" sound uncomfortably like those UFO contactees who fell off the deep end.

Whether the spirits are friendly or not, their communications often sound like the worst kind of gibberish. The Eighth Enochian Key provides one example:

> "The Midday, the first is as the third Heaven made of twenty-six Hyacinthine Pillars, in whom the Elders are become strong; which I have prepared for my own righteousness, saith the Lord: whose long continuance shall be as bucklers to the Stooping Dragon, and like unto the harvest of a Widow."

One way that magicians get around these nonsensical communications from angelic entities is by employing analytical systems like Qabalah. Rooted in the ancient mystical dictum that the universe is made of numbers, Qabalah uses mathematical correspondences of words and letters to find hidden meanings; a word like "hand" could also mean a light, a time of day, or any number of things. Each individual letter in a word may also mean additional words. In this way, a single Hebrew or Enochian word may be interpreted as a complete sentence. The choice of interpretation is often left to the "intuition" of the Qabalist or magician.

Through Qabalah, the (rather common) UFO encounters with aliens making silly statements could really mean something entirely different. When asked, "Where are you from?" the alien response "from anywhere, but we will be in Greece the day after tomorrow" might conceivably hold a Qabalistic message.

Then again, using the Qabalah this way could merely be a torturous excuse for wasting a magician's time. Why don't these spirits just say what they want in plain language, instead of making us jump through these intellectual hoops? The magician's lofty answer is that this way preserves "secret knowledge" from the profane; only "the Wise" will be able to truly understand the messages (implying that magicians using Qabalah are "the Wise").

Of course, if the messages were in plain language, people might judge them to be completely meaningless. Even when translated through these convoluted numerical systems, they rarely display much informational content. Drawing another parallel from UFO lore, could their only real purpose have been to distract or confuse? It's worth remembering Swedenborg's warning to "beware the words of spirits, for they are terrible liars."

The entities of magic have always been associated with certain stars, just like our extraterrestrial friends. Some entities were said to have come down from these stars in prehistoric times to teach the foundations of magic to ancient peoples. The Native American tradition of the Seven Sisters who came down from the Pleiades is one example. Other beings remained at their particular star, but could be contacted at the season when it was closest to the Earth. Polaris, revered by Taoists, and Alpha Draconis are stars of this sort.

The ancient Egyptians celebrated the annual rites of Sothis (their name for Sirius) from July 23 to September 8, at the time when the star is brightest in the sky. During this time, the Egyptian priests could most easily receive communications from the alien entities at the "dog star" Sirius (our name for this time of year, the "dog days," comes from this tradition).

There are many examples of Sirian communications in modern times. One of the most famous is Aleister Crowley's receiving *The Book of the Law* from the alien being Aiwaz, an emissary of the Egyptian god Horus. (The star Sirius is supposed to be the home of Horus and his uncle Seth, who is the origin of the Christian name, "Satan.") The book is considered indispensable by modern practitioners of Crowley's magic.

The material from Aiwaz came through under interesting conditions. Crowley and his current wife, Rose, were staying in Cairo, when Rose began acting strangely one evening, falling into a trance and muttering "They are waiting for you" and similar phrases. Crowley detested spontaneous channeling and was initially frustrated with this behavior, but then devised a number of tests to check "their" level of knowledge. When the beings (or Rose in trance) displayed a high

degree of magical and archeological understanding, he overcame his objections and began writing down the material, reportedly dictated by Rose "in a rich baritone."

The book is a poetic description of a rising current of magical force that is flooding down from the stars to Earth. There
will be profound changes in society and even in the fabric of
physical reality. Not everyone will be able to adjust; some
people will be Masters, others losers. *The Book of the Law* is
written for the potential Masters. "Is a God to live in a dog?
No! but the highest are of us. They shall rejoice, our chosen;
who sorroweth is not of us." Crouched in purple prose, the
text makes reference to the special tools of Crowleyan magicians: sex and drugs:

> "I am the Snake that giveth Knowledge and Delight
> and bright glory, and stir the hearts of men with drunk-
> enness. To worship me take wine and strange drugs
> whereof I will tell my prophet & be drunk thereof!
> They shall not harm ye at all. It is a lie, this folly
> against self."

This "religion," increasingly widespread today, is called
Thelema (for the Greek word for "will"). The main teaching
of Thelema says that "Do what thou wilt is the whole of the
Law. Love is the law, love under will. There is no law beyond
'Do what thou wilt'." Thelema is characterized by ritualized
communication with alien entities from the stars, sex Magick,
psychedelic drugs, ecstatic trance states, a Nietzchean will-to-
power, and the limitless, guilt-free dictum, "do what thou
wilt."

It is worth noting that people around the world still claim
to encounter Aiwaz, and to hear the same message from him.
Many modern Thelemites practice rituals designed to "earth
the current" emanating from Sirius and other places, thereby
paving the way for a New Age. The divine gods will live
again on Earth, and nothing will be the same.

What are these magical entities supposed to look like?
Crowley sketched a drawing of one, named "Lam," who has
a small, slender body, gray skin, diminutive facial features,
and an extraordinarily large head and eyes. Most magicians
consider Lam and his ilk to be no different from the alien

Grays reported to be abducting people. There are now active cults of Lam in Europe and North America, where people enact rituals for contacting these paraphysical aliens.

Another notorious figure who received alien communications from Sirius was psychedelic guru Timothy Leary, who wrote down his *Starseed Transmissions* during the dog days in 1973. Obtained in "nineteen bursts of information," the transmissions again describe an evolutionary leap in which stellar beings unite with humanity.

> "It is time for life on Earth to leave the planetary womb and learn to walk through the stars. The goal of evolution is to produce nervous systems capable of communicating with and returning to the Galactic Network where we, your interstellar parents, await you.
>
> "At this time the voyage home is possible. You are about to discover the key to immortality in the chemical structure of the genetic code, within which is the scripture of life. The time has come for you to accept the responsibility of immortality. It is not necessary for you to die. You will discover the key to enhanced intelligence within the chemistry of the nervous system. Certain chemicals, used wisely, will enable your nervous system to decipher the genetic code."

The literature of magic, like that of UFOs, is filled with alien communications from the stars. Are they separate phenomena, or just different descriptions of the same experience? The similarity in the messages, including an apocalyptic vision of a New Age, suggests that they originate from the same source. Perhaps it is merely temperament that causes one person to become a "scientific" UFO hunter, and another a ceremonial magician or visionary.

The life of the scientist and the magician are not always separate. Jack Parsons (1914–1952) was a rocket scientist employed by the California Institute of Technology, whose work was indispensable to the American space effort. He was also a dedicated member of Aleister Crowley's OTO (Ordo Templi Orientis). In the early 1940s, Crowley made Parsons the titular head of the Agape Lodge (the California

OTO). On his part, Parsons financially supported Crowley in his old age.

Jack Parsons believed that his True Will lay in invoking the goddess Babalon (from the Enochian magical system). This goddess is the "untamable, Divine Feminine who ushers in the New Age." Parsons had strong feelings about the debased role of the feminine in religion.

> "By debasing the mother-image into a demon-virgin-angel, (society) has denied each daughter the possibility of her fulfillment by imputing the concepts of nastiness, dirt, shamefulness, guilt, indecency and obscenity to the entire sexual process, it has poisoned the life force at its source."

Through his "Babalon Working," Parsons felt that he could begin to reverse this damage and regenerate the world. The Working was an eleven-day series of magical operations that produced storms, poltergeist manifestations, alien visitations, and turmoil throughout Parsons's magical community. At its culmination, Parsons received seventy-seven statements or aphorisms that became known as *The Book of Babalon*. Though much of the material was similar to *Liber Al*, Crowley was upset with Parsons's actions and removed him from his leadership of the California OTO.

In his daily life, Parsons's pioneering research in "jet-assisted takeoff" rockets was the forerunner of the larger, solid-fuel engines. Many of his experiments were conducted in a private laboratory in his garage in Pasadena, California. It was here that he was eventually killed, the victim of a chemical explosion.

Though official reports concluded that he had carelessly dropped fulminate of mercury in a trashcan containing cordite, others maintain that he was murdered as part of a conspiracy. Parsons's death was made even more tragic by his mother's suicide immediately after. Crushed by the news of her son's death, Mrs. Parsons swallowed a jar of sleeping pills in front of a frightened, paralyzed friend who was unable to prevent her death.

Parsons may have been a great rocket scientist, but his

writings are often mysterious and inscrutable. In a 1946 essay he wrote:

> "And thereafter he may find the Graal, ultimate consciousness. . . . For it is he, wonderful monster, embryo god, that has swum in the fish, peered from the eyes of serpents, swung with the ape, and shaken the Earth with the tramp of the tyrannosaur's hoof. It is he whose face is reflected in all heavens and hells, he, the child of the stars, the son of the ocean, this creature of dust, this wonder and terror called man."

Is this "embryo god, the child of the stars" our familiar, fetal-looking, gray alien? By saying that he is "reflected in Man," Parsons suggests the face of the alien is our own.

Many magicians now believe that Parsons's work helped usher in the modern age of aliens and UFOs. According to current OTO head Kenneth Grant:

> "The Babalon Working began in 1945–46 . . . just prior to the wave of unexplained aerial phenomena now recalled as the 'Great Flying Saucers Flap.' Parsons opened a door and something flew in."

Qliphoth, a Hebrew word, is the plural of *Qlipha* (harlot). In Qabalistic and magical terminology, Qliphothic entities are semi-intelligent energies left over from the death of a living being or person. Because of their origin, they are also referred to as "shells" or "shrouds." Long after a soul has dissolved or moved on, these Qliphothic beings may remain hovering around the Earth or in other dimensions accessible to the magician. Many of them could be described as energy vampires; others may be responsible for the nonsensical messages coming through some mediums.

The Qliphoth are said to carry some of the memories or habits of their origin. For example, a confirmed hedonist who died in unsatisfied lust may spawn a Qliphothic form that eternally hovers over living people with similar desires, attempting to drain their energies. Qliphothic entities were traditionally viewed as a cause of psychological obsession (a form of possession).

Remarkably, many modern magicians consciously seek out these astral slugs. Practitioners in the increasingly popular OTO tradition (Crowley, Parsons, Kenneth Grant), believe that the nostalgia inherent in these entities make them ideal sources of creative force. They establish a psychic connection with them (like a fictional wizard enslaving a demon), and then use them as magical batteries. Rituals invoking or contacting such entities may often employ sex and drugs.

The behavior of Qliphothic entities (or the Qliphoth-obsessed) is generally chaotic, even malignant. Some accounts list them as taking forms that sound suspiciously like our extraterrestrial visitors. Perhaps what seems to be a medical exam or genetic (sexual) sampling is really a form of vampirism! Scoffers may wish to consider the continuing, unexplained cattle mutilations occurring throughout the U.S. in light of this occult tradition.

If our aliens from space really are somehow related to Qliphothic entities (as many occultists believe), then we should be doubly warned against looking for anything of value in their communications. To quote researcher John A. Keel, "The majority of all supernatural manifestations are harmful, or at least senseless."

One of the most interesting figures in "postmodern occultism" was not an occultist at all. Howard Phillips Lovecraft (1890–1937) is widely considered to be one of the greatest horror writers of all time, ranking just below Edgar Allen Poe. A neurotic, sheltered, intensely private man, Lovecraft came from a family as strange as himself. His father, an ardent Freemason, died of syphilis-related insanity in 1898. His mother reported seeing "weird and fantastic creatures" around the house, and insisted on dressing the young Lovecraft as a girl. When he finally rebelled and adopted male attire, she avoided him and told others that she considered him ugly.

He grew up as a silent, obsessed man who was highly educated in a one-sided, self-taught fashion. He never developed any close relationships, and his one attempt at marriage was a short-lived disaster. His only friendships were all conducted through long, typed letters mailed to other authors (volumes of his fascinating letters are now in print).

Throughout his life, H. P. Lovecraft suffered poikilothermism (a rare medical condition in which the body takes on the surrounding temperature, like a reptile). One biographer writes that "to shake hands with him was like shaking hands with a corpse." Though he always considered himself a rationalist, Lovecraft was continually plagued by strange, vivid nightmares. His "profoundly disturbing dreams" became the basis of his bizarre writings.

Whether the source of his visions were dreams, neurosis, or imagination, Lovecraft effectively described human encounters with the alien. He had little interest in exploring "normal" human fears; for him, the greatest terror was the fear of the unknown, especially the unknown spaces charted by science. His tales frequently describe huge, alien forces from space that seek to invade and transform the Earth. According to him, these "Old Ones ruled Earth once and will rule again . . . when the stars are right."

These qliphothic or cthonic beings were so alien to the minds of humanity that only the most twisted or evil human beings would even consider aligning or communicating with them (though they themselves are neither good nor evil). The mere presence of these ageless forces from space was sufficient to warp the physical laws of reality. When the Old Ones return, as they eventually must, reality as we know it will cease to be.

Lovecraft's themes are curiously prophetic. Writing during the 1920s and 1930s, he frequently described cattle mutilations as an aspect of alien invasions. He emphasized the importance of ancient megalithic sites to cosmic forces, and employed them as "gateways" for the evil forces in his books. His works also contain passing references to Charles Fort and Aleister Crowley.

Lovecraft anticipated modern exobiologists by theorizing that the seeds of alien life might arrive upon Earth upon a meteorite. He also described with horror a chaotic, violent, self-obsessed stage of civilization that would signal the imminent arrival of the Old Ones. It takes little imagination to see the modern world (which he never lived to see) in his descriptions.

Many occultists believe that Lovecraft had access to magical texts of the most advanced kind. Curiously, they see him as an example of a failed magician, who spent his life fleeing in fear from forces that he should have mastered. They see his corpselike, icy physiology as a classic symptom of obsession by astral or qliphothic larvae.

Throughout his writings, Lovecraft made frequent reference to an "evil book" called *The Necronomicon*, or the "Book of Dead Names." Typically, one of his characters will find the book and recklessly read aloud one of the "barbarous invocations," thereby summoning a terrible alien monster with nasty eating habits. Lovecraft's books contain many examples of the "inhuman languages" used to invoke these beings.

Other tales have the protagonist making use of these same formulae from the book to fight the invading beings off. Where did the author find these weird invocations? Though there are persistent rumors that Lovecraft's father possessed a "strange occult manuscript," it had been thought until recently that *The Necronomicon* was merely a fictional device.

Now there are at least three contemporary versions of *The Necronomicon* in print. One is a dark, disturbing art book by the notorious Swiss artist H. R. Geiger (designer of the monster in the film *Alien*); the other two are magical texts containing rituals that you can practice at home. Both these books purport to be translations of extremely ancient texts from the Middle East, specifically Sumer.

The rituals are designed to communicate with what can only be described as "alien monsters"—immense forces of chaos that predate the origin of life on Earth. Like Lovecraft's Old Ones and the radioactive dragons of Japanese films, their mere presence is potent enough to warp the usual laws of physics (and the sanity of those present). Because they were so inimical to normal existence, the "Elder Gods" (different entities presumably on our side) walled them off in alternate dimensions. There they lurk, always hungering to return to Earth. Many of these monstrous "Sumerian" entities have the same names as the beings Lovecraft described, such as Cthulhu, Yog-Sothoth, Nyarlathotep, and Azathoth.

More than just curiosities, the books of *The Necronomicon* have become blueprints for a new generation of practicing magicians. There are now Necronomicon cults and numerous solitary practitioners. Why would anyone want to spend their time invoking such frightening, alien forces? According to the editors of one of the texts:

> "These rituals, incantations and formulae comprise some of the oldest written magickal workings in Western history. The deities and demons identified within have probably not been effectively summoned in nearly six thousand years ... the *Necronomicon* concerns deep, primeval forces that seem to pre-exist the normal archetypal images. These are forces that developed outside the Judeo-Christian mainstream. They are not necessarily demonic or qliphotic in the sense that these terms are normally understood, they simply represent power sources largely untapped and thus far ignored by twentieth-century, mainstream consciousness."

Magicians have traditionally sought power, whether for the noble purposes of High Magic or the material, violent ends of Black Magic. The goal of seeking power, at least something people can comprehend, is not so clear in "Chaos Magic."

Inappropriately named after the modern "Chaos Theory" of fractal mathematics, Chaos Magic seems to disregard the normal procedures and precautions of traditional magic. For example, instead of surrounding oneself with a protective circle symbolizing union with Divine authority, the Chaos magician simply stands on a bare floor. Traditional banishings of the forces invoked may also be disregarded. Perhaps this new breed of magician is more interested in extraordinary experiences (including demonic possession) than in spiritual evolution.

Many Chaos magicians invoke the same Crowleyan forces and deities as do the OTO. In general, sex, drugs, and feverish rituals invoking alien beings are the norm for both sets of practitioners, though serious members of the OTO continue to practice the traditional protective disciplines. Whether OTO or Chaotic in orientation, they hold in common the belief of an alien apocalypse looming on humanity's horizon.

Crowley's last disciple, OTO leader Kenneth Grant, wrote extensively on the re-emergence of the "alien" in modern times. His series, *The Typhonian Trilogies,* revolutionized the modern occult world. Over the past forty years, he reported many encounters between alien monsters, alien humanoids, and magical groups. In many cases, the interaction has not been to the benefit of the humans involved.

In *Hecate's Fountain,* Grant describes a ritual gone wrong. The officiating priestess (also a circus trapeze artist) was named Moola. She and other members of her lodge were attempting to invoke the giant alien being, Cthulhu, who is associated with deep water and deep outer space.

In Lovecraft's works, Cthulhu is an cyclopean, rubbery entity with scales, claws, bat wings, and squid-like facial tentacles. He is able to change his shape and can materialize or dematerialize at will. Truly alien to humanity, Cthulhu represents the inimical forces of chaos heralding the destruction of civilization. He speaks to people through dreams (nightmares) and physically and psychically alters his worshippers. In the Sumerian-influenced *Necronomicon,* he is called Kutulu or Cuthalu.

Moola led a ritual invoking this being while standing on a special swing over the surface of a deep, abandoned well (a symbolic gateway to the realm of Cthulhu). After chanting and ritual movement brought the participants to a state of ecstasy, she cried the invocations to her alien god. Something went dangerously wrong and the waters of the well began to boil. Her supporting ropes snapped, and she plunged screaming into the waters.

The horrified onlookers apparently saw a swaying mass of tentacles wrap themselves about Moola, dragging her down into the depths. According to Grant, ". . . although her body was spewed forth almost immediately in a rain of black fluid, her soul did not return with it. Moola remained mindless until her death."

Grant also researched and met the ancient "Cult of the Ku," which originated in Southeast Asia, but now has adherents in Europe (at least). The three thousand-year-old Chinese hieroglyph "Ku" means both "black magic" and "evil spirit." Grant found texts suggesting that human ghosts can become a Ku. According to the ancient texts:

"The Ku flies about at night and is shaped like a meteor. Its luminosity increases and it projects a human-shaped shadow. The shadow can develop a degree of intensity that enables it to copulate with women. It can then go wherever it pleases and is said to spread calamity throughout the countryside. . . . It also kidnapped human spirits."

Some sorcerers found ways to control these Ku, which sound suspiciously like UFOs. Those who can control the Ku apparently become wealthy and powerful. One way to control them is to provide a source of energy in the form of young women to be debauched and vampirized. Grant goes on to make further comparisons with UFOs:

"It is worth noting that the Ku, like UFOs, seem to avoid populous areas. It lands or earths itself in deserted regions. Another similarity with UFO lore is that the occupants of such crafts sometimes abscond with various parts of the human body (or cattle)."

Old Chinese texts described a humming, buzzing sound heard emanating from the Ku, much like modern contactees hear near UFOs. According to Grant, "the ancient Chinese were compelled to embody their observations in a 'magical' context for want of terms to describe phenomena of extraterrestrial origin."

Chaos magicians state that they are calling on the same order of beings as those who fly about in UFOs. According to messages from these entities in Grant's *Outside the Circles of Time,* the point of interacting with them is to become *as them.* The alien forces of Chaos, so long repressed, are now rising to engulf humanity. The only way to survive the confrontation with Them, they say, is for "Man to become monster." We are told to *become* the Aliens ourselves.

In an article appearing in *The Cincinnati Journal of Magic,* a magician called "Aion 131" describes this unconventional point of view:

"Forgotten memories locked in Sync—All of the Forgotten Ones who came and left, to come again.
Go to the Wild Places, there and there only am I holy, in the cities I can show only a darker mask. . . .

See this seed before thee? Another race to come, and here! One that has found root in the stellar dust.

Spin your Star Webs—I shall flow from chalice to chalice, for naught is alien to I.

Leap in Me, grow through Me, kill in the bloodlust of the animal and I will be.

What is this urge, this stirring within you? GO! Find the Wild Home you abandoned for your petty civilized ways."

Are the uncanny beings and forces described by magical cults around the world really the same as those met by UFO contactees? There are countless similarities in message, alien appearance, and contactee aftereffects. The only real difference seems to be in the opposed belief systems of the magicians and the mainstream. Increasingly, many magicians seem to be consciously pursuing an "alien" set of values.

After encountering many practitioners, I became convinced that High Magic is just as compassionate and spiritual as any other serious religious tradition. High Magic is also supposed to be effective in warding off or controlling demonic spirits, and is in fact more concerned with the human soul than with alien beings. For a contactee in a desperate situation, High Magic may be a viable alternative to psychotherapy. (Certainly, recovered memory hypnotherapy has not been proved more accurate or even more scientific than magic.)

The situation with Thelemic or Chaotic Magic seems quite different from High Magic. Like horror writers, exorcists, or psychotics, these people operate on a daily, intimate basis with alien beings. Some of them seem to be in it only for the perverse thrill of the experience. Like the stilted mediums of the nineteenth-century, their lines of communication seem too corroded for anything of value to emerge.

The image of growing cults of Chaos magicians feverishly invoking monstrous, alien gods in order to overthrow all sanity and reality is somewhat disturbing. Yet outside of isolated criminal acts (Charles Manson was reputedly involved with the California OTO), they probably do not represent a real danger to anyone but themselves and their families. There are very few master practitioners, but many "weekend magicians."

It also remains to be seen if their magical intervention is necessary at all. Our reality seems to be crumbling quite nicely on its own, as the growing numbers of unprovoked alien contacts suggest.

14

PLANETARY ELDERS

Do not fear the terrifying visions;
they are only your own confused projections.

—THE TIBETAN BOOK OF THE DEAD

WHENEVER a culture or civilization loses its way, our traditional response is to explore history for a stronger, earlier model to adopt. It happened during the breakup of the medieval world at the time of the Renaissance; society had lost direction and traditional authority its respect, so people went back to ancient Greek and Roman models and created Classicism. In the face of the monumental changes currently affecting each of us, this seeking for an older way is occurring again. Something inside us longs for the times when things were simpler and models unquestioned.

This longing for the past is obvious in late twentieth-century American politics, in the conservative emphasis on "old-fashioned" family values. It is also to be seen in the worldwide rise of violent, religious fundamentalism, and the terrorism and "ethnic cleansing" of some nationalist movements. However, as in the case of the Classicist Movement, such an impulse is not always unpleasant. Currently many people are attempting to make sense of their paranormal experiences, or even find spiritual illumination, through this principle.

We are now witnessing a huge rebirth of many spiritual traditions once thought lost forever to modernization. Native-American, Shamanic, Tibetan Buddhist, Taoist, Sufi, and Aboriginal teachings are currently undergoing a worldwide renaissance. Unlike most modern spiritual or psychological traditions, these disciplines possess methods for accepting and integrating encounters with the paranormal. Instead of denying the event, or burning unlucky witnesses, they interpret such experiences as a valid portion of each individual's spiritual process.

These lineages hold in common a strong reverence for life and the Earth. The development of wisdom and compassion is seen as of far greater importance than psychic phenomena or material gain. Recognizing that people require rites of passage to mark significant life changes, they offer vision quests, initiatic teachings, meditation retreats, and transformative experiences. In fact, many of their messages and beliefs are nearly indistinguishable from the alien communications reported by UFO contactees.

These "Earth traditions" have always stated that we are not the only intelligent race inhabiting our planet. Whether they were called spirits, dakinis, devas, or genies, these entities were remembered and understood as a part of the invisible world. Some of them were unhealthy or untrustworthy, but others could be spiritual friends and protectors.

One could seek the favors of these forces through austerities or prayers. Why would anyone consciously seek such a contact? After all, people in our culture are mocked or medicated for admitting visionary experiences. The answer is that human beings need a vision to inspire and direct their lives; a book is not always enough.

According to the late Teton Sioux medicine chief Frank Fools Crow, "the entire idea has to do with establishing a state of complete communion with *Wakan-Tanka* (God, or the Great Mystery) and the Helpers." Once this is accomplished, these beings could heal and guide us, providing comfort, strength, hope, and power.

> "The Power that we receive is for curing, healing, prophesying, solving problems, and finding lost people or objects. It is also for spreading love, transforming, and assuring peace or fertility. It is not to give us power over others because the source of power is not ourselves.
>
> "What did they look like? Lights. *Wakan-Tanka* is a huge white light. *Tunkashila* is a huge blue light. Grandmother Earth is a big green light. I speak to it, and a voice answers me out of the light. They help me see and understand what is going on in the world, and

what will be happening in the future. They tell me what I should do about this, and they enable me to prophesy. . . . They help me interpret my visions, and also the visions and dreams of people I am doing ceremonies with."

Like other sages (and contactees), Chief Fools Crow also was taken on voyages to the stars. His experiences sound exactly like those of many UFO contactees:

"I do not feel confined, in fact I am not conscious of any walls at all. It is as if I am floating in space. This is a wonderful feeling, and I wish everyone in the world could share it . . . I go faster than rockets do. I have heard about the speed of light, and what I do is more like that."

Fools Crow was revered by his people for his wisdom and healing powers. The spirits he was apparently in contact with never told him to proclaim his divinity, make money from his visions, or attack others with different faiths. If we apply the dictum, "By their fruits shall ye know them," then Fools Crow was indeed a holy man.

I learned firsthand about the power of prayer, not in a church or in Sunday School, but in a Lakota Sioux sweat lodge. This ancient Native American ceremony takes place in a small dome constructed of willow branches and covered with hides or blankets. Hot, volcanic rocks are brought in from a nearby fire and placed in a central pit. The opening is then covered up and the group sits in total darkness.

Water is splashed upon the red-hot rocks, filling the enclosed space with purifying steam. As the air becomes extremely hot and stifling, people pray aloud for friends, relatives, and all living beings. The greater the discomfort, the more fervently one prays. The discomfort (and claustrophobia) lessens if one prays selflessly.

On many occasions I witnessed examples of "helping spirits" entering a sweat lodge in response to strong prayers. Sometimes a cooling wind would blow through the sealed enclosure; on other occasions, aerial sparks, flashing lights, and strange sounds would be observed by all present. These were generally taken as an indication that people's prayers and intentions were strong and clear. In each case, participants left the lodge feeling strengthened and renewed.

The power and intensity of such prayers has caused many seemingly "miraculous" healings. People with incurable diseases, life difficulties, and relationship problems have experienced drastic improvement. Was it "the spirits" or was it the power of prayer? Teachers in these traditions maintain that it is prayer that linked one up with the Great Spirit, including his "helpers."

Several Native American spiritual leaders have stated that some of the UFO-type experiences people report are encounters with malicious or trickster-like spirits. Such beings prey upon the corrupted or unwary, but are unable to influence people protected by benevolent influences.

I met a deeply religious contactee in Sedona, Arizona. She told me, "Back in the early 1980s, I was driving through the desert east of Flagstaff when I realized that a huge light was flying overhead. I lost consciousness, and then came to in some sort of operating room; I guess it was a spaceship. There were these little, hairless men with huge eyes there. They said that they were going to take me back with them.

"I got really angry; I don't know why I wasn't paralyzed with fear, but I got mad. I started shouting at them, 'This is not lawful; you can't take me like this! I belong to the Light and It won't let you do this. This is not lawful!' "

Her statements appeared to confound the entities, who withdrew to a muttered discussion. Then one of them came back to her and told her that she was correct; she would be released. "The next thing I knew, I was back in my car, stopped by the side of the road. My engine was still running."

Before his death in the mid-1980s, Muskogee Indian elder Phillip Deere described to me the "evil" spirits.

"They play tricks, and cause disease and bad feelings. There's no point to their actions. Sometimes they are the spirits of the dead; other times they are just spirits who have never been alive. Sometimes you can see them flying, like a light in the night sky.

"They can be dangerous if you are not living a healthy life and following Spirit. If you pray to Spirit and purify yourself, then the bad spirits will leave you alone."

The chief rite of passage of most traditional Native Americans is the vision quest. Questers purify themselves, then hike out to a lonely spot in the wilderness to pray and wait for a vision. They carry no belongings or food, and often no water. They will wait and pray, sometimes for many days, until they receive a true vision providing guidance for their life.

There is considerable evidence that similar rites of passage were practiced by traditional peoples around the world, from the jungles of the Amazon to the deserts of the !Kung bushmen. Some scholars suggest that this was even the practice of most European peoples before the advent of Christianity. Ancient humanity, rooted in nature, saw the untamed wilderness as the wellspring of spiritual revelation.

But what happens to participants in such a rite? In most cases, vision questers have meaningful dreams, or strong, symbolic meetings with wildlife. Others encounter lights in the sky, awe-inspiring alien beings, or interior voices. Apparently, the only thing that makes this different from mainstream UFO contacts is that the experience is consciously sought in an attitude of humility and reverence.

I once embarked on a series of short "vision fasts" in the wilderness areas of the Southwest. One of these was in the salt desert of Ah-Shi-Sle-Pah, just outside the rugged land of Chaco Canyon National Park in New Mexico.

This remote area is a strange, surrealistic landscape of narrow ridges and mushroom-shaped stones, prone to sudden changes in weather. Leaving my car on a dirt road, I walked a few miles, finally setting my sleeping bag, groundcloth, and water bottles down under an overhanging rock, close by a huge petrified tree stump. I then began my three-night vigil with some prayers to my personal idea of spirit, asking for help and clarity.

After two days of desert quiet, I was somewhat dehydrated, and beginning to have embarrassing dreams of fast-food stands, or of nonsensical television shows from fifteen years ago. In those two days, the weather literally shifted from one hundred degree heat to thunderstorms to light snow. I spent the second night shivering and sitting up in my bag.

The next day I felt a strange, alert sense of calm. I repeated my simple prayers at intervals, and was answered by the caw of a crow, or the sight of an occasional rattlesnake slithering by. At various times scenes from my personal life came into focus, and I seemed to have that insight that only comes with great distance. This was why I had gone out there, and I was grateful for the experience.

My last night out, I became aware of a strangely luminous quality to the sky overhead. Gazing upwards, I gradually sighted what appeared to be a large, glowing eye looking down. It could have been an atmospheric phenomenon, or a UFO, but that night to me it was an eye. I felt no terror, but instead a strange sense of liberation from my earthly concerns. The eye gradually faded away into the night sky. At dawn, I packed up and went back to the car.

I repeat this experience since many UFO contactees report seeing eyes during their experiences. These eyes may be all over the place (as schizophrenics often report), or they may be the only thing that a witness remembers from a close encounter. Whitley Strieber, author of *Communion,* claimed recurring dreams of a huge eye in the sky gazing down at his house. In occult traditions, the eye is often a symbol for wisdom or the gods (as in the eye of Horus, seen on the American dollar bill).

A good friend, theater director and author Gabrielle Roth, once told me that such experiences are not to be feared, but rather explored. "Shamanic experiences are independent of culture and intrinsic to each individual. People have always had ecstatic or terrifying encounters with spirits and the otherworld, or with their own fragmented selves."

Both spiritual seekers and unwilling contactees encounter nonhuman entities. The difference lies mainly in the value they have for experiencers. The person on a successful vision quest undergoes a deeply transformative experience that instills a sense of purpose and meaning.

On the other hand, many UFO contactees experience a chaotic, seemingly pointless abduction, meeting, or message. Rather than a heightened sense of meaning, they are left wondering if there was any point at all. Their life may be a shambles, or their reputation destroyed. They may find themselves on a never-ending quest to uncover sinister government plots. The contactees who integrate their experience into a meaningful framework are few.

One factor accounting for the difference is cultural. Most moderns are cut off from traditional sources of wisdom, including our most ancient source, the world of wild nature. While writing *The Age of Missing Information,* best-selling author Bill McKibben recorded hundreds of hours of television programming from ninety-three cable stations. He then watched all of this material, seeking to decipher the information locked within our media culture. He then compared his experience with a day spent outdoors in the Adirondack mountains.

McKibben found that the natural world is full of information, and a kind of wisdom, that most people have forgotten. Millions of years of evolution, perceived through all our senses, carry a harmony impossible to find in our popular media. Not only is there information, the information is all interconnected.

Observing a hawk flying through the sky carries more knowledge than any computer bulletin board. As McKibben saw it, the highly touted "information-rich, virtual communities" are a sham, more concerned with politics, entertainment, buying, and selling. The *real information* is found in actually experiencing plants, animals, mountains, weather, and our own bodies and senses.

Little wonder that cut off from the nature of reality, insulated under a layer of cultural egotism, we lose touch with ourselves. If we are not in touch with this natural order, how will we integrate experiences of the kind that UFO contactees and shamans have? So say the traditional shamans.

Wallace Black Elk, descended from the original, famous Black Elk, is a traditional spiritual leader of the Lakota Sioux. Every year, he prays, fasts, and goes "up on the hill" (vision quests) in the mountains. He reports meeting "thunder beings," talking eagles, and "Star Nation people" (beings from space), and hearing the voice of *Wakan-Tanka.* In 1989, in Ojai, California, a small group of us gathered to hear him speak the day before he was to lead a sweat lodge.

"Grandfather" Wallace, in his sixties, is a large, active man with long braided hair. He has a huge grin, despite the almost constant pressure placed on him by radical Native American groups to cease public speaking (to non-Natives). A humble but courageous man, he refuses to bow to the pressure on the grounds that "Spirit has no skin color."

Not really sure of myself, I respectfully asked him about some of the visions he experienced when on vision quest. He was willing to talk, and described the various austerities he put himself through before a vision quest, including fasting from food and water. Though English was not his native language, he communicated clearly and forcefully.

"So when I went on a vision quest, that flying disk came from above. Those scientists call that a UFO—but they're wrong. They're wrong because they are not trained; they lost contact with all the wisdom, power, and the gift. So they have to see everything first with their naked eye. They have to catch one and shoot it down first; and then see how it was shaped and formed. But their intention is wrong, so someone is fooling those scientists that way. They won't learn the truth that way.

"So that disk landed on top of me. It was concave, and there was another one on top of that. It was silent, but it lit up the whole place. It was dark then, but those trees in front of me were luminesced like neon lights. Then these little people came, but they spoke a different language than we do. They could read minds, and I could read their minds. So there was a silent communication.

"They are human, so I welcomed them. I said, 'Welcome. Welcome. Hi, UFOs.' They laughed at that, because they knew I was joking with them. But the one who stood in front of me was dead serious. He never cracked a smile, and never even blinked his eyes. It gave me a funny feeling. It gave me goosebumps down my arms and back and on my legs.

"When I looked into his eyes, it was like a little color TV. I could see a big space back there; I could see everything in the universe through his eyes.

"What I saw in there scared me. I saw these jets flying in formation, and I heard them. Then a light came on, and they just evaporated; they were gone. Then I saw steel tanks in there. When that light came on again, they disappeared too. They sizzled and bubbled, like when you pour water on a hot grill. So I got scared. Where is our military power going to stand when that power comes? They will be no match for it. Everything will just evaporate. It's impossible to challenge the Star Nation people. So I learned a lot from those little people."

Grandfather Wallace went on to tell us that these "Star Nation people" had appeared to him many other times to warn him of an approaching, worldwide disaster. Many Native American shamans have had similar visions of our modern military-industrial might being defeated by a power from the stars, or of a violent, immanent catastrophe. The famous healer and prophet, John Lame Deer, told his vision to author Richard Erdoes:

"Listen, I saw this in my mind not long ago: In my vision the electric light will stop sometime soon. The day is coming when nature will stop the electricity.

"A young man will come, or men, who know how to shut off all electricity. It will be painful, like giving birth . . . a lot of destruction. People are being too smart, too clever; the machine stops and they are helpless, because they have forgotten how to make do without the machine.

"There is a Light Man coming, bringing a new light. It will happen before this century is over. The man who has the power will do good things, too—stop all the atomic power, stop wars, just by shutting the white electro-power off. I hope to see this, but then I'm also afraid. What will be will be."

African shaman and author Malidoma Some warns people that the "presence of the Otherworld is never trivial." He warns that rituals may sometimes backfire if not carried out in the proper respectful attitude. All the Earth peoples repeat this warning, urging practitioners never to perform a spiritual practice without first developing a strong feeling of compassion for all life.

Tibet is another ancient culture with an extensive tradition of UFO-like entities. Tibetan or "Tantric" Buddhism was born in the merging of two separate spiritual traditions, the classical Buddhism of Northern India, and the shamanic Bon religion of the early Tibetans. Bon practitioners, or Bonpos, had a notorious reputation as sorcerers in league with evil spirits. In those days, Tibet was considered an abode of active demons.

In response to the petition of the King of Tibet, the enlightened magician Padmasambhava came to defeat the demons and their human allies. Now revered by Tibetans as a second Buddha, Padmasambhava forcibly converted many of these spirits to Buddhism, posting them as eternal guardians or "Dharma protectors" of the faith.

There are many Tibetan tales of glowing lights that traveled regular routes through the sky for centuries. They were considered to be manifestations of guardian spirits protecting sacred mountains, or Nagas and Dakinis. Nagas are otherworldly spirits possessing great wealth and magical powers, often portrayed as half-serpent or reptilian. They lived in their own societies, had their own separate purposes, and were generally inimical to humanity. Were these Nagas similar to our Grays or Reptoids?

Dakinis are feminine spirits with magical powers that live in another world co-existent with ours. They can disappear or reappear, or simply be invisible. Many of them are "wrathful deities" who manifest as fearsome apparitions. Once again, people's experiences with such beings seem to reflect the amount of spiritual or shamanic training they have had. The Dakinis reserve their most dangerous aspect for those with little love or understanding.

Author and former Buddhist nun Tsultrim Allione teaches the *Chod* tradition founded by the yogini Machig Labdron. In order to reinforce and develop the understanding of egolessness and to develop compassion for all sentient beings, Machig developed the Chod practice. In this practice, after various preliminaries, the practitioner performs an "offering" of his or her body.

" 'Chod' literally means 'to cut,' referring to cutting attachment to the body and ego. First the practitioner visualizes the consciousness leaving the body through the top of the head and transforming itself into a wrathful Dakini. This wrathful entity takes her crescent-shaped knife and dismembers the practitioner . . .

offering the cadaver to every conceivable kind of being, satisfying every kind of desire these beings might have. After all beings have taken their fill, practitioners remind themselves that the offerer, the offering process, and those who have been offered to are all 'empty,' and seek to remain in the state of that understanding."

The Chod practice invokes and overcomes four different demons. Alexandra David-Neel recounted meeting a terrified practitioner of the rite in a lonely place. Realizing that the monk believed he was actually being devoured by literal demons, she sought out his teacher at a local monastery. The senior lama refused to help, stating that his student had to "realize that the demons were only his mind, too." This would probably serve as good advice for many UFO contactees.

There are many stories of Dakinis protecting caches of knowledge or secret teachings. The Dakinis will reveal their secrets when the time is ripe or the correct individual arrives on the scene. Much of these teachings are in "twilight language," which is a symbolic code, often written in the elements. Being able to read the alien language of the Dakinis is a spiritual revelation.

I once registered for a thirteen-day, intensive meditation retreat with Allione focusing specifically on Dakini practices. The night before the event, about to change my mind and not attend, I had a vivid dream. In it, I was shown a huge treasure chest buried deep in the ground. Two transparent "Dakinis" stood on either side of the spot, and the Earth gaped to reveal the chest. Inside the chest were long, ancient tapestries and banners of some heavy brocade.

The tapestries were covered with writing; the individual letters were formed of crusted jewels and gold thread. The shapes were flowing, Sanskritlike symbols similar to the "alien writing" found in contactee literature. To gaze upon the writing was to know the meaning on a very deep level. The material concerned personal suffering, memories of past lives, eternity, wisdom, and compassion.

The dream was also a lucid dream; that is, I knew that I was dreaming. When I awoke, I took it as a signal that I should attend the retreat after all. We learned a meditation practice that included visualizations of a wrathful Dakini dancing on one leg. The last day of the retreat, our entire group left the building we were in and went outdoors.

The sun was bright and the sky was cloudless except for one huge, white cloud directly overhead. The cloud was in the exact shape of the Dakini, down to holding ritual objects in her outstretched hands! All the twenty-five people present saw the apparition clearly and several photographs were taken (the full-color image later appeared in *Women of Power* magazine).

The modern Tantric teacher Sheng-Yen Lu describes invisible entities and secret Dakini realms existing within Lake Sammamish in Washington State:

> "Sometimes, at the lakeside at night, there is a kind of consciousness attached to the water, like 'water spirits.' I noticed them during my first night walks. They also knew that I could help them. They have endured many happenings in the world. Some have committed suicide in the lake. Some have drowned in the lake. Many water spirits look forward to my night walks by the lake. They speak to me and I recite a mantra.
>
> "In my mind, wave after wave of water spirits surge before me. These water spirits, mistakenly feared to be demons by worldly people are not demons but a kind of consciousness who have lost their physical bodies. They attach themselves to the water (or another kind of element) and do not have freedom. They need a goal to follow. They hope to be guided by my Light."

The Tibetan tradition speaks of a "Clear Light" that dissolves inner and outer obstacles, illusions, and distinctions. Recognizing it as one's own mind is to be awakened and to go beyond birth and death. The world-famous Tibetan tradition of conscious dying emphasizes this process. As the awareness of the dying person passes out of the human realm, he experiences a sensation of absolute clarity and lucidity, the Clear Light.

If it is not recognized, the consciousness instead passes into a swirling maelstrom filled with images of compelling power. Both wrathful and peaceful spirits appear to the mind.

If they are not recognized as simply projections of the mind, then they draw the mind back to rebirth in the world of illusion.

This is a description of conscious dying, but it could also be a map for the UFO experience. Some shamans have always said that aliens, elves, or spirits are the same as the dead. The after-death realm is the same as the alien realm.

A similar message is heard overseas, from the traditional Australian Aborigines, who represent the most ancient spiritual lineage on Earth. Compared to our history of cities and civilization (approximately six thousand years old), the age of Aboriginal culture is staggering. They have been living the same way, in the same places, for more than one hundred thousand years (according to both archeologists and their own elders). They are perhaps justified in saying that they, not us, represent "normal humanity." They call themselves "the original people."

Traditional aborigines have no place in their culture for land ownership, clothing, furniture, buildings, or any other modern devices. Yet they have a highly sophisticated tradition of language, music, art, and spirituality. Their intimate knowledge of nature, of plants, animals, and the land is legendary.

Like Native Americans, the Aborigines attest to the reality of spirit beings who sometimes fly through the sky in glowing lights. They say that these entities are associated with certain sacred places, where they appear year after year. There are numerous Aboriginal cave paintings of spirit beings and even of flying disks and globes. Most of these are incalculably ancient, and are painstakingly renewed in annual ceremonies.

The "UFO state of mind," or the spirit world itself, is called by them "the Dreamtime." In this realm, past, present, and future merge into one. The various beings that may appear there are exactly like those described in other traditions. Some are helpful; some are malevolent; still others are mischievous tricksters. A few are the departed spirits of human ancestors or heroes.

Like Native Americans and Tibetans, some Aboriginal elders have stepped forward to explain their natural wisdom before it vanishes completely. They believe that we are entering a final stage of civilization as we know it. To them, the ever more frequent UFO sightings and spirit manifestations are signals of the coming change.

Recently, a remarkable work about traditional Aboriginal beliefs, *Mutant Message From Down Under,* has quietly become a best-seller. The author, Dr. Marlo Morgan, considers herself an average American woman; she is divorced, with a job, and a family. While visiting in Australia, she says she was contacted by members of one of the few remaining traditional tribes and asked to join them on a journey in the Outback. Not really knowing what she was getting into, she joined them.

According to her tale, she found herself wandering in the desert for four months, naked and barefoot, living off the land with the Aborigines. The desert heat often reached from one hundred ten to one hundred thirty degrees during the day. Like she was a child, her guides made every effort to instruct and assist her and she found herself surprisingly comfortable without any of the "necessities" of modern life.

While she lived with them, she witnessed many examples of what we would call psychic healing, prophetic dreams, and extrasensory perception, all considered normal behavior by the Aborigines. They revealed to her that she had been chosen to carry a message back to the modern world.

Since traditional Aborigines justifiably consider themselves to be the mainstream, "normal" humanity, they regard most moderns as dangerous aberrations or "mutants." It seems to them as if all these mutants are engaged in a race to see who can most quickly destroy the Earth's ability to sustain life. The mutants swarming across the face of the planet are wiping themselves, and all other life forms, out of existence.

The message from the "Original People" to the mutants is quite simple, and echoes what those space people have been trying to tell us. "A time of purification is coming. Stop the destruction of life and each other, before it is too late."

The elders told Morgan that they had been living in the same land for countless thousands of years, and that their presence had always helped to sustain the land (a belief shared by traditional native peoples around the world). Now their time was up and they were preparing to leave the Earth to its fate.

> "We, the tribe of divine oneness Real People, are leaving the planet Earth. In our remaining time we have chosen to be celibate and are having no more children. When our youngest member is gone that will be the last of the pure human race. The people of the world have given the soul of the land away.
>
> "Tell your kind that we are going. We are leaving Mother Earth to you. We pray that you will see what your way of life is doing to the water, the animals, the air and to each other. We pray you will find a solution to your problems without destroying this world. Already the rain pattern has been changed, and the heat is increased and we have seen years of plant and animal reproduction lessened. We can no longer provide human forms for souls to inhabit because there will soon be no water or food left here in the desert."

Though some have claimed it is a work of fiction, Morgan's teachings are reaching receptive ears around the planet. Much as in the 1960s, we are in a time when people are dropping the old paradigms and searching for new models. For many people, especially the young, these ancient wisdom traditions offer some hope. There is an emerging culture of those following such traditional spiritual ways embedded in nature.

Many followers of this new paganism display a distinctive appearance. Since the counterculture of the 1960s, it has been associated with tribal jewelry, scarification, natural clothing, and unique musical forms. Currently, full-body tattooing and body-piercing, once markedly eccentric, have become commonplace among American and European youth. The new neo-shamanic or techno-music of these "modern primitives" is matched by the multigenerational "world music" movement that incorporates the languages and rhythms of an older world.

One must be cautious about such fads, however; the original practitioners of these beliefs were concerned with inner growth, not fashion statements. On the other hand, the tribal music and appearances combine to provide a sense of collectivity in a society witnessing the breakdown of the nuclear family and other social institutions.

This is also a community that firmly believes in the existence of extraterrestrial "aliens" and spirits. Many of the topics in this book are articles of faith (or wisdom) for this emerging society. By the standards of previous generations, one could even label these new believers representatives of an "alien culture."

Though we may be witnessing the dissolution of "traditional" Western belief systems, including rationalism, we must also recognize that it is not all superstitious mumbo-jumbo. Most early peoples held belief systems incorporating concepts like Earth-energies, spirits, prophesy, vision quests, and meaningful synchronicities, including the early Christians and Jews. Our ancestors were not foolish; most were eminently practical people who survived a harsh environment to have offspring. They also believed in the unseen world. Perhaps as our own reality becomes increasingly strange, we may find ourselves in need of their more flexible worldview.

It does appear that contactees, magicians, channelers, shamans, and Native American vision questers may all be seeing the same things. When witnesses meet aliens or "lose time" watching UFOs, they may be entering the same Dreamtime that the old Aborigines spoke of. The phenomena is the same; all that we moderns lack are the wise seers and healers back home who can help us make sense of the experience.

15

THE NEW SEERS

*Until you meet an alien intelligence,
you will not know what it is to be human.*

—FRANK HERBERT

TIME and change seem to be accelerating; everywhere people say that "things are moving too fast." Countless new ideas and technologies are rapidly changing our culture into something unrecognizable or even alien. Some of these changes are dismal, such as the rapid destruction of species' habitats. Other developments, such as virtual reality, supercomputers, and chaos mathematics, are hailed as an evolutionary leap forward. Still others are psychic, such as the waves of alien abductions and shamanic experiences.

Whatever our belief system, those able to understand the shifting foundations of reality will be better prepared to face the next century. When entering the future, it helps to have a road map, or many maps. Some people seem to be natural mapmakers.

Many of these mapmakers began with traditional scientific backgrounds, and then found themselves struggling to cope with the reality of paranormal phenomena. In some cases, the shock of these experiences precipitated a radical re-evaluation of consensus reality. Rather than losing their marbles or starting cults, they calmly set out to chart the unknown.

Any list of modern mapmakers must include Harvard Medical School psychiatrist John E. Mack. Mentioned earlier in chapter 2, the Pulitzer Prize-winning Dr. Mack has applied a rigorous science to the formerly vague field of alien abduction. Once he made the decision to investigate, he exhaustively pursued psychiatric illness or other physiological and emotional factors as possible causes for the reports he was hearing from contactees. Only after eliminating all such factors did he leave familiar ground and enter uncharted territory. Forced to at least tentatively accept his clients' statements, he realized that his most fruitful studies were to be of the witnesses themselves. Whether real or not, the "visitors" could be studied best through those who have met them.

In his groundbreaking work *Abduction: Human Encounters with Aliens,* Dr. Mack communicates his realization that these alien experiences were powerful models of *initiation* for his clients. Meaning both "ordeal" and "an introduction to sacred or hidden knowledge," an initiation changes the initiate's life irrevocably.

One of his clients, a teacher of theater and art called "Carlos," experienced a profound transformation in his art and life as a result of an ongoing alien contact. Carlos believes that the aliens (or "light-beings" as he prefers) are here to teach. " 'They are teachers,' he continued, but the experience is in some way reciprocal for 'they are also interested in learning of us.' "

Mack reports that Carlos, and many other contactees, developed an acute ecological awareness. "His experiences seem tied to the fate of the earth and the tearing of the cosmic fabric that the destruction of its life-forms is bringing about." Mack is convinced that within the vast mystery of the alien experience lies the potential for humanity to arrest its self-destructive behavior.

He is frequently asked how an experience that can be so terrifying or traumatic can also be spiritually transformative. For him there is no inconsistency, unless people believe that spirituality is separate from pain and struggle. He notes that some of our greatest spiritual healing and growth is born from challenging experiences.

Dr. Mack is convinced that the phenomenon is very real, but also indirect and intangible. He no longer seeks a "smoking gun," or a purely physical proof. "It may be wrong to expect that a phenomenon whose very nature is subtle . . . will yield its secrets to an epistemology or methodology that operates at a lower state of consciousness." In other words, most researchers have been using the wrong tools; shovels and hammers instead of electron microscopes, bodies instead of brains.

Throughout this work, I have referred to the ideas of veteran UFO researcher John A. Keel. A former news journalist, Keel is widely respected (and resented) for his humorous, open-minded approach to paranormal phenomena and cultists of all kinds.

Keel believes that UFOs are not mechanical machines, but masses of energy apparently able to behave in an intelligent pattern. Like Paul Devereaux, he calls them "Earth lights," because they appear in the same areas year after year, century after century. During a 1993 conversation, he mocked the idea of extraterrestrial origin.

"These lights are obviously not from Mars but from that area, West Virginia or Texas, anywhere all over the world. In ancient times, these lights would appear and we would build a cathedral on that spot. Are there radioactive minerals there, or perhaps some unexplained electromagnetic phenomena? We need to study the Earth itself in relation to these things.

"Everything is tied up in this mystery; there is no subject that isn't included. This is what the ancient psychics and prophets were trying to tell us, but they didn't have the vocabulary. Some of these things may always be basically unexplainable, like cattle mutilations or the crop circles.

"Ivan Sanderson and I sometimes found animals mutilated inside their barns, with no explanation. In one case back in West Virginia, people let their puppy outside, heard a noise and went right out to check. Their puppy was lying dead by the back porch, with a small incision in its chest and the heart removed. *All this took place in a matter of a few minutes.* Studying the mutilations is like chasing your own tail; unless you're medically trained and have a lot of equipment, you don't know what you are looking at."

After a lifetime of studying the Phenomenon, Keel seriously doubts that the United States government is deeply involved with UFOs. "I'd be amazed if the government had any real interest; it seems to be more of a nuisance to them. That Majestic stuff is a hoax, just as rumors of underground alien bases are rehashed versions of the Shaver Mystery in the 1940s. We need to interview these people carefully and look for signs that they were entranced at some point.

"What's doing the entrancing? It depends on each witness's powers of perception. They might see a light at first.

Then it gets closer and closer and they enter a hypnotic trance. What they remember is from the trance, not from reality. We're looking at an age-old phenomenon that goes all the way back to the time of Jesus. Always before, it was seen in a religious perspective. Then there are the women it happened to—starting with the legend of the Virgin Mary—it's another form of incubus-succubus business. We had a lot of these stories in the 1950s, the stuff the UFO buffs wouldn't touch.

"It's also part of the reflective thing—whatever you're looking for, you're going to find. In the 1960s, I experimented with it. I'd look for a weird aspect and it would show up. That demonstrated to me that the whole situation was being controlled. For instance, I focused looking into contactees' birthdates, for example those born on September 6. I'd focus on that date, then all the contactees who came to me were born on September 6.

"If you were looking for scars on the stomach, they came. For example, Budd Hopkins (author of *Intruders*) was searching for scars on the leg, and he found them. The Phenomenon is so controlled that nothing, no data we get has any value. If you're looking for left-handed, red-haired acrobats, you'll get them. So this information is controlled, and it's worthless."

Keel has a controversial name for the mechanism operating the Phenomenon; he calls it "God," well aware of the reaction it can evoke. "The same manifestations that created our religious beliefs, created our UFO beliefs. A serious look at the Phenomenon would cause a revision of our way of looking at religion.

"From my perspective now, the questions worth thinking about are about human perception and our place in the universe. It doesn't make that much sense that people from other planets would come here at all. Instead, the Earth itself may be a living entity and we're seeing things happening that originate, somehow, from the Earth.

"We've got to figure out the purpose of the human race. Charles Fort said that the Earth is property and somebody owns it. Ivan Sanderson said that the Earth is a farm and we're the crop. We may be victims of a thing that we don't understand and may never understand; and It plays games with us."

Some people are starting to learn the rules of the Game. A few years ago, respected Princeton University aerospace scientists Robert Jahn and Brenda Dunne began articulating a new science of the unexplained. By combining their studies of various "topical vectors," such as millennia of human mystical experience, the role of anomalies in scientific method, and the known limitations of statistical science, Jahn and Dunne constructed a theoretical, testable model for apparitional phenomena.

Using high-speed computers to test and measure lab subjects, they were able to explore directly areas of such human potential as psychokinesis (affecting objects with the mind), and remote viewing (observing distant scenes while in a trance). Their work, showing a seemingly definite and measurable perception of "real" remote scenes and events, created a stir within the international scientific community. According to Jahn:

> "The one genre of human experience that has dwarfed all others in its endurance, implications, and resistance to rational comprehension is that associated with the very processes of consciousness upon which all observational and deductive skills are based. Throughout recorded history, instances of inexplicable consciousness-related phenomena have regularly been reported and variously interpreted in such diverse contexts as religion, philosophy, psychology, anthropology, medicine, art, and even high technology."

Dr. Jahn feels that events formerly catalogued as miracles, magic, and UFOs may have a provable scientific basis. Though past scientists failed to define this body of phenomena with any precision, recently a new generation of sensitive experimental tools has become available that permits more credible and controlled research conditions. These more reliable experiments have made it "feasible to move cautiously toward incorporating these anomalies within a better comprehension of the interaction of consciousness with its physical world."

Jahn's work with remote viewing has also been applied to UFOs. In a presentation at the TREAT IV Conference, Edward A. Dames reported on his colleagues' findings regarding UFOs as test subjects for remote viewers. His viewers were carefully trained personnel who were taught to distinguish between atmospheric phenomena, human-made and extraterrestrial technology in their "visions." Dames's bizarre revelations stunned his audience, most of whom were familiar with the concept of remote viewing.

His team frequently observed physical vehicles containing small, gray android-like beings. Since they seemed physical and buzzed around from place to place, these were dubbed "transport vehicles." On the rare occasions that human beings were observed in contact with them, the humans seemed entranced, or in a catatonic state. At first glance, Dames's material seems to corroborate the current viewpoint in the UFO community.

"The first question is whether the beings recognize that they are being remote-viewed. Humans do not. You cannot tell that you are being remote-viewed. Only in two cases in ten years have we ever become aware that someone was aware of a remote observer. We are not so clear about humanoid aliens.

"There are also beings that we have termed 'transcendentals,' which are the formless beings associated with the abductions. These beings are aware of remote viewing. They seem able to edit and affect material, which we were very uncomfortable with.

"We also found a group of normal people, about two or three hundred of them, who are somehow in contact with these beings. We have also seen a physical vehicle in a deep space orbit that is somehow associated with them."

Dames's presentation included information verifying underground bases, alien-induced crop circles, government labs with preserved alien forms, the entire range of UFO contactee lore. What makes this so different from other types of

UFO encounters is that it is induced by the people involved. The age-old methods of shamanic traditions, filtered through modern science, are now being used to access levels of perception where alien phenomena abound. Is it "real"? Like most reports in this book, they are at least real for the people involved.

One theory examining UFO and abduction phenomena from a new angle was birthed in the psychedelic research of the 1960s. During LSD experiments conducted first in the Soviet Union and later at the Maryland Psychiatric Research Center, Czechoslovakian psychiatrist Stanislav Grof uncovered vivid birth memories in his subjects. Based partly on his work, it is now increasingly accepted that a fetus is conscious just prior to birth, and that we may remember our struggle to emerge.

Dr. Grof believes that such images are imprinted at a very deep level, and continue to influence us all our life. He found a basis for correlating certain personality types with their various sorts of "birth imprint." He also believes that exploring or understanding such an imprint is an important part of each individual's struggle to grow mature.

Following up on Dr. Grof's pioneering research, some depth psychologists speculated that alien abduction experiences are unconsciously based on these "perinatal memories." Based on what they considered the lack of physical evidence, they concluded that alien encounters are a form of birth trauma-related hallucination.

Contactees do describe many images that seem lifted directly from Dr. Grof's LSD-induced birth memories. The fetal-appearing aliens, the womblike spacecraft, and a frightening medical operation are the major points of comparison. Some echo the birth memory experiencers with their descriptions of an "oceanic feeling of oneness" or a "primal terror" aboard UFOs. Increasing the comparison with birth are the reported alien exams of reproductive organs or genetic samples, and even stolen pregnancies.

Researchers exploring this "Birth Memory Hypothesis" have found some intriguing connections. A high number of contactees (myself included) experienced difficult births, such as cesarean section or breech births. This presumably led to unresolved issues surrounding birth, and subsequent visions projecting this lack of resolution.

In 1986, I joined a group working with Dr. Grof to obtain first-hand experience. Practicing his nondrug methods of inducing group trance with hyperventilation accompanied by loud music, I found myself plunged into a titanic struggle merely to breathe. It seemed as if I had a strangling rope wrapped tightly around my neck. My pain and panic was so overpowering that I had no idea who or where I was.

The violent feelings lasted for over two hours in which I literally thought that I was going to die. The various screams and thrashing noises from other members of the group having their own experiences added to a scene that must have looked like a chapter from Dante's *Inferno*.

Afterwards, we spoke to the entire group about our experiences. Some people reported ecstatic experiences, others saw images of UFOs, angels, or other lives. Most, however, had images of childhood or of their own birth. My own experience was read as a traumatic birth episode.

I had always known that I was born through cesarean section, but had never discussed it with my mother. Some months later, I asked her about the circumstances of my birth. She remembered that she had started a normal labor until the attending physicians suddenly lost my heartbeat and opted to employ surgery. The doctors found that the birth cord had wrapped around my neck and that I had stopped breathing, just like my "rebirthing" experience of choking.

Though this interlude and a year of follow-up therapy convinced me that we all do carry a birth imprint, I remain unsure of its relationship to abduction experiences. However, I cannot deny that many contactees do seem to have unresolved birth issues.

According to feminist author Donna Haraway, we externalize our fears and separation issues into images of invading aliens on both the psychic and biological levels. This externalizing split has real physical effects, ranging from diseases to imperialism to our interpreting all paranormal experiences in light of our fears. That part of us that creates war and oppression, subjugates indigenous peoples, and contracts AIDS also perceives aliens. Do we need an "alien" in order to feel human?

An increasingly popular author and speaker thinks so. Ethnobotanical philosopher Terence McKenna is hailed by many as the modern successor to Timothy Leary's psychedelic mantle in the 1960s. The comparison may not be quite fair. McKenna is an original thinker whose work is informed as much by scientific theory and Alfred North Whitehead as by shamanism and feminism. Author of numerous books exploring everything from psychedelic mushrooms to virtual reality to UFOs to the new tribalism, his mesmerizing speaking skills and dry wit have rocketed him to cult status speaking to vast audiences in Europe and the United States. If the emerging new order of psychedelic, Earth-centered, computer-literate, tribal culture has a spokesperson, it is he.

I first met Terence at a small conference on the myth of Quetzalcoatl in 1985, and was amazed at his broad grasp of science, history, literature, and philosophy. He is the only individual I have ever met who has apparently memorized every date in history. Maintaining our contact over the next eight years, I found his extraordinary mind and dry sense of humor a continuing source of inspiration.

Terence describes "four abysses" surrounding us. They are abysses because they appear to be dark, vast spaces pregnant with the unknown, or a fear associated with the unknown. The first and greatest abyss in our life is waiting at its end: death. Human history and culture is filled with our attempts to define and understand the immensity that is death; usually, all we succeed in doing is projecting our own fears and desires upon the blackness. The mask it wears is our own face.

Another abyss is the "nightly death," sleep. At the end of every waking period, we surrender both control and consciousness, just as in dying. The plastic realm of dreams again reflects our thoughts and feelings as in a distorted mirror. (Tibetan yogis have always said that the study of dreams prepares us for conscious dying and entering the after-death state.)

A third abyss partakes of the same qualities as the first two. The "abyss of psychedelic experience" is an unknown realm. Few researchers would deny that it too is a black mirror where we see what we fear, or what we most want to see. The sensation of fright felt prior to any psychedelic experience (by anyone sane, that is) is both our fear of the unknown and of losing control.

A final abyss may be best understood by comparing it with the first three. The human encounter with the alien or with UFOs constitutes the fourth abyss. Like death, dreams, and psychedelics, UFOs are a brush with an unknown reality. Such experiences jolt witnesses from their accustomed routines, forcing them to readjust their worldview. As we have seen over and over, the face of the alien looks like what we have been taught to see, or what we are *able* to see.

Could we develop some conscious control over UFO phenomena, much as yogis and shamans reportedly have over the processes of sleep and even death? The first step seems to be stripping away our own distorted projections from the experience. Perhaps the greatest value of maps like the "abyss model" is that they help us recognize UFOs as an essential aspect of the human experience.

Terence McKenna earned his mapmaking stripes by logging countless hours exploring psychedelic space. One of his preferred launch vehicles is the psilocybin mushroom. Psilocybin is a highly visionary natural compound with thousands of years of shamanic use. A tryptamine, it possesses a close similarity to human brain chemistry. Some theorists believe that substances like "magic mushrooms" were humanity's first encounter with the spiritual mysteries.

It should come as no surprise that many people hear a voice speaking while in mushroom trance. Some people, Terence included, call this voice the "Logos," or the primordial voice of humanity's genius. When this voice is heard, one knows oneself to be in the presence of the Divine. Since it emanates blissful, omniscient light, some claim that they are hearing the same source as the "Great Spirit" of shamans, or even the "God" of early Christians and others.

Many people also say they hear the voice of the mushrooms themselves, which claims to be an interstellar being in a symbiotic relationship with countless species on countless worlds (including some humans). The anonymous author of the underground best-seller, *Psilocybin: The Magic Mushroom Grower's Guide,* copied the following communication from the "mushroom entity."

"I am old, older than thought in your species. Though I have been on Earth for ages I am from the stars. My home is no one planet, for many worlds scattered throughout the galaxy have conditions which allow my spores an opportunity for life. . . .

"Beyond the cohesion of the members of a species into a single social organism there lie richer evolutionary possibilities, including symbiosis. Symbiosis is a relation of mutual dependence and positive benefits for both of the species involved. Symbiotic relationships between myself and civilized forms of higher animals have been established many times and in many places throughout the long ages of my development.

"These relationships have been mutually useful; within my memory is the knowledge of hyper-light drive ships and how to build them. I will trade this knowledge for a free ticket to new worlds around suns younger and more stable than your own."

High numbers of mushroom explorers, including McKenn also frequently see "elfis." The experience of encountering diminutive, jolly, trickster-like being of light is especially wid spread among Generation X'ers. Math and physics students the University of Santa Cruz have even dubbed a section woods "elf land" for the high numbers of (mushroom-assiste elfin encounters occurring there.

It is amazing that so many veteran UFO researchers i nore the multitude of psychedelic-induced UFO-alien sigh ings. There are so many correspondences between th psychedelic experience and the "UFO state of consciou ness," it is no longer possible to separate them.

McKenna has his own take on the UFO experience. 1971, he and his brother, molecular biologist Denn McKenna, went into the jungle looking for a legendary ps; chedelic plant. They didn't locate the one they sought, but i stead found many psilocybin mushrooms. Ingesting them ov a period of weeks, they encountered many unusual phenom ena, including UFOs and an alien, "insectoid" intelligence.

"My brother and I discovered during our Peruvian Amazon expedition that psilocybin seems to confer the ability to inhabit more than one world at the same time, as if another world was superimposed over reality. This is a hyperdimensional world where information is accessible in magical ways."

After his Amazonian experiences, McKenna surveyed the literature of mystical experiences, UFO experiences, and systems such as alchemy. He saw that these different traditions were all talking about the same thing. Though the current version of the experience is called "contact with the UFO," it is not reducible to any of the explanations suggested by UFO experts and contactees.

In one late-night conversation, he summarized his thoughts about the UFO mystery, "It is not a contact by a space-faring race, nor is it mass hysteria or psychosis. Many people claim to have seen UFOs, yet science cannot explain them. It seems as if reality is haunted by a spinning vortex that renders science helpless. That spinning vortex is the UFO, and it haunts our history like a ghost."

Terence's own encounters with UFOs led him to view them as phenomenologically real. He believes that UFOs may be intended to "confound" science and reason, because these qualities have begun to threaten the existence of the human race, as well as the ecosystem.

"At this point, a shock or a 'great confounding' is necessary, a shock equivalent to the shock of the Christian Resurrection on Roman imperialism. UFOs are active myths of intervention by a hyperintelligent entity that comes from the stars.

"The UFO would wreck science by a series of demonstrations designed to convince the majority of humanity that the purpose of history is nothing less than total immersion in the teachings of the UFO. Once this message is slammed home via worldwide TV broadcasts, the UFO might simply disappear. Meanwhile, the UFO-oriented religion would embody an archetype of enormous power, able to hold sway in the same way that Christianity halted the development of science for a thousand years."

This Confounding Theory, not so different from tradition Native American or Scandinavian views on "trickster spirits might hold true for individuals as much as for societies. contactee's momentum is indeed halted or redirected by a encounter with a UFO. They come face to face with a "co founding," and their life changes.

While researching this book, I met many people who ha altered their lives after the shock of an alien abduction, channelled communication, or an unexplainable sightin Some had changed their homes or jobs, or moved to anoth part of the country. Others had left or lost their marriages ar families, or had immediately fallen in love with someor who accepted their new belief system. Everyone I met had drastically different worldview after his or her experience.

In such cases, it hardly matters if their encounter was phy ically real, or only psychically or mythically real. The im portant aspect, the one that affected their lives, was the altered belief system. We are now beginning to see large num bers of people changing their belief systems in this fashior

Were their triggering experiences merely a cosmic coinc dence, or is the initial stimulus *intentional?* Physical or no UFO phenomena appear to display some directing intell gence. Is someone or something pursuing a plan to lead us a specific direction? Among others, researcher Jacques Valle believes that humanity is being conditioned to believe certai things.

> "UFOs are part of the control system for human evo-
> lution, like the nuclear process inside the Sun and the
> long-term changes in the Earth's weather. But their ef-
> fects, instead of being just physical, are also felt in our
> belief systems. They influence what we call our spiri-
> tual life. They affect our political institutions, our his-
> tory, our culture."

Vallee refers to the classical patterns of reinforcement use in behavior modification to create new patterns:

> "The best schedule of reinforcement is one that com-
> bines periodicity with unpredictability. It is interesting
> to note that UFOs seem to follow this same structure of

reinforcement. If the phenomenon is forcing us through a learning curve, *it has no choice but to mislead us."*

Like rats in a maze, we are being conditioned by a phenomenon that occurs in regular cycles, yet remains unpredictable. If the stimulus is unpleasant, the rat is under pressure to engage in new behavior. What is that new behavior?

Some of the people we met in this book think that it is an evolving alien-human symbiosis, others a new relationship with Earth and the environment. Still others, like the people involved with the Montauk Project, believe it is a conspiracy to create a society of easily manipulated, superstitious slave workers. No matter "Their" real goal, it is our own beliefs and aspirations, that which makes us human beings, which is manipulated. We can only begin to free ourselves of the manipulation by seeking to understand the phenomenon, including ourselves.

By a roundabout road, moving back and forth in time and culture, we outlined the modern UFO enigma. Only by stepping back from the whole picture have we been able to perceive the vast scale involved. It is clear from human history and mythology that They have been with us since our earliest beginnings. They have always been here. Recently They have reminded us of their presence; we could shut ourselves in, but not shut Them out.

The first UFO sightings of this century, the flying saucers and little green men, were the foundations of a developing mythology, a pervasive, alien worldview that has extended tendrils into every level in our society. Whether the experience takes place in a movie theater or on a country road, in a lucid dream or in missing time, these tendrils of influence touch everyone. Though we cannot see whether it is good or evil, it must still be reckoned with.

They may indeed exist outside us, or represent some aspect of our innermost selves that can reach out and seemingly manipulate the world. Channellers, neoshamans, and scientific researchers alike speculate that humanity is headed toward a drastic reordering and restructuring of what we call reality. Paradigm-shaking scientific discoveries appear almost daily, just as UFO encounters seem to. Those crazy "confoundings" are on the rise. Perhaps we are headed toward a causal collapse, or a reshaping of reality that ignores all the old rules, except those found in old fairy tales. Wherever we finally go, to oblivion or the stars or our ancient past, it is clear that humanity's oldest friends in the UFOs are along with us for the ride.

BIBLIOGRAPHY

PART ONE: MAKING CONTACT

CHAPTER 1 STRANGE DAYS

Blum, Ralph, and Judy Blum. *Beyond Earth: Man's Contact with UFO's.* Bantam Books, 1974.

Cassirer, Manfred. "The Mystery of the Stalled Car." *Strange,* no. 6 (1990).

Chamberlain, David B. *Consciousness at Birth: A Review of the Empirical Evidence.* Chamberlain Communications, 1973.

Clark, Jerome. "Close Encounters of the 3rd Kind: 1901–1959." *Strange,* no. 10 (1992).

Corliss, William R. *Handbook of Unusual Natural Phenomena.* Sourcebook Project, 1978.

Emenegger, Robert. *UFO's, Past, Present and Future.* Ballantine Books, 1974.

Fort, Charles. *The Complete Books of Charles Fort.* Dover Books, 1974.

Gaddis, Vincent H. *Mysterious Fires and Lights.* Dell Books, 1967.
———. *"Strange* Magazine Interview," *Strange,* no. 7 (1991).

Greene, Yvonne. "Fetal Memory Metaphors." *Fortean Times: The Journal of Strange Phenomena.* no. 71 (October/November 1993).

Grof, Stanislav and Joan Halifax. *Realms of the Human Unconscious.* E. P. Dutton and Co., 1976.

Grosso, Michael. "Endtime Anomalies." *Critique: Exploring Consensus Reality.* no. 31 (June–September, 1989).
———. "The Ultradimensional Mind." *Strange,* no. 7 (1991).

Guiley, Rosemary Ellen. *The Encyclopedia of Ghosts and Spirits.* Facts on File, 1992.

Hillman, James, ed. by Thomas Moore. *A Blue Fire: Selected Writings.* Harper and Row, 1989.

Jung, Carl G. *Flying Saucers: A Modern Myth of Things Seen in the Sky.* Princeton University Press, 1978.

————. *The Symbolic Life: Miscellaneous Writings.* Princeton University Press, 1977.

Keyhoe, Major Donald E. (USMC Ret.). *Aliens From Space.* Signet Books, 1973.

Keel, John A. *Our Haunted Planet.* Fawcett Publications, 1971.

————. "Sssseeing Thingsss: Hallucinations, UFOs and Fortean Investigations." *Strange,* no. 3 (1988).

————. "Monsters as Occult Phenomenon." *Strange,* no. 4 (no date).

————. "Investigating UFOs." *Strange,* no. 6 (1990).

————. "Waves of Confusion." *Strange,* no. 6 (1990).

————. "The Occupants." *Strange,* no. 10 (1992).

MacPherson, Euan. "Beyond the ET Hypothesis: UFOs, Ghosts and Time-Slips." *Strange,* no. 4 (no date).

Randles, Jenny. *UFOs and How to See Them.* Sterling Publishing Co., 1992.

Sanderson, Ivan T. *Invisible Residents: A Disquisition Upon Certain Matters Maritime, and the Possibility of Intelligent Life Under the Waters of This Earth.* Avon Books, 1970.

Spencer, John. *World Atlas of UFOs.* Smithmark Publishers, 1991.

Stillings, Dennis, ed. *Cyberbiological Studies of the Imaginal Component in the UFO Contact Experience.* Archaeus Project, 1989.

Thompson, Keith. *Angels and Aliens: UFOs and the Mythic Imagination.* Addison Wesley Publishing, 1991.

Vallee, Jacques. *Messengers of Deception: UFO Contacts and Cults.* And/Or Press, 1979.

————. *Dimensions: A Casebook of Alien Contact.* Contemporary Books, 1988.

————. *Revelations: Alien Contact and Human Deception.* Ballantine Books, 1991.

Walters, Ed and Frances. *The Gulf Breeze Sightings.* Avon Books, 1990.

Watson, Nigel. "The Scareship Mystery." *Strange,* nos. 12, 13 (1993–94).

Willis, Paul J. "The Alien Visitors of Charles Fort." *Strange,* vol. 1, no. 1 (no date).

CHAPTER 2 THE ABDUCTIONS

Alexander, John, and Victoria, eds. *Treatment and Research of Experienced Anomalous Trauma (TREAT) Proceedings.* March, 1993.

Bryant, Alice. *Healing Shattered Reality: Understanding Contactee Trauma.* Wildflower Press, 1991.

Chapman, Douglas. "The Abduction Enigma." *Strange,* vol. 1, no. 1 (no date).

———. "Streiber Ends Communion with UFO Subculture." *Strange,* no. 9 (1992).

Clark, Jerome. "Where Were the Grays?" *Strange,* no. 10 (1992).

Cooper, Vicki. "New Light on Abduction Syndrome." *UFO,* vol. 8, no. 1 (1993).

———. "The Common Ground of Abduction Support." *UFO,* vol. 8, no. 1 (1993).

Earley, George W. "Interview with Budd Hopkins." *Fate,* vol. 45, no. 9 (September 1992).

Fiore, Edith. *Encounters: A Psychologist Reveals Case Studies of Abductions by Extraterrestrials.* Ballantine Books, 1989.

Fowler, Raymond E. *The Watchers: The Secret Design Behind UFO Abductions.* Bantam Books, 1990.

Fuller, John. *The Interrupted Journey.* Berkley, 1966.

Goldfader, Lorne. "Canada's Abduction Scene." *UFO,* vol. 8, no. 1 (1993).

Gotlib, David. "David Gotlib Interview." *UFO,* vol. 8, no. 2 (1993).

Hall, Richard. *Univited Guests: A Documented History of UFO Sightings, Alien Encounters and Cover-ups.* Aurora Press, 1988.

Hopkins, Budd. *Intruders: The Incredible Visitations at Copley Woods.* Ballantine Books, 1988.

———. *Missing Time.* Ballantine Books, 1988.

———. "The Linda Cortile Abduction Case." *Mufon UFO Journal,* no. 293 (September 1992).

Keel, John A. *Strange Creatures From Time and Space.* Fawcett Publications, 1968.

Lindemann, Michael, ed. *UFOs and the Alien Presence: Six Viewpoints.* The 2020 Group, 1991.

Mack, John E. *Abduction: Human Encounters with Aliens.* Charles Scribner's and Sons, 1994.

————. *The Abduction Phenomenon: A Preliminary Report.* Private publication of The Department of Psychiatry, Cambridge Hospital (June 1992).

————. "Other Realities: The Alien Abduction Phenomenon." *Noetic Sciences Review,* no. 23 (Autumn 1992).

————. "Alien Reckoning," *Washington Post,* 17 April 1994.

Meux, Ken. "High Strangeness." *Strange,* vol. 1, no. 1 (no date).

Rak, Charles and Jack Weiner. *The Allagash Incident.* Tundra Publishing, 1993.

Rose, Lauren. "Coming to Terms with UFO Experiences." *UFO,* vol. 8, no. 1 (1993).

Rydeen, Paul. "UFOs and the Cult of Cargo." *Strange,* no. 9 (1992).

Schmaltz, James P. "Alien Insemination: E.T.'s Stole My Baby!" *Far Out,* vol. I, no. II (Winter 1992).

Schwarz, Berthold E. *UFO Dynamics,* vols. 1 and 2. Rainbow Books, 1983.

Smith, Yvonne. "Alien Table Procedures." *UFO,* vol. 8, no. 1 (1993).

Schnabel, Jim. "Memories of Hell." *Fortean Times: The Journal of Strange Phenomena,* no. 71 (October/November 1993).

Spencer, John. *World Atlas of UFOs.* Smithmark Publishers, 1991.

Stacy, Dennis. "Millions of Americans Abducted?" *Fate,* vol. 45, no. 9 (September 1992).

Steiger, Brad. *The Other.* Inner Light Publications, 1992.

Strieber, Whitley. *Communion: A True Story.* Avon, 1987.

————. *Transformation: The Breakthrough.* Avon, 1988.

Swann, Ingo. "The UFO-Extraterrestrial Problem." *Fate,* vol. 45, no. 9 (September 1992).

Thompson, Keith. *Angels and Aliens: UFOs and the Mythic Imagination.* Addison Wesley Publishing, 1991.

Turner, Karla. "Encounter Phenomena Defy Set Pattern." *UFO,* vol. 8, no. 1 (1993).

Webb, Walter. "Sleep Paralysis in Abduction Cases." *UFO,* vol. 8, no. 2 (1993).

CHAPTER 3 HIDDEN AGENDA

Alexander, John. *The Warrior's Edge.* Avon Press, 1992.

————. "Letters to the Editor." *UFO,* vol. 8, no. 1 (1993).

———. Personal communication (1992).

Alexander, John, and Victoria, eds. *Treatment and Research of Experienced Anomalous Trauma (TREAT) Proceedings.* March 1993.

Anderson, Jack. "Hollywood and the CIA Take on Flying Saucers." Jack Anderson column, *United Features Syndicate,* 10 April 1975.

Berlitz, Charles, and William Moore. *The Roswell Incident.* Granada, 1980.

Blum, Howard. *Out There.* Simon & Schuster, 1992.

Boylan, Richard. "Touring Nevada's Outer Limits." *UFO,* vol. 7, no. 6.

Campbell, Glenn. *Area 51 Viewer's Guide.* (self-published), 1993 (reviewed in *UFO magazine* in vol. 8, no. 4).

Claiborne, William. "GAO Turns to Alien Probe." *Washington Post,* 14 January 1994.

Cooper, Vicki. "Possible Covert Operations Targeting Abduction Research." *UFO,* vol. 8, no. 1 (1993).

Eco, Umberto. *Foucault's Pendulum.* Harcourt Brace Jovanovitch, 1988.

Ecker, Don. "Corporate Spooks Ride High at Wackenhut." *UFO,* vol. 8, no. 1 (1993).

Hall, Richard. *Univited Guests: A Documented History of UFO Sightings, Alien Encounters and Cover-ups.* Aurora Press, 1988.

Hough, Peter, and Jenny Randles. *Looking for the Aliens: A Psychological, Scientific and Imaginative Investigation.* Blandford, 1991.

Keen, Sam. *Faces of the Enemy.* HarperSan Francisco, 1988.

———. "Applied Demonology." *Magical Blend,* no. 34 (April 1992).

Lindemann, Michael, ed. *UFOs and the Alien Presence: Six Viewpoints.* The 2020 Group, 1991.

McKenzie, Hal. "Only Politics Can Loosen Knot of UFO Cover-up." *UFO,* vol. 8, no. 4 (1993).

Moore, William. "The Great UFO Con Game." *Far Out,* vol. 1, no. 2 (Winter 1992).

———. "UFOs and the Disinformation Game." *Far Out,* vol. 1, no. 2 (Winter 1992).

Spencer, John. *World Atlas of UFOs.* Smithmark Publishers, 1991.

Steiner, Ralph. "Unmasking the Disinformers." *UFO*, vol. 8, no. 2 (1993).

Stevens, Anthony. "Transcending War: Stop Blaming the Other." *Critique: Exploring Consensus Reality,* no. 31 (June–September 1989).

Stonehill, Paul. "Former Pilot Tells of Captured UFO." *UFO,* vol. 8, no. 2 (1993).

Strieber, Whitley. *Majestic.* Berkley Books, 1989.

Vallee, Jacques. *Revelations: Alien Contact and Human Deception.* Ballantine Books, 1991.

CHAPTER 4 UNKNOWN APES

Berry, Rick. *Bigfoot on the East Coast.* Campbell Copy Center, 1993.

Bord, Janet and Colin Bord. *Alien Animals.* Stackpole Books, 1981.

Cassirer, Manfred. "The Mystery of the Stalled Car." *Strange,* no. 6 (1990).

Chorvinsky, Mark and Mark Opsasnick. "Notes on the Dwayyo." *Strange,* no. 2 (no date).

———. "Hoosier Horrors." *Strange,* no. 2 (no date).

———. "Field Guide to the Monsters and Mystery Animals of Maryland." *Strange,* no. 5 (no date).

Coleman, Loren. "Bigfoot Abduction Excuse Used." *Strange,* no. 2 (no date).

———. "The Abominable Werewolves of the Southwest." *Strange,* no. 7 (1991).

Digregorio, Michael. "Bigfoot-Gate, Part 1." *Far Out,* vol. 1, no. 4 (Summer 1993).

Keel, John A. *Strange Creatures From Time and Space.* Fawcett Publications, 1968.

———. "Monsters as Occult Phenomenon." *Strange,* no. 4 (no date).

Larkin, David. *Giants.* Harry N. Abrams, Inc., 1979.

Opsasnick, Mark. "Monsters of Maryland: Bigfoot." *Strange,* no. 3 (1988).

Pilchis, Dennis. *Night Siege: The Northern Ohio UFO-Creature Invasion.* Privately published by author (no date).

Roe, William. "Formal Affadavit." Edmonton, Alberta, Canada, 1957.

Slate, B. Ann and Alan Berry. *Bigfoot*. Bantam Books, 1976.

Sanderson, Ivan T. *Abominable Snowmen: Legend Come to Life*. Pyramid Books, 1968.

Shuker, Karl P. N. "Red-Eye Glow: A New Explanation." *Strange*, no. 8 (1991).

Spencer, John. *World Atlas of UFOs*. Smithmark Publishers, 1991.

Steiger, Brad, and Alfred Bielek. *The Philadelphia Experiment and Other UFO Conspiracies*. Inner Light Publications, 1990.

Watson, Nigel. "A Gallery of Humanoids." *Strange*, no. 10 (1992).

CHAPTER 5 NIGHT TERRORS

Bearden, Thomas E. *The Excalibur Briefing*. Strawberry Hill Press, 1980.

Ecker, Frances Anne. "Alabama Mutilations." *UFO*, vol. 8, no. 4 (1993).

Fort, Charles. *The Complete Books of Charles Fort*. Dover Books, 1974.

Hough, Peter, and Jenny Randles. *Looking for the Aliens: A Psychological, Scientific and Imaginative Investigation*. Blandford, 1991.

Howe, Linda Moulton. *An Alien Harvest*. LMH Productions, 1989.

———. *A Strange Harvest: A Documentary Film Investigation of the Animal Mutilation Mystery*. LMH Productions, 1980 and 1988.

———. *Strange Harvests, 1993*. LMH Productions, 1994.

———. Personal communication (1992).

Keel, John A. *Strange Creatures From Time and Space*. Fawcett Publications, 1968.

———. "Waves of Confusion." *Strange*, no. 6 (1990).

Lindemann, Michael, ed. *UFOs and the Alien Presence: Six Viewpoints*. The 2020 Group, 1991.

Picasso, Fabio. "Infrequent Types of South American Humanoids." *Strange*, nos. 8, 9, 11 (1991–92).

Rickard, Bob and Paul Sieveking, eds. "Swedish Horse Ripping." *Fortean Times: The Journal of Strange Phenomena*, no. 64 (August/September 1992).

Spencer, John. *World Atlas of UFOs*. Smithmark Publishers, 1991.

White, John. "Psychic Intrigue and Psychotronic Weapons."
    Strange, no. 4 (no date).

CHAPTER 6 THIEVES OF TIME

Bearden, Thomas E. *The Excalibur Briefing.* Strawberry Hill Press,
    1980.

Berlitz, Charles. *The Philadelphia Experiment: Project Invisibility.*
    Fawcett Crest, 1979.

Bielek, Albert. Personal communication (1993).

Cameron, Duncan. Personal communication (1993).

Cathie, Bruce L., and Peter N. Temm. *UFOs and Anti-Gravity.*
    Strawberry Hill Press, 1971.

Chapman, Douglas. "Wilhelm Reich: The Madness in His Meth-
    ods." *Strange,* no. 3 (1988).

Craft, Michael. *Time Travel and the Alien Presence: A Report on the
    Philadelphia Experiment and the Montauk Project.* Unpublished
    article (August 1993).

Davenport, Marc. *Visitors From Time: The Secret of the UFOs.*
    Wildflower Press, 1992.

Grosso, Michael. "Top Secret: Cosmigate Exposed." *Critique: Ex-
    ploring Consensus Reality,* no. 31 (June–September 1989).

Hoagland, Richard. *The Monuments of Mars.* North Atlantic Press,
    1995.

Keen, Sam. "Applied Demonology." *Magical Blend,* no. 34 (April
    1992).

Keith, Jim. *Casebook for Alternative 3.* INE, 1994.

Nichols, Preston. *The Montauk Project.* Sky Books, 1992.

———. Personal communication (1993).

Rickard, Bob. "Alternative 3; Hoax!" *Fortean Times: The Journal
    of Strange Phenomena,* no. 64 (August/September 1992).

Steiger, Brad and Bielek, Albert, and *The Philadelphia Experiment
    and Other UFO Conspiracies.* Inner Light Publications, 1990.

Stevens, Anthony. "Transcending War: Stop Blaming The Other."
    Critique: Exploring Consensus Reality, no. 31 (June–September
    1989).

Sutherly, Curt. "Martian Mysteries," *Strange,* no. 13 (1994).

White, John. "Psychic Intrigue and Psychotronic Weapons."
    Strange, no. 4 (no date).

PART TWO: FIGURES OF EARTH

CHAPTER 7 VANISHING MONSTERS

Bord, Janet and Colin Bord. *Alien Animals*. Stackpole Books, 1981.

Cassirer, Manfred. "The Mystery of the Stalled Car." *Strange*, no. 6 (1990).

Chorvinsky, Mark and Mark Opsasnick. "Hoosier Horrors." *Strange*, no. 2 (no date).

———. "Field Guide to the Monsters and Mystery Animals of Maryland." *Strange*, no. 5 (no date).

Coleman, Loren. *Curious Encounters*. Faber and Faber, 1985.

———. "Other Lizard People Revisited." *Strange*, no. 3 (1988).

David-Nell, Alexandra. *Magic and Mystery in Tibet*. Viking, 1971.

Dash, Mike. "It Came From Outer Space!" *Fortean Times: The Journal of Strange Phenomena*, no. 71 (October/November 1993).

Fort, Charles. *The Complete Books of Charles Fort*. Dover Books, 1974.

Guiley, Rosemary Ellen. *The Encyclopedia of Ghosts and Spirits*. Facts on File, 1992.

Hesiod, trans. by Norman O. Brown. *Theogeny*. Bobbs-Merrill Publishing, 1953.

Keel, John A. *The Eighth Tower*. Signet Books, 1975.

———. *The Mothman Prophesies*. Signet Books, 1975.

———. *Our Haunted Planet*. Fawcett Publications, 1971.

———. "Sssseeing Thingsss; Hallucinations, UFOs and Fortean Investigations." *Strange*, no. 3 (1988).

———. "Monsters as Occult Phenomenon." *Strange*, no. 4 (no date).

———. "Investigating UFOs." *Strange*, no. 6 (1990).

———. "Waves of Confusion." *Strange*, no. 6 (1990).

———. "The Occupants." *Strange*, no. 10 (1992).

Little, Greg. *People of the Web*. White Buffalo Books, 1990.

Magin, Ulrich. "Something Fishy." *Strange*, no. 10 (Fall–Winter 1992).

Opsasnick, Mark. "Lizard Man." *Strange*, no. 3 (1988).

Picasso, Fabio. "Infrequent Types of South American Humanoids." *Strange*, nos. 8, 9, 11 (1991–92).

Rogo, D. Scott. *An Experience of Phantoms.* Dell Publishing, 1974.

Rowlett, Curtis A. "Phantom Black Dog." *Strange,* no. 13 (Spring 1994).

Sanderson, Ivan T. *Things.* Pyramid Books, 1967.

Spencer, John. *World Atlas of UFOs.* Smithmark Publishers, 1991.

Steiger, Brad. *The Other.* Inner Light Publications, 1992.

Steiger, Brad, and Alfred Bielek. *The Philadelphia Experiment and Other UFO Conspiracies.* Inner Light Publications, 1990.

Watson, Nigel. "A Gallery of Humanoids." *Strange,* no. 10 (1992).

CHAPTER 8 THE VERY GOOD PEOPLE

Borgeaud, Phillipe. *The Cult of Pan in Ancient Greece.* University of Chicago Press, 1988.

Chesterton, G. K. *Magic: A Play.* Castle Hill Press, 1958.

Chitouras, Jeff. "Esoteric Sound and Color." *GNOSIS: A Journal of the Western Inner Traditions,* no. 27 (Spring 1993).

Coleman, Loren. *Curious Encounters.* Faber and Faber, 1985.

Corliss, William R. *Ancient Man: A Handbook of Puzzling Artifacts.* The Sourcebook Project, 1978.

———. *Handbook of Unusual Natural Phenomena.* Arlington House, 1986.

Crowley, John. *Little, Big.* Bantam Books, 1981.

Eliade, Mircea. *Shamanism: Archaic Techniques of Ecstasy.* Princeton University Press, 1964.

Evans-Wentz, W. Y. *The Fairy Faith in the Celtic Countries.* Citadel Press, 1990.

Gantz, Jeffrey, trans. ed. *The Mabinogion.* Viking, 1976.

Godwin, Joscelyn. *Arktos: The Polar Myth in Science, Symbolism and Nazi Survival.* Phanes Press, 1993.

Guiley, Rosemary Ellen. *The Encyclopedia of Ghosts and Spirits.* Facts on File, 1992.

Halifax, Joan. *Shamanic Voices.* Dutton, 1979.

Hartland, Edwin. *English Fairy and Other Folk Tales.* Gale Research, 1968.

Hawken, Paul. *The Magic of Findhorn: An Eyewitness Account.* Harper and Row, 1975.

Hodson, Geoffrey. *The Fairies at Work and Play.* Quest Books, 1982.

Holdstock, Robert. *Mythago Wood.* Arbor House, 1984.

Iamblichus On the Mysteries, trans. Thomas Taylor. Wizard Books, 1992.

Irving, Washington. *Rip Van Winkle and the Legend of Sleepy Hollow.* Little, Brown & Co., 1991.

Jacobs, David. *Secret Life: Firsthand Documented Accounts of UFO Abductions.* Fireside Books, 1993.

Kafton-Minkel, Walter. *Subterranean Worlds.* Loompanics Unlimited, 1898.

Keel, John A. *Our Haunted Planet.* Fawcett Publications, 1971.

Lazell, David. "Modern Fairy Tales." *Fortean Times: The Journal of Strange Phenomena,* no. 71 (October/November 1993).

Luna, Luis Eduardo. *Ayahuasca Visions: The Religious Iconography of a Peruvian Shaman.* North Atlantic Books, 1991.

———. Personal communication (1990).

MacDonald, George. *Phantastes.* Schocken Books, 1982.

MacLean, Dorothy. *To Hear the Angels Sing.* Lindesfarne, 1990.

MacLellan, Alec. *The Lost World of Agharti.* Corgi Books, 1982.

Magin, Ulrich. "Yeats and the Little People." *Strange,* no. 4 (no date).

Mebane, Alexander. "The Fairy Ring/Crop Circle Connection." *Strange,* no. 7 (1991).

Norman, Eric. *The Under People.* Award Books, 1969.

Noyes, Ralph, ed. *The Crop Circle Enigma.* Gateway Books, 1990.

Parisen, Maria. *Angels and Mortals: The Co-Creative Power.* Quest Books, 1990.

Picasso, Fabio. "Infrequent Types of South American Humanoids." *Strange,* nos. 8, 9, 11 (1991–92).

Scott, Sir Walter. *Letters on Demonology and Witchcraft.* Lyle Stuart Pub., 1974.

Schefold, Reimar. "Mentawaian Shamans: Mediators Between the Worlds." *Shaman's Drum,* no. 31 (Spring 1993).

Stacy, Dennis. "An Unsolicited Elf." *Fortean Times: The Journal of Strange Phenomena,* no. 64 (August/September 1992).

Stewart, R. J. *Robert Kirk: Walker Between Worlds.* Element Books, 1990.

Strieber, Whitley. *Communion: A True Story.* Avon, 1987.

Thomas of Ercledoune. *The Arthurian Tradition,* C. Matthews. Penguin, 1994.

Thompson, Richard L. *Alien Identities*. Govardhan Hill Publications, 1993.

Tolkien, J. R. R. "Tree and Leaf: On Fairy Stories." *The Tolkien Reader*. Ballantine Books, 1966.

Turner, Karla. "Encounter Phenomena Defy Set Pattern." *UFO*, vol. 8, no. 1 (1993).

Vallee, Jacques. *Dimensions: A Casebook of Alien Contact*. Ballantine Books, 1988.

Weiskopf, Jimmy. "In the Shadow of the Tiger and Boa." *Shaman's Drum*, no. 31 (Spring 1993).

CHAPTER 9 GAIAN MESSAGE

Bartholomew, Alick, ed. *Crop Circles: Harbingers of World Change*. Gateway Books, 1991.

Beaumont, Richard. "Close Encounters of a Circular Kind." *Kindred Spirit*, vol. 2, no. 9 (Winter 1992–93).

Cassirer, Manfred. "Crop Circle Enigma 'Solved' by Circular Reasoning?" *Strange*, no. 7 (1991).

Cathie, Bruce L., and Peter N. Temm. *UFOs and Anti-Gravity: Contact with Earth*. Strawberry Hill Press, 1971.

Chapman, Douglas. "Cropfields Circled." *Strange*, no. 6 (1990).

Chorvinsky, Mark. "Erasmus Darwin on Cropfield Circles in 1789?" *Strange*, no. 6 (1990).

Corliss, William R. *Handbook of Unusual Natural Phenomena*. Arlington House, 1986.

Davis, Beth, ed. *Ciphers in the Crops*. Gateway Books, 1992.

de Chardin, Teilhard. *The Phenomenon of Man*. Harper Torchbook, 1961.

Delgado, Pat, and Colin Andrews. *Circular Evidence*. Bloomsbury, 1989.

Devereux, Paul. *Earth Lights*. Turnstone Press, 1982.

———. "Earth Mysteries." *Strange*, no. 2 (no date).

Devereux, Paul, John Steele, and David Kubrin. *Earthmind*. Harper and Row, 1989.

Fort, Charles. *The Complete Books of Charles Fort*. Dover Books, 1974.

Guiley, Rosemary Ellen. *The Encyclopedia of Ghosts and Spirits*. Facts on File, 1992.

Lawlor, Robert. *Voices of the First Day: Entering the Aboriginal Dreamtime*. Inner Traditions, 1991.

Little, Greg. *People of the Web*. White Buffalo Books, 1990.

Lovelock, James. *Gaia: A New Look at Life*. Oxford University Press, 1995.

MacLean, Adam. *The Alchemical Mandala*. Phanes Press, 1989.

Magin, Ulrich. "Mysterious Craters, Holes and Crop Circles in Eastern Europe." *Strange*, no. 11 (1993).

Michell, John. *City of Revelation*. Ballantine Books, 1972.

———. *The New View Over Atlantis*. G.P. Putnam and Sons, 1983.

———. Personal communication (1993).

Mighty Companions/Echoes 3. *A Crop Circle Compilation*. Mighty Companions, 1991.

Noyes, Ralph, ed. *The Crop Circle Enigma*. Gateway Books, 1990.

Randles, Jenny. "Cropfields Circled: Jenny Randles Responds." *Strange*, no. 7 (1991).

Sanderson, Ivan T. *Things*. Pyramid Books, 1967.

Shoemaker, Michael T. "Measuring the Circles." *Strange*, no. 6 (1990).

Spencer, John. *World Atlas of UFOs*. Smithmark Publishers, 1991.

Stacy, Dennis. "Cropfields Circled." *Strange*, no. 8 (1991).

Steele, John. Personal communication (1993).

Thompson, Keith. *Angels and Aliens: UFOs and the Mythic Imagination*. Addison Wesley Publishing, 1991.

Trench, Brinsley LePoer. *The Sky People*. Neville Spearman, 1963.

CHAPTER 10 ALIEN GENESIS

Bumrich, Josef K. *The Spaceships of Ezekiel*. Bantam Books, 1974.

Bramley, William. *The Gods of Eden*. Avon Books, 1990.

Campbell, Joseph. *The Masks of God*, vol. 1–3. Arkana, 1991.

Charroux, Robert. *One Hundred Thousand Years of Man's Unknown History*. Berkley Medallion Books, 1970.

Corliss, William R. *Ancient Man: A Handbook of Puzzling Artifacts*. The Sourcebook Project, 1978.

Fort, Charles. *The Complete Books of Charles Fort*. Dover Books, 1974.

Gardner, John, and Maier, John. *The Epic of Gilgamesh*. translated from the Sin-Leqi-Uninni version. Alfred A. Knopf, 1984.

Holy Bible, King James Version. World Publishing Company

Hough, Peter, and Jenny Randles. *Looking for the Aliens: A Psychological, Scientific and Imaginative Investigation.* Blandford, 1991.

Huyghe, Patrick. "Antimatter: UFO Update on Erich von Daniken." *OMNI* (May 1994).

Keel, John A. *Our Haunted Planet.* Fawcett Publications, 1971.

Nicholson, Irene. *Mexican and Central American Mythology.* Paul Hamlyn, 1975.

Pauwels, Louis and Jacques Bergier. *The Morning of the Magicians.* Avon Books, 1968.

Sanders, N. K. "Enuma Elish" *Poems of Heaven and Hell from Ancient Mesopotamia.* Penguin Books, 1989.

Schroeder, John. "Ancient Space Travel is Termed Nonsense." *Arizona Republic,* 26 October 1974.

Sitchin, Zacharia. *The Twelfth Planet.* Avon Books, 1976.

———. *The Stairway to Heaven.* Avon Books, 1980.

———. *The Wars of Gods and Men.* Avon Books, 1985.

———. *The Lost Realms.* Avon Books, 1990.

———. *Genesis Revisited.* Avon Books, 1990.

———. *When Time Began.* Avon Books, 1993.

———. "Zacariah Sitchin lecture." Lace Jergensen audiotape (March 1990).

Thompson, Richard L. *Alien Identities.* Govardhan Hill Publications, 1993.

Trench, Brinsley LePoer. *The Sky People.* Neville Spearman, 1963.

von Danekin, Erich. *Chariots of the Gods?* G.P. Putnam's Sons, 1970.

———. *The Gold of the Gods.* Souvenir, 1973.

Willis, Paul J. "The Alien Visitors of Charles Fort." *Strange,* vol. 1, no. 1 (no date).

PART THREE: THE ALIEN CULTURE

CHAPTER 11   ANGELS FROM SPACE

Adamski, George. *Flying Saucers Have Landed.* The British Book Centre, 1953.

Blavatsky, Helena Petrovna. *Isis Unveiled*. Theosophical Press, 1994.

———. *The Secret Doctrine*. University of Theosophical Press, 1988.

Clow, Barbara Hand. *Heart of the Christos: Starseeding from the Pleiades*. Bear and Co., 1989.

———. *Signet of Atlantis: War in Heaven Bypass*. Bear and Co., 1992.

Freixedo, Salvador. *Visionaries, Mystics & Contactees*. Illuminate Press.

Goodman, Felicitas. *How About Demons?* University of Indiana, 1988.

Hastings, Arthur. *With the Tongues of Men and Angels: A Study of Channeling*. Holt, Rinehart and Winston, 1991.

Hawken, Paul. *The Magic of Findhorn*. Bantam, 1980.

Hough, Peter, and Jenny Randles. *Looking for the Aliens: A Psychological, Scientific and Imaginative Investigation*. Blandford, 1991.

Jamal, Michele. *Volcanic Visions: Encounters With Other Worlds*. Arcana, 1991.

———. Personal communication (1993).

Johnson, Paul. "Imaginary Mahatmas." *GNOSIS: A Journal of the Western Inner Traditions*, no. 28 (Summer 1993).

Krafton-Minkel Walter. *Subterranean Worlds*. Loompanics Unlimited, 1898.

Montgomery, Ruth. *Aliens Among Us*. Fawcett Crest, 1985.

Moore, William L. "The Giant Rock Airport Gathering." *Far Out*, vol. 1, no. 4 (Summer 1993).

Parisen, Maria. *Angels and Mortals: The Co-Creative Power*. Quest Books, 1990.

Phillip, Brother. *The Secret of the Andes*. Leaves of Grass, 1976.

Podmore, Frank. *Mediums of the 19th Century*, vols. 1 and 2. University Books, 1963.

Ramsland, Katherine. "Inner Voices: Devil or Angel?" *Magical Blend*, no. 34 (April 1992).

Spangler, David. *Links With Space*. Findhorn Foundation, 1971.

Spataford, Guy. "The Abduction/Out-of-Body Connection." *UFO*, vol. 8, no. 2 (1993).

Spencer, John. *World Atlas of UFOs*. Smithmark Publishers, 1991.

Steiger, Brad. *The Star People*. Berkley, 1981.

———. *The UFO Abductors*. Berkley, 1988.

———. *The Fellowship: Spiritual Contact Between Humans and Outer Space Beings*. Ballantine, 1989.

———. *The Other*. Inner Light Publications, 1992.

Thompson, Keith. *Angels and Aliens: UFOs and the Mythic Imagination*. Addison Wesley Publishing, 1991.

Unarius Academy of Science. *The Arrival: A Space Saga* (videotape).

Wyllie, Timothy. *The Deta Factor; Dolphins, Extraterrestrials and Angels*. Coleman Publishing, 1984.

X-7. *A World Within a World: X-7 Reporting*. Findhorn Press,

ZaviRah, ed. *Lightspeed*, no. 11 (1992).

CHAPTER 12 PROPHESIES AND PANICS

Anchors, William E. "The Invaders." *Epi-Log Journal*, no. 3 (July–August 1992).

Clarke, Arthur C. *Childhood's End*. Ballantine Books, 1953.

Dash, Mike. "It Came From Outer Space!" *Fortean Times: The Journal of Strange Phenomena*, no. 71 (October–November 1993).

Dick, Phillip K. *VALIS*. Vintage Books, 1991.

———. *Radio Free Albemuth*. Avon, 1987.

———. *The Three Stigmata of Palmer Eldritch*. Vintage Books, 1965.

Coleman, Loren and Mark Chorvinsky. "Lizard People of the Movies." *Strange*, no. 4 (no date).

Grossinger, Richard. *Waiting for the Martian Express*. North Atlantic Books, 1989.

Haddon, Jonathon. "Close Encounters of the Film Kind." *Strange*, vol. 1, no. 1 (no date).

Harris, Micah. "Twin Peaks, Fairy Tales, and Rip Van Winkle." *Wrapped in Plastic*, vol. 1, no. 10 (April 1994).

Holmes, Richard J. "New World, New Mind, or Old Mind, End of World." *Critique: Exploring Consensus Reality*, no. 31 (June–September 1989).

Keith, Jim. *Casebook for Alternative 3*. INE, 1994.

Lessing, Doris. *Shikasta: Re. Colonized Planet Three.* Alfred A. Knopf, 1979.

———. *The Sirian Experiments.* Alfred A. Knopf, 1981.

Lloyd, John Uri. *ETIDORHPA: Or the End of Earth.* Simon and Schuster, 1978, first printing 1895.

Lynch, Jennifer. *The Secret Diary of Laura Palmer.* Pocket Books, 1990.

Miller, Craig. "Al Strobel Speaks!" *Wrapped in Plastic,* vol. 1, no. 11 (June 1994).

Morris, Desmond. *The Naked Ape.* Dell, 1993.

———. *The Human Zoo: A Zoologist's Classic Study of the Human Animal.* Kodansha, 1996.

Palmer, Raymond A. "The Shaver Mystery." *Amazing Stories,* vol. 21, no. 6 (June 1947).

Snook, Greg. "Beauties and the Beasts." *Strange,* no. 4 (no date).

Spencer, John. *World Atlas of UFOs.* Smithmark Publishers, 1991.

Stillings, Dennis, ed. *Cyberbiological Studies of the Imaginal Component in the UFO Contact Experience.* Archaeus Project, 1989.

Sutin, Lawrence. *In Pursuit of Valis: Selections From the Exegesis.* Underwood-Miller, 1991.

Thomas, Lars and Soren. "Crypto Movies." *Strange,* no. 4 (no date).

Thompson, Keith. *Angels and Aliens: UFOs and the Mythic Imagination.* Addison Wesley Publishing, 1991.

Vallee, Jacques. *Messengers of Deception.* And/Or Press, 1979.

Watson, Ian. *The Embedding.* Gollancz, 1973.

———. *Miracle Visitors.* Gollancz, 1978.

———. *The Book of Ian Watson.* Mark V. Ziesing, 1985.

Watson, Nigel and Darren Slade. "Supernatural Spielberg." *Fortean Times: The Journal of Strange Phenomena,* no. 64 (August/September 1992).

Wells, H. G. *The War of the Worlds.* Pocket Books, 1988.

Yamashiro, Bryan. "Twin Peaks, Folklore and the Nature of Reality." *Wrapped in Plastic,* vol. 1, no. 10 (April 1994).

CHAPTER 13 CULTS OF CHAOS

Bardon, Franz. *The Practice of Magical Evocation.* Dieter Ruggeberg/Wuppertal, 1970.

Bord, Janet and Colin Bord. *Alien Animals.* Stackpole Books, 1981.

Buettner, John A. "H. P. Lovecraft: The Mythos of Scientific Materialism." *Strange,* no. 11 (1993).

Carroll, Peter J. *Liber Null and Psychonaut: An Introduction to Chaos Magic.* Samuel Weiser, 1987.

Chapman, Douglas. "Jack Parsons: Sorcerous Scientist." *Strange,* no. 6 (1990).

———. "Celluloid Crowley: The Mage and the Movies." *Strange,* no. 7 (1991).

Chorvinsky, Mark and Douglas Chapman. "The Lovecraft Paradox." *Strange,* no. 11 (1993).

Corrales, Scott. "The Thin Black Line." *Strange,* no. 13 (1994).

Crowley, Aleister. *Magick in Theory and Practice.* Magical Childe Publishing, 1929 and 1990.

———. *The Book of the Law.* Magical Childe Publishing, 1990.

Custor, Frater. "Towards an Alien Understanding." *The Cincinnati Journal of Magick,* vol. 2, no. 6, Black Moon Publishing

Delio, Michelle. "The Magical Mark: The Art of Tattoo." *GNOSIS: A Journal of the Western Inner Traditions,* no. 27 (Spring 1993).

DuQuette, Lon Milo, and Christopher S. Hyatt. *The Way of the Secret Lover: Tantra, Tarot and the Holy Guardian Angel.* Falcon Press, 1992.

———. *Aleister Crowley's Illustrated Goetia.* New Falcon Publications, 1992.

———. *Enochian World of Aleister Crowley: Enochian Sex Magick.* New Falcon Publications, 1991.

Guiley, Rosemary Ellen. *The Encyclopedia of Ghosts and Spirits.* Facts on File, 1992.

Grant, Kenneth. *Outside the Circles of Time.* Skoob Esoterica, 1986.

———. *Hecate's Fountain.* Skoob Esoterica, 1993.

Hay, George. *The Necronomicon: The Book of Dead Names.* Skoob Books Publishing, 1992.

Hine, Phil. *Chaos Servitors: A User Guide.* Chaos International, 1992.

Holub, Allen. "The Second Book of the Forgotten Ones." *The Cincinnati Journal of Magick,* vol. 2, no. 6 (no date).

Keel, John A. *Strange Creatures From Time and Space.* Fawcett Publications, 1968.

Lageza, Lazlo. *Tao Magic: The Secret Language of Diagrams and Calligraphy.* Thames and Hudson, 1975.

(NOT FOR USE IN MAGNETIC STRIPE READERS)

ate destination or stop in a country other than the country of departure the Warsaw Convention may be most cases limits the liability of carriers for death or personal injury and in respect of loss of or damage to International Passengers on Limitation of Liability" and "Notice of Baggage Liability Limitations."

CONDITIONS OF CONTRACT

er ticket and baggage check, of which quivalent to "transportation," "carrier" a passenger or his baggage hereunder age, "WARSAW CONVENTION" means ating to International Carriage by Air tion as amended at The Hague, 28th

servants and representatives of carrier and any person whose aircraft is used by carrier for carriage and its agents, servants and representatives.

7. Checked baggage will be delivered to bearer of the baggage check. In case of damage to baggage moving in international transportation complaint must be made in writing to carrier forthwith after discovery of damage and, at the latest, within 7 days from receipt; in case of delay, complaint must be made within 21 days from date the baggage was delivered. See tariffs or conditions of carriage regarding non-international transportation.

lating to liability established by the Warsaw as defined by that Convention.

8. This ticket is good for carriage for one year from date of issue, except as otherwise provided in this ticket, in carrier's tariffs, conditions of carriage, or related regulations. The fare for carriage hereunder is subject to change prior to commencement of carriage. Carrier may refuse transportation if the applicable fare has not been paid.

rriage and other services performed by ticket, (II) applicable tariffs, (III) carrier's nade part hereof (and are available on on between a place in the United States in force in those countries apply.

9. Carrier undertakes to use its best efforts to carry the passenger and baggage with reasonable dispatch. Times shown in timetable or elsewhere are not guaranteed and form no part of this contract. Carrier may without notice substitute alternate carriers or aircraft, and may alter or omit stopping places shown on the ticket in case of necessity. Schedules are subject to change without notice. Carrier assumes no responsibility for making connections.

a full name and its abbreviation being ons or timetables; carrier's address shall eviation of carrier's name in the ticket; in this ticket or as shown in carrier's ger's route; carriage to be performed ingle operation.

10. Passenger shall comply with Government travel requirements, present exit, entry and other required documents and arrive at airport by time fixed by carrier or, if no time is fixed, early enough to complete departure procedures.

11. No agent, servant or representative of carrier has authority to alter, modify or waive any provision of this contract unless authorized by a corporate officer of carrier.

another air carrier does so only as its agent, ply to and be for the benefit of agents,

PRV. 3-89

Lovecraft, H. P. *The Best of H. P. Lovecraft: Bloodcurdling Tales of Horror and the Macabre*. Del Ray Books, 1982.

———. *The Dream Quest of Unknown Kadath*. Ballantine Books, 1970.

Martine, Louis. "The Dreaming of Bes." *The Cincinnati Journal of Magick,* vol. 2, no. 7, Black Moon Publishing, 1989.

Nema. "Panaeonic Magick." *The Cincinnati Journal of Magick,* vol. 2, no. 7, Black Moon Publishing (no date).

Pazzaglini, Mario. *Symbolic Messages: An Introduction to the Science of Alien Writing*. Author-published (1991).

Rydeen, Paul. "UFOs and the Cult of Cargo." *Strange,* no. 9 (1992).

Schueler, Gerard. *Enochian Magic: A Practical Manual*. Llewellyn, 1990.

———. *An Advanced Guide to Enochian Magick*. Llewellyn, 1992.

"Simon," ed. *The Necronomicon*. Avon Books, 1977.

Wilson, Robert Anton. *Cosmic Trigger of the Illuminati*, vol. 1. New Falcon Publications, 1977.

CHAPTER 14 PLANETARY ELDERS

Allione, Tsultrim. *Women of Wisdom*. Arkana, 1986.

Black Elk, Wallace, with William S. Lyon. *Black Elk: The Sacred Ways of a Lakota*. Harper San Francisco, 1990.

———. Personal communication (1993).

Brown, Joseph Epes. *The Sacred Pipe: Black Elk's Account of the Seven Rites of the Oglala Sioux*. University of Oklahoma Press, 1953.

Eliade, Mircea. *Shamanism: Archaic Techniques of Ecstasy*. Princeton University Press, 1964.

Foster, Steven, and Meredith Little. *Betwixt and Between: Patterns of Masculine and Feminine Initiation*. Open Court Press, 1987.

Freixedo, Salvador. *Visionaries, Mystics & Contactees*. Illuminate Press, 1992.

Goodman, Felicitas. *Where the Spirits Ride the Winds*. University of Indiana Press, 1990.

Halifax, Joan. *Shamanic Voices*. Dutton, 1979.

———. *The Fruitful Darkness: Reconnecting with the Body of the Earth*. HarperSan Francisco, 1993.

———. Personal communications (1988–89).

Harner, Michael, ed. *Hallucinogens and Shamanism.* Oxford University Press, 1973.

Harner, Michael. *The Way of the Shaman: A Guide to Power and Healing.* Harper and Row, 1980.

Keel, John A. *Our Haunted Planet.* Fawcett Publications, 1971.

Lawlor, Robert. *Voices of the First Day: Entering the Aboriginal Dreamtime.* Inner Traditions, 1991.

Mails, Thomas E. *Fools Crow: Wisdom and Power.* Council Oak Books, 1991.

McKibben, Bill. *The Age of Missing Information.* Plume Books, 1991.

Morgan, Marlo. *Mutant Message Down Under.* Marlo Morgan Co. (no date).

Norbu, Namkhai, ed. by Michael Katz. *Dream Yoga and the Practice of the Natural Light.* Snow Lion, 1992.

Norbu, Namkhai, ed. by John Shane. *The Crystal and the Way of Light: Sutra, Tantra and Dzogchen.* Routledge and Kegan Paul, 1986.

Somé, Malidoma. *Ritual: Healing, Power and Community.* Swan-Raven and Co., 1993.

Sogyal Rinpoche. *The Tibetan Book of Living and Dying.* Harper SanFrancisco, 1992.

Sullivan, Lawrence E. *Icanchu's Drum: An Orientation to Meaning in South American Religions.* Macmillan Publishing Co., 1988.

Tharchin-Rinpoche, Lama. Personal communications (1991–93).

Thompson, Keith. *Angels and Aliens: UFOs and the Mythic Imagination.* Addison Wesley Publishing, 1991.

Trungpa, Chogyam, and Freemantle. *The Tibetan Book of the Dead.* Shambhala Books.

CHAPTER 15 THE NEW SEERS

Alexander, John, and Victoria, eds. *Treatment and Research of Experienced Anomalous Trauma (TREAT) Proceedings.* March, 1993.

Haraway, Donna. *Simians, Cyborgs, and Women: The Reinvention of Nature.* Routledge, 1991.

Jahn, Robert, and Brenda Dunne. *Margins of Reality.* Harcourt Brace Jovanovitch, 1987.

Levin, Martin. "End of the World or End of the Ego?" *Critique: Exploring Consensus Reality,* no. 31 (June–September 1989).

Mack, John E. *Abduction: Human Encounters with Aliens.* Charles Scribner's and Sons, 1994.

McKenna, Terence. *The Archaic Revival.* HarperCollins Publishers, 1991.

———. *Food of the Gods.* Bantam, 1992.

———. *True Hallucinations.* HarperSan Francisco, 1993.

———. "Radical Mushroom Reality." *Fortean Times: The Journal of Strange Phenomena,* no. 71 (October/November,1993).

———. "Imagination in the Light of Nature." *Psychedelic Illuminations,* vol. 1, no. 4

———. "Questioning Terence McKenna." *UFO,* vol. 8, no. 4 (1993).

———. *The Definitive UFO Tape* (audiotape). Dolphin Tapes, Mill Valley, CA, 1983.

———. Personal communications (1991–93).

McKenna, Dennis, and Terence McKenna. *The Invisible Landscape: Mind, Hallucinogens and the I Ching.* Seabury Press, 1975.

———. *Psilocybin: Magic Mushroom Grower's Guide.* Quick American Publishing, 1991.

McKenna, Terence, Rupert Sheldrake, and Ralph Abraham. *Trialogues at the Edge of the West.* Bear and Co., 1992.

Ring, Kenneth. *The Omega Project: Near-Death Experiences, UFO Encounters, and Mind at Large.* William Morrow and Co., 1992.

———. "Near-Death and UFO Encounters as Shamanic Initiations: Some Conceptual and Evolutionary Implications." *ReVision* 11/3 (Winter 1989).

Rushkoff, Douglas. *Cyberia: Life in the Trenches of Hyperspace.* HarperSan Francisco, 1994.

Siler, Todd. *Breaking the Mind Barrier.* Simon and Schuster, 1990.

Sirius, R.U., ed. *Mondo 2000: User's Guide to the New Edge.* Harper Perennial, 1992.

Stillings, Dennis, ed. *Cyberbiological Studies of the Imaginal Component in the UFO Contact Experience.* Archaeus Project, 1989.

Young, Stanley. "An Overview of the End." *Critique: Exploring Consensus Reality,* no. 31 (June–September 1989).

Zollschan, G. K., J. F. Schumaker, and G. F. Walsh. *Exploring the Paranormal: Perspectives on Belief and Experience.* Prism Press, 1989.

INDEX

Abduction; Human Encounters with Aliens (Mack), 39, 287

Abductions, 24–42, 56, 159–61, 189–90, 287, 292

missing time element in, 152–53

Abe, Shunzo, 170

Aborigine traditions, 282–85

Abramelin system, 255

Abyss, The, 235

Abyss model, 294–95

Adamski, George, 11–12

Advanced Human Technology, Army Intelligence, 59

Advanced Systems Concept Office, US Army, 59

Aetherius Society, 215–16

Age of Missing Information, The (McKibben), 276

Agriglyphs (crop circles), 156–57, 163–73, 177–80, 181–86

Aion 131, 267

Air Force

disinformation and, 62

Project Blue Book, 45, 52

Roswell Incident and, 49–54, 63

UFO research projects, 53–56

Air Technical Intelligence Command (ATIC), 46–47

Akkad, kingdom of, 196

Alchemy, 254

Aleixo, Hulvio Brant, 120

Alexander, Colonel John B., 59–63

Alice in Wonderland (Carroll), 145

Alien Animals (Bord), 130–31

Alien Harvest, An (Moulton-Howe), 88

Alien Identities (Thompson), 209

Aliens From Space (Keyhoe), 52

Allagash Abductions, The (Fowler), 30

Allen, Thomas, 254

Allingham, William, 154–55

Allione, Tsultrim, 279

Alternative 3, 113, 234, 242

Alux, 146

Alvarez, Luiz and Walter, 204

Amaringo, Pablo, 148–49

Amazing Stories, 241–42

Ambrose, David, 113

American Warrior, The (Alexander), 59

Ancient Astronaut Theory, 4, 187–210, 257

ley lines and, 174–75

sacred geometry and, 168–70, 178

sexual encounters, 25

Angels, 141, 213, 222, 227, 232–33. *See also* Magic, cults of

Animal mutilations and deaths, 76–93, 133, 288

Apparitions, 132–37

Aquarius Project, 55–56

Archetypal images, 21–22, 42

Arnold, Kenneth, 5–6, 48

Ascended Masters, 228
Ashtar Command, 225
Ashurbanipal tablets, 196
Aspin, Les, 63
Atlantis, 97, 179–80, 219–21, 253
Aubrey, John, 173
Ayahuasca Visions (Luna), 148

Babalon Working (Parsons),
    260–61
Ballard, Guy W. and Edna, 219–21
Banyaca, Thomas, 169
Barbarous Names, 252
Barclay, John, 6–7
Bartholomew, 214
Barton, "Michael X," 47
Batman, 127
Beamships, 12–13
Bearden, Colonel Thomas E.,
    85–87, 95, 132–33
Bequette, Bill, 5
Bielek, Alfred, 95–101, 105–10,
    114
Bier, Theresa Ann, 72
Bigfoot-type creatures, 66–75, 119
Biopure, 85
Birdlike creatures, 124–28
Birth Memory Hypothesis, 292–94
Black Elk, Wallace, 276–78
Blade Runner, 234, 243
Blavatsky, Helena Petrovna,
    218–19
Bloecher, Ted, 30
Blue Book, U.S. Air Force Project,
    45, 52
Blum, Howard, 53
Blum, Ralph, 10–12
Blumrich, Josef F., 193–94
Book of Babalon, The (Parsons),
    260
Book of the Damned, Lo!, The
    (Fort), 9
Book of the Law, The (Crowley),
    258
Books, alien theme in, 234–36
Bord, Janet and Colin, 73, 130–31,
    136–37

Botanic Garden, The (Darwin),
    172
Boxgrove Man, 189
Brazel, William (Mac), 48–49
Bryant, Alice, 38
Buddha Padmasambhava, 150,
    278–79
Bulletin of Anomalous Experiences
    (Gotlib), 38

Cameron, Duncan, 95, 98–101,
    104–9, 112–13
Campbell, Joseph, 198
Carroll, Lewis, 145
Cathie, "Captain" Bruce, 174–75
Cellular phones, 98
Cereologist, The, 182
Changelings, 160
Channeling, 122, 213–33, 251
Chaos Magic, 265–69
Chardin, Teilhard de, 184–85
Chariots of the Gods (von
    Daniken), 191
Chesterton, G. K., 140
Chevron, 204
Childhood's End (Clarke), 238–39
Chod tradition, 279–80
Clarke, Arthur C., 238–39
Classicist Movement, 270–71
Close Encounters Research
    Organization (CERO), 38
Close Encounters of the 3rd Kind,
    43
Cloudships, 157
Clow, Barbara Hand, 232
Coccioli, Gilberto Gregorio, 122
Coleman, Loren, 73
Collins, "Busty," 165
Communion; A True Story
    (Streiber), 33–36, 275
Conceptual communication,
    179–80
Confounding Theory, 298
Conjunctivitis, UFO sightings and,
    15
Conroy, Ed, 160
Conspiracy theories, 44–65

Cooper, Milton William, 54, 58
Cosmic seeding theory, 203
Creatures, 66–75, 109–10, 119–37
Crick, Francis, 203
Crop Circle Conference, 184
Crop circles, 156–57, 163–73,
     177–80, 181–82
Crowley, Aleister, 249–52, 257–60,
     263
Crowley, John, 145
Cryptobiology, 9, 73
Crystal technologies, 194, 221
Cthonic beings. *See* Qliphothic
     entities
Cultural diffusion theory, 190

Dakinis, 150, 279–81
Dames, Edward A., 291–92
Darwin, Erasmus, 172
David-Neel, Alexandra, 132, 280
Davis, Chris, 71
Davis, Kathie, 31–32, 35–36
Day, Fred, 183
Day the Earth Stood Still, The, 236
Deacon, Terence, 189
Dead orgone (DOR), 102–3
Deardorff, James W., 235
Dee, John, 249, 254–55
Deere, Phillip, 273–74
Defense Initiative Office, 59
Defense Intelligence Agency
     (DIA), UFO Working Group,
     53
Delta Project, 55
Delta-T antenna, 104, 106
Devas, 150
Devereux, Paul, 176–77, 288
Diamond, Jackson County Sheriff,
     10
Dick, Phillip K., 113, 243–44
Dinosaurids, 128–29, 131
Dirigibles, phantom airship
     sightings and, 6
"Disclosure for the Interior and
     Superior Care for Mortals"
     (Harris & Scott), 218
Dolphin channels, 227

*Dolphins, Extraterrestrials and
     Angels* (Wyllie), 227
Dr. Who, 238
Dragon Project, 177
"Dreamland," Groom Lake Base,
     Nevada, 55, 57, 62–64
Duende, 146
Dulce facility, 61, 83–85, 128
Dunne, Brenda, 290
Dwarves, hairy, 119–20, 123–25

E.T., 235
Earth Chronicles, The (Sitchin),
     195
Earth Lights (Devereux), 176, 288
Earth traditions, rebirth of, 270–85
Earth Versus the Flying Saucers,
     234
Eco, Umberto, 64–65
Ectoplasm, 217
Edison, Thomas, 16
Egyptian magical tradition, 254,
     255–58
Eisenhower, President Dwight D.,
     53
Electromagnetic bottle technique,
     100
Electromagnetic disturbances,
     177–78
Electromagnetic radiation (EM),
     low-frequency, 16
Electron capture detector, 180
Electronic voice phenomenon
     (EVP), 16–17
Element 115, 57
Eliade, Mircea, 155
Elves and fairies, 138–62
Energy vortices, 97–98, 100
Enochian magic, 254–55
Enuma Elish, 201
Epic of Gilgamesh, 200–201
Erdoes, Richard, 278
Etidorhpa or The End of Earth
     (Lloyd), 240
Evans-Wentz, W. Y., 142, 153, 157,
     157–60
Excalibur Project, 55

Extra-mundane vandals, 10–12
Extraterrestrial biological entities (EBEs), 53
Extraterrestrial Hypothesis (ETH), 4, 18, 21, 42, 44–45

Fairies at Work and Play, The (Hodson), 140–41
Fairy Faith in Celtic Countries, The (Evans-Wentz), 142
Fairy tradition, 138–62
   rings (crop circles), 156–57, 163–73, 177–80, 181–82
   ships, 6
False Memory Syndrome Foundation, 40
Farfadets, 157
Feng shui, 174
Fiction, alien theme in, 234–46
Film and television, alien theme in, 234–46
Findhorn community, Scotland, 221–23
Fire From the Sky, 29
Fish, Paul, 192
Five Million Years to Earth, 237
Flaps, 86
Flores, Oscar Alberto, 121
Flournoy, Theodore, 7–8
Flugelrads, 47, 110
Fluorescent Freddie, 72
Flying saucer, terminology of, 5
Flying Saucer Conspiracy (Keyhoe), 27
Flying Saucers (Jung), 21–22
Flying Saucers Are Real, The (Keyhoe), 52
Foltz, Charlie, 29–30
Fontes, Dr. Olivio, 26
Foo fighter sightings, 45–48
Fools Crow, Frank, 271–72
Fort, Charles, 9–10, 83, 176, 184, 190, 263, 289
Fortean Times, 9
Fortune, Dion, 249
Foucault's Pendulum (Eco), 63–65
Four abysses, 294–95

Fowler, Raymond E., 30
Fox sisters (Spiritualism), 7, 217–18
Fox Spirits, 150–51
Friedman, Stanton, 49
Friedrich, Christof, 47
From India to the Planet Mars (Flournoy), 8
Frost, Mark, 244
Fuhr, Edwin, 170–71
Fuller, John, 27–28

Gabriel Project, 55–56
Gaia Hypothesis, 163, 180–83, 185
Gardner, Gerald, 185
Geiger, H. R., 264
German UFOs, 46–48
Ghost dogs, 133–37
Ghost lore, UFO sightings and, 18–19
Ghost rockets, 45–48
Giant Rock Airport, 91–93
Gilgamesh, epic story of, 200–201
Girodo, Lou, 87
Glenn, John, 55–56
Gnomes, 144. *See also* Fairy tradition
Gods Must Be Crazy, The, 246
Godwin, Joscelyn, 143
Golden Dawn, Hermetic Order of the, 249–50
Goodman, Felicitas, 229
Gotlib, Dr. David, 38
Gotzen gegen Thule (Landig), 47
Government-alien activities, 44–65
Government Operations Committee, 63
Grant, Kenneth, 261, 265–67
Gravity amplifiers, 57
Grays, 24–25, 34, 39, 51, 53, 56, 57, 84, 106–7, 119, 121, 128–29, 146
Green, Michael, 179–80
Green men, 122
Greenwell, Russell, 124

Gremlins, 46
Grimm brothers, 138
Grimoires, 248
Grof, Stanislav, 292–93
Groom Lake S4 facility, 55, 57, 62–64
Grosso, Michael, 19, 96
Grudge Report, 55
Guest Project, 55
Guided imagery, 40–41
Gulf Breeze Sightings, The (Walters), 14

Hairy dwarves, 119–20, 123–25
Halstead, Millard, 125
Hamilton, Alexander, 78
Haraway, Donna, 293
Hardwick, Gary, 166
Harris, T. L., 218
Hartland, Edwin, 159
Haunted sites, 90
Haut, William, 49
Hawken, Paul, 221–22
Healing Shattered Reality (Bryant & Seebach), 38
Hecate's Fountain (Grant), 266
Hermetic Order of the Golden Dawn, 249–50
Hesiod, 136
Hibbard, Robert, 6
Hickson, Charles, 10–11
Hidden Masters, 220–21
Hill, Betty and Barney, 26–28
Hillenkoetter, Admiral R. H., 53
Hoagland, Richard, 112
Hoax Theory, 163
Hodson, Geoffrey, 140–41
Holloman Air Force Base, 56
Hopi prophesies, 168–70, 181
Hopkins, Bud, 31–36, 39, 289
How About Demons? (Goodman), 229
How to Serve Man, 236
Hronek, Peter, 71
Human Potential movement, 214
Hunt, Robert, 144–45
Hyerdahl, Thor, 190

Hynek, J. Allen, 10
Hypnotherapy, 40–42, 217
abductee experiences and, 31–32, 34

I Am Foundation, 220
Iamblichus, 140–41
Ickleton Mandelbrot set agriglyph, 166–67
Integretron, 92
International Association for Near-Death Studies, 59–60
Interrupted Journey, The (Fuller), 28
Intruders (Hopkins), 31, 32, 289
Invaders, The, 238
"I Remember Lemuria" (Shaver), 241
Irving, Washington, 153
Isis Unveiled (Blavatsky), 219

Jacobs, David, 160
Jacobs, Ted, 35
Jahn, Robert, 290–91
Jeladevata, 151
Jenkyns, Mr. and Mrs. R., 130
Jung, Carl, 21–22, 42
Justified men, 145–46

Kafton-Minkel, Walter, 143
Kaiser, Mr. and Mrs. George, 72
Keel, John A., 14, 19, 20, 59, 78–79, 82, 120, 125–27, 131, 154, 184, 262, 288–89
Keen, Sam, 65
Kelly, Edward, 254–55
Kennedy, Robert, 126
Kennets pictogram, 174
Kerenyi, Carl, 21
Keyhoe, Major Donald E., 27, 52
Killburn, Steve, 30
King, "Sir" George, 215–16
King, Harry, 79
Kirk, Robert, 140, 142–43, 153, 156, 159–60
Klass, Phillip, 14, 28
Klein, Dr. Donald, 34

Ku, cult of the, 266–67
Kubler Ross, Elizabeth, 60

Labdron, Machig, 279
Lake monsters, 129–31
Lam, cults of, 258
Lame Deer, John, 278
Landig, Wilhelm, 47
Language of the Circle Makers, The (Green), 179
Lazar, Bob, 57
Lazaris, 214
Leannain Sith, 160
Leary, Timothy, 259
Lessing, Doris, 239–40
Levi, Eliaphas, 247–48
Ley lines, 174–77
Lilith (MacDonald), 145
Little, Greg, 175–76
Little, Big (Crowley), 145
"Little green men," 122
Lizard-type creatures, 71–72, 121
Lloyd, John Uri, 240
Loch Ness monster, 129–31
Lokapalas, 150
Lovecraft, Howard Phillips, 262–64
Lovelock, James, 180
Lu, Sheng-Yen, 281
Luna, Luis Eduardo, 148–49
Luna Project, 55
Lundy, Ruth, 128
Lynch, David, 244

Mabinogion, The, 139
MacCabee, Dr. Bruce, 14
MacDonald, George, 145
Mack, Bill, 146
Mack, John, 39–40, 286–88
MacLaine, Shirley, 214
MacLean, Dorothy, 141, 214, 222
Magic, cults of, 247–69
Magic of Findhorn, The (Hawken), 221–22
Magic and Mystery in Tibet (David-Neel), 132
Magic Presence, The (Ballard), 219

Magick in Theory and Practice (Crowley), 250
Maidana, Hector, 120
Maiyun, 175–76
Majestic 12 (MJ-12), 53–55, 58
Majority-Majestic briefing, 55–56
"Making Monsters" (Ofshe & Walters), 41
Manisolas, 47–48
Manson, Charles, 268
Mantell, Captain Thomas, 50
Marcel, Major Jesse A., 48
Marduk, planet of, 201–5, 207, 210
Marfa lights, 176
Marian manifestations, 230–31
Mars, visions of, 7–8
Martian pyramids, 111–13
Maryland Bigfoot, 71
Masks of God, The (Campbell), 198
Materializations, 217
Mathers, Samuel Liddell, 249
Mayan ruins, 111, 194, 224–25
McIntyre, Williard, 70
McKenna, Dennis, 296–97
McKenna, Terence, 43, 294–97
McKibben, Bill, 276
Meier, Eduard Billy, 12–13
Men in Black (MIBs), 44, 58–59, 126, 157, 238
Mermaids, 131
Mesmer, Franz (Mesmerism), 216–17
Mexico's Little People (Mack), 146
Michael therapists, 228
Miles, Christopher, 113
Military, UFO-related conspiracy theories and, 44–65
Milk Hill agriglyph, 179
Mind Chronicles, The (Clow), 232
Miracle Visitors (Watson), 242–43
Missing memories, 40–41
Missing Time (Hopkins), 30
Monsters, 66–75, 109–10, 119–37
Montauk Project, 94–115, 234, 299
Montauk Project, The (Nichols), 94–95

Monuments of Mars, The (Hoagland), 111
Moore, Bill, 49, 53–54
More, Henry, 172
Morgan, Dr. Marlo, 283–84
Morris, Desmond, 240
Morrison, Earl, 127
Mother ships, 43
Mothmen Prophesies, The (Keel), 125
Mothmen, 125–26
Moulton-Howe, Linda, 87–89, 128
Mountain peak discharges (MPDs), 177
Mount Shastika, California, 147
Mowing Devil, The, 173
Multiple personality disorders (MPDs), 245
Mushrooms, visionary nature of, 295–97
Mutant Message From Down Under (Morgan), 283–85
Mysteries, The (Iamblichus), 140

Nadu, Tamil, 161
Nagas, 279
Naiman, Dr. Bob, 34
Nathan, Dr. Robert, 14
National Institutes of Health, 85
National Science Foundation, 85
National Security Agency, 57
Nazca Lines of Peru, 191
Nazi flying saucers, 46–48, 100, 110. *See also* Montauk Project
Neanderthal Man, 188–89
Necronomicon, The, 264–66
Nemesis Theory, 204
Neo-Reichian Therapy, 102
Nevada Nuclear Test Site, 55
New Lands (Fort), 9
New Mexico, military research in, 51
Newton, George, 147
Nibiruans, 107
Nichols, Preston, 94–99, 102–11, 113–15

Number-calling phenomenon, 19–21

O'Brien, Ron, 129
Occultism, 247–69
Ofshe, Richard, 41
Olcott, Colonel Henry, 219
Oliphant, Ted, 82
One-eyed creatures, 120–21
Ordo Templi Orientis (OTO), 259–62, 265–66, 268–69
Orgel, Leslie, 203
Orgone energy, 103
Orions, 106–7
Other, The (Steiger), 226
Otis Imperialia (Tilbury), 157
Outer Limits, The, 235, 238
Out-of-place-artifacts (OOPARTs), 190–91, 210
Outside the Circles of Time (Grant), 267
Outside factor, 19
Out There (Blum), 53
Oz Factor, 22–23

Padmasambhava, 150, 279
Paganism, 185, 284
Palmer, Ray, 241–42
Paracelsus, 144, 159
Paranormal phenomena, modern scientists of, 286–300
Parapsychology, UFOlogy and, 19
Parker, Calvin, 10–11
Parsons, Jack, 259–61
People of the Web, The (Little), 175
Pereira, Jader, 121
Perls, Fritz, 214
Persinger, Michael, 177
Personality changes, UFO experiences and, 15
Phantastes (MacDonald), 145
Phantom airship sightings, 6
Phantom trains, 176
Phenomenon of Man, The (Chardin), 184–85
Philadelphia Experiment, 95, 96, 99–111, 114

Philadelphia Experiment, The, 95, 105, 108–9, 234
Philadelphia Experiment and Other UFO Conspiracies, The (Bielek), 95
"Phillip, Brother" (Hidden Masters), 221
Phoenix Project, 103
Piezo-electric effect, 174
Pilichis, Dennis, 66, 69–70
Pilles, Peter, 192
Pipintu, 146
Planet X, 204
Plot, Dr. Robert, 172–73
Popular culture, alien theme in, 234–46
Possession states, 244–45
Possible Extraterrestrial Strategy for Earth (Deardorff), 235
Posthypnotic suggestions, 20
Pounce Project, 55
Powell, James, 80
Princess and the Goblin (MacDonald), 145
Princeton Institute for Advanced Study, 100–101
Project Guest, 55
Projects, UFO military research, 45, 52–53, 55–56, 100, 102. *See also* Montauk Project
Prophet, Elizabeth Clare, 228
Prophetic dreams, 15
Psilocybin: The Magic Mushroom Grower's Guide, 295
Psychotronic warfare technology, 86–87, 94–96. *See also* Montauk Project

Qabalah, 256
Qliphothic entities, 261–63

Radiosonde, 103–4
Rainbow Project, 100
Rak, Chuck, 29–30
Ramsey, Air Force General, 49
Ramtha (J. Z. Knight), 214, 229
Randles, Jenny, 18, 22–23, 173

Raschke, Carl, 245–46
Raths (fairy rings), 156–57, 163–73, 177–80, 181–82
Raybone, Hugh, 166
Rebirthing, 292–94
Recovered memory therapy, 40–42
Redlight Project, 55
Reich, Wilhelm, 94, 100–103
Reptilian creatures, 127–28
Retrocognition, 15
Revelations (Vallee), 85
Rip van Winkle, 153
Roosevelt, President Franklin D., 106
Rosenbaum, Dr. Gene, 28
Roswell Incident, 49–53, 63
Roth, Gabrielle, 275
Ruppelt, Edward J., 46–47
Russell, Dale, 128–29
Ryerson, Kevin, 214

Sacred Magic of Abramelin the Mage, The (Levi), 248
Sagan, Carl, 28, 192
Sages, 270–85
Salem Witch Trials of 1692, 42
Sanderson, Ivan T., 73, 171, 189–90, 288–89
Sayago, Farmin, 121
Scarberry, Mr. & Mrs. Rogert, 125
Schauberger, Viktor, 47
Schiff, Steven, 62–63
Schoenberger, Viktor, 110
Science fiction, alien theme in, 234–46
Scott, James, 218
Scott, Sir Walter, 153, 158
Scully, Frank, 50
Sea serpents, 129–31
Secret of the Andes, The (Brother Phillip), 220–22
Secret Commonwealth of Elves, Fauns and Fairies, The (Kirk), 143
Secret Doctrine, The (Blavatsky), 219
Secrets of the 3rd Reich, 100

Seebach, Linda, 38
Seguin, Ron, 128
Shamans, 155–57, 270–85
Shand, Bradford, 129–30
Shandera, Jamie, 53–54
Shaver, Richard, 242, 288
Shenstone, Peter, 227
Shertzer, Beau, 82–83
Shikasta (Lessing), 239–40
Silbury Hill agriglyph, 168
Simon, Dr. Benjamin, 27
Simonton, Joe, 154
Sirians, 107, 257–59
Sitchin, Zacariah, 107, 188, 194–95, 197, 200–208, 237
Skinner, Bob, 173
Smith, Helene, 8
Smith, Yvonne, 38
Solar System Defense, 112
Some, Malidoma, 278
Songlines, 185–86
South America, monster-UFO reports from, 120–23
Spaceships of Ezekiel, The (Blumrich), 194
Spangler, David, 222–23
Spirits
    communications with, 213–33
    magic cults and, 247–69
    rebirth of Earth traditions, 270–85
Spiritual traditions, rebirth of, 270–85
Spiritualist Movement, 7, 214, 216–18
Star Maidens, 226
Starseed Transmissions (Leary), 259
Star Trek, 234
Stealth bomber, 61, 100
Steele, John, 177
Steiger, Brad, 225–26
Stevens, Anthony, 114
Stevens, Ian, 164
Stewart, R. J., 143
Strange magazine, 9
Strange Harvest, A, 88

Strategic Defense Initiative ("Star Wars"), 51
Streiber, Whitley, 33–36, 160, 275
Stripling, Juanita, 80
Stukeley, Dr., 173
Sullivan, Lawrence E., 146, 157
Sumerians, 195–210
Summit University, 228
Superstition Mountains, 98
Sutton, Elmer "Lucky," 123
Svar direkt, 81
Sweden, animal mutilations in, 80–81
Swedenborg, Emanuel (Swedenborgian movement), 214, 216–17
Symbolic communication, 179–80
Symbolic Life, The (Jung), 21
Sympathetic Magic, 251–52

Taylor, Billy Ray, 123
Telepathy, 15
Television and film, alien theme in, 234–46
Tesla, Nikola, 16, 94, 100–101
Thelema, 258–59, 268
Theogeny (Hesiod), 136
Theosophical Society, 218–19
Things (Sanderson), 171
Thinnes, Roy, 238
"Thomas C.," 83–84
Thomas the Rhymer of Ercledoune (Lord Learmont), 141–42, 145
Thompson, Richard L., 161, 209
Thoth Tarot (Crowley), 250
Thought forms, 132
Thunderstorms, monsters and, 136
Tibetan tradition, 132, 278–82, 294
Tilbury, Gervase of, 157
Time travel, 94–115
Time Tunnel, The, 234, 238
Tolkien, J. R. R., 161
Topical vectors, 290
Total Recall, 113, 234, 243
Transformation (Streiber), 35
TREAT IV Conference, 291

Treatment and Research of Experienced Anomalous Trauma (TREAT), 41
Trench, Brinsley Le Poer, 179
Trickster, legends of the, 21–22
True magazine, 52
Truman, President Harry, 53–54
Tuella, 225
Tulpoidal phenomena, 132–33
Turley, Jonathan, 63
Twilight Zone, The, 238
Twin Peaks, 244–45
Typhonian Trilogies, The (Grant), 265–66

U. F. O., 238
UFOlogy, parapsychology and, 19
UFOs, forms of, 5
UFOs: The Best Evidence, 57
UFOs—Nazi Secret Weapon? (Friedrich), 47
UFO Working Group, Defense Intelligence Agency (DIA), 53
Ultradimensional Mind, The (Grosso), 19
United States Psychotronics Association, 96
Unsolved Mysteries, 63
Unveiled Mysteries (Ballard), 220

V, 238
VALIS (Dick), 243–44
Vallee, Jacques, 42, 85, 154–55, 157, 298
Van Tassel, George, 91–92
Vedas, 209
Villas-Boas, Antonio, 25–26
Vision quest, 273–74, 277
von Daniken, Erich, 191–94, 209
von Neumann, John, 100–101, 106, 107
Voyage to the Bottom of the Sea, 238

Wainwright, Geoffrey, 189
Waite, A. E., 249
Walters, Ed, 12–14

Walters, Ethan, 41–42
Walton, Travis and Duane, 28–29
Walton Experience, The (Walton), 28–29
War of the Worlds, The (Wells), 241
Warrior's Edge, The (Alexander), 59
Watkins, Alfred, 173
Watkins, Leslie, 113
Watson, Ian, 242–43
We Want You—Is Hitler Alive? (Barton), 47
Weiner, Jack and Jim, 29–30
Welch, Russell, 73
Wells, H. G., 241
Werewolves, 77–78
Wetzel, Charlie, 127
Whitehead, Alfred North, 294
Whiteside, Carl, 87
Wilcox, Chaves County Sheriff, 48
Wild Talents (Fort), 9
Williamson, Jim, 80
Wilson, Robert Anton, 241
Window areas, 79
Winged creatures, 124–28
Wise seers, 270–85
With the Tongues of Men and Angels (Hastings), 232
Wombell, Dick, 167
Woodbine creature, 128
World Within a World, A (X-7 reporting), 223–24
World War II, UFO-related conspiracy theory and, 45–48. *See also* Philadelphia Experiment
Worldwide grid, 174
Worthy, Don, 80
Wyatt, L. C., 79–80
Wyllie, Timothy, 227–28

X-7, 223–24

Yeats, William Butler, 159, 249
You Are Responsible! (King), 215

Zimdars-Schwartz, Sandra, 230

ABOUT THE AUTHOR

*It must indeed be true; otherwise,
no one would be able to tell it.*

—THE BROTHERS GRIMM

Michael Craft has been researching Fortean and occult phenomena for over twenty years. He has been the director of three leading West Coast workshop centers. A longtime student of Tibetan, Taoist, Native American, and Western Magickal traditions, he offers retreats and trainings exploring holistic health and personal development.

Like other residents of the strange communities of Crestone and the Baca, Christopher O'Brien was drawn to the sacred valley of Native American myth. He was soon compelled to document, in disturbing detail, the inexplicable events unfolding around him and the questions they raised:

- **What is the truth behind the nightly light show of UFOs pulsing and glowing across the sky?**
- **What are the strange rumbling noises coming from underground?**
- **What is the origin of a mysterious crystal skull found in the Baca?**
- **And most frightening of all, who is responsible for the scores of cattle left bloodless and mutilated in inhuman fashion?**

Including fascinating and sometimes frightening firsthand accounts by residents of the area, *The Mysterious Valley* reveals the story of one of the most bizarre regions on the face of the earth and its chilling implications for the rest of humanity.

THE
MYSTERIOUS VALLEY

CHRISTOPHER O'BRIEN

MIND MEETS BODY...
HEALTH MEETS HAPPINESS...
SPIRIT MEETS SERENITY...

In his writings, spiritual advisor Edgar Cayce counseled thousands with his extraordinary, yet practical guidance to the mind/body/spirit connection. Now, the Edgar Cayce series, based on actual readings by the renowned psychic, can provide you with insights in the search for understanding and meaning in life.

KEYS TO HEALTH: The Promise and Challenge of Holism
Eric A. Mein, M.D.
_____ 95616-9 $4.99 U.S./$5.99 CAN.

REINCARNATION: Claiming Your Past, Creating Your Future
Lynn Elwell Sparrow
_____ 95754-8 $5.99 U.S./$7.99 CAN.

DREAMS: Tonight's Answers for Tomorrow's Questions
Mark Thurston, Ph.D.
_____ 95771-8 $5.99 U.S./$6.99 CAN.

AWAKENING YOUR PSYCHIC POWERS
Henry Reed
_____ 95868-4 $5.99 U.S./$6.99 CAN.

HEALING MIRACLES: Using Your Body Energies for Spiritual and Physical Health
William A. McGarey, M.D.
_____ 95948-6 $5.99 U.S./$7.99 CAN.